BURGER'S DAUGHTER

Nadine Gordimer

BLOOMSBURY

This edition first published by Bloomsbury Publishing Plc 2000

First published in Great Britain by Jonathan Cape Ltd 1979

First published in the USA by The Viking Press 1979

Copyright © Nadine Gordimer 1979

The moral right of the author has been asserted

Bloomsbury Publishing Plc,
38 Soho Square, London W1V 5DF

A CIP catalogue is available
from the British Library

ISBN 0 7475 4979 6

10 9 8 7 6 5 4 3 2 1

Typeset by Hewer Text Ltd, Edinburgh
Printed in Great Britain by Clays Ltd, St Ives Plc

I am the place in which something has occurred.
Claude Lévi-Strauss

ONE

A mong the group of people waiting at the fortress was a
schoolgirl in a brown and yellow uniform holding a green
eiderdown quilt and, by the loop at its neck, a red hot-water bottle.
Certain buses used to pass that way then and passengers looking
out will have noticed a schoolgirl. Imagine, a schoolgirl: she must
have somebody inside. Who are all those people, anyway? Even
from the top of a bus, lurching on past as the lights go green, the
group would not have looked like the usual prison visitors, passive
and self-effacing about the slope of municipal grass.

The schoolgirl stood neither in the first rank before the prison
doors nor hung back. There were several young men in roll-neck
sweaters and veldskoen, men in business suits worn absently as an
outer skin, an old man with a thrust-back head of white floss,
women burrowed down into slacks and duffle coats, one in a long
skirt and crocheted shawl, two in elegant tweed suits, with gold
jewellery and sunglasses worn not as a disguise but as an assertion
of indifference to attention. All were drawn up before the doors,
invaders rather than supplicants. All had parcels and carriers. The
voices of the women were clear and forceful in the public place, the
white-haired man put his arms on the shoulders of two young men
in private discussion, a tall blonde woman moved within the group
with chivvying determination. She it was who borrowed the old
man's horn-headed cane to knock on the door when three o'clock
passed and they were still standing there. As there was no response
she took off her high-heeled sandal and hammered away with that
in the other hand, as well. No one was in a mood to laugh but there
was a surge of movement and voices in approval. The schoolgirl
pressed forward with the rest, turning her head with the bold
encouragement with which glances were linking everyone. A small

3

slotted door within the great double ones opened on eyes under a peaked cap. The blonde woman's face was so close against the door that the warder drew back and in an instant reasserted himself, but as a fair-ground gun meets its pop-up target, she had him.

—I demand to speak to the Commandant . . . we were told we could bring clothing for the detainees between three and four. We've been standing here twenty-five minutes, most of us've got jobs to go back to.—

There was an argument. A man with a briefcase arrived and the group quickly tunnelled him to the fore; he was allowed in through another door within the great portal and then, one by one, the men and women handed over their burdens through this doorway blotted dark by the shapes of warders. The schoolgirl was urged on, given way to by others; Lionel Burger's daughter was among them that day, fourteen years old, bringing an eiderdown quilt and a hot-water bottle for her mother.

Rosa Burger, about fourteen years old at the time, waiting at the prison in a brown gymfrock over a yellow shirt and brown pullover with yellow stripes outlining the V-neck, was small for her age, slightly bottle-legged (1st hockey team) and with a tiny waist. Her hair was not freshly washed and the cartilage of her ear-tips broke the dark lank, suggesting that the ears were prominent though hidden. From the side parting of her hair there was a strand that twirled counter to the lie of the rest and had bleached lighter due to contact with chemicals in the school pool (2nd swimming team) and exposure to the sun. Her profile was prettier than her full-face; the waxy outline olive-skinned people often have, with the cave of the eye strikingly marked by the dark shining strip of eyebrow and the steep stroke of eyelashes, fuzzing at the ends like the antennae of moths. When the girl turned, there were many things disappointing—jaw (she chewed a bit of peanut brittle someone offered) heavy for the small chin, nostrils that cut back too sharply, half-healed and picked-at blemishes round the big soft mouth that curled and tightened, hesitated and firmed when she was spoken to and she answered, a mouth exactly like her father's. But her eyes were light—washed-out grey, at a certain angle so clear the convex

4

of the iris appeared transparent in the winter afternoon sunlight. Not at all like his brown eyes with the vertical line of concern between them that drew together an unavoidable gaze in newspaper photographs. The brown and yellow of the school outfit did not suit her colouring, allowing that she probably had not slept well the previous night and had not had time to eat between hurrying home from school and coming to the prison.

Rosemarie Burger, according to the headmistress's report one of the most promising seniors in the school in spite of the disadvantages—in a manner of speaking—of her family background, came to school the morning after her mother was detained just as on any other day. She asked to see the headmistress and requested to be allowed to go home early in order to take comforts to her mother. Her matter-of-fact and reserved manner made it unnecessary for anyone to have to say anything—anything sympathetic—indeed, positively forbade it, and so saved awkwardness. She displayed 'remarkable maturity'; that, at least, without being specific, one could say in the report. The other girls in her class seemed unaware of what had happened. They did not read the morning newspapers, listen to the news on the radio, nor were they aware of politics as something more concretely affective than a boring subject of grown-up conversation, along with the stock market or gynaecological troubles. After a day or two or in some cases even weeks, the recurrence of their schoolmate's surname in connection with her mother, on the placards of street demonstrators against preventive detention, and the observations of parents, remarking on the relationship—Isn't the daughter in your class?—made her circumstance known and accepted at school. She was granted the kind of sympathetic privileges that served for the crises of illness or divorce at home which were all the hazards the children knew. Her fellow prefects divided her playground and other duties between them. Her best friend (whom she had told about the arrest and detention the first day) said she could come and stay at her house, if she liked—probably without having consulted her own parents. The school was a private one for white

English-speaking girls and they innocently expressed their sympathy the only way they knew how: —Bloody Boers, dumb Dutchmen, thick Afrikaners—they would go and lock up your mom. As if she'd ever do anything wrong . . .

It did not occur to them that the family name was in fact an Afrikaner one.

'Among us was a girl of thirteen or fourteen, a schoolgirl still in her gym, the daughter of Lionel Burger. It was a bitter winter day. She was carrying blankets and even a hot-water bottle for her mother. The relatives of the people detained in a brutal dawn swoop had been told they could bring clothing etc. to the prison. We were not allowed to bring books or food. Little Rosa Burger knew her mother, that courageous and warm-hearted woman, was under doctor's orders. The child was dry-eyed and composed, in fact she was an example to us all of the way a detainee's family ought to behave. Already she had taken on her mother's role in the household, giving loving support to her father, who was all too soon to be detained as well. On that day he had put others' plight before his own, and had been tirelessly busy ever since his own wife had been taken in the early hours of the morning, going from police station to police station, trying to establish for helpless African families where their people were being held. But he knew that his schoolgirl daughter could be counted on in this family totally united in and dedicated to the struggle.'

When they saw me outside the prison, what did they see?

I shall never know. It's all concocted. I saw—see—that profile in a hand-held mirror directed towards another mirror; I know how I survived, not unhappily, if not popular then in unspoken, acknowledged inkling that I was superior to them, I and my family, at that school; I understand the bland heroics of badly-written memoirs by the faithful—good people in spite of the sanctimony.

I suppose I was aware that ordinary people might look down from a bus and see us. Some with wonder, knowing whose relatives and friends we must be—even somebody's daughter, look, a kid in a gym—and knowing why we were there. Flora Donaldson and the others talked loudly in high voices the way another kind of woman will do in an expensive restaurant and, if in very different circumstances, for the same reason: to demonstrate self-confidence and a force of personality naturally dominant of an environment calculated to impress or intimidate. I draw that analogy now, not then; it's impossible to filter free of what I have learnt, felt, thought, the subjective presence of the schoolgirl. She's a stranger about whom some intimate facts are known to me, that's all. We were aware of ourselves and the people belonging to us on the other side of the huge, thick, studded doors in a way that the passers-by would not understand and that we asserted, gave off—Wally Atkinson who had no one inside but had been in many times himself, and came to fly the standard of his white hair among us, Ivy Terblanche and her daughter Gloria, determinedly knitting for Gloria's baby while waiting to hand over pyjamas and soap for husbands who were also father and son-in-law, Mark Liebowitz shaking his weight from one foot to the other in the kind of nervous glee with which he met crises, Bridget—Bridget Sulzer

8

formerly Watkins formerly Brodkin born O'Brien—banging on the prison door with the heel of a multi-coloured sandal from which the worn green leather peeled back, her sexy high-arched foot with thick painted toenails bare in spite of the cold. Even the two women I don't think I knew, the fashionably groomed ones who didn't belong (Aletta Gous attracted the friendship of wealthy liberal women whose husbands, at that time, let them run the risk as an indulgence) had set themselves apart from their background in the strange arousal of the persecuted. One of them had had her cook bake a special wheat-germ loaf (Aletta was always a food-faddist) and the lady argued high-handedly when the warder refused it; I remember because she gave it to Ivy—the queer occasion made such assumptions of sudden friendship possible—and Ivy broke off a bit of crust for me to taste when she gave me a lift home.

I was in place, outside the prison; both my parents had been expecting to be picked up for several weeks. Of course, when it happened, and they took my mother, the reality must have been different from the acceptance in advance; it's impossible to conquer all fear and loss by preparation. There are always sources of desolation that aren't taken into account because no one knows what they will be. I just knew that my mother, inside, would know, when she got the things I was holding, that I had been outside; we were connected. Flora pretended to cuddle me against the cold, but I didn't need her kind of emotional excitement. She talked about 'the girls' in there, and my mother was one of them. Flora was a grown-up who made me feel older than she was.

I knew them nearly all, the people I stood among, and didn't need to look at them to see them as I knew them: as I did the way home, the appearance of a landmark at a certain turn. It was that door that I see: the huge double door under the stone archway with a bulb on a goose-neck looking down as a gargoyle does. The tiny hatch where the warder's eyes will appear could be a cat-door if it were lower. There are iron studs with hammer-marks faceting the white sunlight like a turned ring. I see these things over and over again as I stand. But real awareness is all focused in the lower part of my pelvis, in the leaden, dragging, wringing pain there. Can anyone describe the peculiar fierce concentration of the body's forces in the menstruation of early puberty? The bleeding began just after my father had made me go back to bed after my mother had been taken away. No pain; just wetness that I tested with my finger, turned on the light to verify: yes, blood. But outside the prison the internal landscape of my mysterious body turns me inside out, so that in that public place on that public occasion (all the arrests of the dawn swoop have been in the newspapers, a special edition is on sale, with names of those known to be detained, including that of my mother) I am within that monthly crisis of destruction, the purging, tearing, draining of my own structure. I am my womb, and a year ago I wasn't aware— physically—I had one.

As I am alternately submerged below and thrust over the threshold of pain I am aware of the moulded rubber loop by which the hot-water bottle hangs from my finger, and the eider-down I hold against my belly is my old green taffeta one Granny Burger gave me when I was not old enough to remember her; my father thought my mother's double-bed one was too big and too beautiful to get spoilt in prison. The hot-water bottle is my own idea. My mother never used one; and so—as I prepared the device I imagined her swiftly discovering it—she would realize there must be some special reason for its having been sent. Between the black rubber washer and the base of the screw-top I have folded a slip of thin paper. When I came to write the message I found I did not know how to address her except as I did in the letters I would write when away on a holiday. *Dear Mom, Hope you are all right*. Then this innocently unsuitable tone became the perfect vehicle for the important thing I needed to convey. *Dad and I are fine and looking after everything. Lots of love from both*. She would know at once I was telling her my father had not been taken since she had gone.

My version and theirs. And if this were being written down, both would seem equally concocted when read over. And if I were really telling, instead of talking to you in my mind the way I find I do . . .

One is never talking to oneself, always one is addressed to someone. Suddenly, without knowing the reason, at different stages in one's life, one is addressing this person or that all the time, even dreams are performed before an audience. I see that. It's well known that people who commit suicide, the most solitary of all acts, are addressing someone. It's just that with me it never happened before. It hasn't happened even when I thought I was in love—and we couldn't ever have been in love.

If you knew I was talking to you I wouldn't be able to talk.

But you know that about me.

After the death of her father, someone who had had no importance in their life, someone who stood quite outside it, peripheral, one of the hangers-on drawn by curiosity who had once or twice looked in on it, appeared at her side. Years before, when she was a university student and her father was not yet on trial, not yet sentenced or imprisoned, the young man had come for a Sunday swim at the house. So he said. She must have invited him; many people came on Sundays, it was a tradition. They came when she and her brother were little, they came when her mother was detained, they came when her mother was dying of multiple sclerosis, they came when her father was out on bail during his trial. Nothing the secret police could do could more than interrupt. Life went on; Lionel Burger, in his swimming trunks, cooking steak and boerewors for his comrades and friends, was proof.

This guest was a young man named Conrad. A pale acne-scarred back to the sun, lying in the way of but never putting out a teasing hand to catch the black and white legs of children who raced round the edge of the pool. He rested his chin on his forearms, and sometimes his forehead pressed there. He was not the type looking for commitment. There had been, were some, and they were quickly recognized. Sometimes their potential was made use of. He was not even a paid spy posing as the type looking for commitment; that had become a recognizable type, too. Lionel Burger would not restrict his daughter's normal student sociability for fear she might be made use of by one of those. But this boy was of interest to no one; let him look at them all, if the spectacle intrigued him: revolutionaries at play, a sight like the secret mating of whales. He got his boerewors, hot and scented-tasting, from the hands of Lionel Burger himself, like everyone else. Rosa was a pretty thing as she grew up; many boys would follow her, not knowing she was not for them.

Once or twice during the trial she had noticed this Conrad in the visitors' gallery of the court. She moved inevitably in the phalanx of familiars, the friends some of whom disappeared, arrested and arraigned in other trials, in the course of her father's. Once when she had gone out to telephone from the Greek café nearby, she met the chap on the pavement on her way back to the court-house. He offered her an espresso and she laughed, in her way of knowing only too well the facilities of the environs of this court, always she was aside from her generation in experience of this kind—where did he think you could get an espresso around here?

—You can, that's all.— He took her down a block, round a corner and into a shopping arcade. She understood he must have followed her out of court. Real espresso was brought to a little iron table by a black waiter dressed up in striped trousers, black waistcoat and cheese-cutter. She pulled a funny face behind the waiter, smiled, friendly and charming, any girl singled out by a man. —What d'you think that's supposed to be? In Pretoria!— He pushed over to her an ashtray lettered THE SINGING BARBER.

—What do you think he feels about your father?—

—My father?—

Her beau broke a match between his teeth and waved its V in the direction of the court-house.

Oh, she understood: the blacks, do they know, are they grateful to whites who endanger their own lives for them. So that was the set of tracks along which this one's mind trundled; there were others who came up to her, sweating and pitched to their greatest intensity, Miss Burger you don't know me but I want to tell you, the government calls him a Communist but your father is God's man, the holy spirit of our Lord is in him, that's why he is being persecuted. And there were the occasional letters that had been

12

coming to the house all her life; as soon as she was old enough—her mother knew when that was; how did she know?—her mother let her see one. It said her father was a devil and a beast who wanted to rob and kill, destroying Christian civilization. She felt a strange embarrassment, and looked into her mother's face to see if she should laugh, but her mother had another look on her face; she was aware of some trust expressed there, something that must last beyond laughter. It was a Saturday morning and when her father had come home from his early round of visits to his patients in hospital he had given Baasie and her their weekly swimming lesson; at that moment with the letter before her, 'her father' came to her as a hand cupped under her chin that kept her head above water while her legs and arms frogged. Baasie was afraid still. His thin, dingy body with the paler toes rigidly turned up went blacker with the cold and he clung flat against her father's fleshy, breathing chest whose warmth, even in the water, she felt by seeing Baasie clinging there.

In the coffee bar she was still smiling. She seemed to savour the domino of sugar she held, soaking up dark hot coffee before she dropped it in. —Oh leave the poor waiter alone.—

—No but—I'm curious.—

She nodded in jerky, polite, off-hand dismissal, as if that were the answer to the idle question she didn't ask: What brings you to the trial? A girl in her situation, she had nothing much to say to a stranger, and it was difficult for anyone outside what one must suppose—respect, awkwardly—were her intense preoccupations, to begin to talk to her. An important State witness was due to be called for cross-examination before the court rose for the day; she knew she must drink up and go, he knew she would go, but they sat on for a minute in a purely physical awareness of one another. His blond-brown hand lying across the vice of his crossed thighs, with the ridiculous thick silver manacle following the contour of the wrist-bump, the nave of her armpit in a sleeveless dress, shiny with moisture as she pushed away the tiny cup—the form of communication that is going on when two young people appear to have no reason or wish to linger.

Most of their meetings were as inconsequential. He came to the trial but did not always seek her out—supposing she was right that he ever had. Sometimes he was one of the loose group centred round the lawyers and her who ate sandwiches or grey pies in the Greek café during the lunch adjournment; it was assumed she brought him along, she thought someone else had. He did not telephone her at work but she met him once in the public library and they ate together in a pizzeria. She had thought he was a university lecturer or something of that kind but he told her, now that (without curiosity) she asked, that he was doing a post-graduate thesis on Italian literature, and working on Wednesdays and weekends as a bookie's clerk at the race-course. He had begun the thesis while studying in Perugia, but given it up when he spent a year or so in France and Denmark and England. He was vague about what he had done and how he lived. In the South of France, on a yacht—Something between a servant and a pet, it sounds—

He was not offended by her joking distaste. —Great life, for a few months. Until you get sick of the people you work for. There was no place to read in peace.—

It was a job for which you did not need a foreigner's work permit—he knew all the ways of life that fitted into that category. In London he squatted in a Knightsbridge mansion. He'd fixed up a condemned cottage, in Johannesburg, with the money he'd got for bringing in a British car duty-free, after having had the use of it for a year abroad, an arrangement made with a man who had bought it in his name. —Any time you need somewhere to stay . . . I'm often away for weeks. I've got friends with a farm in Swaziland. What a wonderful place, forest from the house all the way to the river, you just live in a kind of twilight of green—pecan-nut trees, you know.— A casual inspiration. —Why don't you come there this weekend?—

It didn't occur to him: —I don't have a passport.—

He didn't make sympathetic, indignant noises. He pondered as if on a practical matter. —Not even to hop just over there?—

—No.—

14

He looked at her in silence, confronted with her, considering her as a third person, a problem set up for both of them.

—Come to my house.—

—Yes I will, I'd like to see it. Your big jacaranda.—

—Bauhinia.—

—Bauhinia, then.—

—I mean now.—

—I have to go to Pretoria after work this afternoon.— But at least it was a serious answer, a practical matter that could be dealt with.

—There's an adjournment till Monday, isn't there?—

—Yes, but I've got permission for a visit today.—

—It's virtually on your way back.—

The mansion and garden of the early nineteen-hundreds to which the cottage belonged had been expropriated for a freeway that was being delayed by ratepayers' objections; in the meantime the cottage was let without official tenure at an address that no longer existed.

The wavy galvanized iron roof was painted blue and so were the railings of the wooden verandah. From an abandoned tennis court brilliant with glossy weeds a mournful bird presaged rain. The bauhinia tree lifted from shrubs and ornamental palms become a green-speared jungle; the two rooms were sunk in it like a hidden pool. It was safe and cosy as a child's playhouse and sexually arousing as a lovers' hideout. It was nowhere.

She came in out of the sun and the traffic of the highway straight from the prison and he got up from some dim piece of furniture where he made no pretence not to have been lying, probably all afternoon, and kept her standing just within the doorway, rubbing himself against her. The directness of the caress was simply the acting-out, in better and more appropriate circumstances, of what was happening in the coffee-bar. Desire can be very comforting. Lying with the vulnerable brassy smell of a stranger's hair close to her breathing, she saw flies swaying a mobile beneath a paper concertina lantern, the raised flower pattern within the counted squares of a lead ceiling over-patterned with shadows cast from the

15

garden, his watch, where his hand lay on her, showing the time—
exactly one hour and twenty minutes since she had been sitting on
the bench on the visitors' side of the wire grille that fragmented her
father's face as the talk of other prisoners and their visitors broke
the sequence of whatever he was trying to tell her.

—Lucky to find a place like this. It's what everybody always
looks for.—

—Easy. Convincing the rich old girl or old guy who owns it is
the only trouble. They'd have a black if it was allowed to have
blacks living in, because you can control a black, he's got to listen
to you. But a white who will live in a shack like this will always be
young and have no money. They're afraid you'll push drugs or be
politically subversive, make trouble. When I said I worked at the
race-course that was okay; the kind of honest living they understand, although not socially acceptable to them, at least part of the
servicing of their kind of pleasures. You keep your mouth shut
about university, they don't trust students at all. Not that I blame
them. Anyway, suits me. If I can finish the bloody thesis and make
my hundred, hundred-and-fifty a week among those crooks and
suckers at the race-course, I'll push off to Mexico.—

—Mexico now! Why Mexico!—

He got up, stretched naked, yawned so that his penis bobbed
and the yawn became a cat's grin. He put the flat of his hand on
some books on a brass tray with a rickety stand. —No good reason
for people who must have good reasons. If I read poetry or novels I
like then I want to go and live in the country the writer knows. I
mean I just want to know what he knows . . .—

—Lend me something.—

She tried the names on the books he handed her. —Octavio Paz.
Carlos Fuentes.—

He corrected the pronunciation.

—Ah, you've learnt Spanish?—

He came over and touched a breast as one might adjust the angle
of a picture. —There's a girl giving me a few lessons.—

She would not have noticed if he had no longer been about; if he
had disappeared at any time during the seven months of her

16

father's trial, she would simply have assumed he had gone off to Mexico or wherever. In fact, once when, chin on hands across the table among friends and hangers-on, at tea-break while an observer from the International Council of Jurists was commenting on some aspect of the morning's proceedings, he looked up at her under his eyebrows and raised a hand in salute, she recognized the greeting of someone who has been away and signals his return. He took a lift back with her to Johannesburg. He was one of those people who usually wait for the other to begin to talk. The Defence evidence in the afternoon had gone badly; there was nothing to say, *nothing*. She was aware, in the presence of another in the car, only of actions that usually are performed automatically, the play of the tendons on the back of her hand as she shifted the gear-stick, the sag of her elbows on the steering-wheel, and her glance between the rear-view mirror and the road ahead. —How was it?—

—What was?—With an edge of challenge to her preoccupation. Her voice went light with embarrassment. —You've been— where?—Cape Town . . . ?—

—You're always so polite, aren't you. Just like your father. He never gets rattled. No matter what that slimy prosecutor with his histrionics throws at him. Never loses his cool.—

She smiled at the road ahead.

—You must've been very well brought up. No slanging matches and banging doors in the Burger house. Everybody marvellously up-tight.—

—Lionel's like that. Outraged, yes. I've seen him outraged. But he doesn't lose his temper. He can be angry without losing his temper . . . never, I don't remember even once when we were little . . . It's not put on, he just is naturally sympathetic in his manner.—

—Marvellously up-tight.—

She smiled and shrugged.

—The old girl this afternoon. She was a friend?—

—Sort of.—

—Sort of. Poor old girl. Trembling and snivelling and looking down sideways all the time so she wouldn't meet his eyes. Not just the eyes, she couldn't let herself see even the toe of his shoe. You could tell that. And saying everything they'd got out of her, dirtying herself . . . All in front of him. I watched Number One accused. He just looked at her, listening like anyone. He wasn't disgusted.—

—She's been detained for nearly a year.— The driver must have felt her passenger studying her. —She's broken.—

—She was a bloody disaster for your father today. What is this—Christ-like compassion?—

—He knows what's happened to her. That's all.—

Her consciousness of the set of her profile made it impossible for him to say: And you?

To make him comfortable, she gave an aside half-smile, half-grimace. —Not 'well brought up', just used to things.—

The day her father was sentenced he would have been there, the narrow face pale as a Chinese mandarin's with the drooping moustache to match, ostentatiously ill-dressed to rile a stolid gaze of heavy police youths creaking in their buckled and buttoned encasement. She didn't remember seeing him although it was true that she had slept with him once or twice. Family feeling overruled other considerations as at a wedding or funeral; an aunt—one of her father's sisters—and uncle, and cousins from her mother's side came to be with her despite the fact that they had never had anything to do with her father's politics. As at a service in church, the family took the first row in court. The aunt and female cousins wore hats; she had with her in her pocket the blue, lilac and red paisley scarf she put on only when the court rose as the judge entered, each day of the two-hundred-and-seventeen of her father's trial. All around, everywhere except the high ceiling where the fan propellers were still, there were faces. The well of the court was lined with bodies, bodies shifted and surged on the benches behind her, pushed up thigh against thigh, the walls were padded with standing policemen.

He—her father was led up from cells below the court into the well, an actor, saviour, prize-fighter, entering the realm of expectation that awaits him. He was, of course, more ordinary and mortal than the image of him as he would be on this day anticipated; a spike of hair stood away from his carefully-brush— crown, her hand went up to her own to smooth it for him. She saw that he saw his sister first, then the cousins; smiled at her, in remark of the family assembly, then deeply, for herself. Lionel Burger and her father, he gave his address from the dock. She knew what he was going to say because the lawyers had worked with him on the material and she herself had gone to the library to check a certain quotation he wanted. She heard him speaking aloud what she had read in his handwriting in the notes written in his cell. Nobody could stop him. The voice of Lionel Burger, her father, was being heard in public for the first time for seven years and for the last time, bearing testimony once and for all. He spoke for an hour. '. . . when as a medical student tormented not by the suffering I saw around me in hospitals, but by the subjection and humiliation of human beings in daily life I had seen around me all my life—a subjection and humiliation of live people in which, by my silence and political inactivity I myself took part, with as little say or volition on the victims' side as there was in the black cadavers, always in good supply, on which I was learning the intricate wonder of the human body . . . When I was a student, I found at last the solution to the terrifying contradiction I had been aware of since I was a schoolboy expected to have nothing more troubling in my head than my position in the rugby team. I am talking of the contradiction that my people—the Afrikaner people—and the white people in general in our country, worship the God of Justice and practise discrimination on grounds of the colour of skin; profess the compassion of the Son of Man, and deny the humanity of the black people they live among. This contradiction that split the very foundations of my life, that was making it impossible for me to see myself as a man among men, with all that implies of consciousness and responsibility—in Marxism I found it was analysed in another way: as forces in conflict through economic laws. I saw that white Marxists worked side by side with blacks in an equality that meant taking on the meanest of tasks—tasks that incurred loss of income and social prestige and the risk of arrest and imprisonment—as well as sharing policy-making and leadership. I saw whites prepared to work under blacks. Here was a possible solution to injustice to be sought outside the awful fallibility in any self-professed morality I knew. For as a great African leader who was not a Communist has since said: "The white man's moral standards in this country can only be judged by the extent to which he has condemned the majority of its population to serfdom and inferiority."

'. . . The Marxist solution is based on the elimination of contradiction between the form of social control and the economy: my Boer ancestors who trekked to found their agrarian republics, subjecting the indigenous peoples of tribal societies by the force of the musket against the assegai, were now in their turn resisting the economic forces that made their feudalistic form of social control obsolete. The white man had built a society that tried to contain and justify the contradictions of capitalist means of production and feudalist social forms. The resulting devastation I, a privileged young white, had had before my eyes since my birth. Black men, women and children living in the miseries of insecurity, poverty and degradation on the farms where I grew up, and in the "dark Satanic mills" of the industry that bought their labour cheap and disqualified them by colour from organizing themselves or taking part in the successive governments that decreed their lot as eternal inferiors, if not slaves . . . A change of social control in compatibility with the change in methods of production—known in Marxist language as "revolution"—in this I saw the answer to the racialism that was destroying our country then and—believe me! believe me!—is destroying it even more surely and systematically now. I could not turn away from that tragedy. I cannot now. I took up then the pursuit of the end to racialism and injustice that I have continued and shall continue as long as I live. I say with Luther: Here I stand. *Ich kann nicht anders.*'

An hour and a half. Nobody would dare stop him.

'. . . stand before this court accused of acts calculated to overthrow the State and establish a dictatorship of the proletariat in this country. But what we as Communists black and white working in harmony with others who do not share our political philosophy have set our sights on is the national liberation of the African people, and thus the abolishment of discrimination and extension of political rights to all the peoples of this country . . . That alone has been our aim . . . beyond . . . there are matters the future will settle.

'. . . For nearly thirty years the Communist Party allied itself as a legal organization with the African struggle for black rights and the extension of the franchise to the black majority. When the Communist Party was declared a banned organization, and later formed itself as an underground organization to which I belonged, it continued for more than a decade to take part in the struggle for black advancement by peaceful and non-violent means. . . . At the end of that long, long haul, when the great mass movement of the African National Congress, and other movements, were outlawed; the ears of the government stopped finally against all pleas and demands—what advancement had been granted? What legitimate rights had been recognized, according to the "standards of Western civilization" our white governments have declared themselves dedicated to preserve and perpetuate? Where had so much effort and patience beyond normal endurance found any sign of reasonable recognition of reasonable aspirations? . . . and to this day, the black men who stand trial in this court as I do must ask themselves: why is it no black man has ever had the right of answering, before a black prosecutor, a black judge, to laws in whose drafting and promulgation his own people, the blacks, have had a say?'

Not the squat stern pantomime dame in a curly grey wig up on the bench: nobody dared silence him. Not the policemen who had brought him in, between them, not the plain-clothes men as familiar as tradesmen coming to the house since she was a child.

'That is my answer to the question this court has asked, and my fellow citizens may be asking of me: how could I, a doctor, sworn to save lives, approve the even accidental risk to human life contained in the sabotage of selected, symbolic targets calculated not to harm people—the tactic to which the banned Congress leaders turned in the creation of Umkhonto we Sizwe, the Spear of the Nation—turned to after three hundred years of repression by white guns and laws, after half a century of white indifference to blacks' reasonably formulated, legitimate aspirations . . . the last resort short of certain bloodshed to which a desperate people turned as a means of drawing attention after everything else had been ignored—'

One hour and forty-seven minutes.

'My covenant is with the victims of apartheid. The situation in which I find myself changes nothing . . . there will always be those who cannot live with themselves at the expense of fullness of life for others. They know "world history would be very easy to make if the struggle were taken up only on condition of infallibly favour-able chances."'

'. . . this court has found me guilty on all counts. If I have ever been certain of anything in my life, it is that I acted according to my conscience on all counts. I would be guilty only if I were innocent of working to destroy racism in my country.'

They heard him out: the words of the condemned man, and the last judgment on those who had condemned him, the judge learnedly and scrupulously impartial within the white man's laws, the secret police and the uniformed police who enforced them, the white people, his own people, who made the laws. The sentence was what her father knew was coming to him; and she, and the lawyers and everyone around them throughout the trial knew was coming. The newspapers reported a 'gasp through the court' when the judge pronounced sentence of imprisonment for life. She did not hear any gasp. There was a split second when everything stopped; no breath, no heartbeat, no saliva, no flow of blood except her father's. Everything rushed away from him, drew back, eclipsed. He alone, in his short big-headed body and his neat grey best suit, gave off the heat of life. He held them all at bay, blinded, possessed. Then his eyes lowered, she distinctly noticed his eyelids drop in an almost feminine gesture of selfconscious acknowledgment.

She looked straight ahead because she was afraid someone would speak to her or lay a hand on her.

At the back of the court where the blacks were crushed in, standing, so that when the seated whites turned to look up, they were overhung, the shouts flung out: Amandhla!

And the burst of response: Awethu!

Amandhla! Awethu! Amandhla! Awethu!

They fell upon her father: his flowers, laurels, embraces. He grinned blazingly and raised his white fist to theirs.

Then it was over. A thin back went down to the cells between many policemen. It was finished. The groupings dropped apart, lawyers, police, clerks moving across each other. The plump, desperately calm face of her father's counsel, prematurely aged by jowls of tension round his gentle, rosy mouth, looked for her and she struggled to get to him. He kissed her and she sank for a moment into the cushion of that cheek, smelled something he put on when he shaved. A foreigner's British voice was saying past her ear—And here life means life.—

I know those hours afterwards. After someone has been taken away.

After my brother drowned. After arrests. After my mother died at ten past five in the afternoon at the hospital and when we got home the sprinkler was on in the garden and the washwoman's baby was trying to catch the spray in his hands.

I think that while my mother was alive and my brother was a baby my parents arranged their activities so that one of them was in the clear, always, one would always have a good chance of being left behind to carry on the household if the other were arrested. Of course they also calculated on the Special Branch preferring to leave one of them apparently at large, in the hope of being led to others who were working underground. Nobody told me this, nobody discussed it at home—I just knew, as children know about things their mothers and fathers discuss in bed at night. Then when my brother and mother were gone, there was me. If my father were to be arrested, there would always be me.

Afterwards, there are toys, there are cupboards full of clothes, there are bills and circulars from people who don't know the addressee won't receive them. Although there are no documents or letters because people like my father and mother cannot preserve anything that establishes names or connections, there are boxes (an old round leather box with a buckle fastening, I am told people—perhaps Lionel's grandfather—used to put stiff collars in) containing broken things you don't know why have been kept. The furniture in rooms is arranged in accordance with a logic of movement, of currents of life about it that are no longer there.

Theo had wanted to take me home with him but I said I would go back to the house first and come to the Santorinis' later. —To eat with us.—

—Yes, I'll have dinner with you.—

—We'll open a bottle of Dão.— Dão was my father's favourite wine.

Theo could say that to me. He wasn't merely my father's counsel, he wasn't even only a friend. When a hostile colleague had taunted him—lawyers named as Communists by the government are disbarred—with more than professional interest in the Burger case, he had everted his pink, clean lips—Let's say my heart is in it.—

I knew I would have to go through a scene with Lily, and her husband Jamison and any of her other cronies who happened to be gathered at the house. It was she who had given baby photographs to the press when Tony drowned. She had gone into mourning, black from head to toe, with only the salmon-coloured palms of her hands and the whites of her eyes for relief, when my mother died. She did for us all the things white people had taught her one ought to be expected to do. I knew she would be shocked that I did not come back borne along by the aunt and uncle and cousins who had, with the blood-loyalty that was their form of courage or kindness, sat to hear the sentence pronounced. I wanted to take Lily up to my bedroom so that we could sit on my bed and I could put my arms round her and let her have her cry, but she was seated formally among the up-ended *chaises-longues* and pool equipment on the porch outside my father's study with Jamison and the servants from round about who were her intimates, waiting for me. I had told her many times that she must expect my father to go to prison this time for a long time. I had tried to prepare her. But she was sitting there as at one of her prayer meetings waiting for the good news, the Lord's mercy. There was a tray with a jug of orange juice and one glass—for me—on the rusty table with the hole where the sun umbrella used to be fitted. They all got up from the screechy wrought-iron chairs whose cushions she had stored away, and when she saw me coming in, just as I had been day after day for all the time of the trial, she understood there was no good news, no Lord's mercy, and her obstinacy fell away from her. She said with a belligerent sense of tragedy—What they did do to him?—

Then she wept and rolled her head and fiercely waved the others away. Her keening, trilling shrieks seemed about to begin, but some sense in her was watching me and we were making a tacit compact that she would not fall to the floor in hysterics. I stroked her head that felt like a lumpy mattress, her springy African hair divided and plaited in tiny pigtails under her doek (I had often watched her do it, as a child). She rocked me with her. —God is going to stay with him in that place. All the time, all the time. Until he come home.— Here she interceded for us, too, mediating our rejection of belief into the acceptable form, for well-off white people, of merely neglecting to go to church. I don't know what I said; we had our form, too, for correcting without offending—You think of him, Lily. You'll think of him often and he won't be alone.— Something like that.

Arms round each other, just the two of us, we went slowly to the big kitchen where she had cooked so many meals for my father, his family. The alarum clock that she took to her room every night stood on the windowsill above the sink, tacking down the seconds of the end of the first day—*life means life*. At last, she said eggs were finished, and no bread for breakfast tomorrow. So I went out again that day and drove to the Portuguese greengrocer down the road. The west-facing hill where the shops were held the heat of the afternoon sun that made garish the scratches and smears on the car windscreen. Barefoot white children already in their short cotton pyjamas were buying milk and cigarettes and a bonus of chewing-gum or ice-cream cone to take up to the flats above. I was among young women my own age, some with children on the hip or by the hand, their backs and breast-slopes stained deep pink-brown from an afternoon in their swimming-pools; among black men in overalls, silently drinking bottles of coke or orangeade where they stood; among authoritative middle-aged white women bearing the casques of freshly-tinted hair as they selected strawberries and lettuce and lemons according to the plan for a dinner-party. Henriques knew we bought brown eggs, extra-large. My mother must have started the preference; anyway, Lily always insisted on it. Henriques had a smile for everyone in turn; as if, having escaped a poor Madeiran's service in the Portuguese colonial army, he had no right ever to be tired or irritable. He would not dare to flirt with educated South African girls like me, but he expressed a shy preference or longing by the gift of a peach or perfect apple whose price he would wave away. —To-day's unlucky (his English made the liaison). Brown s'come tomorrow, I don' know if you wan' wait.—

Outside the bottle store next door the derelict black women who were always there, not professionals but ready to trade the alleyway use of their unsteady bodies in fair exchange for drink, pleaded with muzzy black building workers. The men went in and out the section of the store where blacks were served, bringing cartons of beer and half-jacks of brandy whose brown paper wrapping was peeled back just sufficiently to unscrew the cap before the bottle passed from mouth to mouth. The quarrelling drunk women shared even a cigarette in this way, parenthetic to their wrangling. One swayed and staggered, her blouse like a grey burst sausage and a blanket hitched round her waist in place of a skirt. In my path, she clutched me: —Sorry missus, sorry.— But the eggs weren't broken.

I felt them click smoothly against each other as ping-pong balls in the paper bag, afterwards.

That was how it was, Conrad. You came round to my father's house that evening to see what it was like to belong to a family where the father could risk going to prison for life, and have it come to pass. I don't reproach you for the curiosity, the fascination this had for you. I was not there; I was with the Santorinis and others who had been part of my father's life. Lily was in the mood for a wake—she needed some sort of ceremony to make the transition to ordinary days when my father would be in prison for life—and you were impressed because she wouldn't let you go before she'd given you a glass of fresh orange juice. You remarked on it later. You were thinking it another interesting example of the 'gracious living' standards of my father's house, jugs of freshly-squeezed orange always on tap. You didn't know it was the glass I didn't drink.

At Theo's we had Dão, Lionel's favourite. The bottles were the remains of a case Lionel had given Theo for his birthday (Lionel was an awaiting-trial prisoner already, then; he'd told me to order it). Everyone there was fiercely proud of Lionel. Yes, that was the mood. Marisa Kgosana, whose husband had been two years on Robben Island, turned up about ten o'clock with her usual bodyguard of huge, silent admirers, and, jerking her beautiful breasts, challenged with a throw-away gesture of hands decked as much in their own blackness as their rings and red-painted nails—Rosa, whose life anyway? Theirs or his?— My father is dead and her husband is still on Robben Island. She has been banned for years. She has many lovers and probably as a husband she has forgotten him, she isn't the Penelope the faithful write about when they find a sympathetic press. He wouldn't expect her to be, because his way, as my father's was, is to go on living however you must. And if he doesn't outlast his jailers, his and Marisa's children will.

Theo thrust on me forms of application for a correspondence course from the external studies university. —You better get cracking with this. Lionel says the registration for prisoners this year closes next week.— And to the others around us, with the assumption of slightly haughty, careless arrogance with which he expressed the intoxication of his association with my father through the trial: —God knows where he found that out. But he did, this last week. With the judgment coming up. And it was the first thing he said when we saw him after the sentence this afternoon. Ay, Rosa? *Don't forget my course.* Anthropology, and if that can't be arranged, the diploma in industrial psychology.—

—Do they offer such a thing?—

—If Lionel says so. Rosa'll have those papers in right away—tomorrow morning, my girl—

Lionel was spending his first night without the privileges of an awaiting-trial prisoner. I think that was what I thought about? They had taken away his own clothes. He had begun an imprisonment that could end only with the end of his life or the end of the regime; not just the government of the day, but any other white government that might succeed it. There was bravado and sentiment in the confidence of the room full of people at Theo's that they were behaving as Lionel Burger would expect, as he would do himself in their situation. That was how they saw themselves. Strong emotion—faith?—has different ways of being manifested among the different disciplines within which people order their behaviour. That was what you were curious—had a sense of wonder about. That was what brought you to Lionel Burger's empty house. I can't tell you anything more because I now see I don't know anything more, myself.

The copper plate at the Burgers' gateway with Lionel Burger's name and medical degrees was kept polished through the months of his trial by the Burgers' servant, Lily Letsile. His daughter Rosa was living at home and working as a physiotherapist at a hospital. She was the last member of the family of five (counting Baasie) to live there, but the household had never matched her doll's house family of mother and father, boy and girl, dog and cat, and even during this period there was usually someone else staying there. Bridget Sulzer's son from the Brodkin marriage came and occupied the garden rondavel while studying for examinations. A political scientist who had been expelled from a neighbouring black state spent six weeks at her own risk (she was an old friend of Rosa's mother), since if the Special Branch came to do one of their regular house-cleanings she would very likely lose the research papers she had brought with her. The old man, Kowalski, his mixed Eastern European antecedents further confused by the turn of speech and demeanour taken on during the years he had lived in a Sophiatown yard, so that even the police no longer could decide whether or not he was the wrong colour in the wrong area, stayed on in a room where there had been many transients. He had turned up destitute at the surgery one day before Lionel Burger was arrested that final time, and been recognized as the champion vendor of the Party paper in the streets, during the period before, in its final avatar, it had been banned.

But by the time her father was convicted, the last of scores of people who had shared the house since she was born there were gone. Her father, allowed to consult with his lawyer on family and business affairs, decided with Theo that the house should be sold. A good job was found for Eilefas Bengu, the gardener, Lily Letsile was pensioned and went home to the Northern Transvaal to reflect upon whether or not she wanted to work again, the Labrador bitch went to Ivy Terblanche where Rosa could come and visit her, the black cat and two tabbies went to the former receptionist from the surgery, the rabbits, the guinea-pigs, the tortoise and love-birds Rosa and her brother had made houses for and slept with and communed with as children had long since died or disappeared. The furniture was sold in a house-auction she did not attend. Three hundred people came (the press reported) and not all to buy; they were curious, too. When Rosa called to pick up some small personal possessions the new owners were there, walking round the swimming-pool where her brother had drowned and replanning, with arabesques drawn in the air and dimensions paced out, the patio area where her father set up his braaivleis and her mother's tree-ferns from Tzaneen had grown so big they lifted the paving. As she was leaving, there was an awkward, undertone conversation and the new lady of the house came running after her. —I wonder—about the plate? The doctor's plate.— The girl apologized; she would get it removed.

She returned before dark with an unhealthy-looking fair man with long hair and a straggling moustache, wearing the fashionable garb of shirt with Balkan embroidery, jeans, and veldskoen. He had a screwdriver but found some difficulty in turning it in the grooves caked with layers of metal polish turned to stony verdigris.

She did not get out of the driver's seat. The oblong where the plate had been showed whitish in the twilight. He put the plate in the boot of her car and they drove away.

Rosa was allowed one prison visit every two months for the first year, while her father was a 'D' grade prisoner. She received from him, and wrote in return, one letter a month not longer than the regulation 500 words. When she exceeded this limit by a sentence, the page was cut at that point by the Chief Warder, who censored prisoners' mail. Her father told her, at her next visit, how he had amused himself trying to construct from the context of the preceding sentence what the missing part would have added. In the July and October of that year, she did not write in order to let her half-brother from her father's first marriage, a doctor working in Tanzania and a prohibited immigrant in South Africa, send a letter. During the second year, her father became a 'C' grade prisoner and was allowed several special visits. Application to take advantage of these visits by Flora Donaldson and Dick Terblanche (Ivy was in prison but her husband's ban had lapsed and had not yet been renewed) were turned down by the Director of Prisons, as was that of an old comrade, Professor Jan Hahnloser, who thought Lionel Burger had foolishly and tragically thrown his life away for political beliefs now long become abhorrent to the professor, but found in the tragedy the necessity to assert the bonds of youthful friendship. The Director did allow a Christmas visit from the aunt and uncle—her father's sister and brother-in-law, a farmer and his wife who had been present in court for the verdict at his trial. It was in the autumn of the second year, when she was allowed to see her father every alternate week, that one of her visits was to the prison hospital because he had the first of the virus throat infections that kept recurring.

She shared a flat for a time with Mark Liebowitz's sister Rhoda, just divorced. Then her flat-mate, the organizing secretary of a mixed trade union of coloureds and whites, began a love affair with a coloured trade unionist and went to Cape Town to be where the man lived even though she couldn't live with him. Rosa disliked the smells of other people's frying that never left the corridors and the noise of other people's radios that gabbled in under the flat door; now she was able to move. She lived with Flora Donaldson and her husband—he was away in Europe on business half the year. It was a house—open house—like their own—her father's—had been; big rooms, with flowers from the garden, friendly talkative servants about, books, pictures, guests, a swimming-pool. She tried a flat again; a small flat, on her own. What she really wanted was a garden cottage. Once she thought she had just what was in mind and then the owners realized who she was and sidled out of the agreement. As they were not open about their reasons she could not tell them the police seemed to be leaving her alone since her father had been serving his sentence. She had not been raided once, in the various places she had lived.

She still had her job at the hospital; she worked mostly in geriatric wards, and with children. Her half-brother wrote from northern Tanzania that if only he had her in his hospital . . . there was no money, no time, no personnel to provide physiotherapy for anyone. She could have gone to work with a doctor friend among rural Africans in the Transkei who needed her kind of skills just as badly—it would have been possible to fly up twice a month for the prison visits—but the Administrator of the territory knew who she was and would not give her permission to live in a black 'homeland'. As it happened, her father's tendency to throat infections appeared to become chronic and she had to be there—at the prison to insist on medical reports from the Commandant; negotiating through Theo for a private specialist to see her father; importuning various officials—available to her father even if she could not see him. She played squash twice a week for the exercise. She went to the theatre when there was anything worthwhile. At parties her bared flesh was as sunburned as anyone's who had long summer holidays at the sea; she did go away from town for a week once or twice, and apparently with a Swedish journalist with whom (it was understood not even her close friends would ever expect information from Rosa herself) she was having a love affair. She took from her father's ex-receptionist one of the kittens produced by the old black cat and set it up with a sand-box in the bathroom of the flat. It was noted that the Swede wore a gold ring, in the custom of married men from Europe. Family friends and associates of her father's generation wished she would get married, to some South African, locally; but no one would have presumed to express this kindly concern to her— of course it was understood she could never leave, leave the country as so many did, now that her father was in prison and she was the only one left to him.

In November, in the second month of the third year of his life sentence, Lionel Burger developed nephritis as a result of yet another throat infection and died in prison.

The prison authorities did not consent to a private funeral arranged by relatives. His life sentence was served but the State claimed his body. A thousand black and white people had come to the funeral of Cathy Burger, his wife and Rosa's mother, some years before. At a memorial gathering in honour of Lionel Burger held one lunch-hour in a small trades hall few of the faces recognized then were to be seen again—the black and Indian and coloured and white leaders gone to prison or exile, or restricted by bans from attending meetings of any nature. Two or three men and women who had been hidden away by house arrest for many years appeared on the platform like actors making a come-back with the style and rhetoric of their time. Some young people present asked who they were? There were babies in arms, and restless children. A tiny Indian boy was given an apple to quiet him. If there were Special Branch men present, they were unobtrusive despite the small number of people, and difficult to spot under the cultivated shabbiness of young white intellectuals and impassively distanced air of black clerks and delivery-men they might have assumed. When the valedictions had been delivered and people were rising from their broken wooden seats, the same tiny boy, seen to have been placed standing on his by his mother, lifted a clenched toy fist and yelled in the triumph with which a child performs a nursery rhyme with exactly the intonation in which he has been rehearsed, *Amandhla! Amandhla! Amandhla!* Faltering response gathered from the sparse crowd trooping out: *Awethu!* Seeing he had done well, he scrambled down among people's feet to retrieve his half-eaten apple. A man who hung around the magistrates' courts to take cut-price wedding pictures and worked part-time for the Special Branch was waiting in the street to photograph everyone leaving the hall.

But people closed around Rosa Burger at the exit; some, with delicacy or embarrassment, pressed her hand and said they would come and see her—nearly three years is a long time and many had lost touch. She looked different, not only in the way in which those to whom terrible events come have faces that are hard to look upon. Her hair was cut very short, curly as the head of a Mediterranean or Cape Town urchin, making the tendons of her neck appear longer and more strained than a young woman's should. There was her father's smile for everybody. But a number of people found they did not know where to reach her, now; she was no longer in her flat: another name was up on the door. Others explained—yes, they'd heard she had found a cottage in somebody's garden, she had moved away, there was no telephone yet. It takes a little time to establish a new point of reference, even cartographically, among a circle of friends. One could always try to reach her at the hospital. Some did, and she came to Sunday lunch. She said the cottage was somewhere in the old part of town near the zoo—a very temporary arrangement; she had not made up her mind what she would do, now. The Terblanches asked if she wouldn't apply again for permission to go to the Transkei. —Why not Tanzania—to brother David! *Why not?* Maybe they're in the mood to relent and give you a passport, now.— Flora Donaldson's husband, who was usually silent in the company of her friends because he was not a political associate, suddenly turned on his wife, reversing the position in which *he* was expected to make the blunders. —Don't be absurd, Flora.— His whole body and face seemed dislocated by insult to Rosa Burger as he moved unnecessarily about the room. —Oh William, what do you know about the issues involved.— —In my ignorance, it seems, a lot more than you do.—

The girl said nothing, tolerantly uninterested in a marital spat at table. But that afternoon she asked William Donaldson whether he would give her a chance to beat him at a game of tennis—it had

33

been a joke, when she stayed with the Donaldsons, that although he played assiduously at some businessmen's sports club to keep fit, he never won a set with anyone but her.

After her father's death, unless the old circle got in touch with Rosa they saw even less of her. The Swede had disappeared; either she must have broken off the affair or he had gone back to Sweden? When anyone did encounter her she often had in tow some young man who looked like a student radical, or fancied himself as a painter or writer—to people of her father's generation he appeared Bohemian, to her contemporaries not much more than a moody dropout and younger than she was. He could perhaps have been a relation, her father's was a big Transvaal family. She could have been keeping an eye on him in town, or offering him a bed for a while. When together they met friends of the Burgers she seemed pleased and animated to chat, and forgot him in his presence; his name was Conrad Something-or-other.

Now you are free.
 I don't know that you said it to me or whether I thought it in your presence. It came to me when I was with you; it came from being with you.

I went to the cottage because it was the place of a stranger who said: any time . . . The others, my father's good friends and comrades, would have been too pressingly understanding and demandingly affectionate. They didn't want me to feel alone, I didn't want to be alone in the flat, but these were not the same thing. You had said long before that if I ever needed a place, I could use that cottage. The suggestion had nothing to do with the death of Lionel. You didn't repeat it after he died. You yourself took what you needed. You used my car. You asked me for money and I didn't ask what the need was. You slept while I was at work and if you were out at night I cooked and ate by myself; the bauhinia tree was in flower and bees it attracted were in the roof, like a noise in the head.

Now you are free.

Conrad went off some evenings for Spanish lessons and sometimes came back with the girl who taught him. Those nights he spent in the livingroom; Rosa, going to work in the morning, stepped round the two of them rumpled among the old cushions and kaross on the floor like children overcome by sleep in the middle of a game.

Conrad and Rosa were often in that same livingroom together on Sundays. The yoghurt and fruit of a late breakfast was supplemented from time to time as she would push onto a plate cold leftovers from the fridge and he would fetch a can of beer and bread covered with peanut butter. Now and then it was bread he himself had made.

The cat she had brought with her skittered among the loose sheets of his thesis buried under Sunday papers. —Shall I put these somewhere safe or put the cat out?—

They both laughed at the question implied. The room filled up with his books and papers, his Spanish grammars, his violin and musical scores, records, but in this evidence of activity he lay smoking, often sleeping. She read, repaired her clothes, and wandered in the wilderness outside from which she collected branches, pampas grass feathers, fir cones, and once gardenias that heavy rain had brought back into bloom from the barrenness of neglect.

Sometimes he was not asleep when he appeared to be. —What was your song?—

—Song?— Squatting on the floor cleaning up crumbs of bark and broken leaf.

—You were singing.—

—What? Was I?— She had filled a dented Benares brass pot with loquat branches.

—For the joy of living.—

She looked to see if he were making fun of her. —I didn't know.—

—But you never doubted it for a moment. Your family.—

She did not turn to him that profile of privacy with which he was used to meeting. —Suppose not.—

—Disease, drowning, arrests, imprisonments.— He opened his eyes, almond-shaped and glazed, from ostentatious supine vulnerability. —It didn't make any difference.—

—I haven't thought about it. No. In the end, no difference.— An embarrassed, almost prim laugh. —We were not the only people alive.— She sat on the floor with her feet under her body, thighs sloping forward to the knees, her hands caught between them.

—I am the only person alive.—

She could have turned him away, glided from the territory with the kind of comment that comes easily: How modestly you dispose of the rest of us.

But he had a rudder-like instinct that resisted deflection—A happy family. Your house was a happy one. There were the Moscow trials and there was Stalin—before you and I were even born—there was the East Berlin uprising and there was Czechoslovakia, there're the prisons and asylums filled with people there like your father here. Communists are the last optimists.—

—. . . My brother, my mother: what's that got to do with politics—things like that happen to anybody.—

He moved crossed arms restlessly, his hands clinically palpating his pectoral muscles. —That's it. To anyone—they knock the wind out of anyone. They mean everything . . . In the end no one cares a stuff who's in jail or what war's on, so long as it's far away. But the Lionel Burgers of this world—personal horrors and political ones are the same to you. You live through them all. On the same level. And whatever happens—no matter what happens—

She was waiting, turned away from him, jaw touching her hunched shoulder in listening obstinacy.

He started to speak and stopped, dissatisfied. At last he settled for it with a strange expression of effort round his hair-outlined mouth; as if he stomached something of both the horrors and his own wonder. —Christ. You. Singing under your breath. Picking flowers.—

She drew her hands from between her thighs and looked at the palms, so responsible and unfamiliar a part of herself, as if they had acted without her volition. The words came from her in the same way. —Nothing more than animal survival, perhaps.—

He disappeared from time to time, once brought from Swaziland a wooden bowl and a piece of naïve wood-carving. The bowl held the sleeping cat or his bread-dough left to rise, the red and black bird was set up where he could see it when he woke in the mornings. When Lionel Burger's big car was sold there was only her Volkswagen, and he assumed use of it, waiting to pick her up outside the hospital without a spoken greeting. Sometimes, not having discussed the intention, they spent evenings in cinemas or, strolling out into the wilderness round the tin cottage, kept walking for miles through the suburbs.

On such a night they walked past her father's house. As she approached it, a passer-by, her tread slowed. Her companion's pace dropped to hers. The lights were on in the upstairs rooms for him to see but only she knew that the watermarks of light behind the dark windows of the livingroom came from a window in the passage to which the inner door must have been left ajar. Only she, her ear accustomed to separating its pitch from all other sounds, could hear that across the garden, beyond the walls, the upstairs telephone was ringing in its place in her mother's room.

He was at ease in the streets as children or black men. A fist knocked on the trunk of the pavement tree they stood under, a caress for its solidity. —How old were you and I when Sharpeville happened?—

No one answered the telephone still ringing, still ringing, not her mother, Lily clopping upstairs in shoes whose backs were bent under her spread heels, old Kowalski obliging, Lionel, herself. —Twelve. About.—

—Just twelve. D'you remember?—

—Of course I remember.—

—I know what I've read, that's all.—

Shifting stains of leaf-shadows over their bodies and faces made the movement of air something seen instead of felt, as in place of feeling her habitation about her, she saw her own shell.

—I suppose in that house there was *outrage*.— In the dark and half-dark each was a creature camouflaged by suburban vegetation.

—Your favourite expression.—

—Lionel found out they'd been shot in the back. I asked my mother and she explained . . . but I didn't understand what it meant, the difference if you were hit in the back or chest. Someone we knew well, Sipho Mokoena—he was there when it happened and he came straight to us, my father was called from his consulting rooms—Sipho wasn't hurt, his trouser-leg was ripped by a bullet. I'd imagined (from cowboy films?) a bullet went right through you and there would be two holes . . . both the same . . . but when I heard my father asking him so many questions, then I understood that what mattered was you could see which side and from which level a bullet came. Lionel had ways of getting in touch with people who worked at the hospital where the wounded had been taken—the press wasn't allowed near. I woke up very late at night, it must have been three in the morning when he came back and everyone was with my mother in our diningroom, I remember the dishes still on the table, she'd made food for people. They didn't go to bed at all. The ANC leaders were there, and the lawyers, Gifford Williams and someone else—it was urgent to go out and get sworn statements from witnesses so that if there was going to be an inquiry what really happened would come out, it wouldn't just be a State cover-up . . . PAC people—Tsolo and his men were the ones who'd actually organized that particular protest against passes at the Sharpeville police station, but that didn't matter, what happened had gone far beyond political rivalry. When I got up again for school Lionel was already shut in with other people, he hadn't had any sleep. Lily gave me a tray of coffee to take to them, and they'd forgotten to turn off the lights in the daylight.—The sort of thing that sticks in your mind when you're a child.—Tony and I kept asking Sipho to show us where his trousers were torn. Sipho said how when the police were loading the dead into vans he had to ask them to take the brains as well— the brains of a man with a smashed head spilled and they left them in the road. My mother got agitated and took Tony out of the room. He was yelling and kicking, he didn't want to go. But I heard how Sipho said they sent a black policeman to pick up the brains with a shovel.—

—Some blacks shot in the back. It's something that changed the look of everything for you, in there (indicating the house) the way firelight passes over a room in the dark. Am I supposed to believe that?—

—But at twelve, you must have been aware—

—Political events couldn't ever have existed for me at that age. What shooting could compare with discovering for myself that my mother had another man? If your father had succeeded in a conspiracy to rouse the whole population of blacks to revolution, I wouldn't have known what hit me.—

—What'd you do?—

—What does Oedipus do about two rivals? I lay on her in day-dreams at school, and when she was serving dinner I stared at her dress where her legs divided—*how awful?* (she could hear in his voice the mimicry of the shocked face he imagined he could see on her in the dark)—I was mad about her; now I could be, with someone other than my father there already. I was in love; you don't think about anything else then.—

Two black men with a woman, arms akimbo between them, went by chattering explosively, servants at home in their white masters' orbit of neighbourly domesticity. They did not notice or did not recognize Rosa. —Your mother—who lives in Knysna?—

—My mother. The same. She's not old now but the other thing—you know, in between. Old at the roots; when her hair grows out half-an-inch white she dyes it again. Never more than half-an-inch old. She's got a better figure than you, in trousers. Lives with my sister, that thoroughly domesticated character who has produced five children. No men around except my sister's little fat stud. They run a pottery school, the two women. She's always bending over the kiln, or something in the oven or grandchildren who need their noses wiped. The same one: I suppose she is.—

The telephone had stopped ringing in the house. Rosa knew by some faint lack of distraction in her ears. Somebody living there now had picked it up.

—Got a match?— She did not smoke.

He paused a second, took out his lighter with thumb scuffing to ignite it. As if guided, he passed the small illumination across the plaque of dimensions that did not cover exactly the whitish square on the brick gateway: the baked enamel profile of a fierce dog, warning emblem of the installation of a burglar alarm system.

—What happened then—

—Nothing happened—not as things were always happening in that house.— They turned away from it, under the pavement trees. —Some of us knew, and some didn't, I suppose. I think our girl did and that gave her a hold over my mother, the white missus was afraid of someone . . . I think I saw that in the way my mother

40

treated her, always flattering her a bit. That's how you learn about power, from things like that. Poor ma. I didn't think of her body any more because I became fascinated by the electrical points in the house.——

The street-lights lost and found them at regular intervals, the street gave way to another. ——I knew from one of those kid's kits I got one Christmas or birthday—no, I suppose I was doing physics at school by then—how quickly two-twenty volts pass through your body. Just a second's contact. You don't have to grasp or thrust. It's not like sticking a knife, or definite as pulling a trigger. Just a touch. I used to stand looking at that brown bakelite thing for minutes at a time: all you have to do is switch on and stick your fingers in the holes. A terrible fear and temptation.——

Their voices rose and fell alone in the cottage. A few steps out into the wilderness and the surge of cicadas mastered, obliterated them as the darkness did their bodies between street-lights; at certain times of day the rise of traffic from the freeways by which they were almost surrounded swirled, isolating words like the cries of birds where the tide engulfs a promontory.

—Didn't you ever imagine killing something, just because it was small and weak? You know how you're obsessed with the possibility of death when you're adolescent. A rabbit that was afraid of you? Somebody's baby you admired in a pram? What it would be like—so easy—to hurt it as a punishment for its helplessness? Rosa? Haven't you even noticed the look of a kid's face sometimes, when it gazes at the infant lying there. A little head you could imagine crushing, while never being able to hurt anything? When you were a kid? What did you make of those feelings?——

Once she appealed, half-angry. —Conrad, you won't believe it. It's like saying to someone you never masturbated. I don't know that I ever had them.——

—The day somebody said look, that's Rosa Burger . . . from the first time . . . I have the impression you've grown up entirely through other people. What they told you was appropriate to feel and do. How did you begin to know yourself? You go through the motions . . . what's expected of you. What you've come to rely on.—

She had taken on a way of sitting up very straight, at once resistant and yet alert to the point of strain. She did not need to look at him.

—I don't know how else to put it. Rationality, extraversion . . . but I want to steer clear of terms because that's what I'm getting at: just words; life isn't there. The tension that makes it possible to live is created somewhere else, some other way.—

Sometimes she parried, insulting in her return to the manner of one who could not be reached by someone like him.

—In the *I Ching*.—

—That crap.— The girl he slept with carried the book as her breviary.

—According to Jung, then.— A book beside the bed.

—But there's something there for you, never mind! One day when he was a kid Jung imagined God sitting up in the clouds and shitting on the world below. His father was a pastor . . . You commit the great blasphemy against all doctrine, and you begin to live . . .—

—*What* tension are you talking about? Why tension?—

—The tension between creation and destruction in yourself.—

Rosa, lips together, breathing fast, the look of someone struggling with anger, dismay or contempt. —Wandering between your fantasies and obsessions.—

—Yes, fantasies, obsessions. They're mine. They're the form in which the question of my own existence is being put to me. From them come the marvels (in that gesture he had from some bar- or bible-thumping ancestor he put the flat of his hand, hard, on Borges' poems she had been reading), the real reasons why you won't kill and perhaps why you can go on living. Saint-Simon and Fourier and Marx and Lenin and Luxemburg whose namesake you are—you can't get that from them.—

When he began to talk (he who had no conversation among other people) she would lose mental grip of what she was occupied with, keeping still and quiet as if to attract something that might approach her. Her hands told the beads of repetitive gesture. Her feet and calves went numb beneath her weight but she did not get up from her place on the floor, the continuance of a sensation holding a train of lucidity.

—Of course I wanted to kill myself. I believed I ought to kill myself for fucking my mother. That's clear and easy to you and me. No difference, when it comes to guilt, between what you've done and what you've imagined. But I had no idea . . . I didn't know the connection existed.—

—You poor little devil.—

—No no no. *Rosa, I'm telling the truth about what matters.* This was just one of the ways I happened to come to reaching the realities: sex and death. Everything else is ducking away.—

She raked the four fingers of her left hand through the stiff, dirty pile of the old carpet, again and again.

—You saw someone dead when you were little.—

—No. Oh a dog or cat. Birds we killed at school, with a catapult. Or at least they did—others. I gave up.—

She smiled. —Why—

—They didn't sing any more.—

—So you chose the 'joy of living'.—

—In my way. Being *told* it was cruel certainly hadn't stopped me.—

Somewhere down in the wilderness outside the cottage the roadmakers had an equipment dump, with mounds of small stones, upturned wheelbarrows treacled with tar, poles and trestles and lanterns for barricades. There was a hut made of sheets of lead ceiling and loose bricks from the demolished mansion. The watchman's brazier, pierced with triangular red eyes at night, smoked through half-bald pepper trees and velour-leafed loquats during the day; outlaw cats waited to streak upon the crusts of burned mealie-meal from the big black pot without a handle that belched on the coals. The sounds of a camp established the direction of the place; there were always hangers-on gathered around him. Rosa came upon the curious stance of the back of a drunk man peeing against a tree; or the cat,

43

sensing the presence of some menace from its own kind, suddenly pinned in thin air an uncompleted gambol.

The watchman gave Conrad money to place bets at the racecourse. The man came regularly to the cottage in the late afternoons; he took off his yellow oilskin hat and asked for the master. If Conrad were not there but might be back soon, Rosa invited him to come in but such a suggestion was incomprehensible to him, he understood it only as the established procedure for approaching a white man's house; sat on the broken step that was all that remained of five that had once led to the verandah, and waited until the white man came.

Conrad squatted down with him there. He read out the names of horses and the odds quoted and the watchman interrupted with throat-noises of assent or sometimes let silences of indecision hold, after Conrad had paused, expecting assent. Conrad pushed the man's paper money into the pocket of his jeans, from which he would use it as ready cash; apparently he took its equivalent from his earnings at the race-course when actually placing the bets at the tote. The watchman giggled with falsetto joy as he was paid out a win. He would take the young white man by the wrist, the shoulder, good fortune made flesh. He would ask, as of right, for a beer. Conrad laughed. —He should be standing me.—

She brought the beer cans. —You're the fount from which all blessings flow.—

Once the black man was emboldened by happiness to talk to her. —Your brother is very clever. I like such a clever one like him.—

—What happens when that watchman loses his money?—

—It's gone. That's all.—

—He can't afford the risk.—

—He can't afford the kick he gets out of winning, either.—

When they went among Conrad's friends she talked easily and he was almost as withdrawn as he was when they encountered the Burger faction. One of his friends was building a sailing ship in a backyard. Rosa laughed with pleasure at the incongruous sight, rearing up between a dog kennel, a garage, and the servant's room where the bed raised on bricks could be seen through the open door. Conrad studied diagrams and charts relating to the ship's construction and the seas on the route proposed. Apparently the idea was that he would navigate from island to island across the Indian Ocean to Australia. The friend looked up at her, casually generous. —Come along.—

—Oh I'd love to. You could drop me off at Dar es Salaam to see my brother.—

It was a game, pretending she had a passport, referring to the son of her father's first marriage, whom she had never seen, as her sibling; her polite fantasy to make herself acceptable among these people absorbed in planing wild-smelling wood and sewing bunk covers. Like a temptation, she returned to its conventions while she and Conrad were cutting each other's hair in the bathroom of the cottage. He had read aloud a poem Baudelaire wrote about Mauritius, translating for her.

—André and his girl have it all out of a manual. I think I'd be scared to go all that way to sea with only one person aboard who knows anything about sailing.—

—So what? You're not scared to stay at home and go to prison.—

She held his head steady to gauge the evenness of the hair-level over the ears. He let her snip towards his lobes.

She took his place on the lid of the lavatory seat. He put round her shoulders the towel furred with his hair, the pale colour and rough as the nap of sacking. —Close your eyes.—

She felt the cold little metal beak along her forehead. —Not too much. Don't scalp me.—

—Don't worry. You look okay. You'll survive.—

She spoke with a change of key. —Why should I go to prison?—

—Well you will, won't you. Sooner or later.—

Her eyes were closed against the falling hair. —If Lionel and my mother . . . if the concepts of our life, our relationships, we children accepted from them were those of Marx and Lenin, they'd already become natural and personal by the time they reached me. D'you see? It was all on the same level at which you—I—children learn to eat with a knife and fork, go to church if their parents do, use the forms of address by which the parents' attitudes—respect, disapproval, envy, whatever—towards people are expressed. I was the same as every other kid.—

—You were not. You are not. Not my kind of kid.—

—*You* were exceptional. From what you've told me.—

—No. Go to church if the parents do. Exactly. You're all atheists, yes? But being brought up in a house like your father's is growing up in a devout family. Perhaps nobody preached Marx or Lenin . . . They just lay around the house, leather-bound with gold tooling, in everybody's mind—the family bible. It was all taken in with your breakfast cornflakes. But the people who came to your house weren't there for tea-parties with your mother or bridge evenings with cigars. They weren't your father's golf-playing fellow doctors or ladies your mother went shopping with, ay?—They came together to make a revolution. That was ordinary, to you. That—*intention*. It was ordinary. It was the normal atmosphere in that house.—

—You have the craziest ideas about that house.— She was brought up short by her own use of the definition 'that house', distancing the private enclosures of her being.

—Keep still. You'll be nicked.—

—You seem to think people go around talking revolution as if they were deciding where to go for their summer holidays. Or which new car to buy. You romanticize.— The cartilage of her nostrils stiffened. The patient manner patronized him, displayed the deceptive commonplace that people accustomed to police harassment use before the uninitiated.

—I don't mean in so many words—their preoccupations supposed the revolution must be achieved; the scale of what mattered and what didn't, what moved you and didn't, in your life every day, presupposed it. Didn't it?—

She had stayed the attack of the scissors, holding up almost aggressively a jagged piece of mirror to see what he was taking off her nape hair. She was murmuring, complaining of him without attentive coherence. —I went to school, I had my friends, our place was always full of people who did all sorts of different jobs

46

and talked about everything under the sun . . . you were there once, you saw—

—What'd you celebrate in your house? The occasions were when somebody got off, not guilty, in a political trial. Leaders came out of prison. A bunch of blacks made a success of a boycott or defied a law. There was a mass protest or a march, a strike . . . Those were your nuptials and fiestas. When blacks were shot by the police, when people were detained, when leaders went to jail, when new laws shifted populations you'd never even seen, banned and outlawed people, those were your mournings and your wakes. These were the occasions you were taught (precept and example, oh I know that, nothing authoritarian about your father) were the real ones, not your own private kicks and poor little ingrown miseries.

—But where are they, those miseries, and your great wild times? I look at you . . .—

—Oh there were parties, all right . . . Christmas trees, weddings. People had affairs with other people's wives . . .—You don't have a corner on that. I don't know about my mother and father—I doubt it. Although Lionel was very attractive to women. You probably saw that at the trial—I think most good doctors are . . . There were terrible rows and antagonisms between people . . .—

—But between the faithful; yes, political ones.—

She continued her list. —And there were deaths.—

In the middle of the night, he began to speak.

—But isn't it true—you had your formula for dealing with that, too.—

She lay and listened to the seething and sweeping of the bauhinia tree against the tin roof.

—Isn't it? A prescribed way to deal with the frail and wayward flesh that gets sick and wasted and drowns. Some people scream and beat their breasts, others try to follow into the next world, table-tapping and so on. Among you, the cause is what can't die. Your mother didn't live to carry it on, others did. The little boy, your brother didn't grow up to carry it on, others will. It's immortality. If you can accept it. Christian resignation's only one example. A cause more important than an individual is another. The same con, the future in place of the present. Lives you can't live, instead of your own. You didn't cry when your father was sentenced. I saw. People said how brave. Some people say, a cold fish. But it's conditioning, brain-washing: more like a trained seal, maybe.—

—What do you do when something terrible happens?— Before he answered she spoke again, from the outline of her profile seen as the valleys and peaks of a night horizon beside him. —What would you do—nothing like that's ever happened to you.—

—Want to pull the world down round my ears, that's what.—

—Pretty useless.—

—I don't give a fuck about what's 'useful'. The will is my own. The emotion's my own. The right to be inconsolable. When I feel, there's no 'we', only 'I'.—

They whispered in the dark, children telling secrets. He got up and closed the window on the swaying, battering windy blackness. He kept a cassette player on the floor beside the bed, and he felt for the keys and pressed one on the tinkly, choppy surprise of Scott Joplin's music. The gay, simple progressions climbed and strutted about the room. Her feet fidgeted under the bedclothes, slowly took on rhythm like a cat's paws kneading. He threw back the covers and they watched the silhouettes of their waving feet, wagging like tongues, talking like hands. Soon they got up and began to dance in the dark, their shapes flying and entangling, a jigging and thumping and whirling, a giggling, gasping as mysterious as the movement of rats on the rafters, or the swarming of bees, taking shelter under the tin roof.

The one in the church-going hat who came to hear sentence pronounced on Lionel Burger was the relative to whom the children were sent the single time when both parents were arrested together. She was a sister of Burger and she and her husband had a farm and ran the local hotel in the dorp of the same district.

Rosa had been armed very young by her parents against the shock of such contingencies by the assumption that imprisonment was part of the responsibilities of grown-up life, like visiting patients (her father) or going to work each day in town (once her mother was banned from working as a trade unionist, she ran the buying office of a co-operative for blacks and coloureds). At eight years old Rosa could tell people the name by which the trial, in which her father and mother were two of the accused, was known, the Treason Trial, and explain that they had been refused bail which meant they couldn't come home. Tony perhaps did not realize where they were; Auntie Velma encouraged the idea that he was 'on holiday' on the farm—an attitude the parents would not have thought 'correct' and that their daughter, resenting any deviation from her parents' form of trust as a criticism and betrayal of them, tried to counter. But the five-year-old boy was being allowed to help make bricks: if he had lived to be a man perhaps he would never have outgrown—given up?—this happy seclusion of what he himself was seeing, touching, feeling, from anything outside it.

Baasie was left behind. Rosa had flown into a temper over this—the way to tears through a display of anger—but she was told by Lily Letsile that Baasie wouldn't like to be out in the veld.

—He would.—

—No, he's scared, he's scared for the cows, the sheeps, the snakes—

49

A lying singsong. Lily and Auntie Velma both used it; whereas Rosa believed her parents never lied. Baasie, the black boy almost Rosa's age who lived with the Burger family, went to the private school run illegally by one of the Burgers' associates that Rosa herself had attended until she was too old and had to go to the school for white girls. He was not afraid of anything except sleeping alone, Alsatian dogs, and learning how to swim. He and Rosa had often shared a bed when they were as little as Tony, they scuttled wildly together from that particular breed of dog and fought for the anchorage of wet hair on Lionel Burger's warm breast in the cold swimming-pool. Baasie was sent to a grandmother; he did not seem to have another mother (he had Rosa's mother, anyway) and his father, an African National Congress organizer from the Transkei, moved about too much to be able to take care of him.

The Nel relatives lived between their farm and their hotel. Three initials and a name over the doorway to the bar and the main entrance from the hotel stoep stood for Uncle Coen. He drove back and forth from his tobacco sheds and cattle to town in a big yellow American car with rubber spats trailing to protect the chassis from mud. Auntie Velma ran the hotel office and drove very fast, in a combi with curtains tied at the waist, from hotel to farmhouse, to the railway station to pick up frozen fish for the second course on the menu, to scattered schools each Friday to fetch children, and to church on Sundays. Tony had his bricks and a cousin not yet of school-going age; Rosa gradually came to make the choice, when car or combi was going back to the farm, of staying at the hotel.

More and more, she based herself in the two rooms marked STRICTLY PRIVATE—STRENG PRIVAAT at the end of the hotel stoep. These rooms had no numbers. There was, instead, outside one, a wooden clock-face with large hands, a wire-and-feather cuckoo, and a poker-work verse: Dear Friend—If you came and we were out/Please before you turn about/Write your name! What time you came! Do call again! COEN AND VELMA NEL. A jotter hung from a string but the pencil was missing. This device was immediately recognizable to any child as something from childhood's own system of signification. Beyond any talisman is a private world unrelated to and therefore untouched by what is lost or gained, disappears or is substituted for, in events of which the child is at mercy. She knew a badge, a password, when she met with one. She never left the Nels' quarters without reaching up and turning the wooden hands to the time she went out the door. (She and Baasie had been given watches for Christmas. She remembered to take hers off before getting into the bath; he had not.)

She would disappear under the dummy cuckoo clock while running down the corridor in the middle of a game with the children of hotel guests. These children would be gone, themselves, in the morning. But no one could sleep in those two rooms STRENG PRIVAAT for one night as they did in the other rooms of the hotel, moving off early for the Kruger Park or the next stop in a commercial traveller's lowveld round, the beds quickly stripped by the maids Selena and Elsie under lights left burning by the decamped, the early morning coffee tray and the night's empty beer bottles standing in the corridor. Numbered rooms were all alike. All the lavatory paper was pink; each narrow bedside rug was speckled mustard-brown; between twin beds a radio was affixed to the wall and above each headboard was a coloured print showing a street scene with similar trees, taxis, people sitting drinking at little tables, and girls with high heels and poodles. Rosa read very well but the shop signs in these pictures were in a foreign language; the word she could recognize was 'Paris'—a place far away in England, she was able to tell Selena and Elsie as she followed them round from room to room, talking above the noise of the vacuum cleaner and the radio they kept turned up while they worked.

The two rooms where no guests were allowed in were exactly as a child would have expected, would have arranged them herself: crowded, overgrown with possessions whose origin was as individual as the standardization of hotel furnishings was anonymous, a shrine of coloured photographs of weddings and babies, souvenirs and natural curiosities. There were no books, no flowers: it was not at all like home—her father's house—but stood in relation to the hotel as the child's cupboard full of treasures does to its parents' domain. The light came through windows safe with burglar-bars, cosy with the domestic lianas of net curtains and wandering philodendron. She lay on a thick carpet the colour of the red you see when you shut your eyes against sunlight and looked at women's magazines and the *Farmer's Weekly*. A parakeet with the digit of a claw missing raised the shutter of one lid then the other. A perlelemoen-shell ashtray, a miniature Limoges teaset, a fossil fragment, tortoise carapace, black-tipped Sacred Ibis feathers someone had stuck in a Vat 69 glass filched from the bar—each was charged with associations she could feel without having to know its history; the rich clutter of private ends pursued was there, in place.

Although no one could enter these quarters, Rosa could come and go as she pleased. With the hotel dog tittuping ahead on three legs she wandered the wide dirt streets behind the main road in the mornings. Scarcely anyone passed her; a white woman going shopping on foot, a bicycle zigzagging. The houses, little and crabbed, with tin roofs, dark stoeps and windows that were never open, or amply haphazard with clumsy gables like dough-shapes, gave no sign of life but the clucking of chickens and the successive frenzies of dogs who, like the one who accompanied her, were all related in the common progenitor of a yappy Pomeranian-Fox Terrier cross. A parallel neighbourly cross-breeding of gardens produced, the length of the streets, the same blinding luxury of cerise bougainvillaea, golden shower creeper, red hibiscus, the same pink and cream frangipani surrounded by a sweet confetti of their own flower-droppings, the same furzy tree-ferns and green-dugged pawpaw palms: the artificial 'tropical' gardens of smart resort hotels, elsewhere in the world. They ravelled out in mealie and pumpkin patches where the dorp ended in khakiweed and rusty metal and the veld merged with it. When she reached these quiet, wild, sleeping limits sudden rustlings aware of her—the presence of rats or snakes, once a nest of kittens that hissed and fled from her—turned her back.

But there were landmarks. She went as far as a broken-paved

space within loops of rusty chain where she puzzled over the letters carved on a stone obelisk, although she was, as Uncle Coen told her, ' 'n Boere meisie' who knew her mother tongue, Afrikaans. The inscription was in Hollands, dating from the time of the Transvaal Boer Republic, commemorating the site of the first Gereformeerde Kerk in the district. Another street ended at the church to which she was taken with the Nel family on Sundays, wearing a borrowed hat. It was a new building of the kind that marked the existence of a dorp from miles away at every turn in the landscape. Its copper-covered spike stuck into the sky like a giant, gleaming, three-sided floor-nail. The street that was in line with the most direct path across the veld to the location was where old black men or women greeted her as if she were a grown-up, black children giggled and talked about her, she could tell, as they passed with a loaf or packet on their heads. Once when a group was playing some sort of tag as they sauntered, and a packet broke, she tried to help scoop up the spilt mealie-meal and realized they couldn't speak Afrikaans or English.

She was resting, in the chair she'd discovered for herself—the solid surface roots of a marula tree, another landmark—when the old oom* who often sat talking on the hotel stoep to whoever would listen, came by. He walked so slowly, appearing to use his stiff hip as a cane past which he dragged his other leg, that she recognized him from a long way. He stopped and spoke in Afrikaans. —What is a child doing out of school, this time?— She could only giggle and say nothing, as the black children had done when she spoke to them. —My child! Go on, now! Go home! Your mother's waiting. Your poor mother, waiting for you to come from school!—

She got up and beat at her dress. The dog sniffed the old man's trousers and jumped away, barking. She did not say to him: my mother's in prison. How could he understand that? The prison was down the road, just behind the police station where the flag flew. A little stone building, and in the yard at the back where the police

* Uncle.

53

van stood, tin sheds with barred windows. The prisoners were barefoot black men in loose shorts whom anyone could see cutting the grass with lengths of sharpened iron outside the municipal offices.

Daniel the bar waiter who served on the stoep sat on an upended beer crate on the pavement when there was nobody drinking. He wore a red monkey-jacket with black grosgrain lapels that smelled strongly of sweat as he moved his arms, a bow-tie, a red-and-black forage cap, and peeling black patent shoes whose shine cracked over the strange protrusions on his feet—like Selena and Elsie, he walked to work across the dusty veld from the location every day. Rosa hopped about on the pavement, coming and going before him while they talked. She described Johannesburg, which he had never seen. —When you going back, me I'm coming there too. I'm going work for your house. Your daddy.— She told him no, Lily Letsile worked for her mother and father. He told her he had five children and would send one of the boys to work in her garden. —How old?—

—Oh he's coming big. I think is nearly thirteen years now.—

—He'll have to go to school, not work in the garden. Children don't work. But he's too big to go to school with Baasie and my school's only for girls.—

Daniel laughed and laughed, as if she were very funny.

Suddenly she told him: —My mother and father are in jail.—

Daniel lowered and waggled his head, gave out grunting yelps, and screwed up one eye to pin reproach on her. —Don't say like that about your parents. Always your parents look after you nice, send you nice school, make everything for you. Don't say those thing.—

The white barman had black sideburns, a bright skin, and wore a belt with a lion's head buckle. Once he took it off and chased Tony and the cousin out of the bar when they were making a nuisance of themselves, but it was only in play. Daniel told Rosa that Baas Schutte used his belt if he found any of the waiters stealing drink; this was the sort of gossip that passed away hours, on the pavement.

—Did you see?— She did not quite believe anyone would hit a grown-up, although she knew some people smacked their children.

—There in the yard! He was holding and that boy he couldn't run away! He's too strong, Baas Schutte!— Daniel was laughing again.

—Which waiter?— She knew them all; they brought her her food, padding heavily in and out the swing doors from the dining-room to the kitchen with its blast of smells and noise, they gambled with bottle tops or flung themselves down to smoke in the sun outside the kitchen.

—Jack? Was it Jack?— She had heard Auntie Velma having an argument with Jack about dried-up mustard in the little metal pots that stood on the tables.

—Jack? Jack he's not waiter for bar! How Baas Schutte can trouble for Jack? That one he's gone away. He won't work here no more in town. He's go away there to his home. He's too frightened for Baas Schutte!— Daniel clapped his hands on his tin tray.

Harry Schutte often took her along for the ride beside him when he drove off in the van that had the name of the hotel and 'Off-Sales' painted on it. Jumping down at the cartage contractor's, the hardware store, the estate and insurance agent's where his girl-friend worked, he seemed to forget Rosa, but would always bring her an ice-cream or a liquorice pipe. The girl-friend leaned on the van window and flirted with him through the child. —Shame, when's your mommy coming back from overseas? Don't you want to come and stay by me so long? I've got a nice house. Haven't I, Harry? I've got two puppies . . . you ask Harry—

Five weeks after she and her brother had been sent away Rosa sat on Daniel's box while he was busy serving the people who filled the verandah tables from mid-morning on a Saturday. A party of schoolgirls voluptuous in track suits jounced down the main street on their way from a sports meeting. Black women selling mealies sat with babies crawling from under the coloured towels they wore as shawls. Farmers whose hats hid their eyes waited for wives and children who trailed and darted in and out of shops, sucking sweets and clutching parcels. Black children coming up behind humble parents were in rags or running barefoot, bundled from above the knees in school uniforms that could be afforded only once in years, so that small boys were tiny within vast clothing, and big boys wore burst and almost unrecognizable versions of the same. Young white bloods revved dust under their wheels, car radios streaming snatches of music. Black youths in token imitations of this style— a bicycle with racing handles, a transistor on a shoulder-strap, or merely a certain way of lounging against the pillars of the Greek fish-and-chip shop opposite the hotel—occasionally crossed, making the cars avoid them, to pick up cigarette butts thrown away by the hotel drinkers on the stoep. Daniel skittered and sweated; the customers climbed the steps past Rosa: huge marbled legs of a young woman who shouted to him for a double rum and coke, dainty little girls with miniature handbags sent off into the hotel hand-in-hand—*Ask the boy where the toilet is*. The parents sat over their beers as if they did not know each other, the grandmothers spread in their chairs like rising bread; there were the fragile grandfathers to whom middle-aged daughters shouted, the sulky young girls who turned away from their families, sucking at straws with eyes narrowed in an assumption of unawareness of passing men. Farmers' wives with cake-boxes exchanged cries of greeting over Rosa's head. The barman's dog ignored her in the bristling pleasure of approaching the town clerk's Pomeranian from whose strain he was distantly sprung. All this ordered life surrounded, coated, swaddled Rosa; the order of Saturday, the order of family hierarchy, the order of black people out in the street and white people in the shade of the hotel stoep. Its flow contained her, drumming her bare heels on Daniel's box, its voices over her head protected her. Her aunt with the confidential, comedian's smile of a woman with a long prominent jaw was suddenly above her. —Guess what? Mommy's coming to fetch you.—

At eye-level, a small boy passed holding in his fist one finger of his father's huge hand.

—And daddy?—

—Not just yet, Rosa.—

Charges against her mother had been withdrawn. Her father was released on bail soon after she and her brother came home, and was on trial for twenty-eight months before the court quashed the indictment against him and sixty other accused out of the ninety-one committed for trial. In the Burger house there was a party, then, more joyous than any wedding, cathartic than any wake, triumphant than any *stryddag* held by the farmers of the Nels' district in celebration of the white man's power, the heritage of his people that Lionel Burger betrayed.

Now you are free. The knowledge that my father was not there ever, any more, that he was not simply hidden away by walls and steel grilles; this disembowelling childish dolour that left me standing in the middle of them all needing to whimper, howl, while I could say nothing, tell nobody: suddenly it was something else. Now you are free.

I was afraid of it: a kind of discovery that makes one go dead-cold and wary.

What does one do with such knowledge?

Flora Donaldson's bossy joy in managing other people's lives saw me taking off for another country: always in Africa, of course, because wasn't that where my father had earned the right for us to belong? Wasn't that our covenant, whatever happened to us there? You saw me in prison. Matter-of-factly, eventually, inevitably. For you, I could not be visualized leaving, living any other life than the one necessity—political necessity?—had made for me so far. You with your navel-fluff-picking hunt for 'individual destiny': didn't you understand, everything that child, that girl did was out of what is between daughter and mother, daughter and brother, daughter and father. When I was passive, in that cottage, if you had known—I was struggling with a monstrous resentment against the claim—not of the Communist Party!—of blood, shared genes, the semen from which I had issued and the body in which I had grown. I stand outside the prison with an eider-down and hidden messages for my mother. Tony is dead and there is no other child but me, for her. Two hundred and seventeen days with the paisley scarf in my pocket, while the witnesses came in and out the dock condemning my father. My mother is dead and there is only me, there, for him. Only me. My studies, my work, my love affairs must fit in with the twice-monthly visits to the prison, for life, as long as he lives—if he had lived. My professors, my employers, my men must accept this overruling. I have no passport because I am my father's daughter. People who associate with me must be prepared to be suspect because I am my father's daughter. And there is more to it, more than you know—what I wanted was to take a law degree, but there was no point; too unlikely that, my father's daughter, I should be allowed to practise law, so I had to do something else instead, anything, something that would pass as politically innocuous, why not in the field of medicine, my father's daughter. And now he is dead! Dead! I prowled about that abandoned garden, old Lolita's offspring caught Hottentot Gods in the grass that had taken over the tennis court, and I knew I must have wished him to die; that to exult and to sorrow were the same thing for me.

We had in common such terrible childish secrets, in the tin house: you can fuck your mother, and wish your father dead.

There is more to it. More than you guessed or wormed out of me in your curiosity and envy, talking when the lights were out, more than I knew, or wanted to know until I came to listen to you, unable to stop, although the shape of your feet held by the sweat in your discarded socks, the doubt whether the money in the two-finger-pocket with the button missing at the waist of your jeans always went where the watchman trusted it to—these venial familiarities of the body's exuding or the mind's deviousness were repugnant to although loyally not criticized or revealed by me. So it was when my brother Tony pinched stamps from my father's desk and sold them at a cent or two in excess of the post office price to the servants round about who wrote to their homes in Malawi and Moçambique, or when he gave himself away by farting with anguish whenever he lied, poor little boy. —The Saturday morning Tony drowned I saw him bringing his friends to swim and I told him not to show off and dive. He promised, but I could smell him.

Still more to it than you knew. My Swede, that Marcus whose name you didn't bring up because you thought it would be painful for me was of no importance, whether he went away or stayed.

What was there between us—as the language of emotional contract puts it? That's easy. He wanted to make a film about my father, in Stockholm. It was going to be a collage of documentary evidence of events and fictional links, with an actor playing the part of my father. I had to look at photographs of Swedish actors and say which I thought would come closest to suggesting Lionel Burger. Because of course Marcus could never see him. Not even as he was then, in prison. We went together one weekend to a Transvaal dorp, for me to show the sort of environment in which my father grew up. We also went together to Cape Town because my father was at the medical school there as a student. That wasn't the reason the Swede gave to the principal. He got into the School to take some footage by telling everyone he was making a film about South Africa's wonderful heart transplants. But the real reason for going to Cape Town was not even the one we concealed, the real reason was to make love at the sea. He had that sexual passion for nature I imagine is peculiarly Northern. Something to do with too much cold and darkness, and then the short period when there is no night and they don't sleep at all. He called it 'dragon-fly summer', just like one long, extraordinary, bright day in which to live a complete life-cycle.

We take nature more easily, the sun's always here. Except in prison; even in Africa, prisons are dark. Lionel said how the sun never came into his cell, only the coloured reflection of some sunsets, that would make a parallelogram coated with delicate pearly light, broken by the interruption of the bars, on the wall opposite his window.

The Swede had buttocks tanned as his back and legs—all of a unity, as if his body had no secrets. He was beautiful. And whether or not I am, he felt the same about me and could coax from me— that is the only way to describe the pride and appreciation, the simplicity of his patience and skill—three orgasms, one after the other, each pleasuring spreading to the limits of the spent one like the water touching to its own tidemarks on the sand. This had never happened to me before. And he wrote to me, when Lionel died. He said he would try to show a rough cut of the unfinished film if the Scandinavian anti-apartheid group held a memorial meeting. He had offered to try through his wife's connections to get a passport for me, abroad, if ever I could leave. Perhaps, from his safety, from his welfare state where left-wing groups were like mothers' unions or Rotary Clubs, and left-wing views did not imply any endangering action, being the lover of Lionel Burger's daughter for a month or two was the nearest he would ever get to the barricades. I don't mind. What else was I?

I told you how my 'engagement' to Noel de Witt was a device to enable him to be kept in touch with when he was in prison. You said with that insistent prurience with which people are curious about that with which they want nothing to do, You mean the underground Communist movement. They used you to keep in touch with him?

Yes of course, it was the obvious, an excellent idea, everyone decided.

—In that house?—

Yes of course, our house; it was natural, no one could suspect otherwise. Noel was one of my father's known associates, he practically lived with us anyway, nothing extraordinary in his supposed to be going to marry Lionel Burger's daughter. And his fiancée had the same privileges as a prisoner's wife has—visits, letters and so on. Without me he would have had no one; he was half-Portuguese, his mother prohibited entry to South Africa because she was a Frelimo sympathizer who had been arrested by the Portuguese at one time, his father disappeared somewhere in Australia. Who would there have been to bring him books and writing paper? My mother and father knew what these things mean when you're inside—the sight of a face that signals the outside still exists, a face whose associations assume that others are carrying on with what has to be done. And even the ingenuity, the blandly-outwitting joke played on the Director of Prisons, who cannot refuse permission for an 'engaged' girl to see her boy, the warders who feel a sneaking empathy even with a Commie when he gazes at his girl across the barrier in the visiting room—that gave confidence. That was one of the satisfactions you didn't have on the list of our pleasures in that house—outsmarting the police. Noel entered gaily into the spirit of the thing. When he noticed the ring that had appeared on my finger for the first visit, he kept asking me whether I was quite sure I liked it? Quite, quite sure?—with all the basking persuasiveness of one who has chosen, he knows, exactly what his darling would want. The ring I wore my mother got from Aletta Gous, remembering that Aletta would rummage for just the right thing—a mean little round diamond thrust up on a mound of filigree steel-coloured metal, indispensable piece of equipment for the dorp betrothal. I don't think it was a fake; somewhere in the nineteen-thirties Aletta had been a young girl in a country town and had nearly married the young man who ran his father's garage and was an usher in the church of a Dutch Reformed sect called the Pinksters. When she outcast herself by running away to the city and taking part in street-corner meetings of the Communist Party, perhaps she flaunted her jaunty contempt for the broken bourgeois convention by keeping its flimsy shackle.

Mine is the face and body when Noel de Witt sees a woman once a month. If anybody in our house—that house, as you made it appear to me—understood this, nobody took it into account. My mother was alive then. If she saw, realized—and at least she might have considered the possibility—she didn't choose to see. Alone in the tin cottage with you, when I had nothing more to tell you, when I had shut up, when I didn't interrupt you, when you couldn't get anything out of me, when I wasn't listening, I accused her. I slashed branches in the suburban garden turned rubbish dump where I was marooned with you. Weeds broke rank where I tramped over twists of newspaper smeared with human shit, bottles and rags cast among the scented shrubs where tennis balls used to be lost. I accused *him*—Lionel Burger, knowing as he did, without question, I would do what had to be done.

Every month I was told what must be communicated in the guise of my loving prison letter. At night, sitting up in bed in my old room in that house, smoking cigarettes at that time, not yet eighteen, I rewrote each 500 words again and again. I didn't know, ever, whether I had succeeded in writing with the effect of a pretence (for him to read as such) what I really felt about Noel so tenderly and passionately. The dates when my duty visits to him were marked on the calendar behind my bedroom door were approached by the ticking off of days in my handbag diary in which (well trained) I never wrote anything that could provide a clue to my life. On the night before the day itself finally arrived I washed my hair; before leaving for the prison I trickled perfume between my breasts and cupped some to rub on my belly and thighs. I chose a dress that showed my legs, or trousers and a shirt that emphasized my femaleness with their sexual ambiguity. Scent me out, sniff my flesh. Find me, receive me. And all this with an unthinking drive of need and instinct that could be called innocent and that you call 'real'. I took a flower with me. Usually the warders would not accept it for him (now and then the sentimentality of one of them for 'sweethearts', or the vicarious sexual stir another got from pandering, would move him to pass the gift). I kept the flower in my lap or twisted the stem in my hand, where Noel could enjoy the sight of the bloom and know it was for him.

Reading in the car while she waited for me outside the prison, my mother would look up, as she heard me return, with her shrewd, anxious, complicit, welcoming expression that awaited me as a little girl when I was released from my first days of school. Had I done well? Here was my support, my reward, and the guarantor to whom I was contracted for my performance. At home, my father, his hands on my shoulders where I sat at table (his way with me, since I had been very small, to caress me like this as he came home from his patients and stood behind my chair a moment) interrogated about what Noel had managed to convey under the lovey-dovey. Was it true that Jack Schultz had been moved to another section of the prison? Had the politicals been on hunger strike for two days the previous week? I always remembered exactly what had been said in the prison visiting-room dialogue between Noel and me, although—as it was to be with my father later—several other prisoners were in their stalls talking to their visitors at the same time, and sentences in many voices crossed back and forth chaotically over his and mine. I remembered word for word, his exact turn of phrase, his cadence—so that, decoding his meanings, glancing from one to another for confirmation of interpretation, my father, mother and I could rely on each nuance being the prisoner's own. It could also be relied upon that I had found the way to convey to him the messages I was entrusted with.

When I had got my driving licence and could go to Noel's prison visit alone, after I had seen him I drove slowly round the limits of the blind red-brick buildings caged in barbed wire with lookouts high up where guns and lights roosted. Round and round, in low gear, as many times as I dared without attracting suspicion. I could see there was no way out. If that was what I was looking for: or for some sign of where, behind those walls whose base not even a weed was allowed to approach, so forbidding and remote yet so ugly, commonplace, he was now back in a cell whose dark, recessed meshed slot might be that one or that one. The effort of following the live impression of him—only just left—into that place, down corridors I had caught sight of, through the smells of lavatory disinfectant, floor polish and sickly stewing meat whose whiff I had got, dazed me. If I looked away from the walls, towards warders' houses, I used to see children playing in the small gardens, creaking the rusty chains of swings provided for them. It was easier to follow him to another life he might be living, on a farm with me (the farm I knew as a child, with tobacco limp as gloves in the drying shed); he wanted to be a farmer (I collected every scrap of information about him) although he had a science degree and worked for a paint manufacturer before he became a political prisoner.—Why should I choose to go to Tanzania or be rescued by Marcus and his wife in Sweden—why could not Noel de Witt and I have gone away to farm, to breed babies from me that would look like him, to grow wattle or tobacco or mealies or anything it was that he wanted to make flourish and couldn't, not so much as a knot of tough grass able to force its way between the bricks of those walls?

I did—as you say—what was expected. I was not a fake. Once a month I sat as they had sent me to take their messages and receive his, a female presented to him with the smiling mouth, the gazing yet evasive eyes, the breasts drooping a little as she hunched forward, a flower standing for what lies in her lap. We didn't despise prostitutes in that house—our house—we saw them as victims of necessity while certain social orders lasted.

When Noel de Witt's sentence was served the prison authorities did what is often done with political prisoners, they opened the doors early one morning a few days before the stated date of his release, and put him out with the old airways bag of clothes and the watch that had been taken from him when he entered two years before. He knew he would be banned or perhaps house-arrested within a week, and he had, hidden away in town, an Australian passport on which he could leave the country if he were quick enough. He did not dare come to our house. From one of those Portuguese greengrocer's shops that open when dawn supplies come from the market, he telephoned someone else, someone on the fringe, who could be trusted to do what was expected now as I had before—someone who had kept safe the Australian passport. When he arrived in England Noel sent a letter through another contact to tell my father these things and there was an enclosure for me, sweet and funny, to thank me for the letters that had cheered him, the visits that had kept him going, the goodies I'd been able to wheedle Chief Warder Potgieter into passing, the cleverly-chosen books I'd managed to get by as essential for his studies. A grateful hospital veteran's phrases. Flowers came without a card and I was told he'd left some of the little money he had, for these to be ordered.

Those were my love letters. Those visits were my great wild times. All this I was free to understand in the tin cottage.

I grumbled one day, some commonplace—I'm sick of this job.—

You were driving me from the hospital where I worked. When we spoke to each other there was the clandestine quality of talking to oneself; the taunting and tempting of mutual culpability. You acknowledged me in you rather than looked towards me. —Even animals have the instinct to run a mile from sickness and death, it's natural.—

The platitude I had used so meaninglessly, harmless remark

belonging to the same level of communication as 'I've got a bit of a headache', broke loose in me. There was no sense of proportion for such things in that cottage; I was taken possession of by chance remarks, images, incidents; the unnumbered pages came up. I read them again and again, their script appeared in everything I seemed to be looking at, pupils of yellow egg yolk slipping separate from whites of eyes cracked against the bowl, faint quarterings of tabby ancestry vestigial on the belly of the black cat, the slow alphabetical dissolve from identity to identity, changing one letter at a time through the spelling of names in the telephone directory. Spoken against the cover of your daily noise on the violin and the bucklings of the tin roof that shifted silences, the chorus of running water in the bath that was furred with putty-coloured lime like an old kettle, the calls of the watchman's drunks making their trajectory over the sough of night traffic, my silence hammered sullen, hysterical, repetitive without words: sick, sick of the maimed, the endangered, the fugitive, the stoic; sick of courts, sick of prisons, sick of institutions scrubbed bare for the regulation endurance of dread and pain.

Yet I left the cottage where this kind of fervid private tantrum was possible.

I left the children's tree-house we were living in, in an intimacy of self-engrossment without the reserve of adult accountability, accepting each other's encroachments as the law of the litter, treating each other's dirt as our own, as little Baasie and I had long ago performed the child's black mass, tasting on a finger the gall of our own shit and the saline of our own pee. Although you and I huddled for warmth in the same bed, I never minded your making love to the girl who taught Spanish. And you know we had stopped making love together months before I left, aware that it had become incest.

It was like an illness no one mentioned, among my father's relatives with whom we stayed when we were little. An illness that proved fatal: they came to pay their respects when they sat, my aunt and uncle, the good and kind Coen Nels, beside me to hear the life sentence pronounced.

Tony was so happy helping to cook bricks in a serious mud-pie game with the farm labourers who called him 'little master' (although that was Baasie's name) and playing with half-naked black children who were left behind when he and cousin Kobus ran into the farmhouse for milk and cake. I understood quite quickly that Baasie, with whom I lived in that house, couldn't have come here; I understood what Lily meant when she had said he wouldn't like to. I forgot Baasie. It was easy. No one here had a friend, brother, bed-mate, sharer of mother and father like him. Those who owed love and care to each other could be identified by a simple rule of family resemblance, from the elders enfeebled by vast flesh or wasting to the infant lying creased in the newly-married couple's pram. I saw it every Saturday, this human family defined by white skin. In the church to which my aunt drove us on Sunday morning, children clean and pretty, we sat among the white neighbours from farms round about and from the dorp, to whom the predikant said we must do as we would be done by. The waiter my uncle's barman beat with his lion's head belt was not there; he would be in his place down under the trees out of sight of the farmhouses, where black people sang hymns and beat old oildrums, or in the tin church in the dorp location. Harry Schutte didn't come to church (on Saturday nights roars of song and the sound of smashing glasses came from the bar, as farmers' rugby teams ended their afternoon's sport) but he had worked hard for his sleep-in and he never forgot an ice-cream for a kid who might have been one of his own (after all, he and my father were born in the same district). Daniel knew the strength of the tattooed arm he was safe from so long as he didn't take the white man's bottle but stayed content to swallow the dregs left in his glass.

For the man who had married my father's sister the farm 'Vergenoegd' was God's bounty that was hers by inheritance, mortgage, land bank loan, and the fruitfulness he made of it, the hotel was his by the sign painted over the entrance naming him as licensee, the bottle store was his by the extension of that licence to off-sales. His sons would inherit by equally unquestioned right; the little boy who played with Tony would make flourish the tobacco, the pyrethrum—whatever the world thinks it needs and will pay for—Noel de Witt would never allow himself to grow.

When the girl cousin who was my contemporary was home from boarding-school for the weekend, we ladyshipped it about hotel and farm together as her natural assumption. Daniel was commanded to bring cokes; the hotel cook was pestered to put our dough men in the oven; a farm labourer mended her bicycle, a child from the kraal brought ants' eggs for her schoolfriend's grass snake, a kitchen maid had to wash and iron the particular dress she decided to wear. Her mother had no other claim, no other obligation but to please her daughter.

With this cousin I shared the second half of my name; it was the name of our common grandmother, long dead. Marie showed me our grandmother's grave, fenced in with several others of the family, on the farm. MARIE BURGER was cut into a mirror of smooth grey stone veined with glitter. On the slab were round glass domes cloudy with condensation under which plastic roses had faded.

You thought I must be named for Rosa Luxemburg, and the name I have always been known by as well as the disguised first half of my given name does seem to signify my parents' desire if not open intention. They never told me of it. My father often quoted that other Rosa; although he had no choice but to act the Leninist role of the dominant professional revolutionary, he believed that her faith in elemental mass movement was the ideal approach in a country where the mass of people were black and the revolutionary elite disproportionately white. But my double given name contained also the claim of MARIE BURGER and her descendants to that order of life, secure in the sanctions of family, church, law— and all these contained in the ultimate sanction of colour, that was maintained without question on the domain, dorp and farm, where she lay. *Peace. Land. Bread*. They had these for themselves.

Even animals have the instinct to turn from suffering. The sense to run away. Perhaps it was an illness not to be able to live one's life the way they did (if not the way you did, Conrad) with justice defined in terms of respect for property, innocence defended in their children's privileges, love in their procreation, and care only for each other. A sickness not to be able to ignore that condition of a healthy, ordinary life: other people's suffering.

Rosa Burger was among city people who ate in a public square at lunchtime. The stale chill of the airconditioned offices she had left evaporated in the sun and the warm sounds of pigeons. There was a statue. The hissing spigots of a fountain donated by a mining company smoothed traffic blare and voices; she had her sandwiches and fruit, bought boxed under a tight membrane of plastic from a shop on the way, others shared a lovers' picnic unwrapped from a briefcase between them on a park bench. Children and greedy waddling birds were fed the same sort of titbits. Indian girls secretively ate daintily with their fingers from take-away cartons of curry. On the grass coloured girls jeered, gossiped and laughed, waving chicken-bones, and black men sat with their half-loaves of bread in wisps of wrapping, pulling out the white centre like cotton bolls. There were bins with advertising legends (Why be Lonely? Step Out Tonight with One of Our Lovely Hostesses) where leavings were thrust, and these were picked over, as the pigeons did what was left on gravel and grass, by various people in various kinds of need. The child who led the blind beggar felt for potato chips and half-gnawed chicken, other blacks shook empty cigarette packs, and there were white men and women, threadbare-neat pensioners and old creatures with sparse orange hair and red lips inexpertly drawn in the light of failing sight who might be obsolescent prostitutes, scratching and peering for finds which seemed to give them satisfaction. The women hid these away in tattered shopping bags; the men smoothed retrieved newspapers.

On the grass black men slept deeply, face down; they might have been dead. On benches avoided by other people, white tramps with drunkard's blue eyes and the brief midday dapperness of hair slicked back in the municipal washroom, approached each other confidentially, came and went with the dogged, shambling dedication of their single purpose—to find money for a bottle. Sometimes one of these who were fixtures along with the pigeons was apart from the others, drunk, asleep, or in some inertia and immobility that was neither. Rosa, seeing one like this, chose a bench on the other side of the walk. But she need not have thought he might make a nuisance of himself; she ate her lunch, two little boys ran up and down twirling plastic whirligigs before him, a girl wearing the name DARLENE in gilt letters suspended on either side by a gilt chain round a freckled neck kissed a young man for the full time it took a pantechnicon, unable to turn at the traffic lights because of a parked car, to manoeuvre its length back into the street from which it had emerged; one of the children was caught and smacked on the back of the thighs by its mother; a fat man in a blue suit dropped an ice-cream cone which was pecked away by the birds; the clock that could be heard only within a radius of three blocks of the old post office struck the single wavering note of one o'clock and then the half-hour; and still the man did not move, sitting with his leg crossed over the other at the knee, arms folded, head sunk forward like that of someone who has dozed during a speech. A pigeon alighted on his shoulder and took off clumsily again.

But that moment in which the bird had paused, cocking its beak, indifferent busybody, changed the awareness of the freckled girl and her boy; of Rosa Burger; of the mother and the two little children, the man in the blue suit. They looked at each other as if each had a sudden question to ask. They all began to watch the man. The children's mouths opened. They pressed back against their mother's side and she moved away from the demand, shifting supermarket carriers as a claim defended, an alibi of the normality of her presence; resting there with her kids in the square, waiting for the time to catch a bus or be fetched by a husband. Now other people from benches farther off, from the grass, approached. Two hobos came over hunched towards each other, hands making intimate sign-language, and the one tried to restrain the other

71

while he took the man on the bench by the shoulder the pigeon had landed on, and called a name. *Hey Doug, come on, man, Doug.* The man did not wake up but did not fall over. He stayed, solid as the statue of the landdrost, as if at the axis where one knee crossed the other he was secured to the bench as the landdrost was fixed to his plinth by bronze prongs.

The two friends backed away, whispering and challenging.

The freckled girl's boyfriend turned to Rosa in triumph, with an answer, not a question. —You know what?—the bloke's dead.—

—Ooooh, I'm getting out of here.— His girl was shaking her hands from the wrists, urgently.

The two little boys moved nearer and were stopped by their mother—Come away!—

No policeman was about but someone fetched a traffic officer and he had in his hand a first-aid box of the kind with a toy axe attached buses carry along for emergencies.

People pressed forward all round Rosa where she stood as if waiting to be told, to have some indication whether to go this way or that. Only the man himself took no notice. The black men who had lain on the grass like dead men got up and came to look at him.

Rosa, moving away out of the small crowd, entered the strands of pedestrians crossing the street, intersecting with the strands coming across from the other side, as a thief makes himself indistinguishable from any other passer-by.

I worked for a trade journal, for a man who imported cosmetics and perfume, for an investment adviser. I gave up my hospital profession when I left you and the cottage. I was living alone for the first time in my life: without a stake of responsibility in that of anyone else. For us—coming from that house—that was the real definition of loneliness: to live without social responsibility.

There had been deaths in my father's house but the death of a tramp in the park was in a sense the first for me. I ate my lunch there nearly always when I was working for Barry Eckhard, the finance man. Up on the twenty-sixth floor the smoked glass windows made the climate of each day the same cool mean, neither summer nor winter, and the time something neither night nor day; I came down into the city to repossess a specific sense of these things. I came to be anonymous, to be like other people. Although Barry's offices concealed their function behind the penthouse style, not only banks' pot plants but also original indigenous sculpture and a chrome table game that, set in motion, illustrated a Newtonian principle of dynamics, he enjoyed revealing to clients who seemed all to be first-name friends that his 'girl Friday' was Lionel Burger's daughter. Sometimes she was invited along with them to expensive restaurants where their simple lunches of grilled kingklip were proof that they were not vulgar tycoons.

In the little public square I went to no one recognized me and so no one saw me. I ate my sandwiches, like everybody else, there, while the man died, or was dead already when we grouped ourselves round him as we did in relation to each other: the black labourers washed up from the streets prostrate upon the bit of grass, not yet ready for the kind of token comfort of white-collar workers so recently opened to blacks by the desegregation of the benches, the coloured factory girls signalling in their teasing manner of eating the sexual self-confidence Indian girls, huddled like nuns, were denied, the couple from the Post Office whose privacy the presence of all of us hedged, I myself making the choice of this bench rather than that because a member of the resident sherry gang sometimes struck up a tedious conversation or—worse—talked to himself. I had quickly discovered it's unbearable to sit on a park bench beside a stranger who is talking to himself aloud as you are doing silently.

The evening newspaper spread across three columns a photograph taken of the dead man on the bench by some keen amateur who happened to have had the good luck to be in the right place at the right time. The space was as much as was customarily given to a daily series of girls on beaches from Ostia to Sydney. The caption drew upon the melodramatic romantic platitude of the 'heartlessness' of the city. (The two little boys were in the picture, mouths open, gazing.) But there was nothing cruel and indifferent about our eating our lunches, making love or sleeping off a morning's work while a man, simulating life with one leg easily and almost elegantly crossed over the other, died or was dying. He looked as if he were alive. He gave no sign of injury, pain or distress, he was not held between the uniformed bodies of custodians, looking out where he could not run, he was not caged in court or cell, or holding out, as a beggar has nothing to present but his stump, a paper for the official stamp that is always denied him. The whole point was that I—we—all of us were exonerated. What could we have done? It was not a matter of help that could be given or withheld. Not a matter of the kiss of life or massaging a heart. Nothing could change the isolation of that man. What could we have known that would have made it possible to understand how he left us while among us, went away without crumpling a paper carton or throwing the skeleton of a bunch of grapes into the bin; stayed with us, as a shape of arranged flesh, when he was not there. The post office clerk and his girl could not do more than kiss. He had to keep his hands off her breasts and keep a newspaper or jacket across his lap to hide the swelling of his arousal to life. But this man who crossed his legs conversationally, whose arms were folded attentively—only his head had nodded off, drooped with the heat or boredom, it could happen to anybody—he carried through the unspeakable act in our presence. He made final the unfinished take-away chicken meal, the fondling half-mating that was as far as DARLENE and her boy could go. He concluded the digestive cycles and procreative tentatives around him by completing the imperative, the ultimate necessity. We saw and heard nothing.

I didn't go back to eat in the square and I didn't cut out the photograph. I knew the arch of the foot that was cocked over the knee, quite a high arch, which gives a foot a nice line, and the shoes not particularly worn since brown suède seems to look right only when rather shabby. The paper said the man's name was Ronald Ferguson, 46, an ex-miner, no fixed abode. He drank methylated spirits and slept in bus shelters. There is an element of human wastage in all societies. But—in that house—it was believed that when we had changed the world (yes, in spite of, beyond the purges, the liquidations, the forced labour and imprisonments)—the 'elimination of private conflicts set up by the competitive nature of capitalist society' would help people to live, even people like this one, who, although white and privileged under the law of the country, couldn't make a place for himself. I had seen my brother dead and my mother and father; each time the event itself, so close to me, was obscured from me by sorrow and explained by accident, illness, or imprisonment. It was *caused* by the chlorinated water with flecks of his pink breakfast bacon in it that I saw pumped from my brother's mouth when he was taken from the pool; by that paralysis that blotted out my mother limb by limb; by the fever that my father smelled of, dying for his beliefs in a prison hospital.

But this death was the mystery itself. The death *you* were talking about; in the cottage. Circumstantial causes are not the cause: we die because we live, yes, and there was no way for me to understand what I was walking away from in the park. There was no way to deal with this happening but to gather the little plastic-foam tray and cellophane from which I'd eaten my lunch and go over and put it, as every day, as everyone else must, in the waste bin hooked to a pole. The revolution we lived for in that house would change the lives of the blacks who left their hovels and compounds at four in the morning to swing picks, hold down jack-hammers and chant under the weight of girders, building shopping malls and office towers in which whites like my employer Barry Eckhard and me moved in an 'environment' without sweat or dust. It would change the days of the labourers who slept off their exhaustion on the grass like dead men, while the man died. The children the white couple would make in their whites' suburb would not inherit the house bought on the municipal loan available to whites, or slot safely into jobs reserved for whites against black competition. Black children—it was promised—would not have to live off the leavings we threw into the bin. Eckhard's clients would no longer get rich by the effort of a phone-call to authorize a sale on the stock exchange. All that might change. But the change from life to death—what had all the certainties I had from my father to do with that? When the hunger ended and the kwashiorkor was wiped out as malaria was in the colonial era, when there were no rents extorted and no privately-owned mansions and cosy white bungalows, no white students in contemplative retreat where blacks could not live; when the people owned the means of production of gold, diamonds, uranium, copper and coal, all the mineral riches that had rolled to the bottom of the sack of Africa—one would be left with that. Nothing that had served to make us sure of what we were doing and why had anything to do with what was happening one lunchtime while I was in the square. I was left with that. It had been left out. Justice, equality, the brotherhood of man, human dignity—but *it will still be there*, I looked away everywhere from the bench and saw it still, when—at last—I had seen it once.

B aasie never came back to live in the Burger house.
Her brother Tony boasted to the little boys of the neighbourhood how he could dive and was drowned in the swimming-pool.

Rosa Burger was unable to make out, driving over the freeway in her car, where the corrugated-iron cottage had been bulldozed. Old loquat trees suggesting those that had grown near the road-makers' camp were incorporated into the landscaping of the shoulders of the freeway, but the bauhinia was not where she would have thought it might still stand.

To be free is to become almost a stranger to oneself: the nearest I'll ever get to seeing what they saw outside the prison. If I could have seen that, I could have seen that other father, the stranger to myself. I seem always to have known of his existence.

I suppose you found another place to live. (Mexico perhaps.) We didn't bump into each other around town (you never knew about the man in the park). But you were the one who had said—Why d'you talk about him as 'Lionel'?—

—Do I?—

—Sometimes even in the same sentence—'my father', and the next moment you switch to 'Lionel'.—

It was something curious, to you who were nosy about what you called the mores of a house of 'committed' people. In me, significant—of what? It's true that to me he was also something other than my father. Not just a public persona; many people have that to put on and take off. Not something belonging to the hackneyed formulation of the tracts and manifestos that explain him, for others. His was different. His may have been what he

77

really was. After he was dead—after I left the cottage where I accused him—that persona became something held secret from me. How can I explain that the death of the man—the man in the park was part of the mystery. As he had died, or the fact of his death existed in my presence without my having been aware of it, so I lived in my father's presence without knowing its meaning.

There were things whose existence was not admitted, in that house. Just as your mother's love affairs and the way your father made his money were not, in yours. My parents' was a different kind of collusion. It surprises me to see, looking at photographs, my mother was actually good-looking. And not only when she was young—in Russia, on some Students for Peace junket, everyone on a railway station holding bouquets big as bundles of washing—but even at that famous nineteenth birthday party of mine that was raided by the police a few months before her illness began. There is supposed to be a particular bountiful attractiveness about a woman who is unaware of her good looks, but if, as with my mother, she literally *does not inhabit them*, lives in purposes that are not served in any particular way by the distinction of a narrow face with deep eye-sockets, a long, straight, slender prow of nose, a skin so fine that even the earlobes are delicately ornamental under early-greying hair, these beauties fall into disuse through something more than neglect. There's a photograph that catches her looking up from a table full of papers, dirty tea-cups, ashtrays, among her plain or brassy women garment workers; magnified by reading glasses, her intricately-marked irises are extraordinary, and the lashes are as thick on the lower eyelids as on the upper. Beautiful eyes. But I see only the interrogatory watchfulness that looked out, looked up at my footsteps displacing the gravel outside my 'fiancé's' jail; the quick flicker of early-warning or go-ahead that went out to my father when she and he were in discussion with the many people who used that house. The lipstick she, in the habit of women of her generation, put on her lips, outlined not the shape of the lips so much as the determined complexity that composed them—a mouth that has learnt to give nothing away when speaking; whose smile comes from the confidence not of attraction but of conviction. I suppose children always think of their mothers as being capable; a rationalization of dependence and trust. She always knew what to do, and did it. The crowds of people who came to her funeral loved her for her kindness; the rationale of her always deciding what action to take, and acting. When Tony lay in the swimming-pool that Saturday morning she jumped in (one of her shoes as she kicked them off hit me) and when she came up out of the water she had him. Lily was holding me and screaming, as if the water would take me, too. My mother hooked her fingers in Tony's mouth and hiked him up with a great effort, she was gasping and coughing, and held him upside-down. The water came out with bits of his breakfast in it, bits of pink bacon I saw. She squatted over him and breathed from her mouth to his, holding his nose shut and releasing the pressure of her hands on his chest. She did this for a long time.

But he was dead.

My father—as a doctor—put her to sleep. The next day he took me to her in their bed; I felt afraid to enter the room. She took me into the bed with her and she was crying, not the way Tony and I did, making a noise, but silently, the tears running sideways into her hair. Lily told me they would 'fill up that terrible hole'—the swimming-pool. Lily said she would never go on that side of the house again, never!

One Sunday soon after, my father remarked that he hadn't timed my crawl once since the school term had begun.

—What about a demonstration this morning? Lovely hot day—

I didn't read the comic supplement spread before me on the floor. My mother ignored the pawing of the cat, wanting to get onto her lap.

—Put on your costume. Off you go.— When I came back he took his car-key out of his pocket and going over to my mother, opened her hand, put the key in it, and folded the hand, holding the fist he had made of it within his own. —You said you'd take the car and fill up for me.—

That swimming-pool was enjoyed by many people. It became the tradition, in summer, for us to keep open house round it at

Sunday lunch—Lionel Burger's braaivleis. My mother swam; she kept a supply of blow-up armlets and it was a rule of the house, dutifully followed by new guests, new contacts, who did not know that the Burgers had had a son, that all children in the pool area had to wear them. Some of the black friends had never been in a pool before; the municipal swimming baths weren't open to them. My father gave their children swimming lessons; they clung to him, like Baasie and me. In that house, we children had few exclusive rights with our parents. Taking into account the important difference that I was a female child and so the sexual implications would have been different, I wonder if the sight of my mother with another man—all right, under another man—would have cracked the shell of containing reality for me, made me recoil entirely into that of internal events, as it did for you? 'I wonder' in the sense that I doubt it; she was Baasie's mother, as well as Tony's and mine, and mother to others from time to time, so perhaps I should not have thought of her and my father, Lionel, as each other's possession. We belonged to other people. I must have accepted that, too, very young, in that house. I became Noel de Witt's girl, if need be.

And other people belonged to us. If my mother had no lover—and although I see I know nothing, nothing about her, I am sure of this—there were other relationships, not sexual, about which there has been speculation. Even in court. The woman who couldn't meet my father's face, looking so gently, patiently at her—who couldn't let herself see 'even the toe of his shoe': poor sniveller, wretched or despicable, she began as one of my mother's collection of the dispossessed, like Baasie or the old man who lived with us. Unlike them, she was not what the papers call a victim of apartheid; she was an old-maid schoolteacher who belonged to a church group that looked for uplifting works to do in the black townships. She must have met my mother through the co-operative's office, in connection with some feeding scheme or other. One of those eager souls who see no contradiction in their protest that they are not at all 'political' but would like to do something effective—something less self-defeating than charity, for what (euphemism being their natural means of expression) they call 'race relations'. Through my mother, she began to teach at the school Baasie and Tony and I had been to, the little school that did not officially exist, where we white, African, coloured and Indian children of my parents' 'family' of associates learned together. So far as she was concerned, my mother had given her exactly what she sought; her gratitude became the kind of worshipping dependency my mother was often burdened with, and we gained another hanger-on in that house. This one was grateful to be in the background: she helped out in my father's surgery when his receptionist was on leave; she would bring home-grown sweet peppers, carrots and radishes from her little garden, for him, who adored to eat raw, bright vegetables; when my mother was ill she wanted to nurse her, although there were others preferred for their skill and the abundant life and vigour dying people need as reassurance.

It is not known when she began making herself useful in other ways. The dates at which the prosecution, for whom she appeared under indemnity as State Witness, suggested she was already acting as a courier predate the illness and death of my mother; but nothing was proved—she wept and insisted she had gone to Scotland for the visit to her elder sister she had been saving for over many years. She produced the inevitable post office book as proof of this monthly scrimping and self-denial, and one needed only to look at her to believe in it.

Maybe my mother knew she could count on the genteel, schoolgirl code of such a person never to enquire about the contents or addressee of, let alone open, letters she was asked to deliver abroad. It was little enough to ask of someone so eager to be needed? This quick realization within my mother would be signalled by that sudden seizing glance, sideways, without turning the head, showing the whites of those eyes shaded not only by their dreamy sockets but also the darkening skin round them, as my mother grew older. I know it well, I'll always know it, that look my mother was unconscious of and that would have amazed— disquieted her: it was a glance that slipped the leash.

When I was the woman of my father's house, after my mother's death, this particular hanger-on scarcely ever came there. Perhaps she knew I had no feelings for her; if anything a young girl's unthinkingly cruel irritation at her self-effacing lack of definition. We didn't notice her absence, as we certainly should have that of Bridget Sulzer, Ivy and Dick Terblanche, Aletta Gous, Marisa Kgosana, Mark Liebowitz, Sipho Mokoena—any of those long-time associates of my mother and father who were still at large, neither in jail, in exile, nor opted out, or even the new frequenters who from time to time were attracted into that house. You were one; Conrad, you never told me whether or not Lionel, in his unique way, making you feel you would be liked, honoured, understood whether you responded or not, tried to recruit you. I wonder if perhaps he did, and you were ashamed that you withdrew from that marvellous ambience? That you never joined Baasie and me in the warmth of that stocky breast? You who had known only a father who prided himself on being self-made on sharp deals in scrap metal and disowned you as a long-haired loafer unworthy of inheriting money and the hard-working tradition in which it was earned. Lionel Burger probably saw in you the closed circuit of self; for him, such a life must be in need of a conduit towards meaning, which posited: outside self. That's where the tension that makes it possible to live lay, for him; between self and others; between the present and creation of something called the future. Perhaps he tried to give you the chance. When you saw that wretched creature in the witness box, she could have been you.

It seems that all the time I thought she'd dropped us, or rather that we had thankfully got rid of her, Lionel was in touch with her. She did the simple things such people are fairly safe for. She kept illegal funds in her bank account. She rented a house where one of the faithful successfully lived underground for several months. It may have been out of some sentiment towards my mother's memory; it may have been because she fell in love, late and hopelessly, with Lionel Burger, who will have made her feel liked, honoured, understood, whether she agreed or not to do what he asked of her, and who will also have—because all women confirm this—made her feel she was a woman. She is the example, in particular, that white liberals give when they point out how Communists, even my father, used innocent people; one could admire the courage, the daring, the lack of regard for self with which a man like Burger acted according to his convictions about social injustice (which, of course, one shares), even if one certainly didn't share his Communistic beliefs and the form of action these took, but the way in which he involved others was surely ruthless? She had never been a member of the Party, or any radical organization. She told the court she 'tried to live according to Christ', and added the rider 'very unsuccessfully'. At that point, as at many during her cross-examination, she wept. Her swollen nose and the torn hangnails that disfigured her hands were distasteful. Those who felt she had been exploited by Lionel Burger expressed their pity and kept unexpressed their disgust at the sight; only he, who had given her her chance, looked and listened without either, ready to meet without reproach the bloodshot eyes that could not look at him whom she had betrayed.

After Lionel Burger's death a number of people approached his daughter with a view to writing about him. As the only surviving member of his family, she would have been the principal source of information for any biographer. One she refused after the first meeting. Another's letters she did not answer. The one to whom she agreed to make material available did not find her very communicative. She had little to offer in the way of documentation; she said the family kept few letters or papers, and what there was had been taken away in police raids in the course of the years. She mentioned she had part of her parents' library but turned aside from suggestions that perhaps this in itself might be interesting to a biographer.

He wanted to go over with her the facts about her father's life—and that implied, from a certain date, her mother's life, too—that he had already collated from written sources, including court records, and the history of the Communist Party in South Africa which he had had to research abroad because most works concerning it were banned within the country. She answered questions in a way he found unexpected—was unprepared for. It was not what she said but the physical aspect of their confrontation. They sat at a table in the sun at the house of a friend of hers through whom he had managed to make contact with her. She kept her arms from elbow to hand resting slack on the table-top most of the time. She spoke without looking at him but at the end of what she had to say turned clear pale grey eyes steadily on him. What was expected of him? He felt inadequate. She at once gave too little and posed something he did not understand.

Lionel Burger had been born in 1905 on the farm 'Vergenoegd' to a wealthy family in the Springbok Flats district of the Northern

Transvaal, but had gone to school in Pretoria and Johannesburg.

Well—she didn't know if they should be called wealthy—they owned land that they'd lived on for several generations.

He began his medical studies at Cape Town, and completed them at Edinburgh University in the late 1920s. He married Colette Swan, a South African girl studying ballet in London, while still a student, and returned to South Africa with her in 1930. They had one son, now also a doctor, and practising in Tanzania. They were divorced—when?

The daughter of the second marriage didn't know. The date of her own parents' marriage was 19th August 1946, the week of the black miners' great strike on the Witwatersrand. Her mother, Cathy Jansen, was twenty-six and the general secretary of a canning or textile union—anyway, one of the three or four existing mixed unions of coloured and white people at the time. The marriage was supposed to have taken place on 14th August but the best man, J. B. Marks, chairman of the African Mineworkers' Union, was arrested on the second day of the strike and this seems to have upset the wedding plans for a few days. Another trade unionist, Gana Makabeni, stood in for Marks. By then, both bride and bridegroom had also been arrested, as a result of a raid on the Communist Party offices in Johannesburg on 16th August. Although her name appeared on the charge sheet as Cathy Jansen, she had become Lionel Burger's second wife while he and she were out on bail, before the preparatory examination opened.

And that was on 26th August?—confirmed. Along with more than fifty other people, black, white, Indian and coloured, many of whom were Communists (and of whom only the few names unforgotten, Bram Fischer, Dr Dadoo, Moses Kotane, would get a mention in the biography) the couple were charged under the Riotous Assemblies Act with having aided an illegal strike and also with having offended against something called War Measure 145. The biographer offered the information that he had looked up War Measure 145: it outlawed strikes by Africans and exposed black strikers to a minimum penalty of £300 or three years. The trial was the most representative, in the country's history, of the different ideologies, skin colours, class interests in opposition to the white regime; it was the first in which her mother and father were indicted together. It was also, in its scope, a shadow cast before the Treason Trial, coming in 1957; the only other, and last trial in which the Burger couple would stand accused together. The trial of her parents before she was born—like the one that was to take place when she would be a child old enough to retain impressions, surely, that could be remembered and recounted?— both ended without Lionel Burger or his wife being convicted.

But two months after they were married, following a new wave of raids on the homes of radicals in all the large towns, Lionel Burger was re-arrested. He and his fellow members of the Central Executive of the Communist Party in Cape Town were charged with sedition as a result of that miners' strike which had postponed but failed to disrupt his marriage plans.

With this observation the biographer provoked a slow wide smile from the daughter of the marriage. For a few moments the list of raids, arrests and trials was the family album: the couple had only just dumped their belongings in their Johannesburg flat when the raid came; there was Lionel Burger's often-heard story of how the police, instructed to search the contents of cupboards and drawers, found these empty, and had to do the unpacking of the suitcases and crates of books instead. He and his new bride simply hung up cups and arranged plates and pots and pans as the police squatted among newspaper and straw, doing the dirty work.

An additional charge against the accused was to do with the Official Secrets Act; again the biographer had consulted the Statute Books, and the supposed breach was a legal technicality relating to a 'Hands off Java' campaign, with a call for boycott of ships passing by way of South African ports while carrying cargo across the Indian Ocean to troops in Indonesia after the Japanese occupation had been ended. But both the biographer and Rosa Burger were too young for campaigns of the immediate aftermath of the Second World War to have much meaning for them.

Cathy Burger née Jansen was not charged in this case, although she and not her husband was a trade union organizer; she was only twenty-six years old and perhaps not prominent enough to have been a member of the Central Executive. The prosecutor accused the Party of having engineered the strike as part of a wider plot to overthrow the government; the accused were cross-examined about Party policy, the role of Communists in trade unions and their attitude to strikes. The biographer had been studying old court records and what had been said by the accused was fresh to him as if it had been spoken in his hearing, and yesterday. Lionel Burger told the court the Communist Party stood for the unity of workers regardless of colour. Communists were required by the Party's policy to be active in unions for which they were eligible. A good Communist must win workers' confidence by proving himself a good unionist. Communists had served the workers' cause by organizing unskilled and semi-skilled Africans, coloureds and Indians, the largest and most neglected sector of the labour force, and through this achievement the Communist Party had made a unique contribution to racial harmony in a country constantly threatened by racial unrest. The strike was 76,000 black miners' genuine and justifiable protest against exploitation and contemptuous disregard of the needs, as workers and human beings, of the 400,000 black men in the industry.

Etc., etc. This rhetoric delivered by her father produced no reaction from his daughter outside the degree of attention that she apparently had decided to apportion the whole interview. It had been spoken in a courtroom in January 1947 before she was born; no doubt her mother was there to hear it. She herself could add nothing about that time, except that as her mother's work was in the unions—a passionate interest, even when banned from labour movement activity and with a child old enough to be aware of evidence of her parents' preoccupations—the double involvement, personal and professional, in that trial must have been intense.

At one point the prosecutor had to withdraw charges because of some irregularity in the prosecution—the biographer didn't want to waste the opportunity to talk to Burger's daughter by going into factual details he could verify elsewhere. Anyway, the accused, including Burger, were re-arrested once again, committed on sedition, and stood trial. The African Mineworkers' Union, led by the black man who was her parents' close friend and first choice as best man for their wedding, was accused of being a concealed wing of the Communist Party of South Africa. The strike of 1946 was alleged to have been engineered by the Johannesburg District Committee of the Communist Party, on which Lionel Burger sat. The Central Executive of the Party, of which he was a member, was accused of having conspired to initiate a strike that resulted in the use of violence against state authority.

Documentation available put beyond doubt of anyone studying it in retrospect that the Communist Party had been and was at the time of the strike closely involved with the miners' union. Since the inception of the Party and its affiliation to the Third Communist International in 1921 (Lionel Burger 16, a schoolboy in Johannesburg), acceptance of Lenin's thesis on the national and colonial question and the consequent task of 'educating and organizing the peasantry and broad mass of the exploited' in addition to 'raising the class consciousness of the proletariat' had been compulsory for the Party. The fact that the organized proletariat of the mines—the basic industry in the country—was white and remained participant in the privileges of the oppressing class, while the black miners, at once peasants and proletariat, were rejected by the white miners' unions, was an adverse reflection on the Party's effectiveness. From time to time there was criticism from the Communist International. The Party had succeeded neither in educating the white proletariat to identify with the black proletariat, nor in organizing the indentured black peasants in their industrialized role as proletarians. For example, the Praesidium of the Executive Committee of the Communist International advised the South African Communist Party to organize revolutionary trade unions of workers. But the Party had no members in the mines, in spite of attempts dating from July 1930 to form a black mineworkers' union, a League of African Rights, and its successor with an African name, Ikaka Labasebenzi—The Workers' Shield. This pioneering was the initiative of Thebedi and Bunting (the latter one of the founders of the Party and stated once by Lionel Burger to have been his early mentor, although records showed that Burger voted for Bunting's expulsion in 1931). Then in 1940 the Party's national conference deputed to the Johannesburg district the specific duty of organizing black miners, whose overwhelming numbers would then benefit the trade union movement and ultimately national liberation, the first phase (bourgeois-democratic/national-revolutionary, varying according to the dissenting views within the Party) of the two-stage revolution to terminate in the attainment of socialism— again in accordance with Lenin's thesis of 1920. (Burger, probably taking along the girl who was to be his first wife, attended the Sixth International in Moscow in 1928, at which the aim of an 'independent Native Republic' had officially replaced the classic Marxist bourgeois-democratic revolution as a first stage for South Africa.) In the trial arising out of the '46 strike, the prosecution's case for a causal link between the Communist Party and the strike relied heavily on the fact that J. B. Marks, chairman of the African Mineworkers' Union, was both a member of the Communist Party and a member of the national council created in 1941 by the black political movement, the African National Congress, for the purpose of organizing black miners.

But the prosecution failed to establish that causal link between the Central Executive of the Communist Party and the strike. Neither could it prove, as evidence of an element of unlawful violence constituting the crime of sedition, the use of knobbed sticks with which (Rosa Burger did remember being told, years after) the black miners danced defiance in the compound yards, or the lashing-shovels with which they defended themselves against the clubs and rifles of the police.

Her father's biographer was eager to expatiate upon his theory, somewhat second-hand, that this trial was a watershed in the relations between liberation movements and the State, and the liberation movements and each other. The documents unearthed and seized during the raids on organization offices and people's homes, then examined as evidence in the trial, provided the secret police with names not only of Communists but of their supporters and any organization or individual who had been associated with them, even during the period when public indignation against Fascism in Europe and among groups of white people at home brought anti-communists onto common platforms with Communists. As a result of the trial, it was possible for the government to pass the Suppression of Communism Act in 1950 and bring about the dissolution of the Party as a legal one. As a result of the information gleaned at the trial, persecution through bannings, spying and harassment of the black political movements brought about an identity of cause that finally erased ideological differences between the African National Congress, the Indian Congress and the Communist Party, and culminated in the Congress Alliance of these movements in the early 1960s; the High Command which directed their underground operations; the new series of sensational political trials in which those taking supreme responsibility were discovered, betrayed, imprisoned, and with which a whole political era, in which and for which Lionel Burger lived, came to an end.

All this, hindsight told the biographer, began when the indictment against her father and his associates in the miners' strike case was quashed, May 1948. It was the month when the first Afrikaner nationalist government took office; that would round off a chapter with a perfect touch of foreboding.

It was the month and year that Rosemarie Burger, hearing him out, was born.

A part from Flora Donaldson, her father's old associates did not pursue her during this time when she kept away from them. Flora had no doubt; the girl needed to live a new life. With managerial kindness and the tact of a well-off woman who fellow-travels beside suffering as a sports enthusiast in a car keeps pace alongside a marathon runner, she championed this course with the gift of a red velvet skirt and a pair of pinchbeck earrings from her own jewel-box. —I'll pierce your ears myself; my grandmother used to do it, I'm an expert.— She returned, for Rosa's own good, to the attractions of Tanzania. She had friends living there, they found the whole place inspiring, it would be a tremendous release to work in a black socialist country. And even London—she no longer thought the idea inconceivable, apparently—all the marvellous people in London! The exiles, Noel de Witt and his young wife, Pauline's daughters, Bridget Sulzer, Rashid's sons—everyone doing interesting, fulfilling work and preparing themselves positively for the day when they'd be able to come back. The Donaldsons had a flat in Holland Park, the key was there for the asking. Flora talked about these things with an air of decisions already half-way taken, when she invited Rosa to dinner and provided as table partners an eclectic assortment of visiting British and Scandinavian left-wing journalists (the latter brought regards from the Swede who briefly had been her lover) and liberal white American congressmen or black sociologists come to visit Soweto from their base in expensive white hotels where only foreign blacks could stay.

The others—her father's closest associates, who ought to have known her best, standing among them outside the prison when she was a child, left her to come to them. Those that there were: who were not in prison or gone into exile. Many were under restrictions which forbade their meeting one another, including her. But this was an ordinary circumstance for them all; there were ways and means. They studied the pattern of police surveillance as surveillance studied them; hiatus will occur, out of habit, in vigilance become routine.

The faithful were there. They did not have to give her any sign. They had always been there. Mark and Rhoda Liebowitz's mother, Leah Gordon, and Ivy Terblanche, danced with her father to the gramophone in the Jewish Workers' Club in the Thirties. Aletta Gous went with Rosa's mother when she was young and Lionel Burger married to someone else, to one of those vast assemblies of their time with names like Youth for Peace, and they were photographed together holding flowers on a Russian railway station. The biographer had borrowed the photograph for reproduction in his book. Gifford Williams, the lawyer with the briefcase for whom the fourteen-year-old had seen the prison portal open, acted for her father for years before he himself was banned, and it was he who had briefed Theo Santorini in the Burger trial.

They were not many. They had been to prison and come out again, lived through two, three, five years of their sentences—just before Lionel Burger died in prison, Ivy Terblanche completed her two years for refusing to testify against him. They lived through years-long bans on their movements and association with other people and often were banned again the week restrictions expired. Except for Dick Terblanche, who was a sheet-metal worker, they had had to find substitutes for work they were debarred from doing. Gifford sold office equipment in place of practising law, Leah Gordon, forbidden to teach, was an orthodontist's receptionist, Ivy Terblanche ran her own little take-away lunch business in the factory area where she had once been a shop steward. Aletta Gous, banned from entry into premises where printing or publishing was done, had lost her job as a proof-reader of Afrikaans textbooks and was working, when last Rosa was in touch with her, with some organization that tried to make popular among blacks a cheap, high protein food.

Lionel's daughter came in through the backyard gate from a lane as she had always done. When she was a child, in homely ease, now because it was not overlooked by neighbouring houses as the front entrance from the street was. As a named person she was forbidden by law to visit Ivy and Dick Terblanche, both restricted people under bans, but their daughter Clare was neither named nor banned and she happened to live with her parents and could receive *her* friends—some sort of an alibi. Dick Terblanche, cleaning the carburettor of Ivy's same old car, lifted a red, yellow-eyebrowed face in whose expression Rosa was long out of mind; but at once came to kiss her. Holding his dirty hands away had the effect of outlining a space round her. Whoever watched the Terblanche house was least likely to be alert on a Sunday morning; the only witness to be seen was a neighbour's child with a kicking rabbit in its arms, watching the car repair. It turned its attention undiscriminatingly to the embrace and then to Ivy, carolling out from the house. Rosa went quickly indoors. A thin old black woman ironing in the converted porch covering the length of the house behind whose louvres the Terblanches followed most of their pursuits, rested the iron end-up. —How's Lily?—

—Fine. She writes sometimes. One of her granddaughters has taken up nursing. Lily's taking care of the little boy she had. He's called Tony, after my brother, you remember?—

—Oh shame, that's very nice . . . And the other daughter, that one the last-born, same age like you?— The black woman frowned shrewdly, laying a claim for old, reciprocal responsibility where it was due. —She's got children?—

—No, no children. She's married to a waiter in a big hotel in Pretoria. He's got a good job, Lily's pleased.—

—Only you's not getting married, Rosa.—

Ivy hitched her Yorkshirewoman's wide rump past the black woman to reach up and disconnect the iron. —Get away with you, Regina, stop giving her hell and give her a cup of tea.—

Dick was scrubbing his hands at the outside sink. His face came up divided by the open louvres of the windows. —Tell Clare who's here.—

There was neither surprise at Rosa's sudden appearance nor reproach at her neglect of them, from the Terblanches. And they were ready to vanish from her company into another part of their tiny house if a knock or the bark of the old Labrador that had once been a Burger family pet should announce the arrival of another guest—perhaps the plain-clothes man whose charge they were. He would find the first guest alone with their daughter.

—Clare's washing her hair, she'll be along.—

Ivy shuffled together papers and newspaper cuttings and dumped them on a chair under a typewriter to weigh them down. Ironed shirts, knitting and cats lay on other chairs, two huge wet pullovers of the kind Ivy had supplied her husband with for many winters were shaped to dry on thicknesses of newspaper. Dick clapped and cats sprang sourly down. Ivy put her hand on her guest's—He wouldn't dare if Clare saw him. She's daft as ever over animals. In her bed every night. Ay . . . you look well, Rosa. Dick, don't you think she's looking better?—

—Since when did she look worse?—

—Flora wants me to throw away all my clothes and buy new ones.—

Ivy cocked her big, wild-haired head. —Oh Flora. Does she, now.—

—You living at her place?— Dick was slightly deaf from working forty years in industrial noise and spoke in a voice pitched to be heard in a machine shop.

—No, no. I see them sometimes.—

—Perhaps William Donaldson will give you a job.— Ivy addressed her husband, taking the opportunity of bringing up tongue-in-cheek, before a third person, something neither would have suggested in private. —He's going to be retired next year in July, is Dick.—

—I'm four years younger than Lionel. He was twentieth November nineteen-o-five, mmh?—

Regina, with the glance from face to face of one who has lost the room's attention, brought in and set out the tea-tray.

Rosa's profile was very like her father's as she looked down with light eyes hidden, sugaring her cup from the bowl Ivy held in a hand from which a cigarette rippled smoke. —When did you get to know Lionel, then—I thought you were together in Moscow that first time?—

—She means 1928.—

Dick and Ivy's response to other people was close as if there existed between them a mutual system of cerebral impulses. —I wasn't interested in the C.P. Soccer mad. And girls. When I was a youngster.—

—We didn't meet until 1930.— Ivy sugared and stirred his tea and gave it to him.

Rosa had her jaw thrust, jaunty, smiling, the young flattering in unconscious patronage of the past: —Girls.—

He nodded, feeling for a spoon with a thick hand pied with scaly pink patches of skin cancer. —*It's stirred.*— Ivy's words issued in smoke as those of comic book characters are carried by a bubble.

—He was too young. I was meant to go but Lionel was already in Edinburgh, it was cheaper to send him from there . . . I'm the one as old as Lionel.—

—Did he take someone along—a girl?—

—Girl! We all had girls.—

But the wife required more female precision in these matters. —What girl?—

—Katya, wasn't it? David's mother.—

—Oh Colette. Could have been. I suppose they must have been together by then. The future star of Sadler's Wells. I don't know when that affair started up—Dick?—

—Were they married when we met?—

But neither was sure.

—She wrote me a letter.— They knew Rosa meant when her father died. Ivy's broad alert face, powdered to the strict limit of jowls, relaxed into a coaxing expression of scepticism and expectancy. The woman Rosa had never seen had been materialized by her. —She did? Where has she landed up by now?—

—She heard via Tanzania. From David. She lives in France. The South of France.—

—D'you hear that, Dick? What'd she say in the letter?— Ivy's lips shaped to lend themselves to the offensive or absurd.

Rosa was odd-man-out in the company of three, one absent, who had known each other too well. She spoke with the flat hesitancy of one who cannot guess what indications her hearers will read in what she is relating. —The usual things.— There had been many letters of sympathy, following one formula or another. But the Terblanches were waiting. Rosa stroked under the hard feral jaw of the cat that treaded her lap and smiled, placing words exactly. —She wrote about here. Well, she said something . . . 'It's strange to live in a country where there are still heroes.'—

Ivy lifted her hair theatrically through the outstretched fingers of both hands, suddenly someone unrecognizable. —About him.—

Dick, commenting, not participating, confirmed hoarsely. —Sounds like her.—

—When I saw the signature it didn't strike me for a moment. She doesn't use Lionel's name.—

—And she calls herself Katya?—

—Ivy, they must have been married already when I met you.—

—You're right. Ay. I don't think he'd've found it easy, otherwise, with her.—

—Perhaps he wouldn't've asked.— Dick drew his lips in over his teeth, turning on his wife an old man's bristled jaw and frown.

Rosa contemplated them as a child opens a door on a scene whose actions she cannot interpret. —It is true you didn't marry without the Party's consent?—

—Some of us were required not to marry at all.— Dick's formal, Afrikaans-accented phrasing quoted; he relaxed the grim jaw and smiled her fondly away from matters she shouldn't bother with.

—Colette Swan was not the wife for Lionel by anyone's standards.— Ivy thrust out the teapot.

Rosa got up to have her cup refilled. —And she wrote about you, Ivy.—

The nostrils opened pugnaciously, the wattles shook at Dick. —Good god, what could she have to say about me.—

He gave his slow, Afrikaner's smile. —Wait, man, let's hear.—

—'You did what she would have expected.'—

Dick pulled an impressed face and Ivy made it clear she hadn't listened; there are people whose approval or admiration is as unwelcome as criticism.

—So it was all right for Lionel and my mother to marry?—

—How d'you mean?—

But Dick looked at his wife and she spoke again. —Cathy was right for everything.—

It was not what the girl had asked. —They were approved first, before they married?—

Dick began to giggle a bit to himself at the past. —Hell, it's not exactly that everyone, I mean it's not as if . . .—

—If you'd ever known Colette Swan you wouldn't talk about her in the same breath as Cathy.—

Like many people who have high blood pressure, Ivy Terblanche's emotions surfaced impressively; her voice was off-hand but her eyes glittered liquid glances and her big breast rose against abstract-patterned nylon. Lionel Burger once described how, when she was still permitted to speak at public meetings, she 'circled beneath the discussion and then spouted like some magnificent female whale'.

—Oh Ivy man! After all, it was someone her father was married to the first time! Have a heart!—

The Terblanche daughter who had stood pregnant outside the prison had left the country long ago with her husband. It was the younger one who came in raking down dun wet hair. —What're you getting het up about now?—

—Nothing, nothing. Things that happened before you girls were ever thought of, nothing.—

With the ease of being a contemporary of the guest, the girl wandered before the glass louvres Dick had fitted, flicking her comb at the avocado pips growing in jam-jars on the sill, her head interrupting the sunlight. —Where're you staying now, Rosa?—

—A little flat, not bad.—

—Sharing?—

—No. It's my own.—

97

—What d'you pay?—

—Clare my girlie, look what you're doing.—

She twisted her head clumsily, sent another shower of drops over her father's bare knees in shorts, laughed—Don't fuss—and mopped him with the end of her long denim skirt. —I mean I've been looking for a place for someone—a girl with a kid, she's coming up from Port Elizabeth—but the rents are terrible.—

—Well, mine's just one room. I don't know whether that would do, with a child. But I know there's an empty flat in the building—or was, anyway, last week.—

Clare poured herself tea, paused critically at the array on the tray, poured the tea back into the pot and filled a cup with milk. —What happened to that garden cottage?—

—It disappeared with the freeway.—

—Not even a biscuit—I've had no breakfast you know. You two have filled yourselves up with scrambled eggs. Why do old people and babies get up so early?—

Ivy took the wet comb from where it had been dropped beside her papers. —Well go into the kitchen and fetch yourself something. There're baked apples. But don't cut the date loaf Regina's made—if it's cut while it's hot it gets sad. She's vegetarian these days, is Clare, and she thinks it gives her the right to priority with everything that isn't meat.—

The girl ignored her mother, amiably sulky. —You're still at the hospital.—

—No, that's over, too.—

Dick had gone into the kitchen and come back with a thick slice of date loaf. —Here, man, eat.— Before Ivy could speak, his patient-sounding Afrikaner voice assured—With Regina's permission.— A quick, comedian's twitch of the nose for Rosa alone.

The skin bridging Clare's heavy eyebrows was inflamed by dandruff. Between bites, she was preoccupied with details of a toilet to which she turned probably infrequently: pushing back the cuticles of her nails with smoke-blued teeth, looking at the strands of hair that came away in her fingers when she tested the length of the ends against her shoulders, noticing intently—as if the presence of the other, Rosa, brought her attention down to these things—her pink feet (thick as her father's hands) like strangers in curling brown sandals.

—You're not looking for a job, I suppose. With us.—

—Us?— Rosa took in Ivy and Dick. Ivy's match waved denial, extinguishing its tiny flame invisible in the sun. —She's working with Aletta.—

—Aletta—oh that's wonderful. How's she these days?—

—A red-head, for the moment.—

—Ma, I must say I think she looks great.—

—But if I did it, you and Dick—

He gazed at Ivy the way familiars seldom consider one another. —You'd look like a bloody Van Gogh sunflower.—

Laughter drew them all together, so that Ivy said what might have been remarked only after she had gone. —And this business of Eckhard—how long's that going to carry on?— A second's glance not at but in the direction of Dick, as if an invisible thread had been tugged, was followed by quick, smooth deflection: —I mean, aren't you bored yet, Rosa?—

The chance given her to speak, if she could. A swift temptation to talk. To ask—

—It's a job.—

Rosa had her old childhood self-possession of being able to evade opportunities as well as advances, stubborn little girl in the woman. And she would not make it easier for anyone by changing the subject; other people were both held off, and held to it.

But an atmosphere of convalescence was still allowed her. Ivy strewed commonplaces over the moment. —Oh it could be quite interesting. Yes, useful, give you a practical insight, the way economic power manipulates in this country . . . one can always learn something . . . for a while, I mean— She looked around generously.

—A job like any other.— Rosa's stillness opposed the other girl's roaming self-awareness, Ivy's ample concern, Dick's restless inklings. He kept nodding, as if patting a hand or shoulder.

Clare spoke without malice. —I suppose it must be something to be decently paid for once.—

—The usual typist's salary. Nothing out of the ordinary. But nothing's expected—of you, either. It's the faceless kind of job 90 per cent of people do. You only really understand when you do it . . . there's nothing to show at the end of the day. Telephone calls and paper looping out of the teleprinter, vast sums of money you never see, changing hands—you never touch the hands.— Her father's smile.

Clare rubbed at the inflamed patch between her eyebrows. —Well come down to our place. We're weighing and lugging sacks about—that stuff we sell smells like baby-sick, Aletta says. No, really, Mum, it's okay at first, you think it's pleasant, but with each load, after a few weeks, it's cloying! Can't get the smell out of your hair and clothes. Tactile and whiffy enough for you, I can tell you. But nourishing, nourishing.— The affectation of a mimicking, didactic air, the eyebrows she had inherited from her father, tousled: —You just have to see Aletta with some of these women who come along. She snatches their babies from them, yelling the place down, prods their pot-bellies—you know Aletta—look at this! look at this!— The girl demonstrated on her own slack body, stretched on the frayed grass matting; wobbled with laughter —And then out with the slides showing what awful things happen to bones when they lack vitamin C and skin when there's not enough vitamin B . . . they get hell for the bits of fur and beads and god knows what they tie round their kids' necks—you know how she is about tribalism. Oh but she's fantastic, eh. They take it from her. They just giggle—Her latest thing, she's going to show them films. This weekend she's seeing that chap who makes short documentaries.—

—A film?— Ivy counted stitches along her knitting.

—Her nutrition education film. I told you. The fellow who borrowed the Mayakovsky. *The Bedbug.*—

—Clare! Get it back from him for me? So that's where it is! I bought that book thirty years ago in Charing Cross Road. I managed to keep it when the police took away everything in sight that was printed. And then some lad of yours walks off with it . . .—

Dick was led to recollect, for his guest. —Colette started a theatre group, you know. Must have been about 1933. She was in charge of the cultural programme, class consciousness through art and that.—

—Invented her own programme for herself, more likely. I don't remember anyone else being asked much about it. Her way of getting out of teaching in the night school. You couldn't get her to work for anything she couldn't take the credit for initiating. Not her! But Clare—I mean it, you tell that young whoever-he-is from me—

—We went in a truck to black townships up and down the Reef, Krugersdorp and Boksburg . . . She made up the plays and I think the songs too. We acted Bloody Sunday and I was Father Gapon. And what was the one about the Gaikas and the British Imperial troops, Ivy? Blacks from our night school were the Gaikas. We used to have the Red Flag flying on the bonnet of Isaac Lourie's old produce truck.—

The laughter of Dick and Rosa attracted his daughter. —Those were the days, old man. We can't even get into the Transkei with our thrilling kwashiorkor slides.—

—Wait until I'm put out to grass next year. I'mna fit you out a mobile unit in a caboose. You'll see. Bappie's promised to get a lot of the equipment through his father-in-law's wholesale business.—

Ivy brought Rosa up-to-date. —Bapendra Govind's home from the Island, you know. Since last month.—

—And how is he? I gather he hasn't been banned again, so far. I haven't seen anything in the paper, anyway.—

—Yes, his wife wants them to apply for exit permits and go to Canada before it comes.— Ivy gestured, letting the knitting sink in her lap. —Leela says she won't go without her mother and father. But you know how clannish Muslims are.—

—What does Leela do?—

—Oh she's been working with me for about six months now. She's an efficient little thing, is Leela! She takes down the sendouts, over the phone, she gives a hand in the kitchen. Oh anything. She goes to the market for me and buys most of my supplies.—

—You have quite an organization, Ivy.—

Ivy looked round. —Ay . . . we all eat. That I can say. Beulah James is in with me, too . . . Alfred has another seven months to go. (They've transferred him to Klerksdorp which is a nuisance for her, Pretoria Central was handier.) We're moving away from the sandwiches and rolls, concentrating more on soup and curry and so on. Hot things are very popular. And then we have salads, of course. I see quite a few of the people I used to work with . . . I may not be allowed to put my nose into factory premises but the whites still send out blacks to buy their lunch . . . Yes, it wouldn't be too bad if we knew what Dick . . . he has to find something to do . . .—

—I wouldn't mind taking Aletta's Follies on a country-wide tour.— Dick grinned; the joke of a man confined to the magisterial district around the house they sat in.

Ivy tensed back her shoulders and stretched the grand folds of her neck, a challenging goose. —I don't think I could face the Bantustans, thank you very much. Even if I could get in. Matanzima, Mangope—any of that crowd—the sight of their 'capitals' with their House of Assembly and their hotel for whites.— A heave of disgust.

—Oh come on, Ivy. If Aletta gets someone in . . . there are still people there . . . old friends. There's work to be done.—

—Where are they? You know where; the black Vorsters have got their detention laws, too.—

—There must be a few still around, contact's been lost, yes—

—You were right not to try it, Rosa. Personally, for me to put my foot in those places . . . It's a denial of Nelson and Walter—of the Island. Of Bram and Lionel.—

The pause settled round the presence of Lionel's daughter. The black woman walked into it. —You having lunch with us, Rosa. I made nice roast potatoes.— But the guest had already risen, she could not stay, they went through the ritual of remonstrances and excuses, Rosa pretending to accept the childhood authority of Lily

Letsile's counterpart, the Terblanches' servant taking upon herself the role of disappointed hostess. Ivy put her arms right round Rosa. —Don't stay away.— The girl called out over the mother's shoulder to the daughter. —Ring me if you want to do anything about a flat.— There was a wave of casual agreement between the two girls.

Dick's tread accompanied Rosa to her car, taking a chance, through the man-high dead khakiweed of the lane, his arms crossed over his chest bundling up the pockets and flaps of his jacket. He stood beside her window and she put the key in the ignition and then did not turn it, looking at him. He was humming softly, stumbling and repeating notes.

—Trying to remember one of the songs . . . Katya . . . Something like this: 'Lift your spade from the field, raise your pick from the ditch, lift your shi-eld, match your step wi-th your bro-ther'— His voice was deep, strangled and shaky, his Adam's apple keeping time under coarse sunburned folds intricately seamed with bristles and blackheads. —Oh lord I haven't thought about it for donkey's years. I never had a memory for that sort of thing. A pampoenhead. When I was in solitary I used to try—even just to remember what I learnt at school, man—you know, poems and that. You read about people who can keep their minds active, saying over whole books to themselves. It's a wonderful gift. But sometimes I—big hands rested on the bevelled edge of the window—I made things, in my mind; I carved a whole diningroom table and chairs, the one for the head of the table with arms, like the one my grandfather had . . . barley-sugar uprights with round knobs on top . . . man, it was craftsmanship . . . But the stoep at home, I planned it when I was inside, it was all worked out to the last inch of frame and pane of glass. And when I checked the measurements, they weren't half-an-inch out, I could go along to the hardware shop, just like that. No problem. I scratched the plans on the floor of my cell with a pin. There was trouble—they were suspicious it was an escape route I was working on. Can you beat it? Anyone'd be stupid enough to draw that where every warder saw it? It was just after Goldreich and Wolpe got away; they were jumpy, I suppose they felt their whole security system had been made nonsense if two politicals could get out on their wits and come back in again without even being seen when arrangements went wrong, *and* repeat the whole business without a hitch the next night . . . Well chances like that won't come again. They're keeping politicals in maximum security these days.—

She was following a current between them on another level. —After next July, Dick.—

He was shyly flattered at what he took to be curiosity about an experience that was approaching him alone. —It's Ivy's worried. I'm not. I'll find something. What d'you think about Flora? Any point? They say her husband wants her to keep clear. She goes for liberal committees and so forth, now. He's warned her off anything else. I don't know whether he'd want to give me a job.—

—There's a kind of obstinacy, always, in Flora.— Rosa was looking at him, suggesting, questioning. —William doesn't get past it, he only circumvents it, whatever he persuades her to do.—

—She's proud of the connection with us. There've been people like that. I know the kind. And even now. She's been useful. Ivy says it's the English middle-class idea of personal loyalty, nothing more. Well, okay. Whatever . . .—

—She'll be pleased if you ask.—

—Anything just to show I'm harmlessly occupied for the next year or two.— He looked away, out over the blackened weed with leonine patience, a restless inward gaze of one in whom will or belief is strength. Then he placed his forearms on the window and carried his face forward, chin held, there, near her. —Not long now, Rosa. Angola will go, and Moçambique; they won't last another year. Someone's just been in touch. There's going to be a revolt in the Portuguese army, they're going to refuse to fight. Gloria's husband's in Dar es Salaam and this—other one—came back from Moçambique—it's true, this time. Someone with strong Frelimo family connections, he's close to Dos Santos and Machel. It's coming at last. Some of us will still be around when it happens. Too late for Lionel, but you're here, Rosa.—

The girl could not speak; he saw it. Her face drew together, the wide mouth dented white into the flesh at its corners, she held a breath painfully and pressed the accelerator, turning the ignition so that the old car engine was startled. Dick Terblanche put a big hand, cuffed quickly and away again over the hair at the curve of her skull to her neck, afraid he had made her weep. And then he jumped back and began to direct the reversing of the car like a parking ground attendant, making feints with his arms, nodding and urging. Rosa saw in the rear mirror his old man's legs slightly bent with effort at the back of the knees, the safari jacket lifted over the behind.

Sweat of wet wool heating up in sun through glass and scent of apples baking with cinnamon.

Those nights talking in the cottage: you wanted to know. The man who was gathering material wanted to know; he supplied facts but it was from me he expected to know.

Noel de Witt's the one with the 'strong Frelimo connections'— that I know. His Portuguese rebel mother. Although Ivy, who went to prison for two years rather than tell in court what she knew about my father, doesn't talk before me of present activities, and Dick, unable not to hint because of whose daughter I am, gave no name. Noel would be the one who reported secret plans for a Portuguese army revolt. The nice new young wife Flora commended would have told no one, even in London, where he was when he went away, because even London is full of informers, and the lines back to South Africa have to be protected. Gloria Terblanche and her husband are in Tanzania, he has a cover job teaching, perhaps sometimes they pass in the street the man who is my brother (although Tony is dead and you I don't see any more)—the son of the woman who went to the Sixth Congress with my father and when he died wrote to me from the South of France.

There are reports from time to time, there are rumours that may be more than rumours. I used to have to try to find some way of telling them to my father when he was alive—but I was well experienced in getting what I needed to past the big ears of warders. Sometimes the sign that it will soon be over is read from an event without, and sometimes it is from within the country. The Terblanches, going from shabby suburb to prison, and back from prison to shabby suburb, growing old and heavy (she) selling cartons of curry, and deaf and scaly-skinned (he) on a pension or charity job from friends—they wait for that day when rumour will gather reality, when its effect will be what they predict, as their neighbours (whom they resemble strangely, outwardly) wait to retire to the coast and go fishing. For the Terblanches even holidays ceased to exist years ago. Their outing is the twice-weekly trip to report at the local police station on the way to or from work, as other people have to attend a clinic for control of some chronic infection. If they get really old and sick I suppose somebody like Flora—someone fascinated by them, shamed by not living as they have lived—will keep them alive on hand-outs of money she is embarrassed to possess. And Dick and Ivy will take it since neither they nor she have petit bourgeois finickiness about such things: they because it's not for themselves but for what lives in them, Flora because she does not believe what she possesses has come to her by right. People like Dick and Ivy and Aletta don't understand provision in the way the clients of the man I worked for do— 'provision' is a word that comes up continually in the market place of Barry Eckhard's telephone: provision against a fall in the price of gold, provision against inflationary trends, provision for expansion, provision against depression, a predicate stored for sons and sons of sons, daughters and daughters of daughters—stocks, bonds, dividends, debentures. In the pulpits and newspapers of my boss's clients the godless materialism of what they call the Communist creed is outlawed; but the Terblanches have laid up no treasures moth or rust will corrupt. For them there is no less than the future in store—*the* future. With what impossible hubris are they living out their lives without the pleasures and precautions of other white people? What have they to show for it—Ivy become a petty shopkeeper, and the blacks still not allowed in the open unions she and my mother worked for, Dick tinkering in his backyard on a Sunday in a white suburb, and the blacks still carrying passes twenty-five years after he first campaigned with them against pass laws and went to jail. After all the Dingaan's Day demonstrations (1929, J. B. Marks declared 'Africa belongs to us', a white man shouted 'You lie' and shot Mofutsanyana dead on the platform, 700 blacks arrested; 1930, young Nkosi stabbed to death, Gana

Makabeni took his place as C.P. organizer in Durban, 200 black militants banished); all the passive resistance campaigns of the Fifties, the pass-burnings of the Sixties; after all the police assaults, arrests; after Sharpeville; after the trials, detentions, the house arrests, the deaths by torture in prison, the sentences lived through and the sentences being endured while life endures. After the shame of the red banner 'Workers of the world unite and fight for a white South Africa', flown in 1922, had been erased later in the 1920s by the acceptance of Lenin's thesis on the national and colonial questions, after the purges when Lionel Burger (who had married a dancer abroad without obtaining his Central Committee's consent) voted for the expulsion of his mentor Bunting, after the Party in South Africa turned right and then left again, after it refused to support the war that South Africa was fighting against racialism in Europe while herself practising racialism at home, after the Soviet Union was attacked and this policy of opposition to the war effort was reversed, after the Popular Front when the C.P. was permitted to work with reformist organizations; after the issue of political versus industrial action (those in favour of political action quoting Lenin's denunciation of the 'infantile disorder of anti-parliamentarianism', those against arguing that in South Africa four-fifths of the working class were black and had no vote anyway); after the banning of the Party, the underground reorganization after 1966, the banishments, the exiles, the life sentences—I didn't learn it at my mother's knee but as you told me, it was the everyday mythology of that house—I breathed it as children must fill their lungs indiscriminately out of mountain air or city smog, wherever they happen to be pitched into the world, and I would like once and for all to match the facts with what I ought to know.

That future, that house—although my father's house was larger than Dick and Ivy's home-improved bungalow, *that house* also made provision for no less than the Future. My father left that house with the name-plate of his honourable profession polished on the gate, and went to spend the rest of his life in prison, secure in that future. He's dead, Ivy and Dick are ageing and poor and alive—the only difference. Dick with those ugly patches on his poor hands said to me like a senile declaration of passion; we are still here to see it. He thought I was overcome at the thought of my father. But I was filled with the need to get away as from something obscene—and afraid to wound him—them—by showing it. It was like the last few weeks when I was working at the hospital; you remember?

They are waiting.

They leave me alone to go my own way because they can't believe—Lionel's daughter—I am not waiting with them. Our kind repudiates ethnic partitioning of the country. They believe I talked of trying to get into the Transkei because I was under orders to find a cover job in a hospital there; I must have taken advantage of my period of 'convalescence' and refused. But one day I won't be able to say no.

Although it's all there, in notes for publication researched diligently from libraries and the memories of exiles, the past doesn't count: the general strikes that failed when the Party was legal, the High Command that was betrayed when the Party was underground. The relic present, when they joke twice a week with the police sergeant as they become signatories to their own captivity, doesn't count. They've lived without fulfilment of personal ambition and it's not peace of mind they're looking forward to in their old age. The defeat of the Portuguese colonial armies in Angola and Moçambique; the collapse of white Rhodesia; the end of South Africa's occupation of Namibia brought about by SWAPO's fighters or international pressure; these are what they're waiting for, as Lionel was waiting, in jail. Signs that it will soon be over, at last. *The* Future is coming. The only one that's ever existed for them, according to documentation. National liberation, phase one of the two-stage revolution that will begin with a black workers' and peasants' republic and complete itself with the achievement of socialism.

And not just waiting. Whatever can be done between one dutiful report to the police and the next will be done by people who, far from poring over the navel of a single identity (yes, a dig at you, Conrad), see the necessity of many. It won't be by chance Ivy has her lunch-counter in an area of heavy industry where thousands of blacks work. And of course the people who pack her cartons of curry and the salads that are so popular are all old associates or their relatives. She put the typewriter down to cover papers she had been working on but when she picked up the comb that was wetting the corner of one sheet she pulled it out to let it dry; I saw it was part of an analysis of wages. She's probably supplying the radical students' black wages commission with material. Dick will tell William Donaldson he wants a job to supplement his pension; but he's looking for what will show him to be 'harmlessly occupied', whatever else he may be doing. It's not easy for families of old lags, like the Terblanches, like the one I'm the remnant of—watched all the time.

They are prepared to be patient with me. It's not sympathy, some pallid underwriting of the validity of self-pity, they offer. I have had a course of action to follow which involved the life of a man who happened to be my father, just as they themselves have had. The consequences for Dick have been periods of imprisonment with my father; for Ivy, imprisonment because of my father. The course of action I have duly fulfilled, with consequences for me some of which were self-evident, foreseen and accepted, just as theirs were, is part of a continuing process. It is complete only for Lionel Burger; he has done all he had to do and that, in his case, happened to imply a death in prison as part of the process. It does not occur to them that it could be complete for themselves, for me.

It is not so easy to shut oneself off from them—these people: Dick with his farmer's blue eyes under those distance-shading eyebrows, his safari suit with shorts that show his strong, vein-tattooed legs, and his jacket decked out with pockets in the style of the old colonial-military, frontier way of life, so that his appearance is innocently exactly that of one of his brother Boers who regard his beliefs as those of Antichrist, the devil himself, and of the capitalist-adventurist European conquistadors he himself sees as the devil; Ivy with her supermarket housewife's body in cheerful prints, her wild, Einstein head, and the unexpected concession to vanity in the evidence—a glossy streak of blonde fringing her upper lip—that she peroxides the moustache with which age is trying to deny her femininity. These two people represent an intimacy with my father greater than mine. They know what even one's own daughter is never told. A biographer ought to be referred to them, Lionel's—what? Friends, associates—comrades, the biographer will settle for as catch-all, but some new term ought to come into being for what I understood, coming back into their presence. It goes beyond friendship, beyond association; beyond family relationship—of course. They will be waiting for me to find what there is for me to do. How they all cared for each other's children, when we were little! In the enveloping acceptance of Ivy's motherly arms—she feels as if I were her own child—there is expectance, even authority. To her warm breast one can come home again and do as you said I would, go to prison.

I found the ring I wore when what I had to do was be a young girl in love. In the leather collar-box from one of my grandfathers, among cards of moth-eaten darning wool and the elastic my mother used to thread through the waist of my school pants. With it were brass serpent insignia of the Medical Corps—my father's cap badges. My mother kept those? My father joined the white South African army, according to the date I've been given, when the Soviet Union was attacked, and was in charge of a hospital in the Middle East. She wasn't married to him then; did she take the badges off old uniforms later, or maybe Tony asked for them, and when the little boy was dead and she found his treasures she didn't throw them away. They could tell any raiding Special Branch policemen nothing about Lionel Burger that should not be discovered. In fact at his trial Theo Santorini included 'a distinguished record of service to wounded soldiers of his mother country' in establishing the standing of such a man: *How easy would it have been, I put it to you, Your Lordship, for him to choose professional and civic honours; and what grave sense of wrongs committed by the white establishment must he have had, in order for such a man to turn his back on the laurels of white society and risk—no, refute outright—*

reputation, success and personal liberty, in the cause of the black people. The army service seems to have lasted two years—like most people, I foreshorten the entire period of life my parents lived before I was alive, and they were strangers to whom I have no relation. Lionel once told me how when he was about fourteen and had just come to boarding-school in Johannesburg he saw torn-up passbooks in the street after a demonstration and curiosity led him to realize for the first time that the 'natives' were people who had to carry these things while white people like himself didn't. For me, this childhood awakening of his is no further away than his reasons for going to war. The war experience gave him the chance to be active (as the biographer's phrase goes) in an ex-servicemen's legion that brought together along with white veterans, black orderlies and ambulance men who had risked their lives but not been allowed to bear arms. The movement broke up, like my mother's attempts to get black workers and white together in trade unions, on the white men's fear of losing the privileges of segregation from their comrades. Yet when the black and white veterans were marching 40,000 strong through Cape Town it must have seemed a sign; soon over, now.

You didn't want to believe that at twelve years old what happened at Sharpeville was as immediate to me as what was happening in my own body. But then I have to believe that when the Russians moved into Prague my father and mother and Dick and Ivy and all the faithful were still promising the blacks liberation through Communism, as they had always done. Bambata, Bulhoek, Bondelswart, Sharpeville; the set of horrors the faithful use in their secretly printed and circulated pamphlets. Stalin trials, Hungarian uprising, Czechoslovakian uprising—the other set that the liberals and right-wing use to show it isn't possible for humane people to be Communist. Both will appear in any biography of my father. In 1956 when the Soviet tanks came into Budapest I was his little girl, dog-paddling to him with my black brother Baasie, the two of us reaching for him as a place where no fear, hurt or pain existed. And later, when he was in jail and I began to think back, even I, with my precocious talents for evading warders' comprehension now in full maturity, could not have found the way to ask him—in spite of all these things: do you still believe in the future? The same Future? Just as you always did? And anyway it's true that when at last the day of my visit came I would be aware of nothing except that he was changing in prison, he was getting the look on those faces in old photographs from the concentration camps, the motionless aspect, shouldered there between the two warders that accompanied him, of someone who lets himself be presented, identified. His gums were receding and his teeth seemed to have moved apart at the necks; I don't know why this distressed me so much. In the cottage I used to see that changed smile that no one will know in the future because the frontispiece photograph I've been asked for shows him, neck thick with muscular excitement, grinning energy, speaking to a crowd not shown but whose presence is in his eyes.

I don't know where you live; maybe in the same city as I am, wherever I go, without either of us being aware of the presence of the other, each running along in a dark burrow that never intersects. You have hired a colour TV in a building round the corner; or you've sailed away from such things, on the ark I saw being built. You never got beyond fascination with the people around Lionel Burger's swimming-pool; you never jumped in and trusted yourself to him, like Baasie and me, or drowned, like Tony. I was fascinated by your friends the boat-builders (you correct me: a yacht is not a boat). They were simple people, not like you; they didn't understand what they were doing when they planed the sweet pine of the bunks for you to sleep in and ran up the curtains that will be keeping out the glare of the sub-tropical sea. But you know that when you take passage with them it's to flee. Because my boss Barry Eckhard and your successful scrap-dealer father proposed to you their fate, the bourgeois fate, alternate to Lionel's: to eat without hunger, mate without desire.

Clare Terblanche sought out Rosa Burger with whom she had played as a child. The shadow wobbling over the blistered glass of the door had no identity; but as Rosa opened her door, compliance came to her face: the matter of the vacant flat she had promised to enquire about.

The other girl swung the worn, tasselled cloth bag that weighed on her hip like a pack-horse's pannier, and took a chair heavily. Her gaze went round the pieces of furniture from the Burger house that stood as if stored in the room. She breathed through open lips, and licked them. —A job to find this place.—

—But you've got my phone number at work? I'm sure I gave it to Ivy.—

—Could I have a drink of water?—

—I'll make tea. Or would you rather have coffee?—

—Coffee, if it's the same to you. Could I get myself some water in the meantime?—

Rosa Burger had the dazed sprightliness of someone who has been alone all day, before interruption. She might even have been pleased the other had come. —But of course!— She was gone into a tiny kitchen. There was the crackling of ice being forced out of its mould, the gurgle and splutter of a tap. The visitor sat as if she were not alone in the room.

When Rosa came back her hair lay differently; she had put a hand through it, perhaps, taking a look at herself in the distorting convex of a shiny surface. She smiled; the other was made aware that sometimes Rosa was beautiful. A knowledge parenthetic between them, briefly embarrassing Rosa.

The water was served with the small attentions of ice and a slice of lemon; the two girls talked trivialities—the neighbourhood, the warmth of the winter day—while Clare drank it off.

—I don't want to telephone you at work.—

The statement was turned aside.

—Oh it's all right, they know I haven't a phone here. I should've let you know about the flat, I'm sorry. I looked at it—but it's a back one, on the ground floor, awfully dark, I don't really think . . . And then when I heard nothing from you—why didn't you pop into the office and see me in all my splendour—

—I don't want to come there.—

Clare handed back the glass. Rosa hesitated a moment, expecting it to be put down on the table.

—Oh.— With the empty glass she accepted that it was not about the vacant flat they were talking. The kettle shrieked like a toy train.

—It's okay. Go on.—

She called from the kitchen, hospitable —Won't be a minute.—

Clare Terblanche was not in the chair but standing about in the room. At the balcony door she rattled the handle but the door merely heaved in its frame.

—The catch is at the top.—

Rosa came and stood beside her for a moment looking out with her at the hillside of roofs and trees dropping away below the building; between blackish evergreens a cumulus of jacarandas, yellowed before their leaves fall, like some blossoming reversal of seasons in the warm winter day. But she was not seeing what the tall girl had in her mind's eye.

—Should we go outside.—

Rosa's lips gave a puff of dismissal. —If you want.— With polite routine consideration she leant over and turned on the portable radio that lay on a pile of newspapers and records. Clare Terblanche's curious expression of finding fault settled at the record player, with its two speakers on the floor. Rosa unplugged the cord; closed the doors to the kitchen and bathroom; sat down—well!—before the coffee. The radio aerial was telescoped into the retracted position and reception was blurred by static interference.

—In that building—where you work now. It's where a lot of advocates have their chambers, isn't it?—

—The whole of the seventh and eighth floors. They've got a communal law library and a canteen—or rather a dining hall.—

The announcer's voice was reciting with the promiscuous intimacy of his medium a list of birthday, anniversary and lovers' greetings for military trainees on border duty. . . . *and for Robert Rousseau—hullo there Bob—Dawn and Flippy, Mom and Dad, thinking of you always . . .*

—Is it true most other people in the building use a photocopying and duplicating room belonging to them?—

Although Clare Terblanche did not see the offices where now and then a pigeon rang against the smoky topaz glass like a shot from the streets far below, breaking its neck, Rosa saw what Clare did, now. *Hennie Joubert, your sweetheart Elsabe . . .* An expression of recognition, of expectation without surprise, a nostalgia, almost, slightly crinkled the delicately darkened skin round Rosa's eyes. —I don't know about most. Quite a few. Barry Eckhard's firm has an arrangement— . . . *missing you lots darling . . . also Patricia, Uncle Tertius and Auntie Penny in Sasolburg . . .*

So the other—Clare—knew; or confirmed a hope: —Eckhard's has an arrangement.— At the inner starting-point of each eyebrow a few hairs, like Dick's her father's stood up—hackles that gave intensity to her face. She rubbed between them with the voluptuousness of assuagement; the peeling eczema danced into life and a patch of red gauze appeared on the white healthy skin of either cheek. —I don't suppose you use it yourself.—

. . . *love you very much see you soon . . .* Rosa Burger was off-hand and informative. It was not easy to hear her; the other girl concentrated on her lips. —Usually there's a clerk who does. If I need photocopying done, I give it to him.—

—And I believe the room's down on the second floor.—

—It is.— . . . *thinking of you god bless thumbs up . . .*

—Is it kept locked?—

—It's open while Chambers are. Same hours as most offices. But Clare, it's no good— With just such a smile, unanswerable, demanding, her father had invaded people's lives, getting them to do things.

Clare Terblanche was confronted with it as a refusal. —Of course I know. You're watched. (There was music now, the muezzin cry of a pop singer.) If you were to start being seen down there we wouldn't last a week. I don't mean *you*. But if you could just get the key for an hour. Just the key. Only long enough for us to have a duplicate made. Who'd ever know? Someone will come in between midnight when the cleaners have left, and the early hours of the morning. The person'll bring our own rolls of paper so that can't be traced; it won't be the paper that's normally used there.—

—It's no good.— A complicated sequence of drumming had taken over from the singer.

—The Eckhard office does have a key? What happens when the courts are in recess, when the advocates are on holiday?—

The moonstone-coloured eyes under dabs of shadow gazed back, sought no evasion or escape. —The photocopying service still operates. We do have a key, yes. In case the office needs to use the room after Chambers are closed.—

—So all the other firms in the building that use the room have keys, too—exactly. We only need Eckhard's for about twenty minutes! Lunch hour; nobody'll be there to notice it's gone before it'll be back.—

Resistance brought them closer and closer to one another although they had not moved.

Rosa Burger's body rather than her face expressed an open obstinacy—the arms thrust down at her sides, the hands, palms on the seat of the chair, pushed in and hidden beneath thighs neatly placed—an obstinacy that came to the Terblanche girl as a demand she didn't understand, rather than a refusal. She trembled on the verge of hostility; they were aware of each other for a moment as females.

Rosa Burger's prim thighs closed at the bony outline of pubis in shrunken jeans, a long sunburned neck with the cup at the collarbones where—she sat so still, no nerves, she did not fidget—a pulse could be seen beating: Noel de Witt's girl; also the mistress of a Swede (at least; of those that were known) who had passed through, and some silent bearded blond fellow, not someone who belonged, not he, either. A body with the assurance of embraces, as cultivated intelligence forms a mind. Men would recognize it at a glance as the other can be recognized at a word.

Clare Terblanche—the old playmate who had been thick and sturdy as a teddy-bear, little legs and arms the same simplified shape, furry with white down that brushed by, in tussles, smelling sweetly of Palmolive soap—her flesh was dumb. She lived inside there, usefully employing now tall, dependable legs that carried one haunch before the other until she found the flat. A poor circulation (showing itself in the pallor and flush of the face), breasts folded over against themselves, a soft expanse of belly to shelter children. A body that had no signals; it would grow larger and at once more self-effacing. Few men would find their way, seek her through it.

There was the table between them at the level of their calves; music and voices, fake sentiment, generalized emotion, public exposure passing for private need. . . . *and one for Billy Stewart. Billyboy I'll bet that's what they call you at home anyway Billy granma and granpa Davis are proud of you keepsmiling allathome love you waiting for you my darling Koosie—*

Rosa suddenly got up and cut off the voice.

—Perhaps you want to look at the flat anyway?—

Clare Terblanche did not answer. She drank from her coffee-mug in slow gulps they both heard. —All right.—

She seemed chastened, chastised.

At the door she stopped, turning back on the girl behind her. —It is just this you won't do?—

I am not the only survivor.

Her crepe soles made the searing squeak of fingers dragged over a balloon that Tony used to torment me with when we were little. I fetched that key at once (she must have found it ironic) from the caretaker and we went down the ringing iron steps of the fire escape. In the empty flat there was an old telephone directory, a population of fish-moth in the bath; cockroaches in the kitchen, a sanitary towel dried stiff to the shape in which it had been worn, left inside the cupboard I opened to show what storage-space was provided. Both were duly shocked at this example of the civilized habits whites were dedicated to maintaining against black degradation (these are the sort of reactions that come to me when I am back among my own kind). Anyway, both of us are nicely-brought-up girls, fastidiously middle-class in many ways—remember the high standard of comfort you remarked in my father's house—although if the class membership of our respective families were to be correctly defined by place in production relations, she was working-class and I was not. Our kind has never been dirty or hungry although prison and exile are commonplaces of family life to us. Being white constitutes a counter-definition whose existence my father and her mother were already arguing between dancing to the gramophone at the workers' club. I shut the cupboard with some sort of exclamation.

Wires were wrenched off at the wainscot where the telephone had been. The smell of her cigarette crept round like a suspicious animal. Freed even of inanimate witnesses, we did not know how to get away from one another—at least, she did not know how to make me feel demeaned by my refusal. On the contrary. I was aware of an unpleasant strength bearing upon her from me. She's

something sad rather than ugly, a woman without sexual pride—
as a female she has no vision of herself to divert others from her
physical defects. The way she stood—it irritated me. Clare
Terblanche has always stood like that, as if someone plonked
down a tripod, without the flow of her movement behind her or
projected ahead of her! There's an ordinary explanation: knock-
kneed. Why didn't Dick and Ivy have her treated when we were
little? The dandruff, and the eczema it caused, they were of nervous
origin. Why did we pretend not to notice this affliction? It was
'unimportant'. She knew I was seeing her clumsy stance, the
tormenting patches of inflamed and shedding skin, stripped of
familiar context. Poor thing; and she knew I thought: poor thing. I
am able to withstand other people's silences without discomfiture.
I felt pity and curiosity, slightly cruel. I might just as well have
reached out and taken her roughly by the shoulder, no one was
there to hear or overhear us, no voice of pulp goodwill overlaid
indiscretion and glossed heresy. I can't speak loudly; it's not my
nature, even in insolence. I said to her, Why do you go on with it?

She was not sure she understood me. Or she understood
instantly; I had an impatient sense that I was part of her mental
process, I was there, taking fright at what exists only once it has
been spoken. She tried an interpretation as a specific reference:
without me, without the photocopies at Barry Eckhard's building—oh, she would find some other possibility. Although (half-
offended, half-appealing for sympathy) for the moment she was
damned if she knew what.

I began to recite a quiet liturgy. —*The people will no longer tolerate.
The people's birthright. The day has come when the people demand*—

She stared at me as if I were shouting.

I spoke with interest, nothing more. —When you see reports of
the evidence in newspapers, doesn't it sound ridiculous? Still the
kits with invisible ink, the forged passports, the secret plans kept
like dry cleaners' slips, the mailing-lists, the same old story of
people who are 'approached' and turn state witness after having
licked some envelopes . . . You want to laugh, you can't help it;
it's pathetic. You'll print your news-sheet or you'll send out your

leaflets. It's all decided already, from the beginning, before you've begun. A few pieces of paper, a few months, and you'll be caught. You'll be traced easily or someone you've trusted will get twenty rand and sell you. *An enemy of the people* . . . You'll disappear into detention. Maybe there'll be a case and a lawyer who tries for mitigation, shaming you by making all the old slogans mean less than they mean.—

Her face slowly thickened and concentrated before me the way the faces of patients at the hospital would register an injection releasing the sensation of some substance into the bloodstream.

—And you'll go inside. Like them. You'll come out. Like them—We saw Ivy and Dick and Lionel.—

Tears pushed magnifying lenses up over her eyes and she had to hold them wide so that I should not see drops fall.

She didn't know how to tell me, me of all people, what she knew we knew. It will be there for everyone to read in the critical study of my father's life—without giving away any useful information about how the struggle is being carried on in the present; of that I have been assured. There is nothing but failure, until the day the Future is achieved. It is the only success. Others—in specific campaigns with specific objectives, against the pass laws, against forced dispossession of land—would lead to piecemeal reforms. These actions fail one after another, they have failed since before we were born; failures were the events of our childhood, failures are the normal circumstances of our adulthood—her parents under house arrest, my father dead in jail, my courting done in the prison visiting room. In this experience of being crushed on individual issues the masses come, as they can in no other way, to understand that there is no other way: state power must be overthrown. Failure is the accumulated heritage of resistance without which there is no revolution. The chapter will be headed by a maxim from Marx which Lionel Burger spoke from the dock before he was sentenced. 'World history would indeed be very easy to make if the struggle were taken up only on condition of infallibly favourable chances.'

Her words threshed about, clutched at indignation and slid into dismay. —But Rosa! They've had the worst of it. It'll be different for us. Whatever happens, we're lucky to be born later—

We were suddenly plunged, reckless in confession, pooling the forbidden facts of life.

—Exactly what your father says. This kind of thing you're doing, does it make sense to you?—

She looked the way I must have, for you, when you described to me watching your mother and her lover fucking in the spare bedroom. She would deal with what was put before her without allowing herself to see it, just as I did. —It's part of the strategy of the struggle. In the present phase—still. That's all there is to it. But you know.—

Of course I know. I could have quoted General Giap's definition of the art of insurrection as knowing how to find forms of struggle appropriate to the political situation at each stage. The huge strikes of black workers in Natal with which her mother will have become involved even if they were spontaneous to begin with, these are an example of Lenin's observation that the people sense sooner than the leaders the change in the objective conditions of struggle, yes. But the necessity for political propaganda remains. Someone must photocopy the open letter to Vorster. At the risk of encouraging adventurism, the necessity remains for the few white revolutionaries to be provided with a role. As long ago as 1962 it is documented that my father was one of those, at last mainly black, at the sixth underground conference of the South African Communist Party who achieved the final perspective, the ideological integration, the synthesis of twenty years' dialectic: it is just as impossible to conceive of workers' power separated from national liberation as it is to conceive of true national liberation separated from the destruction of capitalism. *The future* he was living for until the day he died can be achieved only by black people with the involvement of the small group of white revolutionaries who have solved the contradiction between black consciousness and class consciousness, and qualify to make unconditional common cause with the struggle for full liberation, e.g., a national and social revolution. It is necessary for these few to come into the country secretly or be recruited within it from among the bad risks, romantic journalists and students, as well as the good risks, the children, lovers and friends of the old guard, and for them to be pinched off between the fingers of the Special Branch one by one, in full possession of their invisible ink, their clandestine funds, their keys (provided by another sort of bad risk) to the offices of prominent financiers with photocopiers. Such things are ridiculous (like a child's 'rude' drawing of the primal mystery of the mating act)—she could hardly believe the stupid daring, the lifting of my shoulders against shameful laughter forcing its way past suppression in my face—only if one steps aside out of one's historically-determined role and cannot read their meaning. These are—we are—the instruments of struggle appropriate to this phase. I looked at her, inciting us.

—What conformists: the children of our parents.—

—Dick and Ivy conformists!— Her face screwed towards me.

—Not them—us. Did you ever think of that? Other people break away. They live completely different lives. Parents and children don't understand each other—there's nothing to say, between them. Some sort of natural insurance against repetition . . . Not us. We live as they lived.—

—Oh, bourgeois freedoms. It's not possible for us. We want something else. Christ, I don't have to fight poor old Dick and Ivy for it—it doesn't matter if they bug me in plenty of ways, my mother particularly. They want it too.—

—But were you given a choice? Just think.—

—Yes . . . I suppose if you want to look at it like that . . . But no! Rosa! What choice? Rosa? In this country, under this system, looking at the way blacks live—what has the choice to do with parents? What else could you choose?— She was excited now, had the gleam of someone who feels she is gaining influence, drew back the unfallen tears through her nose in ugly snorts. It's axiomatic the faults you see in others are often your own; the critical are the self-despising. But this's something different. Not a mote in the eye. That girl whom I pitied, at whom my curiosity was directed, so different from me in the 'unimportant' aspects—I watched her as if she were myself. I wanted something from the victim in her and perhaps I got it.

As for her, she mistook the heat of my determination for warmth between us—but that I feel only for her mother and father. She felt she had established fresh contact, other than the outgrown childhood one. Attracted by the possibility of friendship with me—she is graceless rather than shy, used to dodging the cuffs of rebuff—she forgot I had failed her—us—our way of life. As a clenched fist opens on its treasures, bits of stone in the eyes of a stranger, she told me about the man she was in love with, hesitating over his name and withholding it. Then I couldn't stop her telling me that the girl and baby, her friend with a child, for whom she wanted a flat, was married to him although they weren't living together. The girl was 'a terrific person', they 'really get on'. She is the daughter of a professor, an associate of my father who fled long ago and teaches in a black country. The professor's hostage to the future: Clare Terblanche will recruit her, if the remark that they 'really get on' doesn't already mean she is coming up from the Cape because the strategy of the present phase requires this. The lover, the husband—he's one of us, too. Jealousy and anguish between the three of them (perhaps the professor's daughter is really coming to try to get back her man?) is something they will know they must not allow to interfere with what they have to do. Clare Terblanche will rub exasperatedly at the naked patches, like peeling paintwork, on her poor face and snap at her mother, Ivy, who (it comes out between girl-friends in confession) is working with the lover on his Wages Commission. But Clare Terblanche's pride and guilt at sleeping with the other's man, the temptation of being preferred, the pain of being rejected—who knows how it will resolve itself (it's the sort of thing we like to leave to women's magazines)—these will not interfere with the work to be done. It is only people who wallow in the present who submit. My mother didn't, as Lily Letsile demanded, 'fill up that hole' where my brother drowned. The swimming-pool remained to give pleasure to other people, black children who had never been into a pool before could be taught to swim there by my father.

Clare Terblanche decided the flat wouldn't do. Perhaps now that she has told me the special circumstances of her relationship with the prospective tenant she does not want her to live in the building where I might bump into the two of them together, and she would know that I was seeing them in the light of the confidence she had forced on me and already regretted.

Just as we were leaving the place she became absent or even agitated for a moment—I thought she'd forgotten something, left a cigarette not stubbed. Kneeling swiftly she tore sheets out of the telephone directory and then strode over to the cupboard. Picking up the sanitary towel between paper, she lifted it out without touching it with her hands and bundled up a crude parcel. Then she did not know where to put it; no bin in an empty flat. Outside on the fire escape some tenant had abandoned cartons. She lifted the top two and buried her burden, ramming the cartons back, and then stalked ahead of me as if she had successfully disposed of a body.

Only the dove could find you, that's the idea. No claims from the world reach the ark. While you are fleeing, brave young people welcomed by the local newspaper in each foreign port, you scrub the decks in absolution and eat the bread of an innocence you can't assume. Lionel would have explained why. If I do, you will say it's because I'm his daughter, mouthing that spinning-wheels and the bran-and-whole-wheat you used to bake in the cottage cannot restore some imaginary paradise of pre-capitalist production. People won't let Lionel die; or his assumption—of knowledge, responsibility shouldered staggeringly to the point of arrogance—won't die with him and let them alone. But the faithful don't commemorate the date of his death, they don't have to; sentiment is for those who don't know what to do next. Flora sends me Spanish irises on William's account at a florist. The man who's writing the biography phones to ask whether I would prefer to change our today's appointment for another day?

There were two letters behind the locked tin flap bearing my number in the block of mailboxes grey as prison cells in the foyer. The one was from Sweden. I read a whole paragraph before I understood from whom; it was hand-written and any others I had received from him had always been typed. Strange not to know the handwriting of someone with whom you have made love, no matter why or how long ago. He had hoped to be able to tell me that the film about Lionel was at last to be distributed in England, but negotiations had fallen through. He would have to wait until 'something happened in South Africa to rouse interest again'. It was easier to sell material dealing with Moçambique and Angola, at present. He had heard with much pleasure about the wing in the Patrice Lumumba University in Moscow being named after my

127

father. He had written a short piece on this and hoped it would be published soon. Because his film has not realized his hopes that it would make a name for him, that time when Lionel was alive in prison does not seem to him, as it is for Lionel and me, long ago. It is linked to what is as yet unachieved, the Swede's success.

The other letter was not really a letter but a card, closely-written across the inner side of the leaves. I didn't know one could buy cards for the anniversary of deaths—deckle-edged, gilded, posied, that's certainly the sort of thing you're safe from, cut adrift: the ordering of appropriate responses for all occasions, what you used to call 'consumer love', Conrad. I read the signature first; someone had signed for both: 'Uncle Coen and Auntie Velma' but the correspondent was clearly Auntie Velma alone. She was firmly confident as ever in her concept of feelings towards me, the last of her brother's family. I am always welcome at the farm if I want a quiet rest. She does not ask from what activity, she does not want to know in case it is, as her brother's always was, something she fears and disapproves to the point of inconceivability. It's better that way. She offers neither expectations nor reproach. 'The farm is always there.' She believes that: for ever. The future—it's the same as now. It will be occupied by her children, that's all. Maybe there'll be some improvements; change is automation in the milking sheds, and television, promised soon. My cousin, fellow namesake of Ouma Marie Burger, is seeing the world at present. She has a job with the citrus export board and has been sent to the Paris office—isn't that nice? She had to learn French and picked it up very quickly—she has the 'Burger brains, of course'. What Auntie Velma has in mind there is quite simply my father. The Nels have never had any difficulty in reconciling pride in belonging to a remarkable family with the certainty that the member who made it so followed wicked and horrifying ideals. Even Uncle Coen is pleased to be known as Lionel Burger's brother-in-law. Whatever my father was to them, it still stalks their consciousness.

Another thing in the Swede's letter: he wanted a beaded belt like the one he had bought here, did I remember the shop? The shop is a good-works affair, marketing the objects tribal blacks make for their own use and adornment, rather than tourist handicrafts. Like most non-profit enterprises, it is not efficiently run and I didn't have much hope that whoever was in charge would be able to remember let alone be willing to bother to obtain a belt of a particular workmanship—the letter was precise, said Baca, but I didn't think it could be that, more likely from Transkei or Zululand. Sheila Itholeng was there as usual on a Saturday morning to clean the flat and do my washing: the room comes to life. She cooks mealie-meal and I fry eggs and bacon and we have breakfast together like a family. Neither of us has a husband but she has a child. I have bought little Mpho crayons and plasticine but around our legs under the table she was playing at polishing the floor with a bit of rag, her small bottom higher than her head, her pinkish heels turned out just the way her mother's do.

Although Barry Eckhard doesn't make his employees work on Saturdays, I went to town. In the traffic I suddenly began to try to consider this day as something specific as that belt beaded by hand I was going to look for, the duplication of a day in which, this time a year ago, Lionel was still alive, although by midday it was to be the day when he died. He and my mother once went to Lenin's tomb, I'm told. They filed past, muffled up out of all recognition against a cold that doesn't exist here, as an endless queue is still doing. Every November will file past my father's death, the same day over and over again, with summer storm skies and street jacarandas merging hectically in electric purple; seasons can only repeat themselves, they have no future. On the park bench there was also a lying-in-state.

A cordon of police flanked the entire façade of the building where the African crafts shop is. Alsatian dogs strapped to their handlers kept passers-by back but they waited stolidly, blacks holding delivery bicycles, Saturday-shopping families with children, couples with lovers' arms dangling from shoulders or round the waist of one another's jeans, wanting their spectacle, whether it were to be a black pop group that transforms the rhythms of the street, a suicide teetering on a parapet, a bomb hoax. I knew at once what it would be: men and women, ordinary-looking

—amazing!—like themselves, led out under arrest and followed by more policemen, jaws steadying loads of papers and typewriters. The building housed organizations whose premises are often raided. I didn't wait to see which it was this time—the association of black studies or the militant churchmen, all suspected of 'furthering' the aims my father and his associates took so many years to formulate. There was silence from the crowd standing by like tethered horses. A woman with a black woman's bundle on her head and the long-nosed, keen bitter face that often comes with admixture of white blood, drunk or a little crazy, addressed everybody from a round hole of a mouth. —Bloody white bastard. Bloody police bastard.— Two young black men wearing T-shirts with the legends PRINCETON UNIVERSITY and KUNG-FU laughed at her. An older man called deeply, 'Tula, mama' and, a stray not knowing the source of the noise of the tin can tied to it, she grumbled back *Voetsak, voetsak, wena*.

I didn't linger. The police demand identification and search everyone they find in a raided building; why should the Special Branch believe Burger's daughter's presence in the vicinity was to be explained by intention to buy a beaded belt at the request of a former lover? Let others protest their innocence, the water on their hands, like Pilate's. As craziness gave the crone licence to shout at the police, the life sentence gave Lionel licence to say it from the dock: I would be guilty if I were innocent of working to destroy racism in my country. If I'm guilty of that innocence the police will not be the ones with the right to apprehend me.

Some of the big stores have boutiques where they sell African crafts. This follows a demand, the wave of nostalgia for the ethnic in parts of the world where ethnics are put to no sinister purpose. It's currently fashionable merchandise that's on display, rather than anything understood as national culture; *Buy South African* refers to manufactured goods and not to the carved bowls and ostrich-shell necklaces hanging somewhere between small leather-goods and cosmetic counters. The store I tried didn't have beaded belts but I thought the wristbands, athletically, orthopaedically masculine, with bright plastic thongs woven through holes in the tough leather, worn by migratory mineworkers who made them, could be worn effectively by a Scandinavian Africa specialist, and I bought one, god knows why. The huge perfumed street floor of the shop tented the pleasure of people spending money, that peculiar atmosphere of desire and anxious satisfaction evident in the faces, hardly high enough to chin showcases, of children gathered at troughs of cheap array, and women matching colours under the advice of bosom friends, and couples conspiring over price; the spectacle, of objects they can never own as well as those which bait from them the money they have, people yearn for in the countries of the Future my father visited with both his wives. Any one of the coloured artisans and their families or the white student lovers watching arrests a few blocks away was free to enter and see legitimate aspirations that carry no risk of punishment—fully automatic washing machines, electronic watches, cowboy boots, recordings of popular music by heroes who take their groups' names from the vocabulary of revolution. The act of acquisition. You have to acquire a yacht to escape it. A woman beside me as I waited to pay opposed her little boy: But you don't want that? What'll you do with it? It's not a toy! He held tightly a patent fluff-removing brush and would not meet anyone's eyes.

Leaning on her elbow at the cosmetic counter opposite I saw the half-bare back of a black woman dressed in splashing colour which included as overall effect the colour of her skin. The boldest, darkest lines of blue and brown, ancient ideogrammatic symbols of fish, bird and conch were extended in the movement of two rounded shoulder-blades from the matt slope of the neck to their perfect centring on the indented line of spine, rippling as shadowless store lighting ran a scale down it. The cloth suggested robes but was in fact cut tight to the proud backside jutting negligently at the angle of the weight-bearing hip, and close to the long legs. There was a blue turban, and before the head turned, the tilt of a gold hoop bigger than a tiny ear. She could have been a splendid chorus girl but she looked like a queen of some prototype, extinct in Britain or Denmark where the office still exists. She was Marisa Kgosana. We embraced, and the professionally neutral face of the white cosmetic saleswoman, protected by her make-up from any sign of reaction as a soldier on guard is protected by his uniform from blinking an eye before public taunts, awaited the completion of the sale.

To touch in women's token embrace against the live, night cheek of Marisa, seeing huge for a second the lake-flash of her eye, the lilac-pink of her inner lip against translucent-edged teeth, to enter for a moment the invisible magnetic field of the body of a beautiful creature and receive on oneself its imprint—breath misting and quickly fading on a glass pane—this was to immerse in another mode of perception. As near as a woman can get to the transformation of the world a man seeks in the beauty of a woman. Marisa is black; near, then, as well, to the white way of using blackness as a way of perceiving a sensual redemption, as romantics do, or of perceiving fears, as racialists do. In my father's house, the one was seen as the obverse of the other, two sides of false consciousness—that much I can add to anyone's notes. But even in that house blackness was a sensuous-redemptive means of perception. Through blackness is revealed the way to the future. The descendants of Chaka, Dingane, Hintsa, Sandile, Moshesh, Cetewayo, Msilekazi and Sekukuni are the only ones who can get us there; the spirit of Makana is on Robben Island as intercessor to Lenin. Sipho Mokoena who made kites for Tony and showed children the rip in his trouser-leg made by a bullet, Gana Makabeni who was best man at the wedding and Isaac Vulindlela who gave his only son, Baasie, to the care of my father and mother; Uncle Coen Nel's barman, Daniel; the watchman who brought bets for you to place—the creased, pale-soled black feet naked at the swimming-pool as well as the black faces in the majority at the last of the underground congresses my father could attend: in the merger of white Cain, black Abel, a new brotherhood of flesh is the way to the final brotherhood. The middle-aged cosmetic saleswoman and the few customers not too self-absorbed to glance up saw a kaffir-boetie girl being kissed by a black. That's all. They knew no better. That house was closer to reaching its kind of reality through your kind of reality than I understood. You and I argued in the cottage. *Sex and death*, you said. The only reality. I should have been able to explain the element of sensuality that would have qualified the experiences of that house to be considered real by you. I felt it in Marisa's presence, after so long; the comfort of Baasie in the same bed when the dark made that house creak with threats.

Marisa was buying face-cream, testing brands on the back of a hand laid for the saleswoman's attention between them on the counter. The hand wore its insignia of rings and long brilliant nails as a general wears gold braid and campaign ribbons. Didn't I think this smelled too much like a sweet cake? —Over-ripe fruit, to me.—

—Violets, madam— The saleswoman was earnest.

No, no, it wouldn't do; but Marisa wouldn't take the other brand being rubbed onto her plum-dark skin with a rapid to-and-fro of one white finger. —D'you know what they charge for that, Rosa? I'd rather get wrinkles.— The saleswoman had another, a tube, French but not expensive, one need use so little, herb-scented. Marisa had the air of someone who is never undecided. —Okay. That'll do. The nail stuff, the cream, nothing else. But Rosa, if you're working in that building, I'm just around the corner! An attorney's. Someone Theo found—she laughed, sharing our admittance of the use everyone made of Theo, our dependency on him at the trials of her husband, Joseph Kgosana, or my father, as women share faith in a good doctor. —I'd only started, not even a week—then I got permission for a visit. I'm just back from the Island.—

How splendidly she made the trip. In one sentence she and I were alone; even if the elderly blonde, who had put on glasses dangling from a gilt chain to write the sales slip, understood which island, neither she nor the other customers trailing the aisles in perfume and light stood in intelligence of the level of the gaze at which Marisa held me. Hardly a change of tone needed between us. For Marisa it seems easy. She doesn't have to find a solemn face, acknowledge the distance between the prison and the cosmetic counter. She doesn't close away, go to cover, dead still, as I do. She doesn't have to recourse to putting things delicately or explaining herself for fear of being misunderstood or misjudged. Defiance and confidence don't mourn; her beauty and the way she assumes it are stronger than any declaration.

How was he? How are they all? When we talk about them, the prisoners who have survived Lionel, the tone is purposely common-place, an assertion that they can't be shut away, they remain part of ordinary daily life no matter how thick the walls or rough the seas between banishment and home. —He's fine. I was the one under the weather. It's true—really the weather! There was a gale blowing in Cape Town! You can't imagine what it was like. The first day the boat couldn't go at all. The next day the police in my escort weren't too keen either but I said, look, I insist, here's my permit, I'm only allowed out of my magisterial area three days . . . so we got into the boat. I felt terrible—my god, have you ever been seasick? But I held out. And I could see they were much worse than me. First thing Joe said, Marisa! Look at you—there's been something wrong and you didn't say in letters . . . He got his warder to bring me strong coffee—yes, just like that: my wife must have a hot drink—you know? And that one brought it like a lamb.—

—It was a contact visit?— I fall back easily into the jargon of prison visiting. It will always come to me, the language I learnt as a child. At the caprice of the chief warder I would see my father in a small bare room (the furnishings the basic unit for interrogation, two upright chairs and a table, with which the purpose of such rooms was always present) or on the other side of the wire grille through which I could not touch my fiancé's hand.

—He asked about you, he sends his love.— The symmetry of her lovely face smiling made the lie a gift. I hadn't seen her and had sent no word to him through her for so long it was unlikely my name would have come up between them. Experienced people don't waste the precious time of visits; everything to be said by both is thought out and fitted into the allotted period in advance. But there was I, asking about all the others by name, Mandela, Sisulu, Kathrada, Mbeki, the black men with whom my father worked in an intimacy whose nature no one outside it, standing in the street watching arrests of people who haven't snatched pay-rolls or pushed drugs, can understand. Marisa repeated the prisoners' jokes, related what they were studying, whether they'd lost weight or 'put on' as she phrased it, digressed into gossip about the achievements or problems of their families—while checking her purchases, hesitating whether she shouldn't add this or that item, and counting out money from the maw of a big fashionable bag with long fingers grappling at the points of the bright nails, like the legs of some exotic insect feeling out prey. —No, I don't want a parcel—let me have a plastic carrier—one of those over there will do—yes, that's right— As the woman behind the counter turned away to get change: —When you're in a hurry it's best to pay cash . . . If a black produces a cheque book . . . I only use mine when I'm prepared to hang about while they excuse themselves and take it to a-l-l their managers.— And in the same brisk, absent undertone, she made a suggestion, her eyes restless on the sales-woman, her head drawn back to her neck with impatient grace. —My child's gone to get some school-books, I must pick her up. And someone's waiting for me—what's the time, anyway—I said we'd meet at twelve—too bad, can't be helped . . . What are you doing today—this afternoon or this evening?— Marisa did not remember what day this was although she had a few moments before talked of Lionel (as Lionel used to say to Joe, if you can keep your weight and blood-pressure low, man, nothing can get you down). —Come out? You remember my cousin's place, Fats?—

—You turn past Orlando High.—

—Yes, carry straight on, then when you come to the dip, third road on the right—

—There's a shop that sells coal, on the corner . . . ?—

—That's right, Vusili's store—

Between us, while the murmured exchange went back and forth like any other insincere enthusiasm between friends who bump into one another, was the unspoken question-and-answer that our kind follow by gaps in what is said and hesitations or immediacy of response. Marisa is banned and under house arrest. I am Named. The law forbids us to meet or speak, let alone embrace; we take what chances come, of meetings like this, in passing, on neutral and anonymous ground. You taunted me with being inhibited; but you never had anything you valued enough, that was threatened enough for you to hide. Secrecy is a discipline it's hard for old hands to unlearn. People under house arrest cannot receive friends at home or go out at night or weekends; if Marisa could come to town on a Saturday she must have been using a 'spare' day of the exemption granted her for the visit to the Island. She was taking a chance—another—on getting away with going out to someone's house at night. She was unsure whether or not I was banned from gatherings in addition to being named. In fact I was under no ban although I have been refused a passport since before I was named— the very first year I applied. And that application was a secret, too; this time my own, not assumed in common with the others of that house, unspoken between my father and mother and me. She and Lionel did not ever know I tried for a passport when I was eighteen in preparation to follow Noel de Witt to Europe when he came out of jail. He had never known, either; but—de Witt's fiancée and Lionel Burger's daughter—the Minister refused me. In any case, whites are not allowed to go into black townships without a permit, and the presence of the only living member of the Burger family would not be let pass if discovered; if Marisa ignored that she was running a risk, so, if I followed the directions we were exchanging harmlessly, at risk, should I be ignoring my own.

She squeezed my hand and moved away at the same time, our hands remaining linked until they dropped apart, as blacks will do parting on street corners, calling over their shoulders as they finally go separate ways. But she forgot me instantly. In the swaying, forward movement of her crested head as she disappeared and reappeared through the shoppers there was only consciousness of the admiration she exacted, with her extravagant dress, the Ruritanian pan-Africa of triumphant splendour and royal beauty that is subject to no known boundaries of old custom or new warring political ideologies in black countries, and to no laws that make blacks' lives mean and degrading in this one. If the white people in the shop saw only errand boys and tea-girls and street sweepers instead of black people, now they saw Marisa. The saleswoman spoke to me with the smile of one white woman to another, both admiring a foreign visitor. —Where's she from? One of those French islands?—

Seychelles or Mauritius; it was what she understood by the Island. I told her: —From Soweto.—

—Fancy!— she was ready to learn something, her new-moon eyebrows above the golden frame of her glasses.

You were particularly curious about Baasie. You taxed me with him: —That's how you are: here's something that will be important for you for the rest of your life, whether you know it or not. You say you don't 'think' about that kid. Whether you 'think' about it or don't . . . When you were five years old you were afraid of the dark together. You crept into one bed.—

I didn't answer, I kept my head turned from you because I was thinking that that was what I did with you, that was what I was. I was remembering a special, spreading warmth when Baasie had wet the bed in our sleep. In the morning the sheets were cold and smelly, I told tales to my mother —Look what Baasie's done in his bed!— but in the night I didn't know whether this warmth that took us back into the enveloping fluids of a host body came from him or me. You wanted to know what had happened to him. Again and again, in the cottage, you would try to trap me into answering indirectly, unwittingly, although I had told you I didn't know. I didn't tell you what I did know. His father, Isaac Vulindlela, was working with Lionel until the day Lionel was arrested for the last time. He was one of those who left the country and returned under false papers. He managed it successfully twice, helped by his Tswana wife's family on the border of Botswana, who (like Auntie Velma and Uncle Coen?) didn't want to know what he was doing. The third time, when my father was already in prison, I was the one who delivered the new passbook to the drop ten or twenty miles from the border. It was one of the weekends when I disappeared—to show a Scandinavian journalist the scenes of Lionel's boyhood; or to sleep with my Swedish lover entered in a motel register as his wife. The third purpose of the trip was not known to the Swede; I suppose it would give him still greater cachet if he were to learn about it, even now. A better present than a beaded belt or a black migrant mineworker's wristband. My Swede and I were travelling not in my car but the visitor's hired one, as the normal precaution of anonymity he is no doubt used to in his love affairs in the course of assignments that take him from country to country; I told him the spare tyre was soft and I had better see to it as he couldn't speak Afrikaans and at a dorp garage English wouldn't be much use. He stayed in bed, in a room hardly different from those where I followed Selena and Elsie as they cleaned up after the commercial travellers, stroking through the cross of blond hair on his chest and writing an article for *Dagens Nyheter* about the complicity of international industrialists with the apartheid economy.

At the garage on a Sunday morning there was only one attendant; a plump young black whose overalls had no buttons and were clasped together where absolutely necessary by a big safety-pin at the fly. Striped socks and a peaked cap advertising one of the companies my Swede was arraigning from the twin bed under a print of the Arc de Triomphe in spring: the young black man was mending a punctured tube, sitting on oil-stained tarmac with his legs spreadeagled round a tin bath of water. The sleek seal of black rubber bobbed at his hands. For whoever might be passing, I came over, any white missus. —Are you Abraham?— It was the year of the *Smile* button; he wore a big one he had perhaps picked up forgotten by some car full of children piling out to get cokes from the automatic vendor. But he didn't smile. —Yes, I'm Abraham.— We spoke in Afrikaans and in the usual tones, mine kindly but authoritative, his hesitant and unsure whether he was to expect demand, rebuke or a request he would be reluctant to stir for. —Your mother does my washing. She's sent you a letter.—

—Hey? Wat het die missus gesê?— He had heard all right but he wanted to make sure the words were exactly what he had been told to expect. I repeated them and he lip-read as if my voice might deceive but my mouth could be trusted. He wiped a wet hand down the overalls and with that movement my own right hand took the thick envelope out of the straw bag I carried to hold the paraphernalia of a car trip. The envelope passed to him and under the folds of the too-large and filthy overalls, the garb of an anonymously imposed and carelessly assumed identity beneath which, like his hidden body, he kept another, his own. He got up and tramped ahead of me to unhook the hose of the bowser and fill up the car. I gave the usual ten cents in addition to the cost of the petrol and he gave the usual flourish of a dirty rag over the windscreen.

That's how it's done. The cloak-and-dagger stuff. You always wanted to know about such things. But how was I to know, am I to know that you were not there for me to come to out of a calculation of my need? If Lionel Burger didn't recruit you, it could have been that the other side did. You could have been allotted to me and me to you by the men of the Special Branch who have watched me grow up, as the saying goes for any of those adults whom the Nels had us children give the title of honorary 'Oom'.

Whatever else I stood stripped of, teeth chattering in dreadful triumph, in the nights of the cottage, I kept what is second nature become first. I could not shed the instinct for survival that kept my mouth shut to you on such subjects. Unlike the unknown Abraham, you didn't have the background to lip-read me. And in the dorp that Sunday I went back to the hotel and carried a beer, glass down over the bottle smoking cold at the neck, to my Swede. I didn't tell him, either. He cajoled me back to bed and typewritten pages floated away to the floor all round us. The hotel's Selena or Elsie knocked on the door and went away again; hotel servants understand never to ask questions. That's how it's done. He made love to me with the dragon Hoover breathing in the corridor outside and he does not know that the essence on his tongue in the bitter wax of my ear chamber, the brines of mouth or vagina were not my secret. For me to be free is never to be free of the survival cunning of concealment. I did not tell you what I know, however much I wanted to. Isaac Vulindlela was caught with one of those passbooks. That's how it's done. My father's biographer, respectfully coaxing me onto the stepping-stones of the official vocabulary—

words, nothing but dead words, abstractions: that's not where reality is, you flung at me—national democratic revolution, ideological integration, revolutionary imperative, minority domination, liberation alliance, unity of the people, infiltration, incursion, viable agency for change, reformist option, armed tactics, mass political mobilization of the people in a combination of legal, semi-legal and clandestine methods—those footholds have come back to my vocabulary lately through parrying him. I don't know where Baasie is but his father was found dead in a cell after eight months in detention. The police said he hanged himself with his trousers. I managed to convey the news to my father, in prison. Don't ask me how. He didn't know, I couldn't tell him the passbook was one of those I had been able to hand over so easily no one would believe that is how it is done. I find it very hard to tell the difference between the truth and the facts: to know what the facts are? If Abraham at the garage had been a trap the circumstances of my failed mission would have read as ridiculously as any I exposed before poor Clare Terblanche. What was the reality of that weekend in the Western Transvaal dorp? An act in the third category of methods (legal, semi-legal and clandestine) to co-ordinate political struggle and armed activity in creating an all-round climate of collapse in which a direct political solution becomes possible? The material transcendence of a man's span by the recording, for posterity, on film, of landscapes and types of environment that formed his consciousness? The ecstatic energy consumed in the hotel bed between eleven o'clock in the morning when the Dutch Reformed church bells were tolling and midday when the xylophone notes of the lunch gong were sounded, an hour without any consequences whatever except a stain on the bottom sheet—stiff commemorative plaque that a Selena or Elsie would remark, without having her life altered in any manner, before it disappeared in the wash?

Perhaps the way the people in the department store saw me is right. Although it was an article of faith in that house that it is necessary to go beyond the oversimplified race equation—the reformist view of the struggle as between colours, not classes—my mother and father succeeded only in making me a kaffir-boetie.

Baasie's little sibling. Marisa came over me as a sudden good mood. A tenderness softened and livened all round me as I drove home from the city: the Indian vendors with their roses wired like candelabras, and dyed arum lilies; when a red light held me up, the business-like black kid darting, spitting his shrill whistle between the lanes of cars to sell the early edition of the afternoon paper; the huge woman with a full shopping-bag on her head, a tripping child towed at her skirt and that African *obi* made up of the inevitable baby-on-back and swathed blanket thick round her middle, who launched herself, paused—smiled back at me—and scuttled across my path when she should have been waiting at the crossing. The comfort of black. The persistence, resurgence, daily continuity that is the mass of them. If one is not afraid, how can one not be attracted? It is one thing or the other. Marisa and Joe Kgosana have all this to draw on. Lionel and Ivy and Dick, my mother and Aletta; behind *our* kind, who are confined to the magisterial areas of the white suburbs, are people who sent obscene letters calling my father a monster.

I suppose I intended to go into the township to stay in Marisa's orbit a while longer, as people take a second drink to prolong the pleasant effect of the first before it wears off. I don't know; I hadn't decided. The man who is going to write about Lionel was with me in the flat early that afternoon when someone else arrived. Even surprise is something I can't help concealing. I didn't introduce him to the biographer. Orde Greer is a press photographer who knew me by sight, as you did, and whom I knew as I knew you before we had coffee in Pretoria that day, all during the time of Lionel's trial, one of a cast of faces in which I read who I was. In the past few years I've once or twice seen him at a party, fondling an unwilling girl in the indiscriminate way of a man who will not remember next day. He was at the memorial service for Lionel. His name's familiar, as a by-line in the paper; his person was identified for me by a polio limp as mine was for him by my relationship to my father. He greets me in the street and I nod back.

A man wearing veldskoen ankle-boots, rolled-down red socks, shorts and in spite of the summer heat a dusty black, fisherman's sweater—if I hadn't recognized him at once as the one who was handicapped he might have been some athlete jogging round the neighbourhood in training.

—I believe I'm supposed to pick you up. For Fats' place—

And because the biographer was there behind me, I answered as if such an arrangement had been made. —I'll only be another few minutes. Come in.— Marisa's name was not mentioned before a third person; already this established an area where Orde Greer and I knew one another better than by sight. My father's biographer was looking round at him with the frustration, concealed under an

142

affectation of good manners, of one who finds he cannot place someone whose significance he is sure he ought to know. He shuffled notes together and made as if to leave; I apologized firmly for terminating the session, but he was the one who was all apologies. He left; I didn't mention to Orde Greer who *he* was or what he was doing, either.

I didn't know whether Greer was one of us or not; perhaps he was. His *bona fides* was that Marisa had sent him. I offered him a drink if he would give me time to tidy up a bit before we went.

—That's okay. I'm early . . . what's going?—

Sitting in my chair (the old green leather one, the colour of holly leaves, that was in my father's study and that we children used to like to slide on because the friction of bare thighs produced static electricity) he had the air of taking a place he had a right to, would assume with a slightly nervous aggression before challenge. His outfit now suggested ease in the company for which he was bound.

But newspapermen have to be like that—they are used to assuming entry, I know. Afraid of me, and yet familiar at the same time; I had plenty of experience of it during the trial. There was only beer; he paused in mark of regret for the bottle of whisky he had hoped to settle down with: —Beer it is.— Thick hair that tangled with a beard and gave him a consciously noble head, from the front, left him vulnerable when he bent to retrieve the metal loop fallen from the can, showing the hair already rubbed away into the scalp like a baby's tonsured by the pillow on which it lies helpless.

I suppose my experience of journalists makes me stiff in their presence, even so long after Lionel's trial. I become what they caught me as in all the newspaper photographs, the dumpy girl with the paisley scarf doffed, untidy hair springing about, defiant tendons on display in her neck, head turned full-on to the camera because she doesn't have to hide her face like the relatives of a swindler, but eyes acknowledging nothing, because she doesn't need sympathy or pity like the relatives of a murderer. And who are they to have decided—the law did not allow them to photograph *him*—in their descriptions of him in the dock, in the way he listened to evidence against him, in the expression with which he met the public gallery or greeted friends there, that they knew what he was, when I don't know that I do.

This one looked at me from my armchair with the beer-mug sceptred in his hand, marking that I had changed into a pair of well-fitting trousers, not as a man assumes for himself the position of one for whom a girl has made herself sexually more attractive (he wouldn't have dared that), but as a successful intruder notes intimate behaviour that cannot be concealed from him, and from which he will build conclusions that will establish him as an insider. He looked me over—almost. Half-smiling, entirely for himself.

He was one of those people who find it easiest to talk when they are driving and are addressing others only with a voice, body and attention directed elsewhere. In a casual tone by which I understood he had planned to bring up the subject, he wanted to know if I had read a book recently published in England by a former political prisoner in exile.

One of us—I hadn't read it yet.

He offered to lend me his copy. But I thanked him—I didn't need it. I knew that Flora, who so enjoys making 'ordinary' people run mild risks without being aware of it, had arranged for a business associate of William to smuggle copies from London.

—There's quite a lot about you of course. Your father and the family.—

—They were in prison together the last year of my father's life.—

—Oh plenty about that—conversations with your father. How your father ran his own little clinic, more or less, even the warders coming with their aches and pains. They had to decide whether he could be allowed to write prescriptions, and then when he was given pads the politicals used the paper to circulate their own news-sheet . . . it's interesting. But also about the days when . . . the days in the house. The Sundays. That famous house.—

He was taking a route unfamiliar to me.

—I wonder what you'll think of it. How it'll strike you.—

He wanted me to ask why; I understood there must be things in the book I could confirm or deny, things he thought would displease me. If he's one of us it meant partisan sympathy but if he's simply one of them, a liberal journalist observing the 'reactions' of Burger's daughter, enjoying being in the know, it was nothing but the revival of an old newspaper sensation. —Are you sure where you're going?—

He took it as a deliberate change of subject, snubbed himself with a little snigger. —Why shouldn't I be?—

—Just that I've never gone to Orlando this way. You know where Marisa's cousin lives, though?—

—I know.— The shortness rebuked me; he was no tourist in blacks' areas, no Swede in need of a cicerone. He rolled hairs of his beard together between fingers and thumb while we waited to make a right turn across a line of traffic. —I never saw the inside of that house.—

An odd thing to say. To me. And in the manner of someone who is addressing himself in the certainty of being overheard. Did he hang around like you, Conrad? What did he want of us? What absolution did you think you'd find in what my father did!

The journalist and I lost touch once we were at Marisa's cousin's 'place'. Marisa was not there yet; she would 'drop in some time'— Fats was impartially welcoming as the host of a television show. There was the litter of beer, whisky and glasses; three or four black men dressed in tartan seersucker jackets and picture ties, spread thigh-to-thigh on chairs, with among them a runt or two, jeans poked at the knees, laceless running shoes, and the big, sad heads of jockeys or go-betweens for money and sport. There was an insolently handsome boy shaped in his sky-blue denim as Victorian girls were defined by tight-lacing. A middle-aged man with the black school-headmaster's dark suit and neat tie-pin dozed between appearances of being a part of the animation. Men were talking and arguing; Orde Greer stood with a whisky at once in hand, interrupting (Listen—man, listen), cocking his head to take something in, the slight shuffle of lameness making a mendicant of him.

A child bore over to me a cup of milky tea chattering against its saucer. —And how have you been keeping? That's nice!— Fats' wife pushed another child off a dining-table chair with a reproach in her own language, not interrupting the smiling conventions. —I thought maybe you've gone away or something . . . since your father passed on . . . shame— She settled us side by side. —Try a biscuit, Miss Burger, my sister-in-law makes them, she's a really wonderful baker, even wedding cakes, you know. I wish I could be clever like that.— She can never bring herself to call me Rosa. I am part of the entourage of her famous and brave relative, Marisa Kgosana; of the distinction conveyed upon her family by their kinship with Joe Kgosana, on the Island with Nelson Mandela. She caught the hand of a girl who had been stalking in and out of the adjoining bedroom, adjusting the set of the blouse knotted under her breasts and pressing the imprint of one mulberry-painted lip upon the other: —D'you know who this is? This is Lionel Burger's daughter— But the girl did not react to the identity. She gave her hand for a second to a white girl. She said nothing. —Miss Burger, meet my niece Tandi, haven't you perhaps seen that Fanta advert on the big board where you turn off for Soweto?—she's in that—

The girl had already turned away, superior to praise from an aunt who was impressed by whites. She joined a friend, the two braced against the wall from the base of shoes with platforms twice the thickness of the feet they supported, their heads geometrically patterned rather than coiffured with the hair parted in small squares, each drawn tightly to its centre in a tobacco-twist strand pulled to connect it to the next. A baby boy with a bare bottom skeetered into the room from the direction of the smell of food cooking and was pursued by a heavy old woman who held him laughing and kicking while, smiling on an empty mouth, she talked to the two girls. Fats' Margaret was still telling me about her niece, in the English vocabulary of black newspapers—A well-known model and top actress—she faltered in embarrassment over the naked baby, seeing him with eyes other than her own, and scooped him up, also laughing, her pretty, sexually-contented face under her wig and her clumsy voluptuous body, beside the old woman for a moment, a conjuration of what the old woman once was, and the old woman so clearly what the young would be. *Do you know who this is* . . . The grandmother dealt with me in the style of her own time. Her English was the kind white people mimic. She was holding my wrist: —The Lord will reward your fath-a. Yes, he has his reward with Gord. Yes, listen to me, I'm promising. The African people we thanks the Lord for what your fath-a was doing for us, we know he was our fath-a.— Margaret was not embarrassed on her account. Her head tracked, smiling agreement, from the old woman to me. I might have been moved. The afternoon of the anniversary of Lionel's death: but I was aware of those two girls, the one chewing gum with the concentration of an incantation, the other (who had been introduced) a head set like a seal's in a single line with the neck, entirely self-regarding. No, I felt instead only an affinity with them, with their distance, although they were distanced from me, too.

Fats' place, Marisa said. I said. Orde Greer said. Blacks don't talk about 'my house' or 'home' and whites have adopted the term from them. A 'place'; somewhere to belong, but also something that establishes one's lot and sets aside much to which one doesn't belong. So long since I had been with blacks in their own homes that I saw it, Soweto, Orlando, this township house—a year after Lionel was dead—as something apart, apart from my daily life; something from the past. When I was a child I went in and out the black townships with my mother so often and naturally that I embarrassed Auntie Velma and Uncle Coen, chattering of this when Tony and I lived with them. How many months since I had crossed the divide that opens every time a black leaves a white and goes to his 'place'; the physical divide of clean streets become rutted roads and city centres become veld dumped with twisted metal and a perpetual autumn of blowing paper—the vast vacant lot where Orde Greer turned off from the main road that leads from white city to white city; and the other divide, hundreds of years of possession and decision, which lay even between that house where Orde Greer was never invited, that house where the revolution was planned, and the 'place' of those millions who have been dispossessed and for whom others have made all the decisions. From the

147

car I saw it again as I had once ceased to see the too familiar. These restless broken streets where definitions fail—the houses the outhouses of white suburbs, two-windows-one-door, multiplied in institutional rows; the hovels with tin lean-tos sheltering huge old American cars blowzy with gadgets; the fancy suburban burglar bars on mean windows of tiny cabins; the roaming children, wolverine dogs, hobbled donkeys, fat naked babies, vagabond chickens and drunks weaving, old men staring, authoritative women shouting, boys in rags, tarts in finery, the smell of offal cooking, the neat patches of mealies between shebeen yards stinking of beer and urine, the litter of twice-discarded possessions, first thrown out by the white man and then picked over by the black—is this conglomerate urban or rural? No electricity in the houses, a telephone an almost impossible luxury: is this a suburb or a strange kind of junk yard? The enormous backyard of the whole white city, where categories and functions lose their ordination and logic, the ox and the diesel engine, the pig rootling for human ordure and the slaughterer, are milled about together. Are the tarts really tarts, or just factory workers or servants from town performing the miracle of emerging dolled-up and scented, a parody of any white madam, from these shelters where there is no bathroom? Are the ragged boys their brothers? Their children, conceived with lovers in a corner of a room where brothers and sisters sleep? Which are the gangsters, which the glue-sniffers among the young men on street-corners? Who are the elderly men in pressed trousers and ties who sit drinking beer and arguing on a row of formica chairs on the strip of dirt between a house and the street?

I used to know, or think I knew. Baasie looked like one of these children because they were black, like him. He came from streets like these and he has disappeared into them. He is a man, somewhere like this.

The little house into which we were crowded, family, relatives, friends and furniture—familiarity placed it for me without thinking, the bigger type of standard two-roomed township house, three rooms and a kitchen, for which people have to be able to afford (Fats I remembered was a boxing promoter) a bribe to an official.

The diningroom 'suite', the plastic pouffes, hi-fi equipment, flowered carpet, bar counter, and stools covered in teddybear fur were the units of taste established by any furniture superama in the white city. The crowding of one tiny habitation with a job-lot whose desirability is based on a consumer-class idea of luxury without the possibility of middle-class space and privacy; the lavish whisky on the table and the pot-holed, unmade street outside the window; the sense all around of the drab imposed orderliness of a military camp that is not challenged by the home-improvement peach trees and licks of pastel paint but only by the swarming persistence of children and drunks dirtying it, tsotsis, urchins and gangsters terrorizing it—this commonplace of any black township became to me what it is: a 'place'; a position whose contradictions those who impose them don't see, and from which will come a resolution they haven't provided for. The propositions of the faithful that seem so vital to biographical research—I understood them in a way theory doesn't explain, in a way I was deaf to earlier in the afternoon when I was being questioned by my father's biographer. The debate that divided my parents and their associates in a passion whose reality you regard as abstraction far removed from reality; it was based on the fact that they did see. They had always seen. And they believe—Dick and Ivy—they know the resolution and how it will be. Clare still believes; if Lionel lived, if he were to have come out of prison to answer—

But I can't bring Lionel into being for myself, I can't hear responses I ought, on the evidence of biographical data, to be able to predict. After a year, there are new components, now that I have taken apart the whole. I'll never be able to ask my mother, reading her book in the car and hearing my footsteps on the prison gravel, my father opening his arms to Baasie and me in the water, the things I defy them to answer me.

Around me was talk about the selection of black athletes to go abroad with white teams. The argument among the men jumped like a fire-cracker. It landed at my feet; Fats, losing his domination of raised voices, demanded response—My boy has a chance to meet the big boys in West Germany and America—why must I say no?—

But he didn't want to know, he wanted only to show his confidence in worldliness, which quality in him gained the envious support of the schoolmaster, the hangers-on and one or two others, and was despised by his attackers. A handsome man, on the fine line between muscular over-development and fat, on the point of being flirtatious with women and patronizing with men; in shirt-sleeves he had the pectorals softening into breasts that mark an ex-boxer. He rested a promoter's arm round my shoulders a moment, haranguing.

—Boxing's not a team sport, man. It's not a question of selecting for show a black who hasn't had the chance to train like the blokes from white clubs. This business of blacks not having proper facilities like the whites doesn't come into it. I'm not talking about soccer and golf and so on—that's different. A boxer's got his manager, his trainer, his sparring partners—everything. The best.—

—And if he ever gets a fight with a white South African he has to fight as a stranger in his own country, a foreigner, he's a 'Zulu' or a 'Msutu', not a South African like the white.—

Orde Greer had his supporters—When's your great Tap-Tap Makatini going to get a title fight here in S.A.? Yes. Can you tell me that, man?—

Fats answered from the assurance of sources it was implied he wasn't prepared to reveal. —That's coming, that's coming. That's coming soon. You'll see. We're negotiating—

The young man in denims was rocking back and forth on his heels, the muscles of his backside pursed taut. —Your boy can negotiate to go to Germany and America and hell. He's still a 'boy' that's been let out like a monkey on a string.—

The heat was drawn to him and the man who pushed a face forward, shiny with beer-sweat. —Where's it going to get you? All you heroes, man, who don't play sport and want to tell us what to do. Agh!—

—You'll do what the white man tells you.—

—Listen. Listen a minute, man—if my boy wins a big fight overseas—

—So what? You'll make a lot of money and he can show his medal with his pass when he gets back.—

—Then there's no white champ in his weight here who can refuse him a fight and still think he holds the title. Isn't that so? Isn't that true? Isn't that a real breakthrough?—

—You'll do what the white man wants. *Breakthrough* to get *them* accepted back in world sport again. That's it. And when your 'negotiations' for a black to win an overall title here come off, you'll be satisfied. And if next year or the year after white soccer clubs play blacks, and take in black members, the soccer players will shout there's no more racism in sport. But everywhere else in this country the black will still be a black. Whatever else he does he'll still get black jobs, black education, black houses.—

—What do you want, then? I'm talking about *sport*.—

—Blacks will be in sport only if there is one sports body—one controlling council for everyone, every sport. When that happens then you people talk to whites. Not before. If you must talk—if you think playing games with the whites is what we blacks want.—

Orde Greer's patriarch's head was unsteady with excitement, his mouth remained open for a chance to interject. —Is it a question of tactics against racialism in sport or sport as a tactic against racialism—

The collar-bones of the young man in the denim shirt open to the waist moved under black skin with decisive energy. —Tactics! Money money money— He clicked long fingers under our noses to offer the smell.

—We' breaking it down, Bra.— Fats claimed the intimacy of the exclusive (in the basic sense of the word) form of 'brother' taken over by young militants from tsotsi jargon. —What's the good, passing up the openings, saying no all the time—I don't go with that.— He seemed admiring of the vehemence with which he was challenged, inviolably tolerant and masterful. —No, no, no, keep on shouting, boycotting, making the speeches—our guys overseas, SANROC and that crowd, the politicals in exile, and you guys here—that's okay with me. Don't think I haven't got a lot of time for you, my brother . . . But meantime we' the ones giving black sportsmen a go getting up to international standard, we're showing the world what we can do, isn't it? And what about the whites then? It's how you look at it. You only live once, hell—

The young man spoke about Fats as if he were no longer in front of him. —These people will always let themselves be used by the whites. They are our biggest problem; we have to re-educate—

Fats was laughing for our benefit. —I finished Orlando High before you were at your mother's breast. I was ANC Youth League with Lembede at fifteen—

—Always the same story, Mandela, Sisulu, Kgosana on Robben Island—same as Christians telling you Christ died for them.—

Marisa was suddenly there, with her husband's name. She could not have heard the context in which it had been invoked; the perfume and dash of her presence, her gay low voice, surrounded by the wash of her hangers-on as they trooped in, broke up the composition of the room. She held Fats' and Margaret's little boy on her hip a moment; hugging and whispering to him, carried along in the orbit of Margaret and the grandmother; took the smart girls at the wall by the waist in easy schoolgirlish greeting; discovered me. —Rosa . . . oh good! Orde, look, I want to talk to you about something you may be able to do for me. No, Fats— her adorned hands touched from one to the other distributing the unconscious grace of great beauty—just a cold drink. Anything.— In their own language: —It's Tandi's friend—Duma Dhladhla? That's right? You're at Turfloop?— She drew from the young man in denim a punctuation of cool nods and at last a proud curling smile that had not yet been seen, resisting her beauty with his own, as contestants of equal strength entwine forearms and try to force a fist to the table. —You promised to send me your newsletters.— She was as tall as he, he could not look down at her. —The last two happened to be banned.—

—Oh I know that. But that doesn't mean I don't get a copy.—

—I'll see what I can do.—

—Get it to Fats.—

—What's that? Now I'm paper-boy for the students' pamphlets—

She presented him fondly: —D'you know, this is the nicest man in Jo'burg. Whatever you ask, it's never too much trouble. Even if he's my cousin, I have to say it. What'd I do without him, ay, Margaret—

Before her, Duma kept his smile as detachedly as a male dancer holds his stance for the ballerina.

—I wanted to make sure you'd come.— Marisa referred to the arrival of Orde Greer on my doorstep.

—I meant to, anyway.—

—I don't trust you. We should stick together, Rosa. This morning I thought—it's terrible . . .—

Orde was watching us.

She looked at him bewilderedly for a second, but spoke to me. —You remember the night at Santorini's after Lionel was sentenced . . .—

I prompted: —You said, whose life, theirs or his.—

—This morning in the shop I thought: but it was his. I couldn't even go to the memorial meeting.— There were tears in her gaze. She had made a joke and an anecdote of her visit to the Island; a current lover was probably in the room. No one can predict in what form anguish takes hold. She didn't know it was the day, a year ago, my father died but she seemed to me to have given the sign that had not come from me. I felt a dangerous surge of feeling, a precipitation towards Marisa. (The poor creature who betrayed my father must have felt the same impulse towards my mother, in the beginning: an internal avalanche which at last brought her broken to Lionel's feet, unable to look at him.) A longing to attach myself to an acolyte destiny; to let someone else use me, lend me passionate purpose, propelled by meaning other than my own.

—There's no one outside?— Orde Greer meant the sort of discreet car from which the Special Branch agents make their surveillance.

—It's all right. I haven't been back to my place at all, so my man's still waiting for me to arrive from Cape Town.— People like Marisa—like us—are on terms of acquaintanceship with the men who watch their houses and trail them. It's part of the aura that attracts the Conrads of this world to me.

—You could have been followed from the airport.— Greer took on exaggerated whisky-wariness and good sense. He couldn't be one of our kind; we who can't afford not to take chances. Marisa was casual. —No it's okay, I don't think . . . anyway, I've been running around all over the place today, I must've shaken anyone off . . . he'd be dizzy by now . . .— The unshed tears glittered amusement.

—I'm not so sure.— Orde Greer's terse concern suggested a tender authority—surely she hadn't accepted him as a lover? I saw only his inexpressive body, dressed in a confusion that made him somehow physically inarticulate—the foot with the humped, foreshortened arch in boots meant for those who walk or climb, the shorts worn by youths who tinker with motorcycles, the don's black sweater on which his own blonde combings had matted, and the—thinker's? left-winger's? child of nature's? holy man's? down-and-out's?—head blurred with hair.

Tandi and her friend kept pushing cassettes into the player and pulling them out again. Music blared interjection and was cut off while talk kept continuity. Fats' friends were discussing racing bets. Perhaps because I had only been in the midst—listening without speaking—of his argument with the young man Dhladhla who was a student or teacher at a black university, Fats was drawn to secure further witness. He brought me whisky. —They think I can make them rich because of my father. Ha! That's the one for tips. I wish you'd meet him. Marisa's mother's brother, Marisa's mother's my auntie, you know . . . My old man started as a stableboy and now he runs the whole show. Ten grooms and stableboys. The owner wouldn't buy a horse without he says 'go ahead'. He's built a five-roomed house for my father there at the stables near Alberton and when the municipality says, who's staying there? he says—you know what he says to them?— look—my stable manager, I can't do without him, so don't tell me he can't live in a white area. My father's one of the top experts in Jo'burg. In the country! Even the white jockeys come to ask him advice how to handle this horse or that one. I think he's seventy years and you should see him on those race-horses. Those fast things, man! Hell! he loves it.—A man like that—he's happy. You know? Some of these older people . . . I can tell you—he'll say Kgosana's a great man, but himself—he'd be afraid of a black government, d'you know that? These kids with their strong ideas, they don't realize there's a lot of people like that. What can you do with people? Isn't it? They don't want to run to trouble—He gave a confidential tilt of the head towards the kind of life led by Marisa.

—That's exactly what certain whites do realize—bank on.— Orde Greer deferred, was determined to talk to me about such things.

It's easy enough to satisfy; to slip back into this kind of exchange; to toss on the small kindling demanded.

—You're talking about liberals? Or Verligte Nats?—

—Oh both. It's not peace at any price, it's peace for each at his price. White liberalism will sacrifice the long odds on attaining social justice and settle for letting blacks into the exploiting class. The 'enlightened' government crowd will sacrifice the long odds on maintaining complete white supremacy and settle for propping up a black middle class whose class interests run counter to a black revolution.—

The girl Tandi had left her friend and ignoring the rest of us was murmuring in a sulky, flirtatious undertone to Duma Dhladhla, but he thrust his voice back among us—The black people will deal with those elements. The whites won't get a chance. You liberals can forget it just the same as the government.—

—Who says I'm a liberal?—

Dhladhla sharply gestured lack of interest in Orde Greer's protest on grounds of objectivity. —Whites, whatever you are, it doesn't matter. It's no difference. You can tell them—Afrikaners, liberals, Communists. We don't accept anything from anybody. We take. D'you understand? We take for ourselves. There are no more old men like that one, that old father—a slave who enjoys the privileges of the master without rights. It's finished.—

—The black people? You think you're the black people? A few students who haven't even passed their final exams?— The man who looked like a headmaster stood up and ran a hand down his fly in the gesture of setting himself to rights.

Dhladhla gave him a fiery patient glance. —We're bringing you the news that *you're* the black people, *Baba*. And the black people don't need anyone else. We don't know about class interests. We're one kind. Black.—

—Oh you've discovered something in your classroom at Turfloop? Have you ever heard of Marcus Garvey? Yes?—

Orde Greer jolted attention swiftly back to Dhladhla. —But five minutes ago you said 'those people' were the greatest problem. The ones who'll take exemption—in sport, or anywhere, the same thing and they're the same people.—

—We don't deny the problem. We just know that it cannot exist once we rouse the people to consciousness.—

—But it does exist at present . . . a possible future black exploiting class—all right, let's not argue over terms—a group, a sector consisting of quite a considerable number of people. It exists. And the Americans, the British, the French, the West Germans—they wouldn't object either, the Americans would certainly take the heat off at U.N. and in Congress if white South Africa were to opt for survival by taking in that black sector. What I'm asking is just this—could a capitalist society which throws overboard the race factor entirely still evolve here?—

Voices went into the air like caps; from the schoolmaster, the host's other friends, over the heads of the hangers-on who sipped from their beer cans and passed cigarettes between them.

—But definitely, man!—

—All people want is the same chance as whites!—

—That's what 90 per cent are asking for—

—They're asking for what they could never get, because 90 per cent are peasants and labourers who haven't a chance of joining any privileged sector.— James Nyaluza had come in with Marisa, an associate of Joe Kgosana, one of those unaccountably overlooked through all the years of police vigilance. I have known him my whole life. He was in detention in the Sixties, but that was all. Even his continued friendship with Marisa has not saved him from being ignored. He speaks somehow from the margin, one of those fatalistically denied what the Russian revolutionary Vera Figner called living to be judged—'*For a trial is the crowning point of a revolutionary's activity*'. In this sense, Lionel's and Joe Kgosana's lives are fulfilled: and Marisa carried this unspoken assurance around with her in the room as she did the perfume on her body.

Even Fats was treating James with the sort of respect that discounted him. —It's natural—people want the chance to get on. There's always those who can make something of themselves, no matter how poor they are. You take our tycoons here in Soweto, how many of them got more than Standard Six? They come from the farms and the locations. Their mothers were servants in the backyard. Grocer-boys, milk-boys, garage-boys—

The trance of a common resentment fell momentarily upon those who had been bitterly opposing each other and would do so again in the next breath. Dhladhla, James, the schoolmaster, Fats's satellites, celebrated that romance of humiliation by which and from which each in his different way draws strength and anger to revenge it.

—Treated like nothings, living worse than dogs, eating dry mealie-meal, not even shoes for your feet in winter-time . . . today they've got everything they want, man. Businesses, big cars—

—You've got the nucleus of a black bourgeoisie ready and willing to be co-opted to the white ruling class?— Orde Greer had the air of leading towards answers he wanted to be given.

Dhladhla stated and accused impersonally and passionately. —The chance—you know what your chance is? You know what you're talking about? Race exploitation with the collaboration of blacks themselves. That is why we don't work with whites. All collaboration with whites has always ended in exploitation of blacks.—

—Do you believe that was always the whites' object? All whites?—

I spoke to Dhladhla for the first time. My voice sounded to me in a tone of quiet enquiry; Orde Greer's face dramatized it, to me, as tight-lipped.

—Even if they didn't know it. Yes, it was! It is! We must liberate ourselves as blacks, what has a white got to do with that?—

Orde Greer was pressing. —Whatever his political ideas?—

—It doesn't matter. He doesn't live black, what does he know what a black man needs? He's only going to *tell* him—

—You don't believe there is any political ideology, any system where the beliefs of a white man have nothing to do with his being white?—

—I don't say that. I'm talking about here. This place. Where Vorster sits. Some other country perhaps the white man's political ideas can have nothing to do with white. But here, he lives with Vorster. You understand?—

—And if he goes to jail?— Orde Greer was possessed, inspired. So it was all for my benefit, this interrogation.

—To jail with you?—

—In jail!— A splutter of accusing laughter. —He goes for his ideas about me, I go for my ideas about myself— Dhladhla stabbed at his bare chest, a medallion on a leather thong jumping there.

Orde Greer produced me. —He died in jail. This girl's father. You know that?— It was irresistible, inevitable.

I don't know how I look when I'm being used, an object of inquiry, regarded respectfully, notebook in hand, or stripped by you and my Swede to assess my strength like a female up for auction in a slave market. Perhaps I smiled 'offensively' before Duma and Orde Greer; you complained of that in the cottage—I produce a privacy so insulting that those well-disposed towards me don't feel themselves considered worthy of rebuff; even the slap of the 'cold fish' is withheld.

Orde Greer had his drink held in the curve of his hand, away from him, for emphasis or balance. Dhladhla didn't look at me but spoke for me to hear. He was aware I had been watching his face all the time, when he talked and while he was preparing to talk again, his replies flickering over it in soft flashes of energy. It was a face of such plastic beauty, one would think of such a head as 'made of'—that is, solid, cast of a single perfect material all through, smooth

and dark, formed alluvially under the pressure of time and race.
—He knows what he was doing in jail. A white knows what he
must do if he doesn't like what he is. That's his business. We only
know what we must do ourselves.—

The schoolmaster blinked with impatience and distress. —How
many people believe you can turn your back on white people? It's
rubbish! They won't disappear. They'll turn around with guns . . .
and how many blacks want to fight . . . we don't want killing, we
know it's our blood it's going to be. People would rather see some
leaders—(he fended off objections) I'm not talking about the political
leaders in jail, I mean just people in the community who've come up,
even businessmen, big shots in Soweto, people who can meet whites
on their own level in commerce and so on—they'd rather see these
people get a footing from where they can push. Then others feel they
will be able to follow.—They want to be alive.—

James Nyaluza smiled at what he could have expected to hear.
—Of course. But they don't realize the *racial* exclusiveness of the
white ruling class's economic and political power is a *primary*
feature of the set-up. If whites are frightened into taking in some
members of the black middle class, this is only going to be in an
auxiliary and dependent capacity. There wouldn't even be the
perks of political office. Not even a puppet ministry. Not even the
token power you get if you're a Matanzima or a Buthelezi in your
Bantustan 'homeland'.—

—You mean they'd be like the black police are already. As
Dhladhla said—just collaborators in a continued system of race
repression?—

But nobody took up Orde Greer's analogy; he doesn't have the
curious tactfulness necessary towards the question of the black
police who, although they have never yet refused to act against
their own people, are still regarded as fellow victims, bullying and
raiding under the orders of a common oppressor. Whites, not
blacks, are ultimately responsible for everything blacks suffer and
hate, even at the hands of their own people; a white must accept
this if he concedes any responsibility at all. If he feels guilty, he is a
liberal; in that house where I grew up there was no guilt because it

was believed it was as a ruling class and not a colour that whites assumed responsibility. It wasn't something bleached into the flesh.

I was carried into the talk as one's feet carry one into some pattern of movement—a boxer's footwork, a runner's crouch—for which they have been trained. My voice crossed against and raised itself with others. —But is that so, James? In the last ditch, mightn't the whites be prepared to bring in enough black capitalists to create a class-across-colour identity and solidarity—and consequently a common interest in holding down the black masses?—

Marisa spoke with the authority of the Island. —I know that's what Joe's afraid of—he thinks it would link up with the 'homeland' leaders, a way of keeping cheap labour, migrant labour, with a payoff for the 'homeland' crowd and the favoured blacks in the white areas.—

—That's what I mean. The sort of thing the liberal opposition discuss when they try to get together. And the white Progressives are even talking about 'shared power': they actually do have in mind something in the nature of political office—for the 'right' black people, of course. That could have tremendous appeal for middle-class blacks. It goes further than offering Fats a voice on the national Boxing Board, or a black businessman a seat among the directors of Anglo-American.—

Orde put a palm out in a staying gesture to James on one side, me on the other. —D'you think a black group like that can have a place in the national movement?—

James answered as I knew, marking off each word in my mind, he could be counted to. —Never. Its interests would stand in complete contradiction to those of the people as a whole, even in the context of national aims.—

—So what you want me to do?—not let my boy fight overseas until you decide how we're going to smash apartheid?— Fats turned in almost comic dismay to Marisa. —Will it really help Joe and Nelson get out?— He slopped a gout of whisky into James's glass, stopped with a grin before Dhladhla, who did not drink and whose abstinence was eloquent disapproval of the corrupting effect of white men's indulgences on others. —Wait for *him* to raise black consciousness so high Vorster and Kruger are going to see this big thing falling on them?—

—So there's no danger—no hope, if you like to put it that way for some people—that group could have any place in the national movement—

Dhladhla interrupted Greer. —What national movement do you know?—

But it was inconceivable to anyone else in that company that Orde Greer was referring to anything but the African National Congress. —The fact is surely that the African bourgeoisie is being discovered—invented—by whites much, much too late to play the classic role, never mind the one they think it'll serve. That's the point. Not whether some black people want it or not. Do you realize—now he was addressing the room, the house, the streets, the whole 'place' —for you black promoters and businessmen and teachers to come out on top the entire normal process would have to be reversed because the real class formation of a bourgeoisie would have to follow and not precede political power.—

How fascinated he was with his message, bringing in the familiar banned vocabulary the terms of the familiar banned aims of the faithful. They lull me; certainties around me in my childhood. For him they seemed to be discoveries; where had he come lately to them?—but he is a journalist, although it is a camera and not a typewriter he uses, and it could have been that he would make himself a familiar in any milieu, reproducing knowledgeably any jargon appropriate to it. His job exposes him to everything. He's in the know: if he wanted to, he could talk exactly as one would expect from a racing driver at the trackside, or exactly as one would expect from a white Communist close to the ANC.

—*This* and *this* should happen and can't happen because of *that* and *that*. These theories don't fit us. We are not interested. You've been talking this shit before I was born. He's been listening.— Dhladhla pointed at James. —And where is he? And where am I? When I go into the café to buy bread they give the kaffir yesterday's stale. When he goes for fruit, the kaffir gets the half-rotten stuff the white won't buy. That is black.—

—You ignore the capitalist system by which you're oppressed racially?—

—We don't ignore anything. We are educating the black to know he is strong and be proud of it. We are going to get rid of the capitalist and racist system but not as a 'working class'. That's a white nonsense, here. The white workers belong to the exploiting class and take part in the suppression of the blacks. The blackman is not fighting for equality with whites. Blackness is the blackman refusing to believe the whiteman's way of life is best for blacks.— Tandi buried her face against his arm for a moment, threw back her head so that we caught her grin, her tongue curled out pink over her teeth. —It's not a class struggle for blacks, it's a race struggle. The main reason why we're still where we are is blacks haven't united *as blacks* because we're told all the time to do it is to be racist. ANC listened to that—

Marisa laughed. —ANC brought together the widest and biggest black unity there's ever been.— Her tolerance was the professionalism of the imprisoned leader's proxy, aware that the younger generation must be wooed against the day when he returns. Yet she was innocently motherly, if overwhelming sexual charm can ever be subordinate to any other; he was, after all, one of her own, her rebuke was confident. She's ready to move at the head of Dhladhla's students like the splendid bare-breasted Liberty in Delacroix's painting, when the time comes.

The schoolteacher kept trying to make himself heard. —Je-sus. No, I'm telling you!—the things they think they find at Tur-floop—

Dhladhla had the air of seeing over heads, of having his back turned even to those people he was facing. —White liberals run around telling blacks it's immoral to unite as blacks, we're all human beings, it's just too bad there's white racism, we just need to get together, 'things are changing', we must work out together the *solution* . . . Whites don't credit us with the intelligence to know what we want! We don't need their *solutions*.—

Orde Greer drew in his face tight round nose and mouth and closed his eyes a moment. —And white radicals?—

—Aagh! All these names you call yourselves—

—Communists who believe—like you—that reform is not the object. Whether you realize it or not, you've taken from them the idea that racialism is entrenched in capitalism (you turn their very words around, don't you) and you have to destroy one to get rid of the other. They believe it's just as impossible to conceive of workers' power in South Africa separated from national liberation, as it is to conceive of national liberation separated from the destruction of capitalism. A black man had a lot to do with working that out, a black Communist who happens to be called Moses Kotane, eh?— He planted each phrase: —A national— democratic revolution—bringing to power—a revolutionary democratic alliance—dominated by—the proletariat and peasantry. —Except the bit about the dictatorship of the proletariat's been abandoned by Communists in Europe, by now. In Cuba, in Africa . . . it's probably still valid. Isn't that what you want?—

—So what are you saying? There are a few good whites . . . And then? We can't be tricked to lose ourselves in some kind of colourless . . . shapeless . . . 'humanity'. We're concerned with group attitudes and group politics.—

—Communists believe in what you want—no, wait—what you want for *yourselves*. That's right? But they see black consciousness as racialism that sidetracks and undermines the struggle—

Dhladhla held the girl Tandi off from him by the wrist but did not leave hold of her. —Because the problem is white racism, there can only be one valid opposition to balance it out—solid black unity.—

—My god! Now you're quoting Hegel, dialectical materialism in its old-hat form, since then there've been Marxist thinkers who've disproved—

—Our liberation cannot be divorced from black consciousness because we cannot be conscious of ourselves and at the same time remain slaves.—

Slogans in the mouths of those who have re-cast them for

163

themselves regain painful spontaneity for the tags and faded battle cries of causes the speaker doesn't acknowledge.

—Hell, that's beautiful, man?— Fats held his palm up, weighing old words anew for us.

The baby had been making its way through a grove of legs. I picked it up to save it being stepped on, and it examined me, and then put out a little soft pad of brown hand and buffed me on the nose, laughing, laughing until the gurgles became liquid and saliva strung from its amber-pink lip.

—Isn't that beautiful? Duma—if you see my boy giving a knockout against a white fighter, you'll see something beautiful like that, man. I'm not kidding. You'll see he's just like you're saying. Isn't it? Black body and black hands that did it . . . he doesn't care for *any*-body. He feels—he looks—you'll see (Fats appropriated Dhladhla's term; perhaps he would take and keep it, overlay its defiance with the swagger of show-business)—*Black-man*.— His wave of laughter at himself swept round.

James Nyaluza's voice drew aside from it. —Verwoerd and Vorster did it. Fifteen years we haven't been able to reach the kids. It's all words for these kids, just new words . . . When the day comes when you have to act . . . what will they know?—

Duma Dhladhla and Tandi made a couple oddly counterparted by the baby and me. The shift of people as the discussion lost impetus left us in the arena of a moment whose nature was undecided: maybe we would begin to chatter inconsequentially, the obsessive forces charged between all who had been arguing or listening suddenly veering off, leaving little amicable drifts of people, cosy in their silent sociability of shared drinks and smokes on the house, like the huddled hangers-on who now and then loped out contentedly to the lavatory in the yard, or arguing away at treasured points they had not got anyone to listen to yet, like James captured by Orde Greer. Tandi suddenly addressed the baby in my arms off-handedly, in her own language. The baby went still and obstinate. Tandi spoke again. The baby gave a bouncing jerk against me and was quite still again. I was smiling down at him in the homage adults feel they must offer children without knowing why. Tandi held out her arms and at once the baby stretched his to her and was taken from me.

I spoke in the mild intimacy of girls of about the same age. —It is yours?— I meant I had thought the child was Margaret's and Fats'.

—They're all ours.— It was a forked flicker of the tongue; something that the one to whom it was addressed was not expected to understand, had no right to understand. She looked at me for a second; and turned away laughing aggressively, in talk, in their own language, with Dhladhla. She was teasing him, teasing the baby, he half-irritated, the baby half-in-bliss-half-in-tears. Margaret came and took it away from her, while she kissed it passionately and maliciously and it clung to her.

Somewhere near me the white journalist's phrases jingled like a bunch of keys fingered in a pocket. —. . . not peace at any price, peace for each at his—

The women were in and out of the kitchen. I made myself useful with Marisa who at once organized and delegated tasks among the pots of boiled fowl and meat, the potatoes and mealie-pap, the gravy that smelled of curry. Tandi's friend cut bread. Margaret was making her salads dainty with beetroot stars and radish roses.

Thanks madam—the runts waited to be served by me, their fellow-guest, and ate seriously under their caps. Some people left without eating but others came in from the night as a matter of Fats' habitual sociability rather than because they had been invited. In fact I—Orde Greer and I—hadn't been asked for a meal in the way invitations are exchanged among whites, but simply had stayed on after dark until it happened to be the time when Fats' family usually ate. It's in this kind of black sociability, extending to blacks the hospitality already offered to white people in the tradition of my grandmother Marie Burger by Uncle Coen and Auntie Velma, that the Sundays in that house came about. We used to squat round the swimming-pool juggling hot boerewors from fingertips to fingertips; these children shared a dish on the floor, their fingers carefully moulding and dipping balls of stiff mealie-pap in gravy, while the baby and his grandmother ate from her plate.

Sitting on a plastic pouffe between James and Fats I was aware of the figure of Greer always seen from the back, planted with the hopeful and slightly ridiculous air of someone who has determinedly drunk more than anybody else, and makes a nuisance of himself on the periphery of one little group or another, taking with him his set of challenges, so that people might break off what they were saying but would either carelessly absorb his preoccupations or even interpret them wrongly in order to blend them with the direction of their own. He had mushed his food together without eating, already his abandoned plate had the repellent look of leftovers; someone stubbed a cigarette in it. Finally he was before Duma Dhladhla, unavoidable, ignoring the self-sufficiency of the trio, Dhladhla and the two girls. I heard him say very loudly, as if he and Dhladhla were alone—What would you do if you were me?—

Dhladhla took a snapping bite out of a chicken leg in his hand and chewed it with vivid energy, the muscles at the angles of his fine jaw moving naturally in the way of male actors affecting emotion. He looked at Greer, importuned, triumphant and bored.

—I don't think about that.—

Marisa had joined us. —So there was a raid in town today? June Makhubu's detained, and two others, they say. All Sol Hlubi's Black Studies stuff taken away. Even the report on high school children the municipal social welfare people have already accepted as evidence for their official commission . . . I'd like to know how that suddenly becomes subversive . . . They're made . . . Rosa, we were both in town in the morning . . .?—

She assumed I had been as unaware as she. And in this company I understood it was strange, some sort of lapse, from the norm established in me from the beginning of my life, that I should not have told her at once, when we met in the shop.

—Orde probably knows more . . .— Marisa rallied him. —Orde, what was this business at Providence House? Who else did they visit as well as Hlubi's outfit?—

He was stiffly dignified with his red socks sagging over the boots, his hand feeling masturbatorily round his back and chest under the pullover.

He had taken pictures; Colonel van Staden himself led the raid, that meant they were after something big; the intrepid news photographer had doubled up the fire escape and there was one shot of van Staden's man, that lout Claasens—He's holding some chap by the scruff of the neck like a dog, you can see he's got him by a handful of jacket and shirt—man, his feet are practically lifted dangling off the ground—

—But what was happening? Resisting arrest?—

—No—no—Claasens is searching him, with the other hand he's in his pockets—you'll see . . . But you won't because my bloody editor won't publish. He says to me, they'll be down on us like a load of bricks. You'll be in for it too.—You're not allowed to show the police busy in any situation like that. Prejudicial to the dignity of the law. *Their* dignity. *Christ.*—

—Did Claasens see you'd caught him?—

—I ran like hell. One of the others spotted me but when he came after he slipped on the metal steps, down on his backside, the bugger was lucky he didn't fall four flights—

The baby on his grandmother's lap shouted back gleefully at our laughter. An exchange of stories scoring off the police, some of which the tellers had experienced themselves, others belonging to our folklore, was encouraged among Marisa, James and me. —What about when your father and mother got married, Rosa—And I had to describe again, as Lionel told as a political anecdote, a family chronicle, what was really his love affair with my mother: how the police came to raid the first tiny flat and had to unpack the household goods. While I was telling it the baby boy ran over to me and pressed upon me some red knitted garment. I thought it was something of his that he wanted me to help him put on, but he held it away, reaching up towards my head, and then rubbing at his own. What does he want?— I signalled to Margaret and saw the grandmother's gums bared at me in pleasure. But Marisa understood. —He wants to put the hat on you, Rosa. It's for you.— I obliged; bent my head, and the child crowned me with crooked jabs. A cap with a rosette on one side, of the kind black women sell, spread out before them, while they crochet among the legs of passers-by on the city pavements as if they were in their own kitchens. The grandmother was presenting Lionel's daughter with her handwork. I pulled it on and Marisa set it right for me. —The rose shouldn't be in the middle— She tittered delightfully, regarding me, the first knuckle of her slender hand caught between her teeth a moment. Margaret added her touch, rolling up the edge of the thing to make a brim. —No wait— that's it— Marisa pushed all my hair up under it, both of us protesting and giggling. The old woman came over and hugged me. The nine- or ten-year-old girl who had brought me tea in the afternoon hung on my arm with the lovesickness of one who claims an elder sister. Certainly Orde Greer didn't seem in much of a condition to drive; when Fats and his wife urged me to spend the night—the short pile on the baby's head was softly rough under my chin—I was drawn to the idea of staying there among them, in the pawings and touches of the children, the comforting confidence of Fats, capable in corruption, that if the police should discover I was there, he would know exactly to whom to give a bottle of brandy. The vanity of being loved by and belonging with them offered itself. But I know it can't be taken for nothing. Offered freely—yet it has its price, that I would have to settle upon for myself, even if I didn't make a fool of myself, like Greer, asking for an estimate from Dhladhla. We drove under a sky fluttering eyelids of lightning through streets that flattened away into night, low houses shut tight, battened in darkness, barred with tin and iron against thieves and penned against the police, marauders without distinction. The eye in a window was a candle far inside; or only the reflection of the Volkswagen's headlights looking back at me as we shook and swerved our way out. Sudden street-lights, far apart and irregular, make one vulnerable there, passing under them as a target. Smoking like a burned-out site, the miles of townships were all round, dark-clotted, no assertion of tall buildings against the sky, no cloudy alabaster bowl like that inverted above the white city by life that declares itself openly in neon, floodlight, and windows letting lamp-shafts into gardens. A man lay where the road, without a gutter, found a boundary in ruts and pools. Drunk or knifed. It didn't occur to either of us to call out to stop or even pass a remark. Not in that place. Not even if we had been black. Not even though we are white.

Orde Greer got me home all right. He must be used to driving when fairly drunk. The only sound in the car was his heavy breathing and a belching of whisky fumes that buckled him every now and then; he concentrated in a way that excluded my presence. We knew that nothing would happen to us in that car, taking corners fast and wide and pausing with demonstrative caution before crossing against the red light. I can see he's someone perpetually fascinated by the idea of something that may transform him; accidental death is not his solution. And I'm here, the last of my line.

Silkworms of soft rain munching the leaves at two in the morning.

But I hadn't forgotten the red knitted hat; I have that, I put it away in a drawer—the temptation—before I went to bed that Saturday, just as the mild storm reached the white suburbs.

What I say will not be understood.

Once it passes from me, it becomes apologia or accusation. I am talking about neither . . . but you will use my words to make your own meaning. As people pick up letters from the stack between them in word-games. You will say: she said *he* was this or that: Lionel Burger, Dhladhla, James Nyaluza, Fats, even that poor devil, Orde Greer. I am considering only ways of trying to take hold; you will say: she is Manichean. You don't understand treason; a flying fish lands on the deck from fathoms you glide over. You bend curiously, call the rest of the crew to look, and throw it back.

Whatever I was before, you confused me. In the cottage you told me that in *that house* people didn't know each other; you've proved it to me in what I have found since in places you haven't been, although you are exploring the world. But there are things you didn't know; or, to turn your criteria back on yourself, you knew only in the abstract, in the public and impersonal act of reading about them or seeking information, like a white journalist professionally objective and knowledgeable on the 'subject' of a 'black exploiting class'. The creed of that house discounted the Conrad kind of individualism, but in practice discovered and worked out another. This was happening at the interminable meetings and study groups that were the golf matches and club dinners of my father's kind. It was what was wrested from the purges when they denounced and expelled each other for revisionism or lack of discipline or insufficient zeal. It was something they managed to create for themselves even while Comintern agents were sent out to report on their activities and sometimes to destroy these entirely on orders that caused fresh dissension among them, despair and

170

disaffection. It is something that will roll away into a crevice hidden between Lionel's biographer's analysis of the Theory of Internal Colonialism, the Nature of the New State as a Revolutionary Movement, and the resolution of the Problems of the Post-Rivonia Period—the crystal they secreted for themselves out of dogma. What would you do if you were me? *What is to be done?* Lionel and his associates found out; whatever the creed means in all the countries where it is being evolved between the 'polar orthodoxies of China and the Soviet Union' (the biographer's neat turn of phrase), they made a Communism for 'local conditions' in this particular one. It was not declared heretic, although I see it contains a heresy of a kind, from the point of view of an outsider's interpretation. Lionel—my mother and father—people in that house, had a connection with blacks that was completely personal. In this way, their Communism was the antithesis of anti-individualism. The connection was something no other whites ever had in quite the same way. A connection without reservations on the part of blacks or whites. The political activities and attitudes of that house came from the inside outwards, and blacks in that house where there was no God felt this embrace before the Cross. At last there was nothing between this skin and that. At last nothing between the white man's word and his deed; spluttering the same water together in the swimming-pool, going to prison after the same indictment: it was a human conspiracy, above all other kinds.

I have lost connection. It's only the memory of childhood warmth for me. Marisa says we must 'stick together'. The Terblanches offer me the chance to steal the key of the photocopying room. What is to be done? Lionel and my mother did not stand before Duma Dhladhla and have him say: I don't think about that.

They had the connection because they believed it possible.

Rosa Burger did not go back until more than a year after his death to the town where her father had been tried, imprisoned, and died. These occasions for her to visit the town gave rise to no others; he has no grave. But when that summer had already been bisected by the change of the year from old to new in the final digit of the Barry Eckhard organization's desk-calendars, she drove three times to the town and three different addresses there, during February-March. After a period of some weeks, she again began to pay a number of visits (on the 13th and 30th April and on the 7th and 24th May); but these were all to the same address. She was known to have driven to town on these dates and to these destinations by the surveillance to whom all her movements had been and were known, from the day a fourteen-year-old girl, the arteries of her groin painfully charged with menstrual blood, stood with a hot-water bottle and an eiderdown outside the prison. Whether certain purposes those movements concealed—the slip of paper with the child's message to her mother hidden round the screw-top of the hot-water bottle—were always discoverable to surveillance cannot be sure, although for reasons of counter-strategy it is accepted that people like Lionel Burger don't hesitate to make their children adept at feints and lies from the time they're set on their feet. The new occasion for her visits to the town was soon placed: in a category indicated by what the disparate identities of the people she visited had in common. All were people whose allegiance made her father their enemy. All were Afrikaners, whose history, blood and language made him their brother.

Burger's daughter wanted something, then. Something not available to her own kind. She was officially 'named' her kind,

172

high up on the list, not only alphabetically. Although she was not banned, her naming as a Communist was restrictive of associations and movements she would most desire. Perhaps it was a favour she wanted for someone connected with her; but since the affair with the hippy against whom nothing could be found, and the dirty weekends with the Scandinavian journalist (the Department of the Interior had been instructed that he should never be granted another visa, the post office had been instructed to open all letters addressed to him) she seemed to be keeping to herself, except for the old contacts long taken for granted between such people, old lines surveillance can always find its way swiftly along, woken at the epicentre by the tremble of a victim newly trapped. Perhaps she wanted some relaxation of her restrictions; was tired of being a typist and had taken up again the idea of going to work with those two British doctors in the Transkei. Whatever it was, she wanted it badly enough to seek out prominent Nationalists on whom she must carefully have calculated a lien that might lever against the stone slab of fear and resistance her approach would cause to drop into position before them.

It was only when, in April and May, she began to return to one of the three addresses that the exact nature of what she was after began to be narrowed down. The address upon which she had settled her intention, either because she had been rebuffed at the others, or because she had eliminated all but the most useful, was that of Brandt Vermeulen. Brandt Vermeulen is one of the 'New Afrikaners' from an old distinguished Afrikaner family. In each country families become distinguished for different reasons. Where there is no Almanach de Gotha, the building of railroads and sinking of oil wells becomes a pedigree, where no one can trace himself back to Argenteuil or the Crusades, colonial wars substitute for a college of heraldry. Brandt Vermeulen's great-great-grandfather was murdered by Dingaan with Piet Retief's party, his maternal grandfather was a Boer War general, there was a poet uncle whose seventieth birthday has been commemorated by the issue of a stamp, and another uncle interned during the Second World War, along with Mr Vorster, for pro-Nazi sympathies, there is even a cousin who was decorated posthumously for bravery in battle against Rommel at Alamein. Cornelius Vermeulen, a Moderator of the Dutch Reformed Church, was a Minister in the first National Party government after the triumph of the Afrikaner in 1948, when his son Brandt was eight years old, and held office in the successive Strydom, Verwoerd and Vorster governments before retiring to one of the family farms in the Bethal district of the Transvaal.

The sons of distinguished families also often move away from the traditional milieu and activities in discordance with whatever their particular level in frontier society has confined them to. Just as the successful Jewish or Indian country storekeeper's son becomes a doctor or lawyer in the city, or the son of the shift-boss on the goldmine goes into business, Brandt Vermeulen left farm, church and party caucus and went to Leyden and Princeton to read politics, philosophy and economics, and to Paris and New York to see modern art. He did not come back, Europeanized, Americanized by foreign ideas of equality and liberty, to destroy what the great-great-grandfather died for at the hands of a kaffir and the Boer general fought the English for; he came back with a vocabulary and sophistry to transform the home-whittled destiny of white to rule over black in terms that the generation of late-twentieth-century orientated Nationalist intellectuals would advance as the first true social evolution of the century, since nineteenth-century European liberalism showed itself spent in the failure of racial integration wherever this was tried, and Communism, accusing the Afrikaner of enslaving blacks under franchise of God's will, itself enslaved whites and yellows along with blacks in denial of God's existence. He and his kind were the first to be sophisticated enough to laugh at the sort of thing only denigrators of the Afrikaner volk were supposed to laugh at: the Dutch Reformed Churches' denouncement of the wickedness of Sunday sport or cinema performances, the censorship board's ruling that white breasts on a magazine cover were pornography while black ones were ethnic art. He did not shrink from open contact with blacks as his father's generation did, and he regarded the Immorality Act as the relic of an antiquated libidinous backyard guilt about sex that ought to be scrapped, since in the new society of separate nations each flying the flag of its own skin, the misplacement of the white man's semen in a black vagina would emerge, transformed out of all recognition of source, as the birth of yet another nation. He was a director of one of the first insurance companies that had broken into the Anglo-Saxon and Jewish domination of finance when he was a schoolboy, but his avocation was a small art publishing firm he indulged himself with at the sacrifice of losing in it his share of the profits of a wine farm inheritance from his mother's family. At symposia, where he was the invariable choice of white liberals to contribute views fascinatingly awful to them, he was animated on the platform in the company of black delegates, and widely quoted in press reports. *I don't see you through spectacles of fear and guilt . . . my perceptions, like those of my fellow Afrikaner nationalists, are of positive and fruitful interaction between nation and nation, and not of racial rivalry. This will exclude political power-sharing within a single country. Frankly, Afrikaners will not accept that . . . I foresee a future in which the different nations could reach a peaceful co-existence through hard bargaining . . .*

An English-language newspaper exposé once named him a member of the Afrikaner political Mafia whose brethren rule the country from within parliament; and he was interviewed dealing with that, too, smilingly. *Why only the Broederbond? Why not the Ku-Klux-Klan or the League of Empire Loyalists?* So it was not revealed how high his influence in high places might go. He had close friendships in several ministries. An elegant photographic essay, very different from the usual sort of Come-to-sunny-South-Africa information publication, appeared under his imprint in all the country's embassies; there were people in the Department of Information who found 'dynamic' his ideas about improving the country's image without either deviating from principles or being so naïve as to lie about them.

But his closest friendship was placed within the Ministry of the Interior. The ministry where passports are granted; so that was it. It was hardly credible to surveillance that Burger's daughter could expect she might ever get one of those; what was of more interest was what should be making her try. During the April period of her visits to the friend of the departments of Information and the Interior, the Portuguese regime was overthrown in Lisbon, and the lever that had finally dislodged that came from the mutiny of Portuguese troops refusing to fight Frelimo in their final colonial war: it was possible she had lain low on instructions ever since her father's imprisonment waiting to serve just such a situation as this—presenting herself 'clean', she wanted to get out of the country because it was necessary to set up new lines of increased contact to take full advantage of the bases Samora Machel would offer for infiltration from a Marxist Moçambique now established just over the border South Africans unlike her, with passports, used to cross to eat prawns and go spear-fishing. Certainly it was known her kind had had connections with Frelimo all along (that was why the Terblanche woman and her daughter were picked up and put in detention the first week of May, the old man left out to see who would come to him). The solidarity-with-Frelimo 'Freedom' meeting of thousands of blacks, Africans and Indians at Currie's Fountain in Durban brought this connection into the open; interrogation of people arrested there could be relied upon to provide new leads, and no doubt these would double back to the old sources. There was her half-brother in Tanzania; he was surveyed there, too; some of those secretly recruited for military training as Freedom Fighters already have been recruited and receive their little stipend wherever they are. The fact that there was no information she had contact with the brother beyond the two letters after the father died, that indeed it was known he did not have her address after she moved to a flat in the city, did not mean he was not prepared, through a third person, for contact with her wherever she might go abroad, or a welcome for her under another identity in Dar es Salaam. Her father's daughter; she might try anything, that one. But activity within the country suggested by the fact that she should attempt to pass out and in again was what was of concern; there was no hope at all for her that she would get what she had never had, what had been refused her once and for all when she tried to run away from her mother and father after the boy she wanted.

The freeway had been completed since she drove there last; sections, including that which had bulldozed the corrugated-iron cottage and incorporated old loquat trees into landscaping, were linked and distance shortened. The loops hovered at a smooth remove from the milky-coffee river that became a stony ditch in winter, and drowned animals in summer; past country estates where horse-jumps were laid out; cut tracks where an old black man was hauling what was left of a car chassis to a community of Ndebele houses like a mud fort on a horizon of deep veld grasses. Rosa Burger was able to see all these seasons and incidents from then and now; on those other journeys there was room in her for nothing between a point of departure and arrival. The road set her gliding down towards the town between hills softly brilliant with the green of thorn scrub. The monumental shrine to the myth of the volk, shape of a giant's musical-box away on the left somewhere; a signpost for the pleasure grounds of the wild kloof on the right. And then in past the official's house in the fine old garden, the trunk of the huge palm-tree holding up its nave of shade, the warders' houses in sunny domestic order, the ox-blood brick prison with the blind façade on the street—the narrow apertures darkened with bars and heavy diamond-mesh wire, impossible to decide, ever, which corresponded with which category of room for which purpose, and along which corridor in there, to left or right, there was waiting a particular setting of table and two chairs; the police car and van parked outside, a warder come off duty flirting with a girl with yolk-coloured hair and a fox terrier in her arms; the door; the huge worn door with its missing studs and grooves exactly placed for ever. The door was soon passed, and the military headquarters that came next, set back in a gravelled garden with another great palm-tree from the era of the old Republic like the building beside it, a charming example (her father, who had been to Holland, had told her) of Boer colonial adaptation of the seventeenth-century town mansions along the Heerengracht in Amsterdam, built of doll's house bricks and picked out in white along the bungled proportion of gables too small for its height. The suburban post office, where prisoners' visitors and warders made up the queues . . . the Potgieter Street franking enough to convey on an envelope the impress of prison itself.

Rosa Burger went on through the commercial centre of the town in rush-hour traffic of four in the afternoon, glancing at a piece of paper which did not direct her past the Supreme Court or the old synagogue converted for use as a court to which she knew her way. Driving at the pace of one who must make out signs ahead, she found the suburb and street. One of the old suburbs; Straat Loop Dood, a cul-de-sac tunnelled to the barrier of a steep koppie under enormous jacarandas which were not in flower at that season. The houses were those of Boers become burgers seventy or eighty years ago; single-storey farmhouses with dark stoeps where the old people who built them will have sat until they died. The house was like all the others; a pair of horns above the front door, a woody orange tree bearing tiny senile fruit, a wooden balustrade to the red-polished stoep, an oil-drum of Elephant Ear and another from which a flowering cactus clawed up the wall and clung overhead on tentacles like flies' feet. A wasp had plastered a nest against the door. The façade was a statement related to those with which Brandt Vermeulen liked good-humouredly to surprise, to confound disdain in symposia—no, I do not live in accordance with my newspaper image of the worldly man-about-town Afrikaner divorcé, in a penthouse with a sauna and squash in the basement, apeing the parvenu luxury of Johannesburg. He had the confidence to assert (what he would have termed) an indigenous sensibility; appreciation of the privacy, peace and appropriately simple 'environmental solution' preserved in that lovely street, with, of course, another surprise in store—when he opened the humble front door himself, a little tousled, expecting Rosa Burger by telephone appointment but informal by nature, a smiling sun-roused face, he led the way into a huge room that descended on two levels to a glass wall slid back on another garden, a real garden this time. The inside of the house had been knocked apart; it was hollowed out for the space taken up by modern good living. He was barefoot and in white canvas jeans and a checked shirt that smelled of fresh ironing, his hair was wet because—he waved towards the walled garden—he had just had a quick swim. Such a boiling afternoon—would she perhaps like to cool off, his pool was about the size of a bird-bath, no Olympic lengths offered, but there were several bikinis forgotten by various female guests, she was welcome . . .? He chattered in English and appeared to have no curiosity at all about her visit. Should they sit outside under the vine, or in? White wooden *chaises-longues* on wheels were splattered with purple droppings from the Cape thrushes who were feeding their young on the dangling bunches of grapes. —Ah, the mess . . . but the grapes only look pretty, they're those sour little Catawba things, and don't you love the calls of the thrushes? So gentle and inquisitive. And have you seen the size of the babies they're feeding—great fat lumps with spotted breasts, still, but as big as the poor mamma. They just fly in and sit there with their beaks open, look—she sort of posts grapes down them as if they were letter boxes.— The birds skimmed between him and his guest where they stood. —But it's hot. Cooler inside; come, let's sit here.—

The grouping of furniture casually divided the indoor space into comfortable intimacy. Rosa Burger, who had never been in any habitation of this man's before, was settled in the sling of one of the suède and chrome chairs beside a low glass table where he had been working—under a bowl of yellow roses pushed aside, typescript and proofs of book jacket designs lay among newspapers with columns ringed in red. The flat monk's sandals she was wearing let in the long white pelt of a carpet with the feel of soft grass.

Her crinkly Indian cotton dress looked wrung-out round her, limp; to him a statement that the visit was not something for which she had prepared herself in any way. There was no indication of what impression she wanted to make, this girl; but that was, in fact, the impression he had formed the few times, since she was an adolescent, he had encountered her and even from photographs in the papers: she was either so vulnerably open that her presence in the world made an impossible claim, or so inviolable that her openness was an arrogant assumption—which amounted to the same thing. She didn't understand the shame of the need to please, as royalty never carries money. The coolie-pink (he had an affection for these old descriptive terms, so innocently, artlessly insulting)—the purplish pink of the dress made her skin an attractive contrast, almost painterly: greeny-bronze lights slipping over her sallow collar bones and the quiet-breathing dip at the drawstring neckline where the breasts began. The dress was merely uninteresting, not unconventional in the striking way he liked loose clothes on the tall bodies of the Afrikaans state theatre actresses and art school lecturers who were the women he kept around him. It was in spite of her clothes that potent physical appeal remained; unpainted, softly-quilted full lips at rest after a strong polite smile, the water-drop clarity of the eyes and glossy accent of eyebrows in the smokiness of her face. Vitality was suggested by the dark curly head, not tilted in coquetry when she spoke or listened, calmly upright above the chairs when he left her to fetch refreshments.

On one of the walls of this house an oil of heroic proportions: the visitor's eye matched to it a number of others in the room. All were composed radially from figures which seemed flung down in the centre of the canvas from a height, spread like a suicide on a pavement, or backed against a wall, seen from the sights of the firing-squad. Brandt Vermeulen was evidently a patron of the painter. There was also a Kandinsky drawing and a Georgia O'Keeffe lithograph she did not recognize until her host explained his tastes and preferences, much later, because she was rather ignorant of movements in art; a Picasso satyr that was unmistakable even to her, and a group of small, intensely atmospheric Cape and Karoo landscapes that must be Pierneefs. A print from one of the African herbalists' shops, showing the Royal Zulu line from Shaka to the contemporary King Goodwill Zwelithini grouped in cameo portraits round a beehive hut, and framed in pink-striped plastic exactly as it would be in some servant's backyard room, represented quaintly the local naïve tradition, in line (she was later to learn from her host) with Rousseau or Grandma Moses. Standing on an antique Cape yellow-wood kist beside the visitor's chair was a presence, once alone, she became aware of, a life-size plastic female torso, divided down the middle into a blue and a red side, with its vaginal labia placed horizontally across the outside of its pubis, like the lips of a mouth. The tip of a clitoris poked a tongue. The nipples were perspex, suggesting at once the hardness of tumescence and the ice of frigidity.

Brandt Vermeulen carried in orange juice. She was asked to move the roses and he put down the tray among fallen petals. There was a warm loaf-shaped cake—You have to try at least half a slice, my Mina's gingerbread is an experience, and she gets offended—It was delicious, the real thing, he took pleasure in their mutual experience of the pure natural juice and the tender spiciness, helping himself to more cake and gesturing his guest to do so. —It's an old family recipe from my grandmother Mina learnt when she was a piccanin helping out in the kitchen—so she says, but my mother says *she* got it from her mother herself, and taught Mina—maybe your mother had it handed down, too?—

There might be some distant family connection between Brandt Vermeulen and Rosa Burger. It was not on record in Bureau of State Security files. Her mother had been vague about it. Brandt Vermeulen's mother and Rosa's mother could have been third or fourth cousins on the maternal side; he had no need to acknowledge the possibility, nor would Rosa have much ground to claim kinship in the collateral of Afrikanerdom where, if you went back three hundred years, every Cloete and Smit and van Heerden would turn out to have blood-ties with everyone else.—No, she had never tasted such good gingerbread before.

And did she also like pickled pumpkin? Did she know what pickled pumpkin *was*? He thought not! He was playfully boastful about his sensible vegetable patch out there near the swimming-pool; people simply didn't realize how beautiful vegetables were, he must show her his mahogany-coloured brinjals and scarlet chillies, and pumpkins like those plump fancy sofa cushions with a button in the middle. His garden, his paintings, *this* sort of mad venture—he blew rose petals off the jacket proofs—now he was about to lose his boots publishing a book of woodcuts and poetry that was actually erotic but wouldn't run into trouble with the *tannies** because the woodcuts were too abstract and the poems too esoteric for one to expect to sell any copies . . .

He could have gone on quite easily entertaining her with his enthusiasms and ability not to take himself seriously, she could have got up to leave at the end of an hour without having revealed any purpose in coming. Those magnificent pumpkins—Mina pickled them sweet-and-sour, he would give her a jar to take home. —Do you still live in the house—your father's house?—he laughed, he wasn't prying—I don't know, are you married or anything?—

She told him she had lived in various places; now in a small flat.

—So you gave up that house . . . of course. I was there once when I was about fifteen years old—I don't think you were even born—

She smiled, closing her eyes momentarily in an unconscious effort of recall or denial. —Oh yes I was.—

—Well, too young to have been much in evidence . . . I messed up a knee at rugby and the uncle who kept an eye on me while I was away from home at school wanted your father's opinion before he'd take the responsibility for the usual cartilage operation. He swore by the skill of Lionel Burger—may be a red but he's the best doctor in the country! So my father had to give in . . .— He made the transition to Afrikaans, for them, without noticing it—I was a bit nervous, I didn't know what a red would be like, some sort of Antichrist, Frankenstein we kids used to see in the bioscope, but your father was marvellous, we talked rugby—of course he'd been a first team fullback in his medical school days—I decided, what did they mean about this red business!—

—I sold the house, I've given up my old hospital job. Over a year, now.— She was speaking in Afrikaans, too.

* Literally 'aunts'; Mother Grundys.

His beaming, sun-and-chlorine-scoured face composed itself to consider what perhaps his visitor had given up more than a house, a job. Wit and frivolity sank, like kites gracefully grounded.

—I've been working for one of the big investment advisers. The Barry Eckhard organization.—

—I see.— And he was looking, looking at her for what there was to be revealed.

She showed no signs of nerves or embarrassment, yet neither did she have the defensiveness he was used to meeting if someone were to be pressing him. She was mistress of her own silences; as if he were the one waiting for her to speak instead of she herself looking for an opportunity. He folded his arms, workman-like.

She spoke in the tone and cadence she had used to say her mother had not, so far as she knew, been handed down a recipe for gingerbread. —It's not very interesting. In fact, so much less than I thought.—

His bristly blond eyelashes flicked towards the preoccupation on the table. —Ways of losing money are more amusing, unfortunately.—

—I could hardly say I'm tired of it—already. Rather that I don't seem to have made . . . how shall I say . . . contact with it.—

He was drawn into a leading question. —It's not what you need . . .?—

She let his question become a conclusion. Then she spoke not in reflection but directly to him, a quiet statement coming up on him and surrounding him.

—I want to go somewhere else.—

He took time: —Another job?—

—I'd like to see Europe.—

Put like that it seemed so reasonable; he had been back and forth so often; there she was, a girl like any other, a girl in her twenties, of an intelligence, education and class that took experience of the outside world for granted, was it not perfectly reasonable that she was aware of the possibility of other people's pleasures existing for her, too? He could not be less than serious and sympathetic. —Well why shouldn't you! I mean why shouldn't you want to?—

—But I never have.—

—Not as a child?— The telephone had started ringing.

—I've never been able to.— Rosa Burger did not appear to grant tacit permission for him to answer it.

—I thought that once or twice your father— The telephone continued to press its electrical impulses upon them, compressing the isolation of their talk towards a complicity. He got up, shedding that. —Damn it, no one will go.— Old retainers have the disadvantage of being deaf.

From some other room his voice came, lively, cajoling, laughing; when he returned all died quickly from his face.

—Sorry about that.— In a monkeyish gesture his hand darted of itself and tossed a piece of the cake into his mouth.

—My mother and father went several times to the Soviet Union, but before I was born. The last time my father was abroad was in 1950, I was two, he went to England and Czechoslovakia as well. All over—not to America, the Americans wouldn't let him in. It was the last time he or my mother was allowed out. And when I grew up this automatically applied to me, too.—

It sounded like something merely handed down; another family recipe. —Have you never tried?—

—Once.— She smiled at him. —But not very seriously. That is, not in a way that makes any sense. I just went along and filled in a form at the passport office . . . But that was when my mother was alive, and my father.—

—And now?— For the first time, his voice took her on.

She seemed to reiterate, simply: —I want to know somewhere else.— But following the reference to Lionel Burger and his wife, he saw that the statement was different; besides, he heard 'know' instead of 'go': *I want to know somewhere else.* The mother, the father; their destination, here or anywhere, did not have to be hers. He took the soothing, encouraging tone of one who can agree warmly with a move that has nothing to do with him. —Well, why not— naturally—of course.—

—D'you think you can help me?—

He did not evade her gaze; his grin deepened and the skin at the side of his left eye was tweaked by some nerve; he got up suddenly and stood as if he had forgotten what for. He wrestled with pleasantries that wouldn't do, for her; he did not know how to get back onto the plane of soothing empathy without responsibility. She hadn't even given him the conditional 'could'; it was as good as stated: you can help me. More, coming from her: I'm ready to let you.

He scratched both hands up through his short hair, stretched the fingers wide and let his hands fall. Staringly smiled at her, as he kept his good temper, his charm—almost English-gentleman stuff, to faze the English liberals themselves in debate. When he spoke he addressed her with a diminutive in their language, to show—she understood?—he did not repudiate ties that had no need of consanguinity. She and her father and mother belonged with him even though they disowned the volk—nothing could change that, Lionel Burger who died an unrepentant Communist jail-bird also died an Afrikaner. Brandt Vermeulen did not need to tell her her father could have been prime minister if he had not been a traitor. It had been said many times. For the Afrikaner people, Lionel Burger was a tragedy rather than an outcast; that way, he still was theirs. They could not allow the earth of the fatherland to be profaned by his body; yet, that way, they were themselves absolved from his destruction.

—*Kleintjie*, you are not an easy problem . . .—he grinned at her sweetly—ay? It's not just a matter of who will help . . . you know that . . . I don't have to tell you . . . the best will in the world—

—I'm prepared to try. I ask you because no one could ever doubt you—I mean, I can't do you any harm.—

—Look—but you mustn't overestimate what I am . . . my position. I don't just whisper in the Prime Minister's ear . . . and if I did, if I could . . . he is a man of principle, nobody . . . not his enemies deny that. If you mean what you say—you *look* as if you always mean what you say?—

—I want to go out.—

—Believe me, I understand—don't question it, good god, I've

been away, lived abroad myself. It's necessary, it tells you where your home is, it convinces you—you'll see.—

—I hope I'll get a chance to.— They laughed, the tempo quickened between them, in spite of him.

—You'll see—I hope. What we are doing here may frighten the world, but what is bold and marvellous is always a little terrible to some. Your father had the same reaction to *his* ideas, nè . . .? Of course—we who are most diametrically opposed understand each other best! If things had been different—well . . . If your father had lived longer, I think he would have overcome his despair— you see, I think his living as a Communist was an expression of despair. He didn't believe his people could solve the problem of their historical situation. So he turned to the notion of the historically immutable solution . . . yes, he didn't trust us: his own people; himself . . . that's how I see it. But if he had lived a bit longer—I honestly believe a man of his quality—a great man—

Brandt Vermeulen placed the pause for their mutual consideration.

—a man like Lionel Burger, he would have had to have been prepared to acknowledge a discovery: we've gone further . . . I'm convinced. I've often thought—I've wanted to talk to you about this, but I didn't really know you. The dynamic of the Afrikaner— it is not expended, as the social dynamic is in Europe and possibly even America. It's taken many forms since the era of crude conquest, many. Your father's was one. I hear someone's writing a book about him . . . I've often thought I'm the one to . . . I'd like to develop this idea of his having been deflected from his destiny, and why.—

She kept the considering face of one who respects a scholarly approach. Of course, sentiment was too shallow an emotion for someone of her background.

—It's terrible . . . he died much too soon. But in another sense (he found a way to phrase it without sounding callous) you see, it's not long enough ago. You follow? Though to you— He held a deep breath, leaning forward.

—Another life.— She didn't explain; she was putting the

context of her father aside from herself, or in a way so direct Brandt Vermeulen couldn't credit it, made the demand for this: I want to know somewhere else.

—Oh yes . . . one doesn't live in the past—the present is too exciting—well, I mean, alarming, but still!—he did not need to spell out Angola, Moçambique, Rhodesia, Namibia, the border wars their country was fighting, in which he and she might not be on the same side—And that's what makes the whole thing—his hand circled her attention, her face, existence, in the air with the gesture of his red ball-point singling out paragraphs of newsprint. —You simply want to go away? On a holiday?—

—People do every day.—

—On a holiday.—

—Yes.—

—Like anyone else—

He punctuated with nods and smiles, as if she were a little girl giving the right answers.

—If you are just like anyone else . . . just supposing one were to manage some sort of representations on your behalf, just suppose—where to begin—it's quite a thing to expect you to be *regarded* like anyone else?—

—I realize that.—

—You do.— Fingernails very clean, from swimming; he felt with them along the grainy line that crevassed the rosy cushion of his chin. —You do.—

She did not shy away.

He protected himself, for the time being, flattering himself by including her in the bond of not taking oneself too seriously, suddenly flippant. —You'll have to be satisfied with a jar of Mina's pickled pumpkin—I don't know what I can do, if anything—if anything—

—Whatever you offer.—

—It's not what I offer—it's what'll be asked, my girl?— He laughed, they laughed, his hand steadied her shoulder.

No doubt she was reinvestigated, if that was what was meant. At least Brandt Vermeulen got as far as getting his close friend at the

Ministry of the Interior to consent to considering an investigation, instead of dismissing the whole possibility out-of-hand. *That* was an achievement in itself; she gathered it had been accomplished, on subsequent visits to his secluded and charming house whose existence one would not have dreamt of when one knew only the way to court and to prison. He was always apparently pleased to see her; or maintained, in his way, a tradition of hospitality that would be upheld whatever the circumstances. —*Nothing* encouraging to tell you—I must say at the outset—you'll have to be patience on a monument!— (They continued to speak in Afrikaans together, but the tag came in English.) They never discussed anything over the telephone, each for his own reasons observing the cautions of their country. She came in March and April to hear this advice in his presence; it was possible, even likely, that somewhere in the room—behind one of the pictures in his collection, or in the great jars of 'arrangements' his garden provided—was another arrangement that recorded the conversation as part of the investigation. She would have expected this; out of fairness to him, to safeguard his position. Not only did he use her name often, she also used his, calling him Brandt, naming easily and openly, for any monitoring presence, the power she was addressing herself to. He told her the amusing story of how he had come to acquire the plastic torso with the anatomical novelties—as he termed them, again resorting to English—and he returned again and again to the subject of her father's biography. She told him about the young man who was writing it, or at least going about collecting material for it, and what the approach was. They agreed the result wasn't likely to be up to much; an Englishman—Brandt Vermeulen summed up—how could an Englishman expect to fathom Lionel Burger. She never remembered to bring her swimming-costume, although late in April it was still warm enough on one occasion for her (let in at the front door and led to the garden by Mina) to find him in the pool, throwing a ball to a tiny excited black boy paddling around in an old tyre-tube. —Ag, no—you haven't seen my little kaffertjie yet?— Come out to greet her, he spoke affectionately, the child splashing and shouting too much to

189

overhear. It was his Mina's grandson, spending the school holidays pampered in the yard.

Only in May did the other meaning in his remark—It's what'll be asked, my girl?—become operative.

—Of course, I imagine the last thing you'll feel like is getting together with the whole clutch of exiles. In London and so on.— Brandt Vermeulen pulled a respectfully bored face. —The old crowd.—

Rosa Burger smiled slowly; merely tolerantly, he decided, and he went on. —No, of course not. A holiday. That's what I've assured . . .— And then he looked at her for a moment not to be gone back on. She said nothing but the corners of her soft mouth were compressed and her chin jutted as she took the compact steadily. —Good. And while we're about it—maybe the papers overseas will sniff you out.—

—I shouldn't think so.— She did not regard herself as interesting.

—Oh yes. In England—apartheid victim's daughter visits Tower of London, you know the style of thing—

She was shaking her head, chin still forward; to him reassuring, a peculiarly Afrikaner mannerism, typical as a Frenchman's shrug.

—It's understood you won't be giving any press interviews. *You* don't want publicity, it's not your style, no. That's all right? Now I won't make any commitment—I'm not going to give any undertakings you aren't quite clear about, quite happy with. Then that's fine; I'm satisfied. I just hope others will be— He gave his playful, encouraging grin.

—Is there anything else?—

Her conscientiousness made him optimistic. —No. I think things are moving. It's sensible, on both sides . . .— He was quoting an argument he had put forward, somewhere. —*We* don't lack confidence, we don't have to be revengeful, isn't that so? You don't have to be kept prisoner like the Russians do to their dissident families from generation to generation. If there's anything else, I'll tell you, I'll be open. Oh—just one small point— your brother—you've got a half-brother?—

—Yes.—

—You won't be seeing him?—

—If I get a South African passport it won't gain me entry to Tanzania, will it.—

—No, no, but he isn't likely to be in Europe somewhere?—

—I hadn't thought about contacting him at all.—

—Then no problem, no problem.— He didn't want to raise her hopes too high, but sometimes when they had been talking of other things (he kept up with vogue movements in European and American thought, once explaining Monod's theory of chance and necessity, another time something of Piaget and structuralism— it's fascinating—or the writings of Galbraith and B. F. Skinner) he even spoke of addresses he must give her, people she must look up, his good friends.

It was over a year after her first visit to Brandt Vermeulen that Rosa Burger was given a passport. The document was valid for one year, and for the United Kingdom, France, Germany and Italy, but not the Scandinavian countries, Holland or the United States. She told nobody what she had in her possession. She resigned her job with the Barry Eckhard organization without explanation. She said goodbye to no one, except just possibly Marisa. Surveillance was not sure. She said nothing to Flora and William Donaldson, and had not seen Aletta or the Terblanches for many weeks—the two Terblanche women were released from detention but both placed under banning orders. She had no relationship with a man permanent enough, at the time, to require a parting. Not even the Sunday papers discovered she was going; no one but the Department of the Interior, the Bureau of State Security and Brandt Vermeulen (she did not say goodbye to him; it was tacitly understood that he should not have any personal connection with her departure, once it was assured) knew she now had a passport.

It was issued counter to the express advice and instruction of BOSS who could not understand how it could have been granted at all, and therefore disclaimed all further responsibility for the security risk involved. The case became one of those that create interdepartmental hostility and rivalry. Yet nothing could be done to stop her. Rosa Burger sat unrecognized in the departure lounge of the airport early on a Sunday morning. Her legs in jeans and boots showed under the opened newspaper that covered her face but did not hide her; when the boarding call came, the girl lowered the paper and listened as if it were a private summons, only for her. She tramped slowly across the tarmac, disappeared in the shadow of the plane's wing and—there she was—appeared again in the sun. She climbed the metal stairway to the darker shadow of the door, not turning to look back. Surveillance watched her go in.

I do not even know if you are alive. I read of a yacht that has disappeared between Durban and Mauritius. There are photographs of the girls on deck in bikinis 'recalling the high spirits in which the home-built craft set out' only weeks before. Bits of wreckage seen drifting, currents apart, suggest unpreparedness for what could happen: the striped balloon that marked the position of a spear-fisherman, floating from a broken cord, a plastic ice-bucket still decorated with varnished liquor labels washed up among rotting seaweed and flies. At sea, at sea; to circumnavigate is to end up no farther than you started. The world round as your navel. Your contemplation of it in the cottage doesn't serve me any more. I am like my father—the way they say my father was. I discover I can take from people what I need. But I am aware I don't have his justification; only the facility's my inheritance—my dowry, if any man is interested.

Till the last minute, I expected to be stopped. When the boarding call came I put down the morning paper: now: now as I get up the young policeman blinking at the door with his lanyard and revolver and walkie-talkie crackling will ask me to stand aside. I could have stopped early on, before I started, so to speak. The first people I tried were frightened of me; I felt they couldn't have me gone quick enough to wipe my footmarks from the front stoep. Those who were not afraid had no power. I could have given up. It is impossible to decide in advance whether a man like him has sufficient influence. Impossible to find out whether he is in the Broederbond or not. Though perhaps I should have asked him! I'm the one person he might have answered?

The strange thing is, my father had the same kind of illusion about Brandt Vermeulen as he has about my father. Except that my father placed it as something in the past, a lost opportunity, not something that might have come about in one or other of their respective utopias. Lionel shook his head in dry wonderment at the exegesis of apartheid with which Brandt Vermeulen enlightened Rotary Clubs and political seminars. —*Man!*—*he won't scruple to invoke Kierkegaard's Either/Or against Hegel's dialectic to demonstrate the justice of segregated lavatories . . .*— But at the same time Lionel thought Brandt Vermeulen a casualty of his historical situation; with his intelligence, he should by rights have opted for the Future and not the Volk. I might have had this in the back of my mind when I went to him. Anyway, I found he was not afraid.

Not afraid; fascinated. The state of fascination can be a function of vanity. Even the timid woman who betrayed my father was drawn into fascination by an idea of herself as spirited as she would have liked to be, she got from him. Brandt—how quickly he became 'Brandt' and how much it pleased him—was cautious, out of shrewdness, out of care to avoid bungle by haste and lack of strategy, but this was always outweighed by the fascination—not with me, the female thing not at all, but with what he was doing. There I was, final proof of his eclecticism, sitting—at last—in his house beside the torso with the transverse vagina, Burger's daughter named for Rosa Luxemburg and Ouma Marie Burger. I saw, as I continued to present myself there before him, a passport for me would set him free of his last doubts. I offered myself to provide his chance to prove that the volk, become a powerful state in spite of my father and his kind, had no need to fear that in my father which hasn't died, and which Brandt chose to see in me; to prove that an individualist like Brandt Vermeulen could continue to be committed to the volk without sacrificing 'broad sympathies' and 'wide understanding'; that 'pettiness and narrow, punitive restraint' had gone down to the basement of the state museum along with *Whites Only* park bench signs that used to give the country such a bad press abroad.

I hoped to be stopped. 'Détente' (mispronounced and misappropriated) made my passport possible. Brandt Vermeulen wanted to believe in 'the new dynamic' as he preferred to call it; I sat in his lovely old house, one of the exhibits; if he could get a passport for Burger's daughter to travel like anyone else—if Burger's daughter was willing to travel like anyone else—who could say the regime was not showing signs of moving in the direction of change?

When the 24th April came (I know you dislike my habit of naming private events with public dates, but public events so often are decisive ones in my life) I thought I would be stopped. There would be an end of it. Half the white wall fell in on itself; the Portuguese were done for. Dick had not been projecting himself too far into the Future when he talked to me through the car window many months before. But by this time Brandt was deeply committed to his kind of freedom. He had told me how much importance he placed on the *human scale* of policy action (the succinct phrases are his); that meant that when one has found the Kierkegaardian idea for which one must live or die, one must support its policy passionately in theory and at the same time take on the job of personal, practical, daily responsibility for its interpretation and furtherance. He gave me an informal lunch-eon-type address on the honourable evolution of Dialogue, begin-ing with Plato, the dialogue with self, and culminating in 'the Vorster initiative', the dialogue of peoples and nations. With me he was self-engaged in that responsibility on the human scale; for him, his afternoons with Rosa were 'Dialogue' in practice.

Others, less fastidious-minded than he, pursue the human scale in the rooms supplied with only the basic furnishings of inter-rogation, winning over enemies brought out of solitary confine-ment to stand on their feet until they drop, kicked, beaten, doused and terrorized into submission. When I stood watching the wasp delicately plastering its nest for the seconds before the front door was opened to me, I was entering each time a place that didn't exist for my father and that he would never have put me in, never, although he sent me to prisons; that he would never have set foot in himself, although I had inherited from him and from my mother the necessity of deviousness wily enough to get myself there—a place where a meeting was possible between those for whom skin is an absolute value and those for whom it is not a value at all; a place whose shameful existence recognizes a possibility of there being anything to say between migrant miners, factory workers, homeless servants, landless peasants, and the class and colour that lives on them. Peace. Land. Bread. But Brandt knows only the long words—ethnic advancement, separate freedoms, multilateral development, plural democracy. To show the world how South Africa 'beleaguered by hostile states on her own borders', imprisons and detains only those who actively threaten her safety from within, it was more necessary than ever for her to prove her good faith in continuing *daytant* through the right concessionary gestures at home. It was necessary for Brandt to stand firm, with his friends in high places, over the bargain of Burger's daughter. She had accepted that she would contact no one who counted, abroad; she would not even go to Holland or Scandinavia, where anti-apartheid and Freedom Fighter support groups were most active, and her Communist background effectively debarred her from the United States, where black American lobbies would have sought her support for economic boycotts.

Nothing stopped me. Until the very last week I still thought I would stop myself. It's difficult to believe that being too detached to see myself interesting to newspapers could have turned into a guarantee not to be interviewed by the hostile foreign press. It's only too easy to be cold to the prospect of meetings in London with my father's old associates in exile, who would receive me expectant as the old Terblanches and their daughter are; it hardly seemed to constitute an undertaking. And all I had to say about my brother, my father's other son, was to observe that a South African passport isn't recognized in Tanzania. The remark put him as far from me as if he too drowned as a child, or like Baasie, my little kaffertjie, disappeared into some room, some black township, some prison, maybe, where I can't catch up.

After I had taken the passport, after I'd gone—I don't know what they said: the faithful. They would surely never have believed it of me. Perhaps they got out of believing it by substituting the explanation that I had gone on instructions, after all, instructions so daring and secret not even anyone among themselves would know. So my inactivity for so long would present them with a purpose they had always hoped for, for my sake. And by what means I had managed to get papers—that was simply a tribute to the lengths a revolutionary must go. I think about what they must be thinking. Listen to me—Conrad, whatever I may have said to you about them, however they may have seemed to me since I have been free of them, they are the ones who matter.

A donkey. The real reason why I went is something only you would believe. In fact, only if you believe will it become believable, to me. I recognize it as part of the way my life has been coded, since you forced me to read such things in the cottage; but the code is my own, not yours, not theirs. A donkey. A donkey. A matter for the SPCA. Lionel loved animals almost sentimentally, he set the leg of a seagull with sellotape when we were camping at Quagga Mouth when we were children; my mother thought too many people in our country who cared for animals had no care for people—she herself had none over, for beasts. A meths drinker dead on a park bench. A matter for the Social Welfare Department. These are the things that move me now—when I say 'move' I don't mean tears or anger. I mean a sudden shift, a tumultuous upheaval, an uncontrollable displacement, concepts whose surface has been insignificant heaving over, up-ended, raised as huge boulders smelling of the earth that still clings to them. A shift that comes to me physically, as intestines violently stir and contract when some irritant throws a switch in the digestive tract. Earth, guts—I don't know what metaphors to use to describe the process by which I'm making my own metaphors for suffering.

I had the passport on the shelf in the wardrobe. In the leather collar-box with the medical corps brass serpents and my father's watch—I have given away everything of his that might continue to be of use to others, even his medical library, but the only person I'd have liked to have had the watch was Baasie, and I don't know where to find him. The passport was there the day I went to Flora Donaldson for lunch. I thought of it while Flora stood carving the leg of lamb, her voice pitched to penetrate the several conversations at table. —Well-done, pinkish?—would anyone prefer quince jelly to mint sauce— There was childish satisfaction in imagining how she would react (point of knife in air with a bit of meat dangling, face excruciatingly mobile between amazement, curiosity, and indecision whether to be delighted or shocked) if she were to know. She would probably have decided celebration was the correct reaction: —everybody! we have news— William was the one who had been offended by the suggestion, when she was busy managing my life for me just after Lionel died, that I would ever consider leaving the country. He isn't really one of our kind but he understands what it means to be one, whereas good old Flora is an amateur in her perceptions as well as her acts. A talented and brave one, sometimes; the faithful have to be alert for adventurism among themselves, but it can be made use of when it is found in the temperament of others—it was Flora who had Nelson Mandela successfully hidden in her wine cellar when he went in and out of the country illegally before the Rivonia Trial. What her husband William sees in me when I am sitting (a daughter of the house, Flora likes to think of me: Lionel Burger's daughter) on his right at table, is a professional, like my father.

Flora didn't say it was going to be a lunch party. She'd implied wistfully she and William and I had not had a quiet talk and a meal together, just us, for too long. There were three other people; a handsome, semitic-looking Indian lawyer from Durban (for me?—he was allotted to my right at table), a white woman lawyer so perfectly groomed she appeared to be under glaze; and Mrs Daphne Mkhonza, a vast expanse of navy blue crimplene, patent shoes, gilt costume jewellery, like an Afrikaans cabinet minister's wife at the opening of Parliament. Flora still manages to have these 1960s mixed lunch parties although it must be difficult to find blacks, now, who will come to them.

Mrs Mkhonza is often 'featured' in the women's pages of white newspapers as an example of what black people can achieve despite their disadvantages. She is one of the rare black petty capitalists— what Marisa's cousin Fats would call a tycoon, who somehow manages to circumvent some of the laws that prevent blacks from trading on a scale that makes white tycoons. She has petrol service station concessions all over the Transvaal black areas, general stores and—Marisa adds to the story of success and enterprise—is a rent racketeer, obtaining leasehold over township housing by bribing officials, and then profitably letting out rooms in her slum yards to people for whom influx control makes it hopeless to expect to find somewhere to live legitimately. Marisa herself sometimes uses Mama Mkhonza, when it is urgent to find 'somewhere to stay' for one whose presence in Soweto is not open; Mrs Daphne Mkhonza may be an exploiter of blacks, following the example of the whites who admire her self-improvement initiative, but she's also a black woman: she's accepted, like the black policemen.

When we sat down to lunch the white woman lawyer was emphasizing the sociological aspects of legal cases referred to her—she is consultant to an advice bureau dealing mainly with coloured women, squatters, indigents—the prosecutions for incest, rape and desertion as an indictment of living conditions rather than individual criminal tendencies. Whom to punish, how to redress? What she said was concisely analysed, true; her napkin-touched lips shaped and her hands with their pushed-back cuticles outlined human destruction. The smugness of her appearance was perhaps a defence against the self-defeating nature of the good work she did. In such company no one has the bad taste to point out this common characteristic of 'working within the system'. We all listened respectfully under Flora's eye; William with politeness that hopes it will do for admiration or whatever else is called for. The Indian lawyer exchanged a few professional anecdotes in the same context, with a slight change of emphasis—there were laws—did we know?—laws still in force in Natal, whereby an Indian husband could have his wife imprisoned for adultery. A relic of the days when labourers imported from Gujerat were indentured to work in the sugar-cane fields, a perpetuation of the image of the South African Indian as eternally a foreigner in the country of his birth, living by mores that set his behaviour patterns apart. The general theme of conversation and the current pre-occupation of Flora were the same. Mrs Eunice Harwood wanted to make black and white women aware of such rights as they had, over their children, their property and their person, for a start; Mrs Daphne Mhkonza was not only an economically-emancipated black, she was a black woman beating white businessmen with their own marked cards. In her mood of political ecumenism, Flora no doubt saw engagement in a struggle for black rights as a natural extension of the limits of the woman lawyer's scrupulously constitutional commitment, and Mama Mkhonza's recruitment to the system—Orde Greer would expect me to phrase it that way—as a raid upon it. The current ground of common cause was women's liberation, the roast lamb was victualling Flora's little caucus for a meeting that was going to take place that afternoon.

—Where?— If it's true William has decreed Flora must stick to harmless liberal activities these days, he felt obliged to show some interest in them.

She put down her knife and fork and opened her eyes at him, smiling round to draw everyone into the spectacle: —Here, my darling, here. In your house.— The coquettish wifely frankness was that of a woman who no longer has adultery to conceal and enjoys displaying an innocent flirtation. Let him be grateful it was only to be a meeting that was to be there, in his house, quite harmless, too innocuous, maybe, to provide anything much of interest to BOSS, whose man—or rather woman, on this occasion—certainly would be present as a matter of routine observation of any assertion of common purpose between whites and blacks.

And of course I was to be drawn in, too—that was why I had been produced at lunch, although Flora knows quite well that as a named person my position at meetings is a delicate one. Someone like me may attend, so long as the purpose of the meeting is not to be construed as in any way political. One may take part in discussion, yes; but the contribution can't be recorded in the minutes or reported in the press. Meanwhile surveillance has taken down what one has said. And if the subject touches upon political rights, for example the rights of women as our kind (the faithful and their faithful hangers-on, the Floras) see these: the oppression of black women primarily by race and only secondarily by sex discrimination . . . My attendance could bring me into court as a

contravention; Flora offered her statement, prepared for this:
—You're William's visitor, not mine. Mnh? Isn't that so?
Why shouldn't she be? You simply happened to turn up to see
him while I was having a meeting in our livingroom.—

It is true that her friends—of our kind—are old hands at breaking
the minor hobbles of the restrictions on their lives. I should know as
well as anyone how to make a nuisance of myself, using the courts as
the only political platform I could get at, getting my name in the
papers, starkly eloquent of the gag on my mouth I've inherited in the
family tradition, since only my name—Lionel Burger's daughter, last
of that line—can be reported, not my 'utterances'. That's how they
perceive her, people who read the name. I am a presence. In this
country, among them. I do not speak. Except to you, out of a habit,
formed in the dark in your cottage, that came late.

William made objections, naturally. Rosa was not going to run
any risk of being picked up just because of some damn meeting. I
laughed to stop them bickering about me. Mrs Eunice Whatnot,
her face worked-over as if it were a portrait rather than a face,
looked at what a named person was like. Mama Mkhonza majes-
tically bridled on my behalf. —Ter-rible. Honestly! These people!
Really terrible. What do they want with a young girl? Why can't
they leave you alone just to live!—

—Like anyone else: I had undertaken to Brandt Vermeulen.
And I could see, I alone, as I did the passport in the wardrobe,
Flora's meeting as what could stop me. I had only to jeer kindly at
William's fussing, come up to Flora's expectations and sit in
quietly among the women listening to the proceedings; stand up
and have my say. I have faith in BOSS; one of the faces, not so easy
to pick out as the men's usually are, but surely there, would make a
note of the presence—my presence. Unknown to anyone the
passport in the wardrobe nobody knew about would be listed
invalid by the Department of the Interior. The police would
demand its surrender forthwith. I could give it back without
having used it. Maybe there wouldn't be any charge or court
appearance; simply the demand for the passport, their side of the
bargain withdrawn.

—They'll be a mixed crowd of females. God knows. All kinds, I hope. But concerned. We've more or less restricted it to representatives of various organizations, with a few outstanding individuals, old Daphne Mkhonza, yes—we don't just want a lot of do-gooders and church women, we must drop white urban values and rope in some of the toughies with guts, the flamboyant ones. I wish the shebeen queens would come; and white prostitutes—why not? I don't delude myself we'll reach the radical black girls in the student movements, though I've got a hopeful contact or two for Turfloop and the Western Cape. Never mind. Even if we can close up a bit—close the hiatus between the politically-aware young women, those smashing black girls with the *holoha* hairdos—don't you love the way they look? That sort of 'Topsy, and fuck-you'— and the ordinary black woman. Get her to regard herself as someone who can do something again, you're too young to remember, but the women's movement in the ANC was a force—and at the same time get these white suburban good souls (basically, they're really concerned) to tackle human rights *as women* . . . together . . . I think it's possible to tap new resources, maybe—Eunice Harwood's *terrifyingly* professional, isn't she?— Flora had me to herself for a quick briefing away from the others; we buttered scones.

I kept out of the way while people were arriving; William and I sat with the cold coffee cups from lunch, in the little paved courtyard Flora has made off the diningroom, hearing car doors bang and the eager pitch of welcome, the breathy laughter and African organ-note murmur of polite responses, and the enumerative intoning by which introductions could be recognized without names being audible to us. Both too comfortable—too marginal—to get up, he to demonstrate, I to see for myself, we discussed pointing from our chairs how he decided which shoots to train where on the plants he has espaliered against the walls. —Don't you think pomegranates hanging down, that red against the whitewash . . . I want to have a go with a pomegranate. You've seen those miles of peach and pear espaliered on frames along the roads of the Po valley—considerate William at once shifted the tactless reference to the ease with which he could go about the world, making over the question into a small marital joke—Don't see why it's any more unnatural for a pomegranate to be trained to grow in a regular pattern, do you? Flora keeps accusing me, but then so's it 'unnatural' to prune any tree.— The arrivals seemed all to be behind doors, now; each catching the other's eye, we giggled quietly. —Quite a mob.— William assumes in me an affectionate tolerance like his own, for Flora's activities, which he himself is supposed to have circumscribed. When I put down my section of the *Guardian Weekly* we were sharing and went indoors he looked across from the sheets he held but said nothing. The moment in which he might have questioned where I was going was really made by me; I caught myself, an instant almost of shame, in the misreading his concern would be victim of. But I had always made free of their home; I might just as well be going upstairs for a doze on the bed in 'my' room or to the downstairs lavatory with the Amnesty International poster for contemplation on the back of the door.

I skirted Flora's assembly and sat down at the back. The meeting had just begun. After the cube of courtyard sun, dark breathing splotches furred with light transformed the big livingroom. Everyone—I began to see them properly—bunched together in the middle and back seats, the black women out of old habit of finding themselves allotted secondary status and the white ones out of anxiety not to assume first place. Flora's gay and jostling objections started a screech of chairs, general forward-shuffle and talk; I was all right where I was—her quick attention took me in, a bird alert from the height of a telephone pole. After the addresses of the white woman lawyer and a black social welfare officer, a pretty, syrup-eyed Indian with a soft roll of midriff flesh showing in her seductive version of the dress of Eastern female subjection, spoke about uplift and sisterhood. Flora kept calling upon people—masterly at pronouncing African names—to speak from the floor. Some were trapped hares in headlights but there were others who sat forward on the hired chairs straining to attract attention. A white-haired dame with the queenly coy patience of an old charity chairwoman kept holding up a gilt ballpoint. Along my half-empty row a black woman urged between the whispers of two friends could not be got to speak.

In respectful silences for the weakness of our sex, the flesh that can come upon any of us as women, black matrons were handed slowly, backside and belly, along past knees to the table where Flora had a microphone rigged up. Others spoke from where they sat or stood, suddenly set apart by the gift of tongues, while the faces wheeled to see. The old white woman's crusade turned out to be road safety, a campaign in which 'our Bantu women must pull together with us'—she trembled on in the sweet, chuckly voice of a deaf upper-class Englishwoman while Flora tried to bring the discourse to an end with flourishing nods. A redhead whose expression was blurred by freckles floral as her dress asked passionately that the meeting launch a Courtesy Year to promote understanding between the races. She had her slogan ready, SMILE AND SAY THANKS. There was a soft splutter of tittering crossed by a groan of approval like some half-hearted response in church, but a young white woman jumped up with fists at her hips —Thank you for what? Maybe the lady has plenty to thank for. But was the object of action for women to make black women 'thankful' for the hovels they lived in, the menial jobs their men did, the inferior education their children got? Thankful for the humiliation dealt out to them by white women living privileged, protected lives, who had the vote and made the laws—And so on and so on. I saw her falter, lose concentration as three black girls in jeans who had only just come in got up and walked out as if they had come to the wrong place. A white woman had thrust up an arm for permission to speak—We don't need to bring politics into the fellowship of women.— Applause from the group with whom she sat. Black matrons ignored both the white girl and black girls, busily briefing each other in the susurrations and gutturals, clicks and quiet exclamations of their own languages. They responded only to the sort of housewives' league white ladies who stuck to health services and 'commodity price rises in the family budget' as practical problems that were women's lot, like menstruation, and did not relate them to any other circumstances. The black ladies' fear of drawing attention as 'agitators' and the white ladies' determination to have 'nothing to do' with the politics that determined the problems they were talking about, made a warmth that would last until the teacups cooled. Dressed in their best, one after another, black women in wigs and two-piece dresses pleaded, were complaining, opportuning for the crèches, orphans, blind, crippled or aged of their 'place'. They asked for 'old' cots, 'old' school primers, 'old' toys and furniture, 'old' braille typewriters, 'old' building material. They had come through the front door but the logic was still of the back door. They didn't believe they'd get anything but what was cast-off; they didn't, any of them, believe there was anything else to be had from white women, it was all they were good for.

And all the time those blacks like the elderly one near me, in her doek with Thursday church badges pinned to it, a piece cut out of her left shoe to ease a bunion, a cardigan smelling of coal-smoke and a shopping bag stuffed with newspaper parcels, listened to no one; were there; offered only their existence, as acknowledgment of speakers, listeners and the meaning of the gathering. It was enough. They didn't know why they were there, but as cross-purpose and unimaginable digressions grew louder with each half-audible, rambling or dignified or unconsciously funny discourse, clearer with each voluble inarticulacy, each clumsy, pathetic or pompous formulation of need in a life none of us white women (careful not to smile at broken English) live or would know how to live, no matter how much Flora protests the common possession of vaginas, wombs and breasts, the bearing of children and awful compulsive love of them—the silent old blacks still dressed like respectable servants on a day off, although they were sitting in Flora's room, *these* were everything Flora's meeting was not succeeding to be about. The cosmetic perfumes of the middle-class white and black ladies and the coal-smoke and vaginal odours of old poor black women—I shifted on the hard chair, a deep breath in Flora's livingroom took this draught inside me.

Flora touched my hand in passing as we were led into the room where tea was laid out but resisted the temptation to introduce me to anyone and did not even address me by name. There were a few among the black women who knew me, or whom I knew as people who had worked with my mother, in the days of the co-operative. They didn't recognize me, Mrs Cathy Burger's schoolgirl, as a white woman. Among the white women, I saw recognition of my face only in the look of the girl who had leapt up to attack the white members of the meeting—a freelance journalist, Flora mentioned. She did a lot of scribbling on a note-pad. Perhaps she was the one, the one who would have marked my presence for BOSS; an attractive girl with an irreverent expression, in a black leather jacket and ivory and elephant-hair bracelets—if her 'provocative' speech had been meant to encourage others to reveal subversive tendencies it had not succeeded in that gathering. She was eating scones and drinking tea like the rest; as other people receiving their retainer had enjoyed their boerewors among my father's associates and friends at the swimming-pool. When people began to leave there was the usual problem about who, among the few blacks with cars, could give a lift to whom. There were muddles; some people had left without the complement of passengers they'd brought. William was called from upstairs and went off with a car-load to Soweto. I asked Flora if I could give anyone a lift. Her eyes moved quickly. —But where?— I suppose I moved a hand or shoulders. —Perhaps if you could take a couple of women just to the entrance to the townships, or maybe even only to a convenient station—if you are driving that way, anyway . . .— She put her arm on mine, seduced, and spoke in my ear like a lover—But Rosa—not inside, don't go being persuaded to run anyone home to her house, for Christ' sake, please, d'you hear me—

Yet where could she have thought I would be going that was 'on the way' out towards any black townships, now that I had a passport in my wardrobe? Prescient about what she did not know, she was preoccupied with concern at the temptation presented. She looked suddenly alone among her knot of smiling, hand-shaking women; she watched me go with a vividness of attention secret to me.

During those days, that whole time, many months, since I had suddenly begun to go to Pretoria but not to the prison, I did things without a connection made by intention or decision. When three women had fitted themselves and their trappings out of the way so that the two doors of my old car could close, I was going to drop them off somewhere because I was on my way to Marisa. I had avoided her without Brandt Vermeulen needing to mention the precaution. Flora was right. My direction existed. I had not spoken—had not 'uttered'—at the meeting but I felt—can't explain—released from responsibility for myself, my actions, the way I imagine a gambler must feel when he exchanges the last contents of his wallet, down to the lining of his pockets, for a pile of chips and pushes them over the baize. What will be lost is only money; what would be lost was only a passport. It was all external, had nothing to do with, did not match any category of what has really happened to me in my life. Marisa was the one I should have been going to say goodbye to, if I had not been going to be stopped. I try to sort this out in some order, now, of present and future; of logic; it didn't have or need any. You'll understand, you'll approve: one knows best what one's doing when one doesn't know what it is.

Of course Flora was right. An old mama who had confidently lied about where she really lived, climbing into the seat beside me with agreement that her destination was the same as the others', announced when they got out that a bus stop was no good to her at all, she had needed to get to Faraday Station; and even that was no good, she was afraid of tsotsis on the Saturday trains. Composedly sure I would drive her home to her house now that she was in my car, it was natural to her that I did.

She didn't live in an official township at all but in one of those undefined areas between black men's hostels and the mine-dumps on the outskirts of the city. Small industries have taken over the property of worked-out gold mines, the hollows are mass graves for wrecked cars and machine parts, the old pepper trees are shade for shebeens, and prostitutes lie down for customers in the sand of the dumps. There were still hawkers' mules tethered in grazed circumferences of tin-littered veld; a tiny corrugated-iron church with broken windows, and a peach-tree half hacked-away for firewood; in abandoned cottages that had once belonged to white miners, and in the yards built up with shelters made of materials gathered from the bull-dozed mine compounds and the brick shells of concession stores, people were living in what had been condemned and abandoned by the white city. This was the 'place'; she assured me it would do to stop anywhere on the switchback I was driving between dongas and boulders of the tracks that bound bricks, tin and smoke. God would bless me: with this she went off with her stolid side-to-side gait through bicycles and listing taxis hooting at her. Perhaps she didn't really live there—she looked much too respectable for this sort of den existing on the sale of sex and drink to factory workers and railway-yard labourers. It's impossible to say; for Flora's white women to imagine where on earth they come from, these neat black ladies they meet in Flora's house. Probably the old mother thought she'd take advantage of the provision of a car and driver and go and visit an out-of-the-way friend—why not?

I was miles from where Marisa lived, from where I could go to her cousin Fats' place and send someone to see if I could slip into her house by way of yards. I wasn't even sure how to get across to the township without going all the way back through town. There was a woman with a tin of live coal selling roast mealies and I got out of the car to go over and ask directions of her. She didn't know. Orlando might have been at the other end of the world. The ribbed papery husks stripped from cobs made a thick mat all round her, under the soles of my shoes as it was under bare feet when Tony, the other Marie and I pranced with black farm kids around the thresher on Uncle Coen's farm. I made for a gang of black children and youths now, the little ones dancing and jumping among excited dogs to touch a bike with ram's-horn racing handles, a young chap astride it in the centre of other adolescents sharing smokes and a half-jack of something wrapped in brown-paper. I called to them but they only catcalled and laughed back in wolf-whistle falsetto. I was approaching—smiling, no, be serious for a moment, tell me—I heard the hard ring of struck metal and saw the fall of a stone that had hit my old car. I drove away while they went on laughing and yelling as if I were at once prey and a girl for teasing. I took wheel-tracks deep enough to be well used that seemed to lead over the veld to a road away on the rise in the right direction. The hump of dead grass down the middle swished against the belly of the car and now and then the oil-sump scraped hard earth. The track went on and on. I was caught on the counter-system of communications that doesn't appear on the road-maps and provides access to 'places' that don't appear on any plan of city environs. I was obstinate, sure the track would be crossed by one that led to the main road somewhere; there was a cemetery half a kilometre across the veld with the hired buses as prominent as sudden buildings, and the mass of black people and black umbrellas like the heap of some dark crop standing on the pale open veld, that mark a Saturday funeral. I gained a cambered dirt road without signposts just as one of those donkey-carts that survive on the routes between these places that don't exist was approaching along a track from the opposite side. Driver's reflex made me slow down in anticipation that the cart might turn in up ahead without calculating the speed of an oncoming car. But there was something strange about the outline of donkey, cart and driver; convulsed, yet the cart was not coming nearer. As I drew close I saw a woman and child bundled under sacks, their heads jerked rocking; a driver standing up on the cart in a wildly precarious spread of legs in torn pants. Suddenly his body arched back with one upflung arm against the sky and lurched over as if he had been shot and at that instant the donkey was bowed by a paroxysm that seemed to draw its four legs and head down towards the centre of its body in a noose, then fling head and extremities wide again; and again the man violently salaamed, and again the beast curved together and flew apart.

I didn't see the whip. I saw agony. Agony that came from some terrible centre seized within the group of donkey, cart, driver and people behind him. They made a single object that contracted against itself in the desperation of a hideous final energy. Not seeing the whip, I saw the infliction of pain broken away from the will that creates it; broken loose, a force existing of itself, ravishment without the ravisher, torture without the torturer, rampage, pure cruelty gone beyond control of the humans who have spent thousands of years devising it. The entire ingenuity from thumbscrew and rack to electric shock, the infinite variety and gradation of suffering, by lash, by fear, by hunger, by solitary confinement—the camps, concentration, labour, resettlement, the Siberias of snow or sun, the lives of Mandela, Sisulu, Mbeki, Kathrada, Kgosana, gull-picked on the Island, Lionel propped wasting to his skull between two warders, the deaths by questioning, bodies fallen from the height of John Vorster Square, deaths by dehydration, babies degutted by enteritis in 'places' of banishment, the lights beating all night on the faces of those in cells—Conrad—I conjure you up, I drag you back from wherever you are to listen to me—you don't know what I saw, what there is to see, you *won't* see, you are becalmed on an empty ocean.

Only when I was level with the cart, across the veld from me, did I make out the whip. The donkey didn't cry out. Why didn't the donkey give that bestial snort and squeal of excruciation I've heard donkeys give not in pain but in rut? It didn't cry out.

It had been beaten and beaten. Pain was no shock, there is no way out of the shafts. That rag of a black man was old, from the stance of his legs, the scraggle of beard showing under an old hat in a shapeless cone over his face. I rolled to a stop beyond what I saw; the car simply fell away from the pressure of my foot and carried me no farther. I sat there with my head turned sharply and my shoulders hunched round my neck, huddled to my ears against the blows. And then I put my foot down and drove on wavering drunkenly about the road, pausing to gaze back while the beating still went on, the force there, cart, terrified woman and child, the donkey and man, bucked and bolted zigzag under the whip. I had only to turn the car in the empty road and drive up upon that mad frieze against the sunset putting out my eyes. When I looked over there all I could see was the writhing black shape through whose interstices poked searchlights of blinding bright dust. The thing was like an explosion. I had only to career down on that scene with my car and my white authority. I could have yelled before I even got out, yelled to stop!—and then there I would have been standing, inescapable, fury and right, might, before them, the frightened woman and child and the drunk, brutal man, with my knowledge of how to deliver them over to the police, to have him prosecuted as he deserved and should be, to take away from him the poor suffering possession he maltreated. I could formulate everything they were, as the act I had witnessed; they would have their lives summed up for them officially at last by me, the white woman—the final meaning of a day they had lived I had no knowledge of, a day of other appalling things, violence, disasters, urgencies, deprivations which suddenly would become, was nothing but what it had led up to: the man among them beating their donkey. I could have put a stop to it, the misery; at that point I witnessed. What more can one do? That sort of old man, those people, peasants existing the only way they know how, in the 'place' that isn't on the map, they would have been afraid of me. I could have put a stop to it, with them, at no risk to myself. No one would have taken up a stone. I was safe from the whip. I could have stood between them and suffering—the suffering of the donkey.

As soon as I planted myself in front of them it would have become again just that—the pain of a donkey.

I drove on. I don't know at what point to intercede makes sense, for me. Every week the woman who comes to clean my flat and wash my clothes brings a child whose make-believe is polishing floors and doing washing. I drove on because the horrible drunk was black, poor and brutalized. If somebody's going to be brought to account, I am accountable for him, to him, as he is for the donkey. Yet the suffering—while I saw it it was the sum of suffering to me. I didn't do anything. I let him beat the donkey. The man was a black. So a kind of vanity counted for more than feeling; I couldn't bear to see myself—her—Rosa Burger—as one of those whites who can care more for animals than people. Since I've been free, I'm free to become one.

I went without saying goodbye to Marisa.

Someone threw a stone, yes. Perhaps one of the little ones with baby brothers or sisters humped on their backs, shouting voetsak! at the dogs, flung a stone not meant for me. If someone did report I'd been at a public meeting with a possible political intention, there were no consequences. Nothing and nobody stopped me from using that passport. After the donkey I couldn't stop myself. I don't know how to live in Lionel's country.

Conrad. I did not tell you before. The yacht was never found. I may have been talking to a dead man: only to myself.

TWO

To know and not to act is not to know.

　　　　　　　　　–Wang Yang-ming –

The silk tent of morning sea tilted, pegged to keyhole harbours where boats nosed domestically like animals at a trough; Vauban's ancient fort squatted out to the water; two S-shaped buildings towered, were foreshortened, leaned this side and that of the wing, rose again. Lavender mountains with a snail-trail spittle of last winter's snow swung a diagonal horizon across the fish-bowl windows. Down to earth, the plane laid itself on the runway as the seagulls (through convex glass under flak of droplets) breasted the sea beside it.

Passengers who disperse from the last step of a plane's stairway all hurry but their oncoming seems slowed, their legs don't carry them, they're seen through the horizontal waverings-away of a telescopic lens. The long last moment before anybody is recognizable: a woman tipped into her mouth the drop of melted sugar settled in the bottom of an espresso thimble and stood at the glass wall. Her eyes held the moving figures, her expression becoming an offering like a bunch of flowers held ready, but her head hawked forward in tense curiosity.

She left the bar and hurried to the little crowd gathered at the barrier before the passport officers' booths. Among the elegant homosexuals with bodies of twenty-year-olds and faces like statues of which only the head remains of the ancient original, the blonde with nipples staring through her shirt, the young man with a Siamese cat on a leash, the well-preserved women wearing gold chains and sharkskin pants attended by husbands and poodles, the demanding American children with wet gilt hair, the black-clad grandmothers borne up emotionally by daughters and the frilly infants held by young fathers in leather jackets, she was the one: rounded knuckles of cheekbone, brilliant blue dabs under clotted

219

lashes, wrinkled made-up lids, tabby hair. The one with the neck rising elegantly although the bosom was big and she was low in the welcoming crowd—stocky, and when they could be seen the legs had the ex-dancer's hard lumpy calves and fleshless ankles.

Her gaze, pushing through the queue bunched behind the immigration booths, setting aside this one from that, passed over once and then returned, singled out. She was watching the approach of a girl sallow and composed with fatigue. The girl had curly hair—dark girl—and a look around the jaw, a set of the mouth (that was it: the woman's expression deepened strongly) although the eyes were clear and light, not what she was looking for.

They had seen each other. The understanding spun a thread along which they were being drawn together while the girl took her turn; almost at the immigration booth, now; now there, putting the green passport on the counter for an official hand to draw under the glass partition; bending suddenly to dig in the bulging sling-bag (a hitch? a document missing?—the woman craned on her toes). The eyes-down face of someone under surveillance. A faint, sideways smile to the woman watching. (Nothing wrong; just the usual traveller's start of anxiety that something has been remembered too late.) The girl was pushing the green passport into a pocket on the outside of the bag. She drew the zip firmly closed. She moved on, she was in: received. Coming across the few yards, through the barrier, the whole of her could be seen clear of other people, small girl with a sexy, ignored body (the mother had always somehow ignored her own beauty, found it of no account) dressed in the inevitable jeans outfit yet never in a thousand years would have passed for one of the young from yachts and hotels and villas wearing the same thing. Pretty. But not young-looking. A face seen on a child who looks like a woman.

The corners of the mouth dented but the lips remained tightly closed, the strangely light eyes were fixed on the woman with an expression of self-amazement, as if the girl doubted her own existence at that moment, in that place.

They had never seen one another before. The woman's worn

lilac-coloured espadrilles splayed sturdily in welcome. She held her arms in a wide tackle and her mouth was parted, smiling, smiling.

The aircraft Rosa Burger boarded was bound for France. The destination on her ticket was Paris but after two nights in a small hotel where she did not unpack she flew back in the direction she had come from, south, to Nice. There she was met on a beautiful May morning by a Madame Bagnelli, who when she was very young had gone to the Sixth Congress in Moscow, had been or tried to be a dancer, was once married to Lionel Burger. She had a son by him living in Tanzania whom she had not seen since he was a student; she took his daughter home to her house in a medieval village, preserved to make money out of tourists, where—the people who had known her in South Africa heard—she had been living for years.

She talked all the way above the noise of the old Citroën into which she settled herself like a sitting hen. There was an impression of speed beyond the car's capacity, because of her style of driving and the jig of windows that opened like flaps. She had had a terrible feeling it was the wrong day—she should have been at the airport yesterday—she had rummaged everywhere to check with the letter—put away too carefully—that was why she was so excited, relieved when she saw—

—You'd given me the phone number.—

—Oh I was afraid if you arrived and I wasn't there—you'd just have gone off again—I was so worried—

Changing from lane to lane of traffic along a sea-front, bursts of conversation in another tongue, scenes from unimaginable lives in the space of a car window and the pause at a red light, palm-trees, whiffs of nougat against carbon monoxide, pink oleanders, fish shining in a shop open to the street, pennants fluttering round a car mart, old men in pomponned caps bending over balls, shop-signs silently mouthed—Oh that—fort, château, same thing, all their castles were fortifications. That's Antibes. We'll go one day—the Picasso museum's inside. Good god, what's he think he's doing, *quel con*, my god, *ça va pas la tête, êh?* These kids on scooters, they attack like wasps. It's twelve o'clock, that's why this town is hell, everyone rushing home for lunch . . . don't worry, we'll make it, I just must stop for bread—are you hungry? I hope you've got a good appetite, mmh?—Would you rather have lettuce or cress? You must say. Start off the way we're going to go on, you know— I'm not going to treat you like a visitor.—

She came out of the baker's and pushed a baton of bread through the window. At the greengrocer next door she turned to smile at her passenger. In the wisp of tissue-paper that belted it, the bread crackled under the pressure of Rosa Burger's hand; she sniffed the loaf like a flower; the woman's smile broadened and mimed—go on, take a bite. Children in pinafores were being dragged past by brusque young women or old ones in slippers who blocked the pavement while they gossiped. On balconies, men ate lunch in their vests. The tables outside a bar were tiny islands round which people greeted each other with a kiss on either cheek. Rosa Burger sat in the car like an effigy borne in procession. Out of the town, past plant nurseries and cement works, the light on the new leaves of vines hunched like cripples, grey-headed olives surviving among villas, the sea appearing and disappearing from bend to bend: —They told me over the phone, a direct plane *tonight* so of course I thought my god I've—then I told myself, stop fussing . . . I'm so glad you've come before the pear and apple's quite over—look— up there, d'you know whose house that is? Renoir lived there—

A frail foam pricked through by green on trees hollowed like wine glasses; where? where? The girl gazed at a day without landmarks. No sooner was something pointed out than it was behind; to the driver all was so familiar she saw what was no longer visible. The car began to buck up a steep gravelly way between the park secrecy of European riverine forest, roadside tapestry flowers ashy with dust. Like the sea, a castle turned this way and that. —Poor things, more tin cans than fish in our river these days, but they keep trying. You actually do see some with a tiddler or two . . .— A child's pop-up picture book castle at the pinnacle of grey and yellow-rose houses and walls, rising from the apartment blocks that filled the valley like vast white ocean liners berthed from the distant sea. Awnings bellied; leaning people were dreamily letting the car pass across their eyes an image like that in the convex mirror set up at the blind intersection. Shutters were closed; unknown people hidden undiscoverable behind there. A woman on a vélo with a child dangling legs through the parcel-carrier was drawn level with, greeted, wobbling and puttering, overtaken. —She does for me, you'll meet her on Tuesday, what hell with that child when it was little, peed on my bed and when it started to crawl! It was into everything, biscuits crumbled on my papers and books— how do you feel? About children? I am a grandmother I suppose, but for me it's so long since I handled . . . How old are you, Rosa? I was thinking last night, how old can she be, that girl—twenty-three? No? Nearer twenty-five? Seven—my god.—

A woman with gold tinsel hair in the sun leaned on a cane to let them pass, a middle-aged man spilling belly over jeans gestured with his pipe, the girl with a smile of oriental persistence held out of the car's way a spaniel dancing about her on its lead: the driver waved to all without looking. —You're in a room at the top, a lot of stairs to climb, I'm warning you—but there's a terrace, the roof of the adjoining house actually but they let me fix it up. I thought you'd like to be able to step out when you wake up in the mornings. Sunbathe, do what you like. Get away from me or anyone, quite private. If you'd rather you can have the smaller room on the first floor?—well, you'll see . . . a jumble of a house like all the houses, the whole village's a warren, every one's built against the next, if my plumbing goes wrong you have to go to the neighbour's to find the leak . . . you'll see, you'll just say if you'd rather come downstairs. But that room adjoins mine; *I* don't mind, but you might . . . we could close off the door between us, of course. The top room used to be Bagnelli's room, when he was home . . . I should tell you, he died four years ago. It was fifteen years. We never actually married, but everyone . . .—

Suddenly the car braked, the forearm tanned with tea-leaf marks went out to stop Rosa from pitching forward.

—Didn't I tell you. So there you are! *The* day, *the* time, everything. Pure nerves. What a state Madame Bagnelli was in

223

about your arrival. I had to dash after her with the eggs she left in the *épicerie* this morning. You don't look too forbidding to me— A man's voice with the precision of an English stage vicar, and a long, thick beardless face under a captain's braided peak bent to the window.

—Yes, safe and sound—Rosa Burger, Constance Darby-Littleton. Are you walking up the hill . . .?—

—Of course I want to walk. It's my constitutional. I thought everyone was perfectly aware of my habits by now— Night-blue slits between puffy lids had no whites, no eyelashes, and moved from driver to passenger like mechanical eyes set in one of those anthropomorphic clock-faces. The car passed on at the level of matron's breasts slung under a checked shirt.

In a parking ground scooped out below trees a fat young Bacchus wearing cement-stained cowboy boots leapt from a pick-up loaded with broken tiles and window-frames. —*Madame Bagnelli*— Loud, indignant and laughing exchange; not necessary to understand the language adequately to be able to follow that this was workman and client taking up some long-standing wrangle. —He came around and couldn't get in! Now isn't that just too bad! How many days I've waited in for nothing! I won't see him for another six weeks and after another dozen phone-calls. He's supposed to put a floor in my *cave*—rather the junk-pit that's hopefully going to be a *cave*. He gets whatever's there.— The car was held on the clutch at the top of the spiral where the road forked at a broken city wall. The castle waved bright handkerchiefs of unidentified nations. The car announced itself with a gay warning blast, turning right. Greasy locks and a beautiful, lover's face were approaching. —*Madame Bagnelli*—the man counted out three letters from his mail-bag and presented them to her; they thanked each other as if for the pleasure of it, using that language. Rosa Burger was presented by a new name with the accent on the final syllable: the friend—all the way from Africa!—who would be getting mail so addressed.

The car swung past the postman into a steep little alley blocked by a studded double gate and she was about to get out to open it for the first time on a house where she was told she would sleep, up flights of stairs, a room with a terrace: for that moment, there was nothing behind that gate with its push-button bell and card under a plastic slot, *Bagnelli*.

—What do I call you?—

—Call me?—

—Do I call you Madame Bagnelli, or— (Colette was the name, 'Colette Swan'. 'Colette Burger'.)

The woman pressed back from arms braced against the steering wheel; she relaxed suddenly, turned her head full on with an expression of sly voluptuous complicity, as if her hand closed on the shy, casual question as on some inert but electrified shape that came to life on contact. —Katya. You call me Katya.—

On the gate there was a note under Scotch tape and a big dried sunflower like a dead burst star. MADAME BAGNELLI URGENT— exclamation mark scored within its outline. The gate dragged screeching across courtyard paving; the smell of stony damp and a perfume never smelled before; and then it brushed Rosa Burger's face as the door was opened, the suitcase bumped through: lilac, real European lilac.

—Dah-dah-dah-dah; dedah—well that can wait. Why the hell should I phone *the moment I come in* . . .— The note flew into a straw basket. —You want to go straight up? No—let's just dump everything. I've got a little (swimming colours, fronds blobbing out of focus and a sea horizon undulating in uneven panes of glass)—just a little something ready—the glass doors shook open, the new arrival was on a leafy shelf of sun, offered to the sea midway between sky and tumbling terraces of little dark trees decorated with oranges. She smelled cats and geranium. The elaborate toy villas of the dead in a steep cemetery took on their façades the light off the sea. She felt it on her cheeks and eyelids. She saw—saw a crack up a white urn that was a line of ants, a tiny boat like a fingernail scored across the sea, saw the varicose vein wriggling up behind the knee of the ex-dancer putting down the tray with the bottle of champagne in a bucket.

They drank leaning together on the balustrade, great open

spaces of the sea drawing away the farting stutter of motorcycles and gear-whine of trucks, music and voices wreathing their own, from other terraces and balconies. Now and then something came tinkling-clear to Rosa Burger: once a man's sudden derisive laugh, the gobbling bark when a dog has a cat treed; a woman's yell to stop someone driving off. These shattered lightly against her; her palm felt the still cold of the glass and her tongue the live cold of the wine. They sat in tilted chairs with their feet up on the balustrade among falls of geranium and ice-plant drowsy with big European bees in football stripes. The woman toed off the heel of each espadrille and ran the arch of her bare foot over the head and back of a Manx cat. (—Not mine but he likes me better than his owner.—) Out of her boots Rosa's feet were released cramped and marked, her jeans were pushed up to the knee. The woman was telling the history of the village with the enjoyment of one who projects herself into the impression it must have for someone who has never seen anything like it before. —A nobility of robber barons, from the crusades to the casinos, a suzerainty—do I mean sovereignty—these weren't kings— They laughed together in seraglio ease. —Feudal exploitation (these terms slipped in as an old soldier will use the few phrases he remembers from a foreign campaign, when he meets a native of that country) right up to the time of the French revolution. That big garden with the cypress and fig, here behind us, just below the castle, you must have noticed the trees as we drove—it was a monastery. My friend Gaby Grosbois' house is part of the monks' pig-sties. But after the revolution the new industrial entrepreneurs and businessmen bought up these church properties for nothing and used them as their country houses, they lived like the aristocrats. During our war the Resistance in this part of the country had its headquarters in the cellars. Oh you'll hear all the tales, they love to have someone who hasn't heard them before—everyone a hero of the Resistance, if you want to believe—but a few years ago—Bagnelli was still alive, no; just after—it was going to be made into an hotel, some actor was interested in the investment. It came to nothing. Now it belongs to an arms dealer, not that they ever come here, no one sees them . . . the old Fenouil couple keep up the garden. The suzerain changes his nationality . . . Japanese are the ones buying up big properties here now; North Africans are the serfs making roads and living in their *bidonville*—squatters. And people like me (laughing)—we manage to survive in between.— Again and again, the cat slid under the high-arched foot. —I can imagine how you've been brought up (eyes closed and smiling face tilted back into the sun a moment) . . . here you forget about degrees of social usefulness—good god, nobody would understand what on earth I'm talking about. But on the other hand I suppose you'll be surprised at the way anybody will do anything; no question that what you do's infra dig— Back and forth the cat raked by maroon-painted toenails. —I cook for Americans sometimes, in the summer—I know the kind of French food they like. Solvig pays me to vacuum her books and pack away her winter clothes once a year. She's a friend, but she's the widow of a big Norwegian publisher, she's got money, and so . . . I look after the local hardware shop when the owner goes skiing for her two weeks every January. Cold little hole, selling toilet rolls and plastic dishes . . . when the French are concentrating on making money they make no attempt to be comfortable. Other friends, a Greek painter and his boy-friend—they take jobs at the race-course when the trotting season starts. But women aren't hired. Oh I patch up old furniture—'restore antiques'—sounds better, eh. Sometimes I get a chance to give English lessons—I taught dancing at the Maison des Jeunes until I got so heavy the floorboards quaked.—

—And your husband? What was he?—

—Bagnelli?— A long-drawn ah-h-h-h, amused, the touching on things that couldn't be explained even in the easy lucidity of wine and fine weather, in half-an-hour's understanding. —D'you know what he was when I met him—a captain in the French navy. In Toulon. But here, oh he did a lot of things up and down the coast, a wine agency, once it was motor-racing, a tin mine in Brazil—oh lord. And always yachts, yachts—he had shares in them, or was promised shares in them, he sailed them for other people, he even designed them—

—I shared a cottage with someone who planned to go round the world. But to see a yacht being built in a backyard four hundred miles from the sea—

—You?— The smiling woman allowed herself to look at the girl as she had wanted to since she first settled recognition upon her at the airport.

Dissolving in the wine and pleasure of scents, sights and sounds existing only in themselves, associated with nothing and nobody, Rosa Burger's sense of herself was lazily objective. The sea, the softly throbbing blood in her hands lolling from the chair-arms, time as only the sundial of the wall's advancing shadow, all lapped tidelessly without distinction of within or around her. —Like someone in prison. Everything it might do or be—but it couldn't function. Locked. Landlocked.—

—You never saw it launched? When they slip into the sea—oh yes, it's true, marvellous, it's a coming to life—I used to cry— The woman produced liquid brilliance in her eyes, a past seductiveness. The carefully-oiled and tanned flesh between her breasts wrinkled shinily under the pressure of folded arms like a skin forming on cooling fatty liquid. —Tell me—did you know me? Or—(the girl's down-turned considering smile)—of course you saw I was the one who'd recognized who you were and so—I mean have you ever seen a photograph?—

—When I went through Lionel's things. There were one or two taken in England and in Russia. Damn it—I should have brought them. The Soviet Union ones—one can recognize them at once, even if the background doesn't give much indication. The same with those of my mother; you know Ivy Terblanche? And Aletta?—

—Oh I knew them all, all of them. So long ago!—

—My mother with Aletta on a railway station, holding flowers. You can see at once which are the Russian ones—you all look so exalted.—

—Yes, yes.— A wailing laugh. —Like pop-star fans. Come. The last drop between us. Although it's warm by now. Warm champagne makes you drunk.— She sat with her knees apart and her belly forgetfully rolling forward. —Moscow, Moscow, Moscow! I auditioned with the Maryinsky, you know. What a wonderful time we had. Too late, too old, nineteen or twenty, lazy already—but they took a fancy to us and what a time we had. Their parties went on all night; you breathe vodka like a dragon, after. I had to ask the maid in the hotel to change the pillow-cases—they gave back vodka fumes just from our breathing. We missed whole sessions of their bloody Congress; well, one whole session . . . Lionel—that father of yours—(a pause, genuine or assumed, of incredulity, looking at the girl lying in the chair) he gave them a most convincing yarn about having to sit up all night preparing papers for a committee, what a reputation for Party diligence but it started with a different kind of party . . . You look like him. In spite of the eyes. You wouldn't be able to judge, because you think of him as he is—was. But then in Moscow . . . I see it while I look at you! You know, when you have lived with different men, lived a long time, like me, you'd be surprised, you forget what they really were like. When I wrote to you when he died, it was a public figure that I . . . looking at you I see that: because here he is as he really was, in Moscow. Like your father . . . but I think—I should say, after being with you for exactly—what?—one-and-a-half hours—after this long acquaintance, my dear Rosa, I would say you are more your mother. Yes. I didn't know her well—although in the Party we all 'slept in each other's underwear' (I'll never forget: someone once shocked us stiff by telling us that, someone who'd been expelled, *naturally*—I'll never forget the blasphemy against the comrades!). How could I know her well—anyway, she was so young. It must have been round about 1941. Your mother was simply—at once—my idea of a revolutionary.—

She was looking at her daughter, the girl smiling, fending off with a languid fascination the play of attention that quickly shifted again.

—Me in a cloche hat? Down to my eyebrows? Oh my god— The body squatted, spread-kneed, as if on the lavatory; nowhere to be found in this woman the marmoset face showing itself out of fur hat and fur collar, the slim pointed shoes lined up beside Lionel

Burger's outside the hotel bedroom. Laughter and chatter trailing behind or bursting ahead, the solid, over-blown figure came and went, preparing food, between rooms vague and dark with objects not yet seen as more than shapes, and the radiance, the sweet hum of the village, on the terrace. The innocence and security of being open to lives all around was the emotion to which champagne and more wine, drunk with the meal, attached itself. All about Rosa Burger, screened only by traceries of green and the angles of houses, people sat eating or talking, fondling, carrying out tasks— a man planing wood and a couple leaning close in deep discussion, and the susurration of voices was as little threatened by exposure as the swish of shavings curling. People with nothing to hide from, no one to elude, careless of privacy, in their abundance: letting be. The food was delicious and roused a new pleasure, of greed. Rosa Burger had not known she could want to eat so much; but the Manx cat sniffed the fish-bones fragrant with herbs as an everyday offering. An Englishwoman came in the tight little hat, chiffon scarf and gloves of one who keeps up some bygone standard. She forestalled any possibility that she was unwelcome by the air of having her mind on more important matters than her friend's guest, and being too busy to be expected to stay. —I've an appointment at the bank.—

—You know the bank doesn't open till three. Come on, Alice—

—Not just the bank. There are plenty of things I have to see to.—

—Such as, for instance?—

—Don't pry into my affairs, Katya.—

Madame Bagnelli laughed, pouring coffee. —Ah, if you had any, Alice, I'd be dying of curiosity. Here, just as you like it, strong, in a thin cup. We saw Darby on the way to her liquid lunch.—

—In the bar tabac?—

—No, on the hill.—

—Oh yes. She must have been down to the *aide sociale* office about her rent.—

—Not on a Tuesday. Thursday's for interviews.—

—What's today? Are you sure? Well perhaps she went to the

clinic. She never tells when there's something wrong. Likes to think she's not flesh and blood like the rest of us. But I notice how she's short of breath on the stairs. I can hear her when she goes past my door up to the second flight.—

—And who else did I see, before I went to the airport—Françoise, yes, Françoise *without* Marthe, trying to make up her mind whether to buy sardines at five francs a kilo. She didn't see me.—

—Oh Marthe's in Marseilles. Didn't you know? For three days. She came round to ask if she could do anything for us, there. Darby said some of those green peppercorns we had last time.—

—Well she probably phoned. I've been in and out—Rosa coming. But you can get them here, why bother?—

—Not the Madagascar kind.—

—Yes, the Madagascar ones. In the shop behind the post office. Yes, yes, right there, Monsieur Harbulot has them. *Exactly* the same, I assure you.—

—Well I'm not so sure. Have you seen Georges?—

—They've gone to Vintimille to buy shoes. And some place where they get their olive oil. Manolis doesn't like any other.—

—He's lucky if Georges can afford to indulge his whims, that's all I can say.—

—Donna and Didier went along.—

—What for?—

Madame Bagnelli appealed to her house-guest against the absurdity of the question. —For the ride. For fun.—

—Spoiling that boy, too. Just as she did the others. You'll see.—

A French voice flew through the house like a trapped cuckoo. Another woman arrived and the same sort of conversation continued in French. The first woman stopped in the doorway to talk another five minutes. —Well, I hope you enjoy your holiday or whatever it is. Did Darby meet her, this morning?—

—Of course, for a moment. Why?—

With the Englishwoman hardly out of earshot Madame Bagnelli was explaining: —Wanted to be the one to tell Darby she'd met the girl at Katya's—did you see that!— It was repeated in French and she and the Frenchwoman rose to a heightened pitch of laughter, each cutting across the comments of the other. There was an anxious attempt at English now and then. —But *you* have the beautiful sunshine too, êh . . . it's a wonderful country? I know. I like to go there, but— The Frenchwoman pulled the enchanting face of a woman twenty years younger and rubbed first-finger and thumb together. The two women then fell into a discussion about money, serious and with twitches of pain in the expression about their mouths, calculations reeled off in which Rosa distinguished only *milles* and *cents* colliding along chains of hyphens as the bees did sottishly round the dregs of wine. A young man had appeared; she turned her chair away from the sun, and found the battlements of the castle up there behind her in the sky, the flags luminous as stained glass, and down in the indoor shadowy hush of the house was aware that one of the objects detached itself and moved into human shape. She saw him eavesdropping before he made himself known. Out in the light of the terrace, he had come upon them all on bare feet, tightly bound in blinding white pants to just below the navel and naked above it. Two sea-pumiced brown hands over Madame Bagnelli's eyes and she seemed to know the touch instantly.

—But you're in Vintimille—What happened?—

He bent round to her face and kissed her, then ceremoniously, leisurely, went over to bend to the face of the Frenchwoman. When he had kissed her she took his face in her palms and said something whose cadence was adoring and admiring, motherly-lustful.

—What are you doing here? Didier!—

He leaned against the balustrade before his audience. —I didn't go.— In a dark-tanned face the nostrils had the pink rawness of one who has been diving.

—And Donna?—

—She went.—

—Didier? But why?—

The Frenchwoman said of the lost opportunity, things were so much cheaper over the border in Vintimille; he had seen the leather coat Manolis got there last winter?

—Didier? What've you been doing all day alone, then?—

—Fishing. Spear-fishing. You don't need anyone to do it with.—

They were introduced but he didn't address himself to Rosa Burger. The questions and comments of the women fawned round him inquisitively and appreciatively; he seemed not to address anyone, eyeing himself in an accompanying vision of himself, like a mirror. He went purposefully about the table under the awning finding morsels he ate quickly, licking his fingers. He waved down offers to fetch something more for him to eat; wiped round the salad bowl, soaking bread in the oil, served himself cheese wrapped in straw, with a certain professional deftness. His dark cloudy blue eyes under lashes so long he seemed to trail them on his cheeks, his chewing jaw, followed the return of the women's talk to the subject of taxes. Now and then he put in an objection or correction; they argued. He belched, hit flat belly-muscles, ran fine hands over smooth pectorals. They laughed: —Like that cat, Didier. Come for titbits and just stalk off.— He was embracing the women again, swinging gracefully from one to the other. He said goodbye to the girl in English used in the casual manner of an habitual tongue but with a marked French and slight American accent.

—When are they coming back?—

The voice was caught before the slam of the door. —How should I know?—

—Naughty boy! What are you sulking about?— Madame Bagnelli yelled, bold and laughing, out of range. She performed a little caper of activity and swooped on the table, scooping up dishes, emptying bees and dregs among the flower-urns. The Frenchwoman left. They tidied away the remains of the meal, lingering in the cool livingroom to talk, Madame Bagnelli's voice flitting without cease from where she bent into the refrigerator in the kitchen, or sank suddenly, legs crossed at the ankle balletically, to a little sofa. Her guest had opened the suitcase and brought out the offerings that are part of the ritual of arrival. The girl eyed them warily now that they had found their recipient—safe options chosen for someone not known, they might seem only to do for *anybody*, the interchangeable airport gifts she herself had had her share of, all the years she had stayed at home. Only one suggested a particular being imagined, asserted associations that might not exist, or might be unwelcome: a double necklace of finely-carved hexagonal wooden spools separated by cheap store beads.

The woman looked at it looped in her hands; quickly at Rosa Burger; at the necklace, and parted a bead from a spool. —See what they're strung on. What's it called . . . that palm . . . *Ilala*. Ilala palm thread spun by rolling the fibres up and down on your bare thigh. I've seen them do it. Look, not cotton! Ilala palm— She broke into pleased pride at the verification, identification in herself. —And the wood—don't say, wait— His daughter stood there before her. —Tambuti. Yes? That scent! It's Tambuti.—

—I think so. They're the things the Herero women wear. There's a shop . . . very occasionally you find something—

—It's from Namibia—even the Afrikaners don't call it South West anymore, eh?— She wandered round her livingroom considering the disposition of a strange blood-dark head of Christ on leather embossed in flaky gold, staring almond eyes; a picture of a nude girl with an eel or other sea-monster mutilated beside her; a great iron key; jagged with age and an ancient fervour that had hacked it from the whole, a fragment of a rigid wooden saint raising a pleated hand and upright finger over the fireplace. She hung the necklace from a candle-bracket marbled thick with the lava of wax. —When I'm not wearing it, I want to enjoy seeing it.—

—The day before yesterday's. I thought you might like to— Rosa Burger hesitated before dumping along with crumpled wrappings the South African newspaper that had been standing up from her bag when the woman first singled her out.

—Good god. How many years . . .— Madame Bagnelli sank down holding the paper at arm's length. —Same old mast-head . . . In the kitchen, you'll see a pair of specs. Probably on the shelf where the coffee-grinder . . . on the fridge or *in* the fridge— sometimes I take something out and put them down without . . .— She dismissed herself with a twirl of fingers. —You were still there. Only the day before yesterday.— She was looking at Rosa Burger as at someone whose existence she, too, could not believe in. His daughter wagged her head slowly; they were together. —Have you ever been out before?—

The head weaved, making its way, setting aside in the soft confusion of wine all that had been emerged from.

—Never.—

—Of course *never*.—

—And you have never been back.—

The woman drew her elbows against her body, rocked herself cherishingly, fists together under her chin, the newspaper fell. —Ah, they wouldn't get me. Never.—

She sprang up on her wide-planted feet; balance and agility contradicted bulk. —Can we do the monkey-trick? Up my staircase, swing by tails—

There was scarcely room for her to pass between wall and wall with a thick silky cord, a theatre prop, swagged up one in place of a rail. As she led she was explaining how to manage some eccentricity of the hot-water tap in the bathroom; she panted cheerfully.

At the top was a room clear with different qualities of light. It brimmed against the ceiling; underneath, patterns and forms showed shallowly ribbed. A big jar of lilac, scent of peaches furry in a bowl, dim mirrors, feminine bric-a-brac of bottles and brushes, a little screen of ruched taffeta for sociable intimacies, a long cane chair to read the poetry and elegant magazines in, a large low bed to bring a lover to. It was a room made ready for someone imagined. A girl, a creature whose sense of existence would be in her nose buried in flowers, peach juice running down her chin, face tended at mirrors, mind dreamily diverted, body seeking pleasure. Rosa Burger entered, going forward into possession by that image. Madame Bagnelli, smiling, coaxing, saw that her guest was a little drunk, like herself.

If I'd been black that would at least have given the information I was from Africa. Even at a three-hundred-year remove, a black American. But nobody could see me, there, for what I am back where I come from. Nobody in Paris—except, of course, there's the cousin. The daughter of Auntie Velma and Uncle Coen, with whom I share our grandmother's name. She was in Paris, with me, selling South African oranges somewhere in these buildings flaring to a prow from diminishing perspectives where two streets merge V-shaped, in my single evening, walking them. I could have looked up the Citrus Board under its French title in the directory. The boerevrou with her tour group's pin beside me in the plane remarked as we chatted in our language, it's a great pity we Afrikaners don't travel enough. Stick-at-homes, she said. True, for one reason or another. She at forty-three (she confessed) and I at twenty-seven (she asked) going to Europe for the first time.

I knew from books and talk of people like Flora and William I was in the quarter tourists went to because the nineteenth-century painters and writers whose lives and work have been popularized romantically once lived there. Thousands of students seem to occupy their holes of hotels and haunts now, blondes and gypsies in displayed poverty the poor starve to conceal, going in fishermen's boots or barefoot through the crowds, while back on Uncle Coen's farm people save shoes for Sundays. Girls and men whose time is mine, talking out their lives the way clocks tick, buying tiny cups of coffee for the price of a bag of mealie-meal, drinking wine in the clothes of guerrillas surviving in the bush on a cup of water a day. Dim stairs, tiny bent balconies, endless dovecotes of dormer windows were nearly all dark; everyone in the streets. I walked where they walked, I turned where they turned, taking up

236

the purpose of these or those for a few yards or a block. They met and kissed, kissed and parted, ate thin pancakes made in a booth glaring as a forge, bought papers, paraded for a pick-up. If students play charades, there were surely others wearing the garb playing at being students, and still others wanting to be taken for their idea of models, actors, painters, writers, film directors. Which were the clerks and waiters off duty? How could I tell. Only the male prostitutes, painted and haughty enough to thrill and intimidate prospective clients, are plainly what they are: men preserving the sexual insignia of the female, creature extinct in the preferences of their kind. One went up and down before the café where I sat with the drink I bought myself. He wore a long jade-green suede coat open on a bare midriff with a silver belt round it and his face of inhumanly stylized beauty was a myth. If I had been a man I would have approached just to see if words would come from it as from any ordinary being.

The Boulevard Saint-Michel was my thread back to the hotel with its cosmetic gilt-and-glass foyer and old-clothes cupboard of a room with the bidet smelling of urine. I kept wandering down side streets to the sight of eddies of people in the soft coloured light from little restaurants and stalls of bright sticky sweetmeats and lurid skewers of meat. Under the sagging, bulging buildings of this Paris along streets that streamed into one another was a kind of Eastern bazaar; more my idea of a souk, where also I have never been. Bouzouki music wound above the heads of people in sociable queues outside small cinemas burrowed into existing buildings. The cobbled streets with beautiful names were closed to traffic; from the steep end of one called Rue de la Harpe, a crowd pressed back to form an open well down which I looked on a man from whose mouth flames leapt and scrolled in a fiery proliferation of tongues. I was moved into the crowd, kneaded slowly along by the shifting of shoulders. There were still heads in front of me but I could see the man with his anxious, circus-performer's eyes sizing up the audience while he turned himself into a dragon with a swill of petrol and a lighted faggot. He pranced up and down my patch of vision between collars, necks and the swing of hair. I was enclosed in this amiable press of strangers, not a mob because they were not brought together by hostility or enthusiasm, but by mild curiosity and a willingness to be entertained. I couldn't easily move on until their interest loosened, but closeness was not claustrophobic. Our heads were in the open air of a melon-green night; buoyed by these people murmuring and giggling in their quick, derisive, flirtatious language, I could look up at the roof-tops and chimney-pots and television aerials so black and sharp and one-dimensional they seemed to ring out the note of a metal bar struck and swallowed into the skies of Paris. Close to bodies I was comfortably not aware of individually and that were not individually aware of me, I instantly was alive to the slight swift intimacy of a movement directed only to me. As swiftly, my hand went down to that flutter of a caress; I seized, as it slid out between the flap of my sling-bag and my hip, a hand.

I held very tightly.

The fingers were pressed together extended helpless and the knuckle bones bent inwards across the palm to the curve of my grip, unable to make a fist. The arm above the hand could not jerk it free because the arm was pressed shoulder to shoulder with me, the body to which the arm belonged was jammed against mine.

Still locked to that hand I couldn't see, I turned to find the face it must belong to. Among this crowd of strangers in this city of Europe, among Frenchmen and Scandinavians and Germans and Japanese and Americans, blue eyes and curly blondness, Latin pallor, the lethargic Lebanese and dashing Greeks, the clear and delicate-skulled old Vietnamese who had passed me unseeingly, the Arabs with caps of dull springy hair, pale brown lips and almost Scottish rosiness on the cheekbones whom I had identified as I heard their oracular gabble on the streets I walked—among all these a black man had been edged, pushed, passed along to my side. The face was young and so black that the eyes, far-apart in taut openings, were all that was to be made out of him. Eyeballs of agate in which flood and volcanic cataclysms are traced; the minute burst blood-vessels were held in the whites like a fossil-pattern of fern. If he hadn't been black he might have succeeded in looking like everybody else—sceptically or boredly absorbed in the spectacle of the fire-eater. But the face could not deny the hand in anonymous confusion with like faces. He was what he was. I was what I was, and we had found each other. At least that is how it seemed to me—this ordinary matter of pickpocket and victim, that's all, nothing but a stupid tourist with a bag, deserving to be discovered.

A twinge moved a muscle beside the straight, wide-winged nose. I pretended to be innocent of staring at the face of a stranger. He had round his thin neck with pimples like gravel under the silver-black skin there, a chain with an animal tooth bobbing with his heart-beat, one of the bits of home I'd seen blacks like him selling, all day, bean-necklaces and crude masks and snakeskin wallets, shaking West African rattles in the Tuileries to attract custom. I heard or felt something drop. I said to him—I don't know what—and it was in English, of course, or maybe in Afrikaans (because that was what I had spoken on the plane and my tongue was still coupled with that speech centre). He wouldn't have understood, anyway, even if he had not been deaf with fear, because I was not speaking in French or Fulani or whatever it was would have meaning for him. And if I had appealed to the people around us—they wouldn't have understood either. I didn't know the French, didn't have the words to explain the hand in mine.

I let go. I let him go. He couldn't run.

Somehow I managed to butt down and feel for my purse or wallet of traveller's cheques or passport. I brought up from among feet a little black book; he had felt for leather, and come up with the address book in which, anyway, I have been trained to record nothing more valuable than the whereabouts of hotels and American Express offices. We were still close. His fear of me melted to a presence of connivance and contempt; because if I wouldn't denounce him while I held him, no one need believe me now that I had set him free. It was a secret between us, among them; a ridiculous position we were in, until leisurely—he couldn't hurry like a thief—he made himself appear to be pushed again, to drift on, moving thin shoulders swinging in a tenth-hand aspiration, someone's once-plum-coloured jacket with the hunched cut I'd seen that day on sharp young Frenchmen dressed as they thought the rich and successful did.

I went by way of Paris not to lead to you: my father's first wife. Brandt Vermeulen didn't think of her when he was making sure I'd understood whom I was expected to keep clear of. Yet no one who has ever been associated with my father will ever be off the list of suspects that is never torn up. If it could have occurred to anyone hers was the village, the house, she the one for whom I would make when they let me out—but who remembers her?

I feel an ass, among them: thinking how I came among these people who know such tactics only in their television *policiers* (the old Lesbians are addicts); for whom running down to the baker is a sociable act by which everyone else knows what time they've got up for breakfast, and whose contact with the police is an exchange of badinage about the inside story of the latest bank hold-up in Nice while they stand together with their midday pernods in Jean-Paul's bar. Out of place: not I, myself—they assume my life is theirs, they've taken me in. But the manner of my coming—it doesn't fit necessity or reality, here. Lionel Burger's first wife. You are not to be found in Madame Bagnelli, their Katya. I could see that the particular form of baptism by which she got that name came back to her when I asked, the first day at the gate (before I'd seen my lovely room, this cool belfry of a house where their voices fly around) what I should call her. For them you're Katya because in a small community of different and sometimes confused European origins mixed with the native French, diminutives and adaptations of names are a cosy *lingua franca*.

I suppose for them the name places you vaguely among the White Russians. Like old Ivan Poliakoff whose love stories you type at four francs a page. When I met him, with you in the village, he kissed my hand, lifting it in one so frail I felt the blood pushing slowly through the veins. I ask what the stories are about? Such a very old man, one can't imagine he can remember what it was like—love, sex. You tell me you have suggested he write romantic historical stuff about the affairs of counts and countesses, Russian aristocrats, using the setting of the great country estates where he spent his childhood.

—At least the background would be something he knows. But no, his characters are groupies who get picked up by American film actors at the Cannes Festival or teenage heroin addicts who are saved by devoted pop-singers. He thinks he's learnt the vocabulary from telly—hopeless, the manuscripts come straight back. And then he expects me to lower my rate to three francs!—

People here don't know I'm as removed from young life around the Cannes Film Festival as the ancient Russian count who won't tell his age. —What's a groupie?—

Their Katya's complaining about Poliakoff becomes a performance she improvises along our laughter. —Look at the handwriting. Need a bloody code expert to unhook his G's from E's—a *wire* cutter never mind a magnifying glass—can you believe it? B's like those old-fashioned carpet-beaters—and on top of everything he writes in bed at night after he's put his face-pack on—d'you see! page all smeared with cucumber milk or yoghurt and egg-yolk or whatever it is he concocts—sometimes I just make up a sentence myself to fill in, *Delphine sniffs cocaine from Marcel's manly armpit*, he doesn't notice the difference . . . more likely sees I've improved the thing and too jealous to admit—

—What's a groupie, anyway—

—You know. One of those girls who follow singers and actors around. Tear the shirts off their backs. Or they just worship with fixed eyes—Ivan's do.—

I giggle with *their Katya* like the adolescent girls at school, who were in that phase while Sipho Mokoena was showing Tony and me the bullet hole in his trouser-leg and I was running back and forth to visit prison, the first prison, where my mother was. The oriental-looking head of Christ that is half-painted, half-stamped on leather is a present from Ivan Poliakoff—the first ikon I have ever seen. You took me to an exhibition of famous ones on loan from the Hermitage in Leningrad; Gregorian chants were being relayed as we spent a whole morning looking at the face of the pale and swarthy outcast. You said, He's so beautiful I could believe in him. In some examples his crown of thorns was spiked with red jewels, to represent blood, I suppose. A beige-and-white couple whose silk clothes suggested they were worn once and thrown away, examined the rubies and garnets close-up, silent, she with a pair of half-lens gilt glasses, passing the catalogue between their hands soft and clean as new kid gloves, clustered with gold. Coming around behind us was a young American with an arm along his wife's nape, a baby in a seat on his back and a five- or six-year-old by the hand. He showed the little boy the Christian mask that represents the world's suffering the way Japanese masks represent various states of being, in the theatre. —See Kimmie, that's our Lord, he probably looked a whole lot more like that than the man with blue eyes and blond hair they show you in Grade School.—

Then we went to swim at one of the coves between Antibes and Juan les Pins Katya's friends regard as their own preserve, keeping among yourselves the difficult and unexpected way to get down, trespassing and scrambling past restaurant dustbins. I could lead anyone, by now. We pooled our picnic lunch with Donna and Didier. It was the last time this summer they would come there, she said, the Swedes and Germans arrive after the middle of June; one will have to swim off-shore from the yacht. She's very orderly-minded; impulse does not rule this woman who can do whatever she likes. I gather from conversations she sails to the Bahamas in November, goes skiing in January, and likes to travel somewhere she hasn't been before—in the East, or Africa, say, for a month late in the European summer. She's surprised I don't know the African countries where she has gone game-watching and sight-seeing. She talks about them and I listen along with the other Europeans like Gaby Grosbois, for whom Africa is a holiday they can't afford. It's not possible to say how old this Donna is—again something she has determined with all her resources, the great-granddaughter of a

Canadian railway millionaire, you tell me: this woman with long, pale red crinkly hair tied back from a handsome, naked face, a shine of bright down around the mouth and lower cheeks in the sun, has the same kind of frontier background I have. The Burgers were trekking to the Transvaal when the great-grandfather was laying rails across Indian territory. It's an accident of birth, that's all, whether one has a grandfather who has chosen a country where his descendants can become rich and not question the right, or whether it turns out to be one where the patrimony consists of discovering for oneself by what way of life the right to belong there must be earned by each succeeding generation, if it can be earned at all. I suppose her hair has faded. There may even be white strands blended into its thickness, one wouldn't notice. She is probably forty-five or more, once a big pink-faced girl who still has mannish dimples poked reddening into the parentheses enclosing her smile. Sometimes when she is following what someone is saying to her she bares her teeth without smiling, a mannerism like a pleased snarl. I notice this habit because it's the only sign of the strong sexuality I would expect to find in a woman who feels the need to buy a young lover. You and Gaby—Madame Bagnelli and Madame Grosbois—agree that this one is the best she's had, not 'a little bitch' (you use the derogatory inversions of Lesbian friends) like Vaki the Greek, his predecessor.

What happened to Vaki-the-Greek?

I pipe up from time to time, like a child listening to folk-lore. I am beginning to understand that there is a certain range of possibilities that can occur within the orbit of a particular order of life; they recur in gossip, in close conversations at the tables big enough only for elbows in the back of Jean-Paul's bar, in noisy discussions on the terrace of this one's house or that. Vaki-the-Greek went off to South America with the director of a German electronics company he picked up here in the village, on the *place*, Darby witnessed the whole thing and told Donna after the little bitch had disappeared with the Alfa Romeo that had been registered in *his* name, for *her* tax reasons. Didier is straight (I don't know whether by this is meant not bisexual) and although he rightly expects to be treated generously, he's not likely to be a thief—never! —When he goes, he'll just go.— Gaby approves, endorsing Katya.

Didier knows his job. How to please them; all of you. How to please Donna, although that may require some skill, at times he opts out of the company, sets up in the ivory tower of his youth to remind her of his confinement, at other times he is a shrewd and haughty personal aide confronting the garage over the price charged for repairs, going with her to argue with her lawyers—whatever the relationship is between them, I notice it is never so smoothly bonded as when we meet them either before or after one of their sessions with the lawyers, sharing the same preoccupation as other lovers would fondle under a table. And there are the occasions, perfectly timed, when I see him turn and go back to the room he is leaving as with some premonition of the significance of the moment, to kiss her once, on the mouth, holding her gravely by the upper arms. She is never the one to make the move to fondle him in public. That must be one of the unspoken arrangements between them, to save her face before other women? By some sound instinct he knows when to make the move towards her that she cannot allow herself to make towards him.

His professionalism extends to me. He and Donna exchange the left-and-right cheek-greeting with me as everyone else has been doing since my first few days in your house but he doesn't flirt with me as he does with women older than Donna. Heterosexual or Lesbian, you all belong to a category that cannot challenge her. That's the code. There was that particularly hot day when Donna's yacht was being painted and he decided to come with us to swim from one of the beaches too polluted for her. Katya, Madame Grosbois, Solvig—he lies among them safe from demands as they are. If I try to describe him to myself in a word it's to call him precocious—a boy at home with preoccupations on the other side of test and struggle. To be made rich is ageing, if you are young. On the beach, even the sexuality of his body, the curve of his genitals making a shield of the white trunks, was not aggressive. The Norwegian lady took off her bikini bra, Madame Grosbois displayed a belly puckered and loosened by child-bearing long ago. His body's presence didn't shame any of you. I begin to see here that modesty's really a function of vanity. When the body is no longer an attraction, an expression of desire, to bare your breasts and belly is simple; you lay like old dogs or cats grateful for the sun. No offence was meant.

We swam the waveless peacock-shaded sea, Rosa, Didier, Katya—you talking and calling and flinging away from yourself bits of floating plastic board as if you believe, like an early navigator, somewhere there is an edge of the world over which they'll be carried and break the global cycle by which what you rid yourself of returns. You tired and floated; Didier and I swam on round a small headland into a stripe of deep blue and came ashore among rocks, where I cut my toe on a sardine-tin. Threadworms of blood came from me in the water; when I took my foot out, from under an eyelid of skin red pain runnelled. I hopped over the pebbles. It hadn't hurt after the first stab, in the water, but now it was seared by the air. We examined my toe together; blood; the reminder of vulnerability, life always under the threat of being spilled. A little ceremony of blood-brotherhood, every time.

—We need something to tie.— He was very severe.

Well, two people in a bikini and trunks; we didn't have it. I smiled—it would be all right, the water would wash out the cut well on the swim back.

I must hold the foot high to reverse the flow. I said no, no, it was all right, the chill of the water would staunch it.

—But it hurts you, no?— Water was shaken on him where he crouched with my foot between his knees. The sprinkle on his face already dried stiff in the sun came from my hair, he called —Hey!—flashed me a squinting annoyed look against the light. My toe disappeared from the exposure to pain; I felt it surrounded by gentle warmth and softness. Because his head was ducked I felt before I saw that he had my toe in his mouth. Ridiculous— ridiculous at the same time as sensual, as so many sensual moves are, if you set yourself outside them. But it was done with such confidence I understood it as I was meant to.

As he squatted there before me I saw and felt his head, his tongue as if it were between my legs—he knew it.

—My dirty foot! I walked all round the valley early this morning.—

—How can it be dirty, your foot—out of the sea, Rôse, tell me— He held it between his palms like a rabbit or a bird, and he knew he was holding it to suggest this.

—Come on Didier. We must swim back.—

He mimicked. —Come on Didier, we must go—Rôse, it's true your feet are a bit broad, peasant feet, but you have a beautiful navel, it's really like the one on the top of an orange—now why do you pull your face, why shouldn't we laugh together—Rôse—

—Didier, not with me.—

—With you?—

—You don't have to.—

—What do you mean, don't have to. I don't have to do anything. I do what I feel.—

—I put it badly.—

—Rôse, you are talking—what are you talking.—

—You know. If a new woman turns up—a girl, among the friends, you . . . it's like being nice to the older women; appropriate—

—But we're young, Rôse— He seems sometimes to take up lines of dialogue he has heard in television serials. —Mnh? It's natural, êh. We are the only young ones!—what's the matter with you?—

I said to this strange being, as if I knew him: —You think it's wrong then, with Donna, unnatural—making love, living with her?—

He frowned sceptically.

—Because she's so much older? A sacrifice? She owes you something?—

—What? Donna is a generous woman.—

—Me. Owes me to you.—

He made a mouth like the mouths of cherubs blowing the four winds in the Italian pictures in Solvig's collection. They tell me this part of France was Italian a hundred years ago; I see faces I

247

thought belonged to the eighteenth or nineteenth century. —She doesn't expect I should not like girls. She must understand, êh. She likes a young man.—

If I am curious about them, these people, to me it seems they allow me to be so because I am a foreigner. But I see it's that they are not afraid of being found out, the nature of their motives is shared and discussed; because the premise is accepted by everybody: live where it's warm, buy, sell or take pleasure honestly—that is, according to your circumstances. They recognize their only imperatives as dependence on a tight-knotted net of friendship, and dedication to avoiding tax wherever possible while using all the state welfare one can contrive to qualify for—the rebates, allocations, grants and pensions they are always discussing, whether rich or poor. —So it's all right, then?—

He was still playing with my foot, but one of the grey beach pebbles would have been the same, to his hand. —It's fine. We go along very well together. She's a good business woman, you know. She looks after her money.— (Doesn't he know about Vaki the Greek? Of course he does; what went wrong there is regarded by him as a calculated risk in relations of the category of hers with Vaki and himself: I'm learning.) —She knows how to enjoy it. I've been around the world. We go wherever we like.—

—And it's your whole life?—

—Oh, I'll do other things. I've got ideas.—

His sulks are a ploy, then, something to bring Donna to an edge of apprehension about holding him. He feels free, this kept boy: free to be one.

—Things you'd be doing if you weren't with her.—

—Not necessarily. I have a good friend in America—we want to set up in Paris what they have at the Metropolitan Museum there (I shook my head, I have never been to the Metropolitan Museum)—get a franchise for making reproductions of works of art to sell in the French museums. Egyptian cats and imitations of jewellery and so on. It's a good thing. Nobody in France thought of it before. You just have to be the first—the same with everything. Donna and I are looking into the possibility of bringing truffles by air from the desert somewhere near where you . . . I forget. We are meeting a man about it in Milan.—

—But you don't work, here. You do feel it's your life, this?—

—Why not? You'll find somebody. You can't go back, êh?—

—Katya must have said that.—

—Donna mentioned . . . I suppose they talk. *Botswana*—that's the name. The man in Milan says the natives in the desert sometimes have nothing to eat but truffles . . . the poor things, êh . . . 600 francs a kilo . . .!— He began to link his fingers through my toes again, prepared to give himself a second chance at rousing me. —I know a lot—well, not a lot—about where you come from. I'm from Maurice, you know that?—Mauritius, you call it. Nearly Africa! Oh god . . .— He was laughing. —It's nothing for me. Filthy. Poor. Sometimes I like to make Donna sick when I tell her how the dogs, some dogs in Port Louis have ruptures here—he drew a breath to suck in his narrow belly— they hang down right onto the street.—

He laughed again, at my face, but he didn't see the donkey that still exists somewhere.

—Donna goes crazy.—

—I don't know why Katya should have said that.—

—Africa is no good for white people any more. Same on the islands. It was okay when I was a kid.—

—I was born there. It's my home.—

—What does that matter. Where you can live the way you like, that's what counts. We have to forget about it.—

—My father died in prison there.—

—You know why we went to Maurice? My father was a collaborator with the Germans and he was sent to prison after the war. People only talk about their families who were in the Resistance. Oh yes. Nobody thought maybe the Germans were going to win—oh no. Donna makes me swear not to tell anybody! She's from Canada, what does she know about it, can you tell me! I know people whose mothers had their hair shaved off for sleeping with Germans. We have to forget about them. It's not our affair. I'm not my father, êh?—

He helped me back into the water, supported by my arm round his neck. There was nothing sexual about the closeness; it was the huddle of the confidences common among all of you, the friends in the village—the divorced women and women widowed, like Madame Bagnelli, by lovers, the old Lesbians and young homosexuals. When we got back to you on the beach he must have remembered my stupidity, not having taken the easy opportunity of making love, and he was cool to me and sharp with Donna for the next few days when she and he were in my presence. Sometimes he trails a caress as I pass him; but it's only to see if I will pounce. It's playful and even derogatory.

A morning can be filled by shopping in the market. Not in the sense of passing time; filled with the peppery-snuff scent of celery, weak sweet perfume of flowers and strawberries, cool salty secretions of sea-slippery fish, odour of cheeses, contracting the nasal membranes; the colours, shapes, shine, density, pattern, texture and feel of fruits and vegetables; the encounters and voices of people handling them. By the time Madame Bagnelli and her guest had moved along the stalls—meeting acquaintances, admiring dogs or children entangled with their legs—comparing prices between this vendor and that, had bought a pot-plant not on Madame Bagnelli's list and eaten a piece of spinach tart, they needed an espresso at the bar on the corner where the young workmen were coming in and out off their vélos and the old men in casquettes deciding bets for the tiercé were already drinking small glasses of red wine. By the time the women got back up the hill to her house, Madame Bagnelli had tooted at someone who asked them in for an aperitif, or Gaby Grosbois and her husband Pierre dropped by to take theirs on Madame Bagnelli's terrace—Pierre and the little Rôse drinking pastis, and the two older women following Gaby's *régime*, telling them how good vegetable juice was for ridding the body of toxins.

Madame Bagnelli carried whatever she had to do out onto that terrace. Squatting on a stool in her frayed espadrilles she picked over herbs she had gathered with her guest on the Col de Vence and was going to dry. She sand-papered an old table she had bought cheaply when they went to the street market near the old port in Antibes, and hoped to sell to some Germans who had taken a house next door to Poliakoff; her chin settled into the flesh of her neck and flecks of gilt caught on the clotted mascara of her

251

eyelashes. In the same position, uncomfortable-looking for a woman her size, with her sewing machine on a low table between her legs, she made the flowing garments Gaby Grosbois cut out —I tell her, Rôse, she is still a woman, êh, men still look . . . she must know what to wear. This year nobody is wearing like this— tight, short—for her the style is good, very loose, décolleté—no, no, Katya, you have still a beauty, I'm telling you— The two women laugh, embracing. —If with Pierre everything was still working— (more laughter, her mouth playing at tragedy) —I will be worried—

Reading in the room that had been waiting for her, Rosa Burger was aware in the afternoons of Madame Bagnelli's activities down there, the scissors snapping at threads like a dog at flies, the slap and slither of a paint-brush; the striking up of the record she had set playing indoors. The Goldberg Variations, the first side of the Christmas Oratorio, some Provençal songs punctuated by clucks as the needle rode a scratch, and now and then accompanied by a second voice—Katya's, following and anticipating phrases she knew so well the recording had become a kind of conversation. At some point it would become a real one: that was the masculine croak of Darby and the hoarse patter of one of her cronies. Their voices were changed by age like schoolboys' at adolescence, so that the one who had been as famous in Paris as Baker and Piaf—people in the village told Rosa again and again: You know that Arnys lives here?—could not be distinguished from the Lesbians who had perhaps cultivated the lower register or the old Americans, ex-patriate for thirty or forty years, who had 'granulated the vocal chords' (Madame Bagnelli's attempt at translating a local expression, 'la voix enrouée par la vinasse') with deposits from the alcohol they had consumed.—At 33 per cent flat rate he surely might be better off . . . but if you have a fluctuating income coming in from a dozen different sources? . . . it only makes sense if you're certain you can't spread your assets in such a way that you can get into a lower tax bracket—The English comes from Donna, and the wriggling, ticklish laughter means the Japanese girl with the dog.

—You will be a nice friend for me. We are same age.— The

text of a children's first reader; the Japanese girl said it at one of those daily meetings at the top of steps or on the *place*, when people ran into each other and stood about talking. The girl prattled to her beautiful dog in some anthropomorphic game—Rosa looked down from her own private roof-top and saw her, so pretty in tight French trousers and high clogs she wore with the close-elbowed, close-kneed femininity of exotic dress, turning up a smiling, wide-jawed face on its frail stem. She lived with an Englishman Madame Bagnelli's guest hadn't yet met. He passed below on a morning walk with a stick, the girl and the dog; a white-haired man with the majesty of a slow-grown tree casually carried in the denim egalitarianism first taken over by students from peasants and labourers, and then from the young by the rich. He was a Lancashire shipyard owner—had been, everyone had been something else before they came to live as they wanted to, here—for whom Ugo Bagnelli, whose name Madame Bagnelli continued although she had never been married to anyone but Lionel Burger, had worked. —If Tatsu invites you, you should go—just to see what Ugo did. Everything in that boat's his idea. He fitted out . . . must have been three or four—a whole succession of yachts and cabin cruisers for Henry Torren. Oh Henry happened to like him . . . not many that one does. He's a solitary. Apart from whatever young woman he marries or lives with. He's never mixed here. He likes to think he's not like us . . . there're so many failures, you know? But people who haven't got money also do what they like, here. I don't think he approves of that, it spoils things for him, ay? He would like to think he doesn't enjoy the things the rest of us do! Not a snob, no, no, you have to know him . . . we get on all right. A puritan. Ugo never charged him—w-e-ll, so little it was nothing. Ugo loved luxurious things—he lived with them—oh-ho in style!—in his imagination, you know?—while we were eating nothing but spaghetti. He could design them and make them but he knew he would never have them for himself. In a way it was the same thing . . . why do I fall for such men? Rather why did I . . . And now— The gesture, the face of mock abdication learned from Gaby Grosbois when she talked about Pierre, her husband.

Madame Bagnelli and Rosa Burger did not deliberately talk about Lionel Burger but did not avoid doing so: he was a fact between them. It changed them, each for the other, at different times and in different contexts. They had not known each other before they became a middle-aged woman and her young guest fortunate to find themselves in a state that could not have been anticipated, arranged for or explained. Compatible: that was enough, in itself; comfortably, they began to exist only at the moment each turned out to be the one the other was looking for on an airport. That fact—the fact of Lionel—when the passing of daily life thinned or shifted to reveal it, made, like a change of light transforming the aspect of a landscape, the two women into something else for each other.

As Madame Bagnelli was talking, the girl was looking at the woman who had fallen in love with Lionel Burger. The woman felt the way she was suddenly seen, and became Katya. —We were young, all the ideas were so wonderful. You've heard it all before, god knows. But they were. 'We were going to change the world'. When I tell you even now—I could still begin to tremble, my hands . . . you know? And I thought that was going to happen! No more hunger, no more pain. But that is the biggest luxury, ah? I must have been a stupid little creature—I was. Unattainable. Not to be achieved in our lifetime; in Lionel's. He understood that. He was prepared for it, don't ask me how.—But if it should be never? What then? I couldn't wait, I can't wait, I don't want to wait. I've always had to live . . . I couldn't give it up. When I saw your mother—you remember I told you?—I thought: that's the end of me.—

The girl corrected her. —No, you said—you could see she was a 'real revolutionary'.— A precisely-imposed pause. Smiling. They were skinning big sweet peppers that had been grilled.

—Yes, that's what I mean. So that was the end of me. I wouldn't stand a chance against her. The end of me with him.— The skin of the peppers was transparent when it lifted in finicky curls and the hot flesh beneath was succulent, scarlet; the tips of their fingers burned. —Like this, about half-an-inch, don't worry if they're not

regular— Rosa watched while she laid strips of flesh in a bowl.
—But I was also free of *them*. That was something. Those bastards.
I was wearing a pair of shoes once, summer shoes, very pretty ones.
Everyone wore white shoes in summer in those days. I must have
innocently let slip the servant girl had blancoed them for me. The
next thing, a complaint at a meeting: Comrade Katya was showing
bourgeois tendencies not fitting in a Party member. They wouldn't
be specific. Nobody admitted it—I lost my temper and screamed at
the meeting—I knew it was the shoes, nothing but a bloody stupid
pair of white shoes—Now a little dribble of oil between each
layer— Her stained fingers, followed by those of the girl, dripping
juice to the wrists, arranged a lattice of gleaming red. The girl
looked at her; she answered, prompted: —A sprinkle of salt.—

In the bar tabac young Swedes and Germans, Englishmen and
girls crushed in to drink something labelled *La Veuve Joyeuse* and in
the evenings Madame Bagnelli's friends moved over instead to
Josette Arnys' bar for the summer season. The old singer was
surrounded by young homosexuals as by a large family, affectionate, bored and dependent. Some served behind the bar or were
served as clients, indiscriminately; Madame Bagnelli had towards
them the easy, bossy, cuffing and teasing manner that all the
women in the village who for various reasons had denuded
themselves of their own children, adopted towards young men.
—Oh pardon! Je m'excuse—je suis désolée, bien sûr . . . Je vous
avais pris pour le garçon . . . Rosa Burger's French was beginning
to piece together whole patches of talk but comprehension tattered
when jokes and insults began to fly between Madame Bagnelli and
some distant-faced young man taking up his wrist-strap bag,
cigarettes and gilt lighter. One of them cooked for Arnys in
the cellar-kitchen off the cove of tiny tables beside the bar. Paper
place-mats painted by another advised the choice of *spécialités
antillaises* (among the old recordings that played continuously
was the voice of Arnys in the Thirties singing of 'the island where
Joséphine Beauharnais and I were born'). In the white toque worn
as a transvestite wears a wig, gold chains tangled with the blond
hair on his chest, her chef sat most of the time playing cards with

Arnys in her corner under photographs of herself with Maurice Chevalier, Jean Cocteau, and others whose names were not so well known to a foreigner.

The bar counter was central and majestic as a fine altar in a church. When Rosa Burger lost track of the talk she could follow with her eyes again and again the spiral of magnificent dark oak corkscrew pillars that flanked the mirror where they were all reflected—Darby's captain's cap, Madame Bagnelli's breasts leaning on the mahogany surface, Tatsu's eyes opaque as molasses, the gaze of one of the homosexuals flirting with himself, the detachment of a French couple dazed by sunburn and love-making, the excited hunch of Pierre Grosbois as he gave his frank opinions, his warnings on this or that subject to Marthe and Françoise, the shrivelled, bright-lipped pair with long cigarette-holders whose flowery courtyard bordering the *place* was a shop where feather boas, old bathtubs with dragon's feet, the broken faces of romanesque angels, wore price-tags as trees are named in a botanical garden. The oak pillars—when Pierre explained something to Rosa he considerately used a special, didactically-enunciated French—were screws from old olive presses that had been numerous in the countryside round about, from Roman times (What are you saying! And long before that!—his wife thrust her face over her shoulder) until the end of the nineteenth century (—The '14–'18 war, Pierre!—).

Madame Bagnelli had not yet shown her guest Alzieri's olive oil mill, the last of the old ones still in use, but she and Rosa had taken *pan-bagnat* and wine and spent the midday hours in the olive grove that was Renoir's garden. The valley of his view to the sea was raised to a new level with cheerfully ugly flat buildings. —People don't want gardens they have to work in, they want balconies to tan on, to be just as good as the tourists who can afford to come here only to *bronzer*. That's democracy in France— The flesh of Madame Bagnelli, dozing on her back on the grass, wobbled a little with laughter. —But look—the way the light falls on us, it's the light he painted, isn't it?—

The caretaker came to describe his noises in the head to her; she must have been in the habit of going there often. Rosa fell asleep and woke, under a tree that hung a tarnished silver mesh of foliage over its black trunk and her body. —Were they growing here before the house?—

—Oh probably before the revolution. If you live in Europe . . . things change (a roll of the untidy head towards the cement glare in the valley) but continuity never seems to break. You don't have to throw the past away. If I'd stayed . . . at home, how will they fit in, white people? Their continuity stems from the colonial experience, the white one. When they lose power it'll be cut. Just like that! They've got nothing but their horrible power. Africans will take up their own kind of past the whites never belonged to. Even the Terblanches and Alettas—our rebellion against the whites was also part of *being white* . . . it was, it was. But here you never really have to start from scratch . . . Ah no, it's too much to take on. That's what I love—nobody expects you to be more than you are, you know. That kind of tolerance, I didn't even know it existed—I mean, there: if you're not equal to facing *everything*, there . . . you're a traitor. To the human cause—justice, humanity, the lot—there's nothing else.—

—Had you decided that when you went away?—

The older woman sat up slowly, enjoying the leverage of muscles, rubbing upper arms, marked by the grass, like a cat grooming itself after a sand-bath. —Oh I don't know. I accept it. But there is the whole world . . . I have forgotten I ever thought of myself like that.— The girl might have been showing curiosity about an old love affair. —To live with a man like Ugo—how can I explain—? He was in his life as a fish in water, with him you just stopped gasping and thrashing around . . . In Europe they don't know what conflict is, now, bless them.—

At the bar Grosbois' voice was always unmistakable; while he talked he kept his right hand slightly in the air ready to intercept interruptions from his wife. —Thirty years?—what is that? Are we all dead? We don't remember? What have we French to be ashamed of that we don't celebrate what we fought for, any more? If Giscard was worried about offending the Germans, that's too bad. *I'm* not worried. The French people are not worried, êh. They took our food, they moved into our houses. We hid in the cellars and the mountains and came out to kill them at night in the streets. Should we forget all that?—The little house across the street from us, a boy of nineteen was taken hostage, they killed him—his mother is still living there.— I walk through Paris and see the plaques where they shot down people in '44—

—He's right, he's right.—

—Yes, but what does the 8th of May celebration every year mean? Just another demo in the streets . . .—

—*Exactly*—no public recognition of the glory of the French nation, all that is thrown away—pouf! The President of the Republic finds it vulgar, êh. Thirty years ago we rid our country of the Nazis and that is nothing to go on marching in the streets about. But the students, êh—the clerks from the Banque de France, the PTT—every little man who wants a few francs more a month—that's a spectacle for Paris.—

—In Vincennes they're showing fascist films to the students—

—Ah, no, *Françoise*. That's something different. That's to warn them—

—Oh yes? She's right—what's the difference, the kind of film they'll see and the way they already behave? They smash and destroy their own universities. They—excuse me, êh—they actually piss on the desks of their professors. It can only encourage them—

—What? Nazis kicking Jews and dragging women off to the camps—

—People don't see anything wrong with violence. Since May '68, it's a general way to get what you want. Am I wrong? You saw on television last night—that gang in Germany. The trial that's begun . . . The Baader-Meinhof lunatics—they are the result of what happened in '68. People only disapprove of each other's aims, maybe, nowadays. They all use the same methods, hijacking, kidnapping—

—What was the name of the boy, the redhead, you should see, he's become quite fat and middle-aged! (Gaby's blown-up jowls in the mirror.) Really. There's an interview with him in *Elle*—

—She means Cohn-Bendit.—

—In your women's magazine? What do they dig him up for?—

—But of course! Ponia's lifted the interdiction against him, he's in Paris autographing some book he's written.—

—Pierre, I'll show you the article. It's in the bathroom—I was reading while my tint was taking. Nobody's noticed my hair . . . isn't it a sexy colour?—

A young man came over to look more closely. —What did you use? I want to streak mine.—

—I've got half a bottle left, Gérard. Come past tomorrow morning, you're welcome to it—

—They charge 60 francs in Nice. And I'm going to have to move out of my room, as it is—

—No? But why?—

—She can get double for it in summer. She needs the money, too. Her husband's on pension and the granddaughter's got herself pregnant, stupid little *nana*, I could see her asking for it.—

A man Rosa Burger greeted as she did many people because they passed one another so often in the village, at last came up to her in the bar with the formality with which Frenchmen approach women as a prelude to expectations of intimacy. Would she have a drink or a coffee with him?

—You are English?—Ah? I had a friend who went down there, in the building trade, like me. He's making a lot of money. 12,000 francs a month—new francs, I'm talking about. But there's trouble there, êh? . . . I don't want trouble . . . And you like France? The coast is beautiful. Of course. There are some good places to go dancing—you've been to Les Palmiers Bleus, it's just near Cap Ferrat? Don't your friends take you dancing?—

She had seen a man and girl at a café table, tossing a snapped-off flower back and forth between them; the exchange, in any language, was as simple as that to manage. —I'm staying with Madame Bagnelli.—

—That's the one in the little house just above the old Maison Commune? But she's an English lady.—

—Only the name's Italian.—

259

—No, no, Niçois, plenty of French people with those names around here. My name: Pistacchi, Michel Pistacchi—you can say that? I'll take you to Les Palmiers Bleus—you'll like it. Why do you laugh? You find me funny?—

—We won't be able to talk—you can hear I don't speak French—

—I am going to ask Madame's permission to take you dancing.—

—Ask her? What for?—

Like most gregarious men, he was drawn to girls who appeared to be set apart from the company in which he noticed them. As if to confirm his instinct for such things, the foreign girl's face broke with vivid amusement, she was generously promising when she laughed.

He brought roses for Madame Bagnelli. Wearing an elegant navy blue blazer he came to fetch Rosa Burger in a sports car— Not mine but it's nearly the same thing, you understand—when my friend finds a good buy in a newer model, I'll take over this from him.— He ordered an elaborate dinner and expanded volubly in the busy to-and-fro of tasting each other's dishes. —This's what I like, to be with a girl who appreciates good food, an atmosphere—I don't go out if it's not somewhere first-class. No discos— He danced expertly and his attempted caresses as they danced were as expertly calculated not to exceed the line at which they could, for the time being, be ignored. She understood most of what he said; when she did not follow the words, could follow the dynamo that moved him, the attitudes and concepts turning always on his private needs, fears and desires. He boasted innocently of familiarity with his *patron*—I'm at his house for *casse-croûte* every day—at the same time as he complained of the responsibility he was expected to carry in comparison with what he earned, the taxes he paid.

—But isn't your union a strong one, in France?—

She hadn't got it right; he was eager to guess past her mistakes. There was laughter and he squeezed her a moment.

—Ah, but you're intelligent, you know what's going on in the

world, I can tell . . . What a pleasure, to be with a girl you can talk
to . . . and you tell me you can't speak . . .! Let me explain, the
unions—they don't work, those fellows—we work for them, and
they get fat on it—

The subject distracted him from his awareness of her body and
his determination to make her aware of his; she could see in his face
he didn't want to get caught up in such talk, yet someone who
would listen was not to be resisted, either.

—And if the socialists come to power?— She had to construct
sentences experimentally in her mind, before she spoke.

—Mitterrand? He would sell out to the Communists—

—Then the workers will be strong. Not the *patrons*.—

He stopped dancing, broke the rhythm. He held her away from
him. —I want what is mine, êh? My parents worked for it. When
my father dies, his house is mine, êh? The Communists won't allow
that. I would be robbed of my own father's property—you know
that?—

Katya called him 'Rosa's mason': —The first time you've been
out with a brick-layer, I'll bet.— The two women were amused at
this example of sheltered childhood.

—I want to see the house you are going to inherit.—

—*Comment?*—

Again her sense was not clear; at last he understood, but was still
surprised. —Ah it's nothing to see. Old people without money, it
needs a lot of fixing up—

It was a small farmhouse-cum-villa with the burnt umber and
rose tiles the people of the region had always used, and an
automatic washing-machine in the kitchen. His mother brought
out fancy glasses and the father a bottle of his own wine; they
exchanged smiles with the strange girl but did not attempt to talk
to her, and she could not make out the dialect they spoke with
their son, only that the conversation was the kind that takes the
opportunity to cover a lot of ground when parents have a chance to
consult with an adult son or daughter. The three became a family,
briefly, while she walked with them down the hillside garden: the
son leaping ditches in his elegant boots, the mother and father

padding along in muddy slippers, all talking, explaining, object-ing. Father and son were absorbed in disagreement over how to deal with a tree that threatened to fall. Rosa was taken by the mother to see drills of young vegetables she bent to lift, here and there, rumpling the grey soil; through leafy shelters and rickety sheds where seedlings were green and transparent, past baskets of stored walnuts and a bucket—alive as a cheese with worms—of swarming snails gathered for eating. Under olive and cherry trees a long table was covered by flowered plastic below a lamp wired in the branches: there was a pet sheep staked to mow the grass within the radius of its rope, and a swing for grandchildren. Rosa sat eating the cherries the father filled her lap with, and the son ran at her, head lowered to make them all laugh, and sent her up into the air; she got back to her feet at last, laughing, holding her throat as if something were about to fly from her. —I like your inheritance.—

—Ah, when the mistral starts, that tree's going to smash the power line—that will cost plenty! I've told my father. It's a serious offence in France to obstruct installations—

Madame Bagnelli invited the friends Georges and Manolis to share the home-grown asparagus Rosa was given. One of the intimates 'smelled them cooking' as Madame Bagnelli said, and called up, at the gate just as Rosa carried the settings for the table onto the terrace. Bobby was the immensely tall Englishwoman with beautiful legs who at sixty still wore without looking ridiculous bullfighter's pants that ended at the knee, and toenails shaped and painted like fingernails. If Rosa came upon her sitting on the *place* on her usual bench she seemed to think they might have had an arrangement to meet; she would jump up, moving her mouth welcomingly, kiss the girl and insist on buying her a coffee, taking up as if the two had been involved in it together some local story of a dispute or crisis in the village. —Well, the great event didn't come off yesterday, after all. They waited for a phone-call, but it was only when the brother-in-law turned up—you know, the little fat one, from Pegomas, unappetizing if you ask me— In the straw bag she carried rubber gloves and often a newspaper, magazines (that was the source of the *Vogues* and copies of *Plaisirs de*

France Katya placed in her guest's room) or a flowering branch from the large, locked house with a majolica virgin on the façade she looked after for absentee owners. As far as Madame Bagnelli knew, she was smuggled into France by a Free French officer who had fallen in love with her when she was in the British women's navy during the war. The village crones derided the claim that she had been in the Resistance. —She was part of the village when I came. He used to have a house, he used to come every few months—they tell me at one time he actually lived there with her. Since I've been here, he would come when he could, just like Ugo . . . We were waiting for his wife to die. Well she was so ill . . . We used to ask about that woman's health, it seemed so hopeful, she had every disease you could wish for. He died first. Oh I don't think by then . . . Bobby never expected—she's lived here so long, she has her ways . . . Sometimes now if you mention her Colonel she'll answer as if she knows who you're talking about but it's the way you cover up when you haven't really caught on.—

Manolis's voice preceded the pair of invited guests, giving directions in his Greek French as if advising how to steer an awkward burden through Madame Bagnelli's dark little house. The fragile cargo was Georges manoeuvring himself. —He has hurt his leg. Last night. He should not walk up steps, I tell him.— Manolis switched to the English he had learnt from Georges, so that it was spoken with both French and Greek accents. His smooth, narrow, yellow face with its dark moles and sorrowful glittering black eyes was dramatic in haughty disapproval and anxiety. Georges made an entrance, leant on a cane. —I had to ask one for him all around—in the end, it was old Seroin, but what a trouble: it's from his papa, it's from when he was a *gouverneur en Indochine*, if it should be damaged ta-ra-ra—

Georges grinned with a free arm held out for the women to come and kiss him. —Manolis had new curtains ready, I was standing on top of the armoire, you know, the treasure Katya found for us in Roquefort-les-Pins—yes—I must have fallen two metres— He smelled of suède (the supple shirt he wore) and lemon cologne and his blue eyes and white hair cut like Napoleon's were close to Rosa, a presence sure of its androgynous vitality, while he talked past her ear and hugged her. Bobby looked on with head raised from the preoccupations she carried comfortably around like a piece of invisible needlework. —Outside my door it's been like that for a month. You could break your neck. Not a light, pitch dark. The gang of Arabs just leave their picks and spades at five o'clock— they don't care.—

—But here we've got exactly the person you need. Let Rosa see, Georges. Come quietly into my bedroom—get on the bed—let a qualified physiotherapist examine you . . . it's free!— Madame Bagnelli presented her house-guest in another capacity, as much to be taken on trust, for the others, as the wild stories of the country she came from.

—You're a nurse?—Manolis was strict.

—A doctor is the only one to touch it.— Bobby spoke confidentially to Madame Bagnelli, wrinkling her nose. Her voice was louder when she thought she was whispering.

—Not the bedroom—I won't move now I'm here—Manoli, put the cushions on the floor—

Madame Bagnelli, curtseying easily up and down, weighty on her thin ankles, arranged it all swiftly.

—I'll take off his shoes, no?—

The girl was in charge, smiling, her chin lifted. —Roll up your trouser-leg. That's no good—right up. No—you wear your pants too tight around the thigh: take them off.—

—She's not slow, êh? All right, if you say—

They laughed down at him as he pulled in his waist nattily, unfastened belt and flourished zipper. Manolis drew the pants off with the air of preparing a corpse, bringing more laughter. Georges's chin pressed on his chest in a grimace showed teeth worn laterally to the bone that were more of a private vulnerability revealed than was the body he wore like an outfit he knew would make a good impression. Rosa Burger's hair had grown enough to fall across her face; they saw only her mouth firm in professional concentration. Her hands moved with the grip and sensitivity they had not put to use for a long time. The doctor says there's no crack

264

in the patella? You were x-rayed? And there was no dislocation?

Manolis appealed to everyone: —Nothing is wrong! But look how Georges is, he cannot even turn in the bed!—

—I might be able to ease it a bit. Give me half-an-hour.—

They deferred to her, Manolis going off to finish setting the table and Madame Bagnelli trailing Bobby into the kitchen where she added final touches to the sauce.

Several glasses of wine released the urbanely concealed concern over himself Georges had been keeping from his lover. The tone meant specifically for him reached Manolis as he swabbed vinaigrette with a piece of bread; at once his attention fixed in his great dark, mournful gaze (when Manolis laughed, those eyes shone as if he were crying) and his lips drew tensely against other chatter.

—It's better. I said: I think it's definitely better. It'll be all right. I can move the knee—well, I won't but I feel I *could*.—

—We were supposed to be going to the Algarve next week. A great day, to be able to go to Portugal. We've waited a long time for that.—

The two men lifted their glasses with ceremony.

Madame Bagnelli assured: —Of course you're going. Rosa will come and massage Georges every morning won't you? Of course—

—I shouldn't have thought it was such a wonderful thing—people I know've been having holidays there for years, it was so cheap, even cheaper than Spain.—

—We wouldn't have gone ever while Salazar lived, even for nothing.—

Bobby was unaware of reproaches as she was of being ignored.

—Of course they say it's finished now—people have been chased out of their houses by the Communists—English people who've retired there, put every penny—

Georges took more sauce, miming a kiss to Madame Bagnelli in praise of its excellence. —If we couldn't afford Chile under Allende, at least we can afford Portugal under Gomes. I wouldn't miss it. People in this village! Did you hear what Grosbois said? If everything's so fine in Portugal now, why haven't all the Portuguese who're digging the streets here with the Arabs gone home

. . . There has to be prosperity overnight, êh, or that's proof the Left is making a mess of things— One year, that's all it is—

It was true that Madame Bagnelli could still take on, like an old challenge to all comers, something like the blazonry of attraction and sexuality; a kind of inward caper to match the boxer-like prance—hefty, light on her feet—she sometimes broke into about her terrace. —It was lovely, last year when we all danced on the *place*—Georges?—

Georges indicated her to Rosa. —You should have seen her, with a red carnation behind the ear.—

—And you? We all went crazy. Oh some people just thought they were at the battle of the flowers in Nice—never mind . . .— Manolis and Georges had brought a special white wine; she lifted the third bottle dripping high, from the bucket, and was going round with it. —And what about Arnys? Rosa—Arnys didn't know any Portuguese revolutionary songs so she sang one she remembered about La Pasionaria, from the Left Bank in '36—she cried to me afterwards, she says she once had a great love in the International Brigade.— Madame Bagnelli stood with her glass in her hand as if she were about to make a speech or sing a song herself. —Where this girl comes from, April meant the end of the whites in Moçambique, right next door . . . you realize what that must have been?—

Manolis regarded Rosa the way he did when she had taken charge of Georges professionally. —What an experience. To be down there in Africa—êh.—

The girl stood up, too, palms on the table. She could see the flood-lit castle behind the black paint-brushes of cypress; music and voices were the single insect-chorus of the summer night. She looked from one face to another at the table in expansive impulses, even affectionate, even appealing. —There were no red carnations.—

But Georges and Manolis prided themselves on being thoroughly informed. They stirred, reflective. Bobby politely, pettishly mouthed that she wanted another piece of bread.

—Black people were ecstatic—Frelimo fought for eleven years

. . . But if you came out in the streets—that's impossible there
. . . You wouldn't dare celebrate. There was one mass meeting,
people went to prison—

—Not just *overnight*, waving banners, and headline interviews
with the heroes in the papers next day, like it is here when there's a
political rumpus— Madame Bagnelli kept up a counterpoint of
emphatic interruption.

Manolis waved her aside to exact acknowledgment; he had the
experience of the Greek colonels in his blood although he had not
been in his country during their rule. —And the white people? Of
course they are afraid the same thing will happen down there,
that's it?—

—The refugees kept coming in, people looking like us, you
know, people could look at themselves, and them—bringing their
grandmothers and refrigerators, white people— Rosa's light eyes
were indiscreet, trusting. She was her own audience, ranged along
with the faces.

—What can they expect! They've asked for it. They allowed
themselves to be brain-washed into believing they're a superior
race. Running with refrigerators! It will come. Three hundred
years, enough! You are outcast . . . they throw you in prison to die
if you try to change them— Madame Bagnelli had the air of one
carried away by whatever company she found herself in to profess
preoccupations and opinions at one with theirs. With the Grosbois, she was as animated a participant in their decision to eat
organically-grown vegetables or Gaby's interest in the alterations
Nice-Matin reported were being made to the villa of the Shah of
Iran's sister.

—This girl could make a good living here. She would do well. I
mean it— Georges leant forward to draw everyone to the sudden
idea of supporting their own local political refugee. —The yacht
people, there are always pains and aches when you take too much
exercise . . . they hurt themselves water-skiing and I don't know
what. Really, it's amazing, how my leg feels, you know, relaxed—
the muscles— The convinced shrewdness of his blue eyes can-
vassed.

—And even in the village!—

—No one who does that kind of work—

—Aië, aië, what about papers?— Madame Bagnelli looked at Rosa gaily in the enthusiasm of Georges and Manolis. —She has to have permission to work, a permit—

Georges mimed away the maunderings of despised officialdom. —Pah-pah-pah. She doesn't ask. No one knows. She gets paid in cash, she puts it in her pocket.— Fingers extended fastidiously, with the ring set with a gold seal from the reign of Alexander the Great worn in betrothal to Manolis, the palm of one hand wiped itself off against the other.

Katya took Rosa to hear nightingales. They locked the gate but rooms were open behind them, the candles smoked on the littered table. Up on the terrace, they might still have been there, in the warm still night voices hung.

Down the steep streets with gravity propelling them gently, under street-lamps fluttering pennants of tiny bats, shouldered by the walls of the houses of friends, through lilting staccato-punctuated voices swung about by music coming from the *place*, whiffs of dog-shit and human urine in Saracen archways, arpeggios of laughter flying in the chatter of knives and dishes from the restaurant where a table of French people sat late under young leaves of a grape-vine translucent to the leaping shadows of their gestures. (—You never understand what makes them so euphoric in the ritual of feasting together—not even when you understand their language perfectly.— Katya was proudly fascinated by the tribal impenetrability of the people she lived among.) Past the little villas of the dead with the urns of their marble gardens sending out perfume of cut carnations as from the vase in any family livingroom; the hoof-clatter of linked couples approaching and trotting away on their platform soles, the stertorous swathe cut by motorcycles, cycles, the quiet chirrups of older people wandering the village as at an exhibition of stone, light, doorways fringed with curtains of plastic strips, the faces of carved lions melted by centuries back to the contours of features forming in a foetus. In the remnant of forest ravine all this familiar element was suddenly gone like torn paper drawn up a flue by the draught of flames. It had lifted away above the flood-lit battlements of that castle domestic as a tame dragon. Katya plunged through littered thickets, some quiet vixen or badger of a woman, cunningly coexisting with caravan parks and autoroutes. Rosa strolled this harmless European jungle.

—Wait. Wait—

Katya's breathing touched her as pine-needles did. All around the two women a kind of piercingly sweet ringing was on the limit of being audible. A new perception was picking up the utmost ring of waves whose centre must be unreachable ecstasy. The thrilling of the darkness intensified without coming closer. She gave a stir, questioning; the shape of Katya's face turned to stay her. The vibrating glass in which they were held shattered into song. The sensation of receiving the song kept changing; now it was a sky-slope on which they planed, tipped, sailed, twirled to earth; then it was a breath stopped at the point of blackout and passing beyond it to a pitch hit, ravishingly, again, again, again.

Katya hooked the girl's arm when the path widened. Their feet carried them towards the village. —It goes on all night. Every summer. If I can't sleep, I just come out at two or three in the morning . . . Oh I have them always, every year.—

In the middle of winter, seven months pregnant, to teach night-classes in some freezing old warehouse . . . okay, I was 'disciplined'—how ashamed I was!—had to be disciplined because of my bourgeois tendencies to put my private life first. I remember I cried . . .

Murmuring, up there, like schoolgirls under the bed-clothes. Laughter.

Once I was suspended from the Party for 'inactivity' . . . when they gave something a name, I can tell you . . . it meant anything they decided. 'From each according to his ability' . . . I was dancing in some bloody terrible revue six nights a week—can you believe it? I had to—Lionel was an intern earning almost nothing, he walked the floor with the baby when he came home. But on Sundays I used to take my little street theatre group I'd got together out to the black townships on the back of a furniture remover's lorry . . . oh baby and all. They had it in for me. I wouldn't go to their old lectures on Marxist-Leninism—I could read it all for myself?—no, you were supposed to sit there listening to them drone on. One poor devil, I forget her name—she was even accused of trying to poison the comrades by boiling water for tea in a suspect-looking can. One of the Trotskyites who was expelled . . .

What did he say?

I've never talked with anyone as I do with you, incontinently, femininely.

Dick was the only one . . . well, he didn't exactly defend me, how could anyone—I suppose I really wasn't good material. But there was some sort of little (an amused pause, mutually culpable in the understanding of our sex)—*something—going on at one time. Much later, during the war. I knew he really liked me. He thought I was an extraordinary creature . . . a few kisses managed in the most unlikely circumstances . . . oh innocent Dick. We despised the subjection of women to bourgeois morality but he was*

270

scared of Ivy and he had schoolboy feelings of honour and whatnot towards
his comrade. He worshipped him. He once told me: Lionel will be our Lenin.
I think—now yes, don't let me lie, we actually slept together once. In Ivy's
bed! Good god. Don't strange things excite men? Funnily enough, I
remember the sheets. I've never forgotten her sheets. They were embroidered,
chain-stitch daisies and so on, bright pink and blue—she always wore such
awful clothes! She was away at some conference in Durban with Indians.
We were supposed to be roneoing pamphlets. Sweet Dick. But compared with
somebody like Lionel . . . the affair didn't have much of a chance. It wasn't
exactly anything to worry about. I can't imagine what he'd look like now
. . . his jacket always used to be hitched up on his bum, quite unaware of
himself, I used to feel the giggles coming on . . .

What did he say?

You've never asked me why I came and I don't ask that, either.
You tell me anecdotes of your youth that could transform my own.
Several times I could almost have exchanged in the same way an
anecdote about how I used to dress up and visit my 'fiancé' in jail,
wearing Aletta's *verloofring*. I could imitate the way the warders
talk, and you would laugh with the pleasure of the softened
reminiscence. That's exactly it!—the brutishness and guileless
sentimentality of grandmother Marie Burger's *taal* in their
mouths. Of course I know what we're like when there's some
little thing going on—when Didier gave me my chance, taking a
toe for nipple or clitoris. What'd he say, your husband, when his
dancing-girl was disciplined? It must have seemed so petty to
him—the blancoed shoes, your tears. Or maybe he saw this
ideological spit-and-polish as essential training for the unquestion-
ing acceptance of actions unquestioningly performed, the necessity
of which was to come later. He may have smiled and consoled you
by making love to you; but seen the faithful go ahead and
discipline you because you preferred amateur theatricals to Marx-
ist-Leninist education.

The little something going on with comrade Dick—what'd he
say then? Perhaps he didn't notice. You deceived him because you
were not of his calibre; it was your revenge for being lesser, poor
girl, you were made fully conscious of your shortcomings by his not

even noticing the sort of peccadilloes you'd console yourself with.

All these things I see and understand while we're shelling peas, ripping out a hem with an old blade, walking in the cork woods, watching the fishermen put out to sea, slumping with our bare feet on the day-warmed stone after your friends have gone home to bed. It's easy, with you. I'm happy with you—I see it all the way he did; smiling and looking on, charmed by you although you've grown fat and the liveliness Katya must have had has coarsened into clownishness and the power of attraction sometimes deteriorates into what I don't want to watch—a desire to please—just to please, without remembering how, any more.

A little something going on. What did he say?

He couldn't say anything because by then there was the real revolutionary: you recognized my mother the first time you saw her. Nobody has ever told me, but the accepted version, the understanding is that Katya left Lionel Burger—that was in character for someone so unsuitable (even she recognizes this, in later life) for the man he was to become. She left him for another man or another life—same thing, really, what else is there for a woman who won't live for the Future? You haven't contradicted this version. But I see that whatever you did, you and he and my mother knew he said nothing because of her. Back there where we come from someone's writing a definitive life in which this will be left out. Anyway, if you *were* to ask me—I didn't come on some pilgrimage, worshipping or iconoclastic, to learn about my father. There must have been some strong reason, though, why I hit with closed eyes upon this house, this French village; reason beyond my reasoning that surveillance wouldn't think to look for me there.

I wanted to know how to defect from him. The former Katya has managed to be able to write to me that he was a great man, and yet decide 'there's a whole world' outside what he lived for, what life with him would have been.

It was easy for Rosa Burger to turn aside from the calculated pleasures of Didier; she had never been the same age as Tatsu, playing with her dog in the old man's garden. At one of the summer gatherings she told a man she had never met before and probably would never meet again her version of an incident in Paris when a man tried to steal money from her bag. —He found me out.—

—In what?—

—I thought someone else might be keeping an eye on what I was doing.—

—A pickpocket. Poor devil.—

—Yes.—

—A black man.—

—Yes.—

The Frenchman she had had this conversation with in English was still in the village on Bastille Day—some of these friends-of-friends were about only for a weekend; names and faces introduced with enthusiasm as a brother-in-law, a cousin, a 'colleague' from Paris or Lyon, his transience giving the host a dimension of connection with seats of government, commerce and fashionable opinions. He was on the *place* like everybody else dancing, watching others dance, and applauding and kissing when the fireworks went off from the top of the castle. Katya and Manolis, Manolis and Rosa, Katya and Pierre, Gaby and the local mayor, Rosa and the car-salesman son of the confectioner, hopped and swung past Georges snapping castanet fingers; some beautiful models from Cannes stood about tossing their hair like good children told not to romp and spoil their best clothes; and he was one of the city Frenchmen with neat buttocks, fitted shirts and sweaters knotted by the sleeves round their necks, whose cosmopolitan presence strengthened the family party against the tourist element. He danced with her, rather badly, twitching a cheek at the painful music coming from a festooned platform. He was at the other end of the table when eight or ten of the friends ate at a restaurant together after loud and serious discussion about dishes and cost. Gaby Grosbois had taken charge. —I will arrange a good price with Marcelle. Moules marinières, salad—what do we drink, Blanc de Blanc . . .?— She strode off to the whistling of the Marseillaise, swinging her backside with a mock military strut.

The tiny restaurant was a single intimate uproar. Marcelle's barman sang in *argot* and in the course of one song snatched a curved *ficelle* from the bread-basket and jigged among the tables holding it thrust up from between his legs with priapic glee. It wagged at shrieking women—Katya, Gaby—Mesdames, just look, don't touch— With a flourish, like someone putting a flower in a buttonhole, he stuck it in Pierre Grosbois' groin, from where, to the applause of laughter, Grosbois, by tightening his thigh muscles, managed to rap it against the table.

In the disorder of chairs pulled back and the face-bobbing goodnight embraces the stranger paused vaguely at Rosa. —We'll go and have a drink.—

They lost the others in the jostle of the *place*.

—Where?— He stopped and lit a cigarette in a dark archway; for him, she was the local inhabitant.

They went to Arnys, who did not seem to recognize the foreign girl outside the context of her usual company. The old woman went on playing patience in the chiffon dress that rode up on huge legs stemming from little tight pumps like satin hooves. Her blind, matted Maltese dog came over and squirted a few drops at his chair: *Chabalier*, he was writing for Rosa, on the margin of a newspaper lying on the bar, *Bernard Chabalier*.

—Where do you stay when you come to Paris?—

—I don't come to Paris.—

—You thought you were being followed.—

—Ah that. Two nights; I was on my way here. The first and only time.—

His hunch of face against hands accepted that he had not been answered. —Do you want more wine? Or coffee?— For himself he spoke to the barman plainly and severely, as if to forestall any irritating objections. —I know it's summer. I know it's Quatorze Juillet. But you have lemons? I want lemon juice—hot.—

—No more wine. I'll have that too.—

—You're sure you'll like it? Not some exotic French drink, you know, just sour lemon juice.—

—I understood.—

—When I was a student in London I used to ask the way on a bus. They would tell me, ten kind people at once . . . Yes, yes, grinning at them, thank you—but I was lost. It's a matter of pride, standing up to the chauvinism of the foreign language. At press conferences you hear a visiting statesman so eloquent in his own language—and then suddenly he tries a few words in French . . . an idiot speaking, an analphabetic from some wretched forgotten hamlet learning to read at the age of seventy.—

The girl did not seem intimidated. —I'm used to it. I've been speaking two mother-tongues all my life and I've always been surrounded by other languages I don't understand.—

—I speak English—

She gestured his competence; he was not impressed by his achievement—Well I worked there six years—but I don't know that we'll understand each other, êh.—

—Why not?— She took up the formula for a man and woman amusing themselves for half an hour.

—If you talk like that, yes. I say what I think will flatter you and make myself interesting. *I like this. Don't you think that.* Each makes an exhibit— I can't go through that. That's not what I . . . That's right, don't answer . . . it's embarrassing not to flirt, not to spread the tail-feathers and cocorico—

One of Arnys' young men looking down his cheeks glided two glasses in saucers before them. The man poured the little packet of sugar into the cloudy liquid and stirred medicinally; Rosa did the same. He reached for more sugar.

—What did you do?—

275

She felt again the grip in which she held a hand in the street named Rue de la Harpe. He waited for her to answer and she tasted the lemon juice and took swallows in sips because it was very hot.
—Nothing.—

She turned to him for a verdict, proof of his own words—he would not understand.

—I have done nothing.—

—What could you have done?—

—Ah, I can't explain that— She looked indulgently round the bar at the young men like chorus girls touching at their hair and clothes in perpetual expectation of making an entrance, the old singer satisfying a sense of control over all she had lived by the resolution of the right card coming down.

—There are many things I could say you could've done. Girls in the streets of Paris like tourists with their tired feet and *Guide bleu* who are hijackers on the run. Little students with art nouveau tresses who have cocaine for sale in their satchels. Deputies dining at the Matignon—silver hair, manicured—Anne-Aymone talks gardening with them—who are selling arms to both sides in the Middle East, Latin America, Africa, anywhere.—

—None of those.— He did not have a pullover knotted round his neck (a worn leather jacket had been put down on the bar stool beside him); he separated from the awareness in which a few common characteristics ran into one. A high forehead with distinct left and right lobes was almost a pate; thinning curly hair edged it against the light and straggled out in wings above and behind the ears. A wide thin mouth, with mobilities of muscle that modelled in the firm flesh around it expression more usually conveyed by lips.

—W-ell. There are also those who imagine they must have committed something, they feel they're being followed. It's all right.— The thick eyebrows that compensate men for losing their hair lifted with tolerance. The eyes had a trance-like steadiness, showing the arch of the eyelid rather low over the eyeball in a hollow of bone.

—I don't imagine. There's nothing either neurotic or mysterious— She had a need to be plain; as he had said, to make oneself 'an exhibit' was not acceptable. —If you are followed by policemen you get used to it, so do they. You know whether they fall asleep waiting for you and whether they slip away at regular times for a beer. I've known them since I was a child. But in a foreign town, it wouldn't have been so easy to recognize one. I don't know the sort of person who'd do the work, here—the kind of clothes, the haircut—

She gave up, smiling.

—If you don't live like that—haven't . . . And here—even I— if one isn't living like that—

He was looking at her with detached respect. —You've been in trouble. All right. I told you, it's impossible . . . I know about it but I haven't been in it.—

—First of all, I don't think of it like that—as 'trouble'—

—No of course not. You see? It's less and less possible for me. When I said we wouldn't understand each other I didn't think it would be something like this. I was thinking only we wouldn't admit why I said come and why you came. About the things between men and women. You attract me very much—you know it, and you answer it by leaving the others, with me. Perhaps you haven't found a man you want among all those who must have shown themselves interested?— Oh yes. But you couldn't tell me . . . And how would you understand about me. I am eating the food and drinking the wine of friends I don't think much of, living on them . . . and perhaps I also think a new girl is part of my little sabbatical . . . I don't know. You know that I'm a teacher. 'Professor'—we were introduced yes, but names . . . Every Frenchman who teaches in a lycée is a professor, every German is Herr Doktor. The people I'm staying with will tell you I'm writing a book—in their house, it's a wonderful process to them. Would I tell you it's my old Ph.D. thesis I entered myself for at the Sorbonne three years ago and that I hope maybe—maybe— someone will publish it if it is ever finished.—

—You can tell me.— She could laugh, unembarrassed. She put out a hand, tendons spoked widely on the back, and felt down round the spiral of the olive-press pillar she had followed with her eyes when she had been with other people.

A woman's voice recorded thirty years before was singing about the island where she and Napoleon's Joséphine were born. He had fished the slice of lemon out of the bottom of his glass and was gobbling the skin with a mouth drawn by the zest. —A pig. Excuse me, I love it.—Do you know what that is? That's Arnys singing—unmistakable. She was the best of the lot. Like some voice coming up from the street when you're falling asleep or not really awake yet.—

Rosa leaned to whisper and was touched by the springy hair behind his ear, smelled him for the first time. —That's Arnys there. It's her bar.—

—Ah no.—

—People keep on telling me. It doesn't mean much to me.—

He was looking at the old woman in some kind of partisan pride and bravado at endurance. —You chose Arnys' bar. Something like that happens . . .— He swung down from his stool and was over to the old woman; she looked up, mouth parted girlishly as in the photographs on the walls. He spoke low and fast in French. She growled an uncertain Monsieur?—a bass note with snapped strings. And then one of those extraordinary bursts of French animation broke out. They protested to each other, they talked both at once, lifting faces like birds challenging beaks, Arnys half-closed her eyes, they laid hands upon one another, Professor Bernard Chabalier repeating with reverent formality, *chère madame, Josette Arnys, Josette Arnys*. Her dog struggled under her arm to get at him or be let down.

He came back laughing privately past amiable glances; he might have been showing himself appreciative of any other local landmark. —*Very modest*—d'you know what she says?—she told me there will never be anyone like her. 'This whole feminist thing' means women won't be able to sing about love any more, they'll be ashamed. So I said but the island song, it's not about love, at least not that kind of love, it's about origins, it was even romantically political, êh, in advance of its time (I didn't say that to her)—the

Antilles, the hankering of Europe for a particular humanism it believes to flourish in a creole world? But she says the real source of song remains only one—look at the birds, who can sing only because they must call for a mate.—

—Hadn't you ever seen her before?—

—Where would I see her? In Paris nightclubs when I was a kid? We have some old records at home—my wife's family is the kind that never throws anything away—we play them once a year or so, when there is a party, you know, like tonight—everybody drinks too much wine and jumps round . . . Are you working tomorrow?—

—I'm not working.—

—Oh god, I will have to drive myself. The whole year I say: if I could get away from the flat, children, committees, Sunday lunches, everybody, if I could have three weeks, that's all. And now I'm alone with my thesis I'm always talking too much about. The whole summer has been arranged around me, my wife and children given up their holiday, even my mother writing me letters saying don't reply, you are too busy concentrating.— He drew back from himself. —Do people like you have holidays? Can you say, *arrête*. Set a date for the *rentrée*.—

—I promised.— She was deeply tempted, since this man had not proved never to be met again, to place something else before him as she had five minutes in the Rue de la Harpe. —I undertook to have a holiday. Like everybody else.— Her manner was teasing.

—We'll come tomorrow.— He spoke as if they had agreed to shelve some decision. —Does she open in the middle of the day? About twelve.— On the way out he returned to the old singer and kissed her hand. There was another flurry between the two. —She wants to open a bottle of champagne. Her boys would be jealous, êh, she obviously didn't stand them a Quatorze Juillet celebration. I told her, tomorrow.— As the girl's head preceded him into the street he was at once pleading and strict. —I'll be waiting here.—

There were times when she was there before him. He began to make it a rule that he got up early enough to have worked three hours before he appeared for her through Arnys' tabernacle-shaped doors with the panes of syrupy amber blistered glass at the top. They opened inwards and usually only for him; hardly anyone came in the mornings. Pépé or Toni or Jacques—whichever had happened to take the keys for Arnys when the bar closed at four or five in the morning—prowled listlessly between the hole of a kitchen, the restaurant alcove smelling of corks swollen with wine and corners where the Maltese had leaked into the sawdust, and the espresso machine set gargling and spitting into cup after cup taken up with dirtied, delicate, trembling ringed hands. The self-absorption of the young homosexual was strangely restful. He would drink the coffee as if it were the source of existence, smoke as if what he drew into his lungs and elaborately expelled through mouth and nostrils was a swilling-out with pure oxygen; reviving, his closed face marked by sleep and caresses like a child's by forgotten tears and a creased pillow would change and flicker with what was passing in his mind. Now and then he would give the bar counter a half-moon swipe. In the presence of a creature so contained, Rosa came to awareness of her own being like the rising tick of a clock in an empty room. She had a newspaper, or a book she and Bernard were exchanging, but she didn't read. The huge wooden screws of the olive press, the mirror wall behind the bar, the photographs whose signatures were a performance in themselves, the green satin that covered the walls of the alcove, held in place where it was coming loose by the pinned card, *Ouvert jusqu'à l'aube*; the china fish with pencils in its mouth, the bottles of Suze, Teacher's, Ricard, Red Heart, ranged upside-down like the pipes of an organ, the TV on the old rattan table facing the kitchen at the whim of whoever currently was cook, so that he could be seen in the evenings, cutting or chopping or beating while he watched; the ribbons saved from chocolates or flowers curled like wood-shavings among the bill-spikes on Arnys' roll-top desk: in a state exactly the reverse of that of the young homosexual, all these were strongly the objects of Rosa's present. She inhabited it completely as everything in place around her, there and then. In the bar where she had sat seeing others living in the mirror, there

was no threshold between her reflection and herself. The pillars s.
had noticed only as a curiosity she read over like a score, each nick
and groove and knot sustaining the harmony and equilibrium of
the time-space before the door pushed inwards.

—You choose something you hope someone else isn't writing
about already. That's the extent of the originality— The irony was
not unforgiving, of himself or others. He held her innocent of the
pettiness of Europe. He took her hand a moment, in her lap. —I
also wanted to give myself time.— He pulled a comic, culpable
face. —If you are too topical, the interest will have passed on to
something else before you've finished. And if it's something purely
scholarly, well, unless you are a great savant . . . what will I
contribute . . .? No one will take the slightest notice. But the
influence of former French colonists who've come back to France
since the colonial empire ended—I haven't got a working title
yet—that's something that will go on for years. I don't have to
worry. At first I thought I would do something about the decline
of Latinity—in fact I've given a few little talks on the radio . . .—

—To do with linguistics?—

—No, no—the decline of the Latin source of the French
temperament, ideas and so on—I don't know, it sounds a lot
of shit? You know it's true the life of the French becomes directed
more and more by Anglo-Saxon and American concepts . . . It's
tied up with the Common Market, OTAN . . . god knows what else.
If you want to be fancy you can compare it with the destruction of
the ancient culture that flourished in southern France and Cata-
lonia in the Middle Ages, the *civilisation occitane*: instinctive,
imaginative, self-renewing qualities losing out to sterile techno-
logical and military ones. But I don't much like it. What d'you
think? Too nationalistic. And it leaves out of reckoning Descartes,
Voltaire . . . Where does that kind of thing end? But of course I
make a big fuss like everybody else when I see old *bistrots* like this
disappearing and being replaced by drug-store bars, and markets
pulled down for supermarkets . . . oh on that level . . . *Enfin*—
when I was playing with the Latinity idea, I spent some time
around Montpellier, in the Languedoc (the region's named after

of that civilization—the tongue they spoke was _~~gue~~ d'oc_ . . . 'oc' simply means 'yes', that's all . . .). I was also in Provence. Provençal isn't just a dialect, ~~it~~'s one of the _langues d'oc_. Not much more than a remnant, ~~but~~ there still are attempts at publishing works in it, but the great Provençal revival took place in the last century—Frédéric Mistral, the poet—you've heard of him?—yes. Well then I found I was beginning to think about something different, though in a way . . . related, because migrations, social change . . . I began to think about the _pieds noirs_ concentrated in Provence, here on the coast particularly, and what effect _their_ mentality is having on modern French culture. Part of the consequences of colonialism and all that. Ouf— He had gestures estimating how little all this was worth in the intellectual market. But he was practical. —They've come back—some after generations in Algeria, Tunisia, Morocco. What gives the idea an interesting nuance, most of them came from this part of the world—their families, originally; southern France, Corsica, Spain. It even relates a bit to the old Latinity business: they have in their blood somewhere the qualities of the ancient cultures, the temperament, but they now bring back to France from her imperialist period the particular values and mores colonizers develop. The locust people. Descend on the land, eat the crop, and be ready to fly when the enslaved population comes after you . . . Anyway, there are hundreds of thousands back here and they're very successful. That ancient spontaneousness, capacity for improvisation, alive in their veins? Maybe. A million unemployed in France this summer, but I don't think you'll find one among them. Many have their money in Monaco—tax reasons. I've been to talk to some people . . . d'you know that 2 per cent of the population there is _pied noir_ . . . Not a bad subject, êh. It's just controversial enough.—

—Why must it be a thesis? It would make a good book.—

—Rosa. Rosa Burger.— He leaned back, elbow on the bar, picked up the china fish and put it down again.

—Oh the style of a thesis—the long-winded footnotes. What you want to say gets buried.—

—I'm a schoolteacher. If I don't get a Ph.D. I won't get a job at a university. We have it all worked out—such-and-such a number of francs against such-and-such at the lycée. We can buy a piece of land in Limousin or Bretagne. In so many years build a small country house. To take a chance on a book—you have to be poor, you have to be alone, you can't have middle-class standards.— He caught her by the wrist, persuasively, smiling, as if to make fall a weapon he imagined in her fist. —You don't know how careful we are, we French Leftist bourgeoisie. So much set aside every month, no possibility of living dangerously.—

She was considering and curious. —Who need live dangerously, in Europe?—

—Oh there are some. But not the Eurocommunists . . . Not the Left that votes. Terrorists holding one country to ransom for horrors happening in another. Hijackers. People who push drugs. No one else.—

—One of the people you thought I was.—

—I know who you are.— The third time they met he returned with this discovery. He did not so much mean that someone had told him, as one of Madame Bagnelli's friends no doubt had: her father was on the side of the blacks, out there—he was imprisoned, killed or something—a terrible story. *Bernard Chabalier* was among the signatures of academics and journalists that filled sheets headed by Sartre, de Beauvoir and Yves Montand on petitions for the release of political prisoners in Spain, Chile, Iran, and on manifestos protesting the abuse of psychiatry in the Soviet Union and censorship in Argentina. He had once signed an Amnesty International petition for the release of an ageing and ill South African revolutionary leader, Lionel Burger. 'At a time' (it was an expression he used often, not quite English, and somehow thereby more tentative than in its correct form) there had been a suggestion he should be on the anti-apartheid committee in Paris. He had spoken a short introduction to a film made clandestinely by blacks showing the bulldozing of their houses in mass removals. The facts came from the black exiles who were hawking the film around Europe; his ability to communicate with them in English was his primary qualification. —And I gave it as a talk on *France Culture*—I sometimes get asked to do things; usually the sociological consequences of political questions—that sort of programme.—

—I'd like to hear you. If I could understand.—

—I should talk only French to you, really . . . you'd improve quickly . . . But you'll never say anything real to me except in English. I won't give that up.— Before there was time to settle an interpretation, he became practical and amusing. —If I had a tape recorder here I could do an interview with you for the radio, you know. They'd buy it I'm sure. We'll split the fee. A grand sum. What could we do with it? Change our brand of champagne?— They drank every day without remarking it the loving-cup of the first meeting, the same *citron pressé*. Pépé/Toni/Jacques prepared it each time as if he had not known what the order would be: a signal of contempt for heterosexual trysts. —We could buy two cheap tickets to Corsica. On the ferry. Vomit all the way—I am terribly seasick. I know you will not be.— A moment of gloomy jealousy.

—I've never been on board a ship.—

—But it would be good—people would hear your voice, and I would translate you (finger-tips pursed together by the drawstring of a gesture, then opening away)—im-pec-cable.—

—I promised. I can't speak.—

Arnys was at her old roll-top desk as soon as she arrived; she spent the first hour of her day in meditative retreat behind three walls of minute drawers and cubby-holes: her misty spectacles hung on the little pert nose of the celebrity photographs and her hands went about spearing invoices on spikes with the brooding orderly anxiety, over money, of hardened arteries in the brain. Their voices came to her as the voices of so many who were lovers or would be lovers, whose intense abrupt interrogations and mono-logues of banalities too low to be made out sounded as if secret and irrevocable matters were being discussed.

He put aside what he had said like a trinket he had been playing with. —Who was it you promised?—

Rosa caught the abstracted peer above the old singer's glasses, tactfully dropped in respect for sexual privacies everyone knows

from common experiences and indulges. The protection of Arnys'
unimaginable life, and the life to which the one called Pépé was at
that moment connected on the phone—the pillars, the enclosed
reality of the mirror—all contained her safely. —That's how I got
here. How they let me out.—

—The police?— The awkward respectful tone of initiative
surrendered.

—Not directly. But in effect, yes. Oh don't worry . . .— Her
eyes moved to smile, a parenthetic putting out of a hand to him.
—I didn't talk. I made sure I had nothing to talk about before I
went to them. But I made a deal. With them.—

—Sensible.— He defended her.

She repeated: —With them, Bernard.—

—You didn't betray anybody.—

'Oppress'. 'Revolt'. 'Betray'. He used the big words as people do
without knowing what they can stand for.

—I asked. No one I know would do that. I did what none of the
others has done.—

—What did they say?—

—I didn't tell anyone. I kept away.—

He was working well; the regulation of his days had fallen into
place round the daily meetings in Arnys' bar, hardly open for
business but tolerant of certain needs. She saw in the rim of
shaving-foam still wet on an earlobe that he had broken off
concentration at the last minute, jumped up in the virtue of
achievement to prepare himself for her. He was superstitious about
acknowledging progress, but the calm elation with which he slid
onto the stool beside her, or the gaiety of his exchanges with Arnys
were admittance.

—I'd like to have you there in the room. I've always resented
having anyone in the same room while I work.— It was a
declaration; a reverie of a new relationship. But he refused himself.
—I'll make love to you, that's the trouble.—

After the first Sunday of their acquaintance, when each had been
committed to excursions with other people, they had gone on
Tuesday straight from Arnys to the room where he lived. —I

thought of an hotel. I've been worrying since Quatorze Juillet, where can we go?— His hosts were out; but it would not often happen that the house would be empty. —Do you know that little one in the street near the big garage? Behind the Crédit Lyonnais.—

—You mean opposite the parking ground where they play *boule*?—

—I like the look of those two little windows above.—

—There's a bird-cage outside one.—

—You saw it too.—

—That's the little restaurant where Katya and I eat couscous— they make couscous every Wednesday. Fourteen francs.—

His suitcase lay open on a chair, never unpacked but delved into, socks and shirts that had been worn stuffed among clean shirts carefully folded in imitation of the format of the shirt box and clean socks rolled into neat fists. Someone had packed shoe-trees for him. They were serving to hold down piles of cuttings and papers sorted on the bed.

It was exactly the hour of the day when she had arrived and come out into the village on Madame Bagnelli's terrace. He moved his papers in their order to the floor, already naked, with the testicles appearing between his thighs as his male rump bent, equine and beautiful. They emerged for each other all at once: they had never seen each other on a beach, the public habituation to all but a genital triangle. He might never have been presented with a woman before, or she a man. Tremendous sweet possibilities of renewal surged between them; to explode in that familiar tender explosion all that has categorized sexuality, from chastity to taboo, illicit licence to sexual freedom. In a drop of saliva there was a whole world. He turned the wet tip of his tongue round the whorl of the navel Didier had said was like that of an orange.

In the heat they shut out, people were eating in soft clatter, laughter, and odours of foods that had been cooked in the same way for so long their smell was the breath of the stone houses. Behind other shutters other people were also making love.

The little Rôse has a lover.

I spend less time with you; you understand that sort of priority well. You were the one who said, Chabalier, why go home—stay tonight and we can make an early start in the morning. The little expeditions to show me something of the country are arranged by the two of you, now. The big bed in the room you gave me—the room I'll be able to keep the sense of in the moments before I have to open my eyes in other places, as Dick Terblanche knew the proportions of his grandfather's dining-table when he couldn't remember poetry in solitary confinement—the bed in my lovely room is intended for two people. Once dragged shut the heavy old black door doesn't let through the sounds you have known so well, yourself. If they are audible through the windows they merge with the night traffic of motorbikes and nightingales. When the three of us have breakfast together in the sun before he goes off to his work I notice you make up your eyes and brush your hair out of respect for male presence and as an aesthetic delicacy of differentiation from the stage in life of a young woman in perfect lassitude and carelessness of sensuality—I can't help yawning till the tears come to my eyes, thirsty and hungry (you buy croissants filled with almond paste to satisfy and indulge me), spilling over in affection towards you a bounty I can afford to be generous with. Bernard says to me: —I am full of semen for you.— It has nothing to do with passion that had to be learned to deceive prison warders; and you're no real revolutionary waiting to decode my lovey-dovey as I dutifully report it.

With Solvig, with old Bobby (rambling off over her own hopelessly philosophical grievances in a bright English voice:

—I used to do all Henry Torren's correspondence at one time. Ten francs an hour! You couldn't get someone to wash your floors for that. How many millions d'you think he's worth! Oh but I don't really mind. I don't expect anything different. His grandmother wore clogs, a cotton-hand, it's true, my dear—)—with all the little group of you who once lived with lovers: I imagine in your voices down there on the terrace or in the kitchen a discussion of the prospects, for me, you all know so well.

Manolis was having an exhibition of his paintings on glass; Georges, reversing their roles and taking up housewifely responsibility for the opening, calculated with Madame Bagnelli the number of people for whom he was on his way to order *amuse-gueules* from Perrin: Donna and Didier, twelve, Tatsu—and Henry; maybe—fourteen, you and Rosa and Chabalier, seventeen . . . Pierre Grosbois had built himself an 'American barbecue' and the Grosbois initiated it with a party—No madonnas and flying donkeys (he looks too much at Chagall, êh), the bouzouki records his boyfriend buys him were the only Greek inspiration, what did you think? But I also can make things with my hands—*and the little Rôse will bring her professor, of course.*

Gaby suddenly cut out a dress for her; there were fittings with Rosa standing on the terrace table, waving to acquaintances who happened to look up and see her aloft, and the children of neighbours, curious and shy. The equidistant sea and sky were divided for her by the line of gravity like an hour-glass, through which a ship wrapped in pink-mauve haze passed from one element to the other, coming down over the horizon. Gaby and Katya pinned and tacked; while Rosa recognized the car-ferry boat from Corsica or Sardinia Bernard identified when they were walking round the ramparts, Gaby was telling Katya about a book she had ordered from Paris. —*La Ménopause effacée*, apparently if your doctor isn't a complete idiot you can avoid the whole thing. It simply doesn't have to happen to you— Being Gaby, she gurgled with laughter, tipped over into the uncontrolled improvisation and patter that sometimes seemed to become compulsive, she would talk at a street-corner or at the door, unable to free people of herself. —You can go on for ever. In theory. Not that anyone would want to, my god . . .

With Pierre, *mon pauvre vieux*, it's not much point . . . and where would I find someone in this place . . . Can you imagine, like Pierre's dentist's wife—you remember, I told you?—she takes a policeman to the Negresco on his day off every week, she picks him up from the préfecture in Nice, they have a good lunch— She pays for the room . . .— The laugh rose to a wail—Madame Perrin's second daughter is at the reception there now—the old Perrin said, it's *comme il faut*, mind you—not as if it's some type picked up on the beach, he's from the préfecture, *a family man*.—No—but look, my eyebrows are getting coarse, like an old man's. Look at these marks on my hands—

—Keep out of the sun, Gaby.—

—Keep out the sun!—it's not the sun, you know it, Katya. My doctor says there's nothing to be done. He's a man, what does he care. But it's not so sure, not at all. We should have been taking hormones years ago, Katya . . . they say deterioration can't be repaired but it can be arrested—Like that!—ah, that's better, that's the way the skirt should hang . . . This girl won't ever need to get old, who knows?—

The ship was growing from veil to solidity, from pink to white, and as it listed imbedded itself out there in an ocean laid like a Roman mosaic pavement in wavy bands of pollution to the inshore limits. She and Bernard Chabalier might take a ship, one day; they could be standing somewhere on that advancing object, approaching again the chalky-lavender mountains beyond Nice and the white buildings nested up the cliffs, flashing a fish-scale tiled cupola, blue, green or rose with a gilt spike, and the towers on the shore towards Antibes that spouted up over the sea, leaning, turning slowly on their axes under the wing of the plane, built in the spiral—that aspiring, unfinished figure—that was reduced to the scale of her hand in Arnys' bar. Rosa took in a great lungful of air out there, causing pins to give way, and the women protested indulgently. —I take the pills he gave me, yes—but I wonder if it's the best thing? according to what I've read there're new discoveries all the time. I'm going to take the book and simply say, tell him— But Katya—you examine your breasts, don't you? It's essential. You don't neglect yourself?—

—You're the only one who goes to a private doctor. You miss the girls' gatherings at the clinic; Bobby, Françoise and Marthe, Darby in his oldest cap (afraid they'll reassess pensions and charge if you look too prosperous). We all have our pap test. You're crazy to pay.—

—Pierre's idea, not mine. He doesn't trust the clinic doctor— for my part ours is a *vieux con*. But the breasts—you must do that every month. Just in the bath, I lie in my bath and like this— carefully—I close my eyes and feel—you must concentrate—

Katya put out a brisk hand to Rosa. —Come down. You seem to like it up there.— Now and then when the French people became absorbed in discussion of bowel movements or other regulations of their bodies' functions, she could be distinguished as a foreigner among them still. She spoke English, to redefine herself for the eyes of the girl; a comment on preoccupations deftly quitted, disloyally leaving her friend to them. —If someone would write the book that tells how to get old and ugly and not mind.—

—I don't understand you too well . . .?—Gaby looked from one to the other.

Katya said it for her in French.

Gaby put on her show of jostling gaiety—Look at that, look at that one!—but Katya, you have still a beauty, êh.— An impressed face pausing at Rosa. —Listen to her—when you have like this (an imitation of the mouth of Françoise or perhaps it was meant to be Marthe) like the anus of a hen . . . when you are gaga like Poliakoff . . . then you can complain, êh— She was a dancer, you know that? The muscles are still supple—The Ballet Russe . . .— A career was built up in the air.

Katya seized and crossed hands with her friend in the position of the *corps* of cygnets, jerking her head to the burst of 'Swan Lake' she sang. Their breasts' bulk shifted from side to side like pillows being plumped.

Pierre had come up out of the dark of the little stairway and the house, a lonely bald child in search of playmates. He looked at his wife laughing and panting, intimated to Rosa, by drawing up a chair and placing himself carefully, that she and he were the only reasonable beings present.

Gaby was over at once. —How do you like it? Isn't she beautiful? I'm proud of myself, frankly—

Her husband gazed, not to be influenced. —Wait. Sit down, Rôse. A dress can't be judged until you see a woman coming and going, standing and sitting—am I right?—

—But it's good! The colour, with her skin? The tiny design—real *satin fermière*—I think the fashion's amusing—

—Wait. Yes. It's good.—

Rosa walked up and down for them, smiling over her shoulder as she turned the body Chabalier defined for her with his hands, the face he watched with an attention that was only for her.

The girl's strong awareness of herself brought to Katya the physical presence she had known, and overlaid by many others: Lionel Burger's young flesh and face that was always under an attention beyond desire, a passion beyond theirs on the bed, the passion-beyond-passion, like the passion of God, although for him there was no such concept: he was on his own; a frightening being, the young man who thrust his heat inside her in the coldest cities of the world.

Pierre carried the glass of pastis that was his avuncular intimacy with the girl and tackled her round the neck in a moment's hug, murmuring with generosity and sense of celebration that needed no tact—The little Rôse *en pleine forme*, everything is wonderful with you, êh.—

There's the desire to create a little store of common experience between lovers, foreigners: while she was living with the Nel family in the dorp hotel on the Springbok Flats, a youth of eighteen was taking his baccalauréat at the Lycée Louis le Grand. The pictures of street cafés, awnings and poodles in the hotel rooms—I told the cleaning girls, that's Paris, a place in England.

—You were a show-off and ignorant as most show-offs. Whereas of course I could have put my finger just *exactly* on the map of Africa where your aunt and uncle had their small hotel— He stroked away on her eyelids and in the bend of her elbows the years and places that could not exist, his for her, hers for him. Those of the present and immediate past did not seem to have much importance. Since she had taken down the plate and sold that house, she had lived with friends; in a flat; in a cottage with some young man who had paused in his wanderings about the world; and then a flat again, the same city. —It's a condominium in the *quinzième*, not bad, Christine found it when they were re-planning the interior so it's more or less according to her idea. At least I have a small room to work in—before I used to have my table in the bedroom, and if I wanted to work late . . . the other person gets fed up, wants to go to bed. There's a big terrace where the kids can keep their bicycles—but she's cluttered it with a lot of plants, I'm not so keen—

Rosa Burger and Bernard Chabalier were easily matched to these contingent circumstances; wearing the same clothes covering the same newly-discovered minutely-known bodies they could be set walking along streets that had scuffed the shoes they wore now in each other's presence, could be seen standing in grey European raincoat on a metro platform, turning home into one of the new rectangles pushed between florid nineteenth-century mansards and frail yellowed walls of earlier buildings, or followed—a small, strong girl whose shoulder-muscles of an open-air country's physique moved in a bare-backed dress, like the one she was wearing—through traffic of black men on bicycles and women with bundles on their heads that was familiar footage from television news.

When their delight in each other brimmed and its energies turned outwards, they liked to go fishing. The old car borrowed from Katya tackled tracks tunnelled beside the Loup; they shared the modest opportunities of a catch with young husbands in caps given away at petrol stations, old fellows with wives who knitted and minded paper bags holding bait, bread and wine; and all were startled together by the descent of wandering bands of hoarse teenagers who pushed one another about, splashed and went away, leaving the shuddering markings of light and shade to settle again on figures and water, working them over in a way that broke up limits and made one single state of being for a whole summer afternoon.

They looked at paintings. —In Africa, one goes to see the people. In Europe, it's pictures.—

But she was seeing in Bonnard canvases past which they were being moved as if processed by the crowd, a confirmation of the experience running within her. The people she was living among, the way of apprehending, of being alive, at the river, were coexistent with the life fixed by the painter's vision. And how could that be? —When you look at a painting, it's something that's over, isn't it?— it's a record of what's already passed through the painter's mind, both the event of seeing and the concept that arises from it—the imagining—are fixed in paint. So a picture is always abstract, to me—the style of painting hasn't much to do with it. But when Katya and I go and lie under the olive trees . . . even my room, you know, the room she gave me—the flowers in a jar on the floor, and his flowers, this bouquet of mimosa . . . These pictures are proof of something. It *is* the people I'm living among I'm seeing, not the pictures.—

—And do you know why, my darling? This woman here

stepping through the leaves, and this mimosa—the woman he painted in eighteen-ninety-four (look in the catalogue, it's written), the mimosa in '45 during the war, during the Occupation, yes? All right. In the fifty years between the two paintings, there was the growth of fascism, two wars—the Occupation— And for Bonnard it is as if nothing's happened. Nothing. Look at them . . . He could have painted them the same summer, the same day. And that's how they are, those ones up there round the château—that's how they live. It's as if nothing has ever happened—to them, or anybody. Or is happening. Anywhere. No prisoners in Soviet asylums, no South Africa . . . no migrant workers living without women just down the road . . . no 'place of protection' at Arène— right under our noses, over there in Marseilles—already this year seven thousand poor devils have been locked up there like stray animals before they're deported . . . To be alive day by day: the same as in Bonnard—tout voir pour la première fois, à la fois. Until the age of eighty. Oh that's charming . . . of course, if you can manage it. Look here—and there—the woman's flesh and the leaves round her are so beautiful and they are equal manifestations. Because she hasn't any existence any more than the leaves have, outside this lovely forest where they are. No past, no future. The mimosa: fifty years later, it's alive in the same summer as she is. There hasn't been any Hitler, concentration camps— The slow-moving surge of people in holiday clothes pushed them away out of the galleries to the shallow steps and down to a courtyard of sculptured figures elongated as late shadows. His muscular legs with their shining straight black hair, and his pale European hands with the thin gold ring of his family status shone softly in the shade. —no bombings, no German occupation. Your forest girl and the vase of mimosa—c'est un paradis inventé.—

They were both wearing shorts and as they strolled his leg brushed hers like the weaving of an affectionate cat.

—If I did come to Paris—

—You will come, you will come— He went ahead along a narrow path under pinkish-blue-trunked pine trees, putting out a hand to lead her behind him.

—I can't imagine how it would be—work out. How I would see you.—

—As you are seeing me now. Every day.—

—I'd be—where?—

—Some nice little hotel. Near the lycée. So that I can come quickly to you. I want first to show you *la dame à la licorne* in the Cluny.—

—You will arrange treats for me.—

—What is that?—

—When you take children out to amuse them.—

—Ah no. I love her, I can't let you go any longer without knowing you have seen her too.—

Rosa leant beside him on a stone wall, looking on slopes with vineyards spread out to ripen in the sun and olive trees stooped along abandoned terracing broken by old farmhouses and new villas. A shirtless man was tiptoeing across a tiled roof he was repairing; a woman's arms and stance were those of someone yelling up at him, although she was too far away to be heard. Farther still, on the strip of sea threaded behind the sandcastle towers, flags and belfries of hill-top villages, a ship like a spouting whale sent up white smoke. She followed the woman stepping back and back to see the man on the roof as if completing a figure that was leading to a tapestry on a museum wall from a room in an hotel that would be particular among streets of such hotels. Her chin was lifted and she was smiling, grimacing with lips pressed together in some shy and awkward mastery. Bernard saw the man on the roof: —The belly he's got on him. Il va se casser la gueule, vieux con . . . Maybe even a little apartment. It's not easy, but I have a few ideas. I know just what you'd like—a little studio in an old building . . . but usually they are stinking . . . the passages . . . you can't imagine. No, we'll find something better.— He no longer saw the man on the roof, the woman, the valley; eyes were drawn as if against glare, against thoughts in the language where she could not follow him. —Mind you, an hotel—then there's always the concierge, if you need anything and I'm not— The long mouth with the thin upper line reacted with sadness and shrewd obstinacy to objections she did not know about; the steady eyes came to a warm, assuring focus, denying them. —I'm absolutely sure something can be done through the right people. The anti-apartheid committee can get you temporary residence and even a work permit. If not for you, then who the hell? But discreetly . . . Though of course they'd love to have you on a platform, Rosa, you can believe it . . . And we could get that film of your father, it would be—but no, of course not, not until you have French papers. They'd jump at the idea of you—probably they'll make a job for you right away. And there are my contacts. Not bad. Quite a few black academics who have influence in French-speaking African countries they come from—There are so many projects and never enough people to go. It's possible you could get a job doing wonderful work, medical training in Cameroun or Brazzaville, somewhere like that—I've many times been offered a lectureship at one of those black universities there, a year's contract, there wouldn't be any question of moving the family.—

They had taken on without thinking one of the ancient group-ings of the couple; found a place in the grass where she folded her legs beneath her and he laid his head against her belly, feeling it shake when she laughed and hearing the muffled questioning sounds of her gut as a child of his in her would. —I'll come alone. We'd have a whole year.—

—I was talking with the dear boys before you came to Arnys' yesterday. They were consulting their horoscopes in *Marie-Claire*. Very serious. You know, I just found I had the words, I could put them together without thinking— The face turned up to hers was the face he must have had ten years earlier, a face to be curious about, smoothed like a piece of paper under the heel of a hand, unmarked by lines of ambitious anxiety, and as it was before the chin-crevice was deepened by sensual intelligence. —Oh your French will be fine. You'll manage perfectly all right. Maybe in Africa I'll even finish my bloody book. Ah, that's very good: one of the reasons for my taking the job after all will be that it's necessary to go back to colonial sources and so on.—

All practical matters were open between them; a wife and two children, a responsibility assumed long ago by a responsible man. The attitude on which Bernard and Rosa's acceptance of this circumstance rested was based on one of the simple statements of a complex man: —I live among my wife and children—not with them.—

The statement, in turn, seemed to seek an explanation from Rosa she could not give; but in the saying, the burden of it was shifted a little, her shoulder went under it beside his. They had no home but he was living very much with her. The security was almost palpable for him in the vigour and repose of her small body. Resting there, he gained what she had once and many times at the touch-line of her father's chest, warm and sounding with the beat of his heart, in chlorinated water. Her eyes (the colour of light, creating unease; Boer eyes, *pied-noir* eyes?)—moved above his head among trees, passers-by and—quick glance down—in a private motivation of inner vision as alert and dissimulating as the gaze her mother had been equally unaware of, looking up to see the daughter coming slowly over the gravel from the visit to her 'fiancé' in prison.

The young smooth face spoke out beneath hers; from what he had been and what he was: —You are the dearest thing in the world to me.—

At gatherings they lost each other in the generality and then would become aware, near by, of the back of a head or a voice: she heard a slightly different version of Bernard Chabalier giving a slightly different version of what he had said about the painter. —fifty years, fauvism, futurism, cubism, abstract art—for him everything passes as nothing. 1945 is 1895. Maybe what is complete is timeless . . . but events change the consciousness of the world, it shakes and the shocks register seismographically in movements in art—

Donna was obliged to entertain an English friend who was the property of her family—the sort of single example, culled by them from the politico-intellectual circles whose existence they ignore, that is the pride of a rich family. He would take himself at their valuation of his distinction. He would expect to have a party given for him; Donna had had to round up, among the usual people she knew, a few that he would feel were on a level to appreciate him. Her explanation of what he was or rather did was unsure; had been a member of parliament, something to do with the fuss over Britain's entry into the Common Market, something to do with editing a journal. She couldn't remember how good his French was; the Grosbois, the Lesbians from the *brocanterie* and other people of her local French contingent collected in one part of her terrace, happy to make their own familiar party, anyway; Didier in an exquisite white Italian suit (only Manolis recognized pure raw silk) asserted his own kind of distinction while moving about swiftly serving drinks in the preoccupied detachment of someone hired for the occasion. His contribution to proper appreciation of the guest of honour was instinctively to take on a role in keeping with the position of Donna as the host of James Chelmsford.

Chelmsford himself was got up in shirt-sleeves, blue linen trousers, espadrilles showing thick, pallid blue-veined ankles, yellow Liberty scarf under a shinily-shaven red face, drinking pastis; making it clear he was no newcomer to this part of the world. Donna shepherded round him a little group that included Rosa. It attracted one or two others who had opinions to solicit as an opening to giving their own—a journalist from Paris who was someone else's house-guest, a construction engineer from the Société des Grands Travaux de Marseille.

—Why has it taken Solzhenitsyn to disillusion people with Marx? Others've come out of the Soviet Union with the same kind of testimony. His Gulag isn't something we didn't all know about—

Chelmsford was listening to the journalist with an air of professional attention. —Well, for that matter of course, one might ask how since the Moscow trials—

—No, no—because they belong to the Stalinist period and the Left makes a strong distinction between what died with Stalin, that's the bad old days . . . But dating from the new era—post-Khrushchev—the thaw, the freeze again—everyone's been aware the same old horrors were going on, hospitals the latest kind of prison camp, new names for the old terror, that's all. Why should Solzhenitsyn rouse people?—

—But has he?—

The journalist gave the engineer the smile for someone of no opinion. He addressed his reaction to the others. —Oh without question—after that creature so tortured, so damaged—who could meet his eyes on television, sitting there at home on a Roche-Bobois chair with a whisky in your hand. I know that I . . . that face that looks as if it has been hit—slapped, êh?—so that the cheeks have no feeling any more and the mouth that makes itself (he drew up his own shoulders, shook his clenched hands, and bunched his mouth until the lips whitened)—that mouth that makes itself so small from the habitude of not being allowed to speak freely. The Western Leftists don't know how to go on believing. They don't know what to defend in Marx, after him.—

—It's not easy to answer.— The engineer spoke up friendlily to

Rosa as if for them both; he had the scrupulously tolerant manner of some new kind of missionary, his feet in sensible sandals, his blond head almost completely shaven for coolness in the river-mouth swamps of Brazil and Africa where (he chatted to her) he prepared surveys of prospective harbour sites. —Perhaps it's the approach, something in his style? The writing, I mean. Something Victor Hugoish that appeals to a wide public, much wider . . .—

—The public. The public in general were always ready to believe the Communists are nothing but beasts and monsters anyway—it's the intellectual Left that's rejecting Marx now—

—Well I doubt whether the same kind of thing can be said of England—but then I doubt whether we can be said to have an intellectual Left in the same sense. One could hardly put up Tony Crosland as a candidate among café philosophers . . .— The French didn't understand the joke.

—And even rejecting Mao—you can't 'institutionalize happiness'—from the same people who were the students in the streets in '68!—

The journalist and the engineer singled each other out, constantly interrupted, above the heads of others. —No, it's not quite true, Glucksmann *attacks* Solzhenitsyn for saying Stalin was already contained in Marx—

—We-ell, they put up some kind of half-hearted show . . . I mean, of course you don't come out and say, I was wrong, we brilliant young somebodies, the new Sartres and Foucaults, our theories, our basic premises—blood and shit, that's all that's left of them in the Gulag, êh?—

—Of course one shouldn't overlook that Solzhenitsyn's basic pessimism has always made him a plebeian rather than a socialist writer—

—But how will we change the world without Marx?— (The engineer admitted as if smilingly confessing to have been a football first-leaguer, although his build wouldn't credit it: —I was out in the streets in '68.—) —They do still agree it must be changed.—

—I wonder. Hardly. Even that. What have they between their legs, never mind in their heads. Political philosophers . . . They'll capitulate entirely to individualism. Or get religion. Either way, they'll end up with the Right.—

—Well, for a start, we must disown Marx's eldest child. La fille aînée. We must declare the Soviet Union heretic to socialism.— Bernard Chabalier joined the group; she heard the interjection among others. He had the elliptical gestures of one who has slipped back into the shoal.

—No, no, let's be clear: there's a distinction between the anti-sovietism of the Right and the new anti-sovietism of the Leftist intellectuals. The Left now may *seem* to define the evils of Soviet socialism just as reactionary thought always did: pitiless dictatorship over forced labour. But what they condemn isn't the *difference between* Soviet socialism and Western liberalism—which is roughly speaking the thesis of Western liberalism and even of the enlightened Right—that's true in England?—

—M—y-es, I suppose one could say we believe we know what human rights we stand for but we don't want nationalization and unrestricted immigration of blacks. That's why the Labour Party's going to come to grief.— The French laughed with the guest of honour this time and he tailed off into vague assenting, dissimulating, scornful umphs and murmurs that dissociated him from that particular political folly.

—Neither is it the orthodox apologist thesis that what's happened to socialism in the Soviet Union has something to do with a legacy of Russian backwardness—that old stuff: her state of underdevelopment when her revolution came, the economic setback of the war, the autocratic tradition of the Russian people and so on. The Left's theory is that if Stalin was contained in Marx, it's because the cult of the state and *la rationalité sociale* already were contained in Western thought—it's this that has infected socialism. The *phenomenon* of Gulag arose in the Soviet Union; but its *doctrine* comes from Machiavelli and Descartes—

The distinctively-modelled forehead with the fuzz of hair behind each ear tipped back, the lids dropped, intensifying the gaze. —So all that's wrong with socialism is what's wrong with the West. The fault of capitalism again—

—Let me finish—therefore the anti-sovietism of the Western Leftists is an anti-sovietism of the *Left*, quite different.—

—and let me tell you—Bernard burst through the hoop of his own irony—it's the tragedy of the Left that it can still believe all that's wrong with socialism is the West. Our tragedy as Leftists, the tragedy of our age. Socialism is the horizon of the world, Sartre has said it once and for all—but it's a blackout . . . close your eyes, hold your nose rather than admit where the stink is coming from.—

—The important thing surely is—

The engineer's voice ran up and down themes that pleased him: —I wish I could arrange my convictions with the genius of a new *philosophe* . . . and they talk about Manichean . . . they accuse Giscard . . .—

—Surely the important factor is—the Englishman had drawn up his belly and lifted his chest, holding his opinions above argument—. . . at least these fellows may have the sense to have done with total ideas and the total repression indivisible from such ideas. When you get someone saying the twentieth century's great invention may turn out to be the concentration camp . . . when you start coming out with thoughts like that, we may be getting away at last from the lure of the evil utopia. If people would forget about utopia! When rationalism destroyed heaven and decided to set it up here on earth, that most terrible of all goals entered human ambition. It was clear there'd be no end to what people would be made to suffer for it.—

Bernard saw her, Rosa, looking at them all, at himself as one of them. Her cheekbones were taut with amazement; her presence went among them like an arm backing them away from something lost and trampled underfoot. —'You can't institutionalize happiness'?—In all seriousness? As a discovery . . .? It's something from a Christmas cracker motto . . .—

The engineer was charmingly quick-witted. —Perhaps they meant freedom, somehow they're—I don't know—a bit too shaken these days to use the word. In the Leftist view of life, anyway, the two are as one, more or less, aren't they, they're always insisting their 'freedom' is the condition of happiness.—

She weighed empty hands a moment—Bernard saw what was underfoot taken up and shown there—then hid fists behind her thighs. —Don't you know? There isn't the possibility of happiness without institutions to protect it.—

The Englishman smiled on a grille of tiny teeth holding a cigar. —God in heaven help us! And up goes the barbed wire, and who knows when you first discover which is the wrong side—

—I'm not offering a theory. I'm talking about people who need to have rights—*there*—in a statute book, so that they can move about in their own country, decide what work they'll do and what their children will learn at school. So that they can get onto a bus or walk in somewhere and order a cup of coffee.—

—Oh well, ordinary civil rights. That's hardly utopia. You don't need a revolution for that.—

—In some countries you do. People die for such things.— Bernard spoke aloud to himself.

Rosa gave no sign of having heard him. —But the struggle for change is based on the idea that freedom exists, isn't it? That wild idea. People must be able to create institutions—institutions *must evolve* that will make it possible in practice. That utopia, it's inside . . . without it, how can you . . . act?— The last word echoed among them as 'live', the one she had subconsciously substituted it for; there were sympathetic, embarrassed, appreciative changes in the faces, taking, amiably or as a reproach, a naïve truth nevertheless granted.

The Englishman set his profile as if for a resolute portrait. —The lies. The cruelty. Too much pain has come from it.—

—But there's no indemnity. You can't be afraid to do good in case evil results.— As Rosa spoke, Katya paused in passing and put an arm round her; looked at them all a moment, basking in the reflection of a past defiance, an old veteran showing he can still snap to attention, and went on her way to sponge a stain of spilt wine off the bosom of her dress. —This terrible balcony of mine, it catches every drip.—

The Englishman's authority reared and wheeled. He took

another pastis from Didier's tray without being aware of the exchange of his empty glass for a full one. —Not a question of moral justification, we must get away from all that. The evil utopia—the monolithic state that's all the utopian dream is capable of producing has taken over moral justification and made it the biggest lie of the lot.—

—Yes, yes, exactly what they are saying—whether it's the Communist Party or some giant multinational company, people are turning against huge, confining structures—

—Our only hope lies in a dispassionate morality of technology, our creed must be, broadly speaking, ecological—always allowing the premise that man's place is central—

Bernard met Rosa in the thicket of the others' self-absorption. —For them, it livens up a party.—

She shrugged and imitated his gesture of puffing out the lower lip: for all of us. She gave a quick smile to him.

They moved away as if they had no common destination, would separate and go to Didier's bar or join the Grosbois faction where Darby was being egged on to growl out some story which brought down upon her such bombardments of laughter that Donna watched, annoyed. They moved measuredly, like a pair meeting by appointment to exchange a message under cover of the crowd. He suddenly began to speak. —There's plenty you can do, Rosa. In Paris, in London, for that matter. Enough for a lifetime. If you must. But I begin to think— He stopped; the two moved slowly on. —Ah, my reasons are not theirs—

He couldn't have said what he did, anywhere else; not alone with her; the presence of the crowd made it possible, safe from any show of emotions let loose. —I want to say to you—you can't enter someone else's cause or salvation. Look at those idiots singing in the streets with shaved heads a few years ago . . . They won't attain the Indian nirvana.— Her head was down, bent towards his low voice. They might have been murmuring some gossip about the group they had just quitted. —Oh I know, how can I compare . . .— He paused for her quick glance but it did not come. —The same with your father and the blacks—their freedom. You'll excuse me for saying . . . the same with you and the blacks. It's not open to you.—

—Go on.— She held him to it in the knowledge that he might not be able to find the time and place where he would dare to speak again: a meeting away from the lovers Bernard and Rosa.

—Not even you.—

But he was afraid. He disappeared into thoughts in his own language and the surf of human company broke high all around them. The view of the sea from Donna's terrace was paraded by red and blue and yellow sails of the local people's tiny pleasure craft on a Saturday afternoon all tacking in and turning at the buoys that marked the limit of sheltered waters. He could see Corsica wavering through the distortion of distance. —I really feel like pushing off to Ajaccio. You know? We ought to get the feeling of what's going on there. The cellar the autonomists occupied when they killed those two gendarmes belongs to one of my *pieds noirs*. The French Algerians are making a fortune in Corsica. I'd like to talk to them.—

—Was the rioting actually against them, or was it also against French rule—to put it the other way about, I mean was the choice of that particular man's cellar deliberate?—

He took pleasure in explaining what interested her; in her practised understanding of the way things happen in events of that category. —Oh the two are closely connected, the moving in of settlers from Algeria is seen by the independence movement as part of France's colonialist exploitation—when they got kicked out of Algeria, they came nearer home to another one of France's poor 'colonies', though Corsica's supposed to be part of metropolitan France . . . So it's the same thing. The French Algerians represent Paris, to the Corsicans. They even reject Napoleon as some sort of sell-out: the great hero of the French, the assimilator. The Simeoni brothers who lead the independence movement have taken up Paoli as hero. Ever heard of Pascal Paoli? In the eighteenth century he fought the French for an independent Corsica . . . It might be fascinating, for us now . . . and for my book. A popular revolt that's actually within its scope—the riots are the most serious trouble there's been in Corsica. Make a good chapter.—

—It'll be enough to take your mind off your stomach.— When lovers cannot touch, they tease each other instead.

—We'll fly. To hell with the ferry.—

—I wanted to go on that lovely white ship.—

—Good god, I don't want you to see me vomiting . . . it's not a lovely ship, my Rosa, it's just a floating belly full of cars.—

—When? There's no problem about visas, I suppose? They'll let me in?—

—You are in. I told you, it's colonized, it's France—

He gripped her wrist where she leaned on her elbow, wrestling with their joy.

Georges and Manolis joined them. Didier had put on an old Marlene Dietrich record and pulled up Tatsu from the cushions piled on the floor as in a stage harem. She did not grin and giggle when she danced; hers was another face. Manolis was letting Didier's tango lead his eyes: —I was saying to Georges—beau, mais très ordinaire—

Dancing, the Japanese girl's face was as it has never been before, grave, dreamy, fully expectant, and I felt what she had wanted—one age, with her. Something is owed us. Young women, girls still. The capacity I feel, running down the sluiced alleys under flower-boxes to meet the man who tells me his flesh rises when his ears recognize the slither of my sandals, the flashes of bright feeling that buffet me at this point where I see the sea, the abundance for myself I sense in whiffs from behind the plastic ribbons of open kitchen doors and greetings from the street-cleaners paused for a glass of wine at the bar tabac. School comes out for lunch and a swirl and clatter of tiny children giddy round my legs, they clasp me anywhere that offers a hold, I dodge from this side to that like a goal-keeper, arms out . . .

I see everything, everything, have to stop to stroke each cat taking up the pose of a Grimaldi lion on a doorstep. Or I go blindfold in the darkness of sensations I have just experienced, deaf to everything but a long dialectic of body and mind that continues within Bernard Chabalier and me even when we are not together. Suddenly a woman stood before me; the other day, a woman in a nightgown stopped me in one of these close streets that are the warren of my loving.—One of the old girls, the Lesbians or beauties from the nineteen thirties.—I thought for a moment it was Bobby there.

She clutched me by the arm; the nerves in her fingers twitched like fleas. I saw that there were tears runnelling the creases of her neck. *Help me, help me.* I broke surface into her need with the cringe and bewilderment at the light of a time of day or night one doesn't recognize. And that was what she herself inhabited: *What time is it?* She wanted to know if she had just got up or was ready to go to

bed; she had slipped the moorings of nights and days. When I
asked what was wrong she searched my face, gaping tense, the
lipstick staining up into the vertical folds breaking the lips'
outline: that was what was wrong—that she didn't know, couldn't
remember what it was that was wrong.

I took her away from the street that exposed through folds of blue
nylon the dangle of dark nipples at the end of two flaps of skin. The
door to a little house—*Lou Souliou* in wrought-iron script—stood
open behind her. I offered to help her dress or get back to bed
(supposing she had been in bed; she couldn't say). But as soon as we
were inside she began to chatter with matter-of-fact, everyday
animation. We did not mention what had happened in the street.
She put on something that looked more like an old velvet evening
coat than a dressing-gown. She offered me coffee—or vodka? There
should be a bottle of vodka in the fridge, and some tomato juice?
When she heard my French pidgin she answered in English with a
formal American turn of phrase like a character out of Henry James.
Photographs and mementoes in a dim, cosy room—like all the
houses where women live around here. A free-range life; some of the
things looked Peruvian, Mexican—American Indian. The Provençal
panetière with books and small treasures behind its wooden bars, the
curlicued spindly desk—it was stacked with rolls of unopened
newspapers. —You're Arnys' little friend, aren't you? That's where
we've met. Arnys loves young people— Bernard is Arnys' little
friend, but I suppose this must have been one of the women who have
seen me in the bar so often this summer. When I come back another
year they may even remember, your—Madame Bagnelli's—girl, the
great love of the Parisian professor who was writing a book.

I wanted to go and she wanted to keep me with her in case the
woman I had met in the street took possession of her again. I came
flying up the hill to look for you singing while you upholster an
old chair or paint a brave coat of red on your toenails. I wanted to
ask who she was and tell you what happened. But when I saw you,
Katya, I said nothing. It might happen to you. When I am gone.
Someday. When I am in Paris, or in Cameroun picking up things
that take my fancy, the mementoes I shall acquire.

The prospects: what are the prospects? For Burger's first wife, Ugo Bagnelli's mistress, for Rosa Burger.

You have your nightingales every May and the breasts that gave such sweet pleasure are palpated clinically every three months in the routine of prolonging life. The bed Ugo Bagnelli came to when he could get away from his family in Toulon—I sleep in it with Bernard, now—will not be filled with another man of yours. As Gaby Grosbois says, there could only be an arrangement, one pays for the hotel room oneself, like Pierre's dentist's wife and the policeman. And dear old Pierre in his blue Levis—it does not worry his wife that he might still find you desirable; there's nothing for it but to make a joke between you of his impotence. You laugh at her when she says 'You have still a beauty, Katya'; today I saw you in the good light that's only to be found in the bathroom, of the dim rooms in this house I wish I could stay in for the rest of my life—I've seen you plucking bristles from your chin.

It's possible to live within the ambit of a person not a country. Paris, Cameroun, Brazzaville; home. There's the possibility with Chabalier, my Chabalier. He tells me that once installed in Paris, I'll have my Chabalier who is the only one who counts. He's not disloyal. He doesn't say he doesn't love his wife and children; 'I live among them, not with them'. We don't say ritual words between us; I don't want to use the ones I had to use to establish bona fides for a prison. How is it he knew that—he was somehow recognizing that, in his distaste for going through the motions of flirtation the first night in the bar.

'I have to satisfy her sometimes.'

I have asked him outright: you will have to make love to her when you go home. We knew I meant not only when he goes home from here, but when I am living 'near by' the lycée and he has been with me. He never lies; and mine was a question only a foreign woman would ask, surely. I realize that. I feel no jealousy although I have seen her photograph—she was on one he showed me when I asked to see his children. She is a pretty woman with a pert, determined head whom I can imagine saying, as you told me Ugo's wife did: You can have as many women as you like so long as you don't bring them into my home and I don't know about them. —An indestructible bourgeoise—you said of Ugo's wife, and you laughed generously, Katya. —That was good. I didn't want to destroy anyone; I didn't want anything of hers.— And you had your Bagnelli for more than fifteen years. Bobby had her Colonel. It's possible.

We could even have a child. —You're the kind of woman who can do that— He's said it to me. —I wouldn't be afraid to let us have a child. I don't agree in general with the idea that a girl should go ahead and have a child just because she wants to show she doesn't need a husband—like showing one can get a degree. It's no easier than it ever was. A child without a family, brothers and sisters . . . But ours. A boy for your father.—

When I'm middle-aged I'll have with me a young son at the Lycée Louis le Grand named after Lionel Burger; he would have no need to claim the name of the Chabalier children. We have kin in Paris, my child and I: I think sometimes of looking her up one day when I'm living there, cousin Marie who promotes oranges. In Paris there will be no reason to avoid anyone once I have new papers. Free to talk. Free. If I should meet Madame Chabalier accompanying her husband at one of the left-wing gatherings? —It doesn't matter. You will probably like each other. You'll chat like you do with anyone else who has political ideas more or less in common . . . that's all. She tries to keep up.— He scoops the soggy slice of lemon out of my glass when he's eaten his own, and sucks that. —You haven't done her any harm.—

I don't want to know more about her; don't want to know her weaknesses or calculate them. What I have is not for her; he gives me to understand she would not know what to do with it; it's not her fault. —One is married and there is nothing to be done.— Yet he has said to me, I would marry you if I could, meaning: I want very much to marry you. I offended him a bit by not being moved. It's other things he's said that are the text I'm living by. I really do not know if I want any form of public statement, status, code; such as marriage. There's nothing more private and personal than the life of a mistress, is there? Outwardly, no one even knows we are responsible to each other. Bernard Chabalier's mistress isn't Lionel Burger's daughter; she's certainly not accountable to the Future, she can go off and do good works in Cameroun or contemplate the unicorn in the tapestry forest. 'This is the creature that has never been'—he told me a line of poetry about that unicorn, translated from German. A mythical creature. *Un paradis inventé.*

When I saw you plucking the cruel beard from your soft chin, I should have come to you and kissed you and put my arms around you against the prospect of decay and death.

After a short trip to Corsica in pursuit of research for his thesis, Bernard Chabalier put his mind to discovering some sound reason why he should need to go to London, as well. He was good at this; extremely skilful and practised, beginning by convincing himself. Once this test was made—his face that habitually flickered with ironic scepticism and amusement at doubtful propositions accepted this one as passable—he was confident he could convince whoever was necessary. —I ought to spend a few days in London to talk to a British colleague—yes, of course the LSE— he's doing the same sort of research. The influence of the counter-emigration in Britain. Not bad, 'Counter-emigration'. I think I've invented it. The settlers who returned from Kenya, the Rhodesians who have been slipping back since UDI, Pakistanis, that goes without saying, West Indians. As a comparison: a short chapter for purposes of comparison. The mutation of post-colonial Anglo-Saxon values as against . . . Such things are good for a thesis. Erudite touches. Impress the monitors.— These points would scarcely need to be led before his wife (Christine is her name) and his mother for whom the demands of the thesis come before everything. —If sitting on top of a pillar in the middle of the desert was the best way to get my doctorate, they would send me, no mercy, a bottle of Evian to make sure if I was dying of thirst I wouldn't drink water with germs. Ambitious for me, oh, I can tell you! They make sacrifices themselves, it's true . . .—

Four days and three nights together in Corsica had given Rosa Burger and Bernard Chabalier a taste of the experience of being alone, a couple in the pure state, the incomparable experience they were in no danger of losing in the attempt at indefinite prolongation that is marriage. But the joy without demands—because the

313

night-and-day presence of the other, sensation and rhythm of breathing, smell, touch, voice, sight of, interpenetration with was total provision—becomes in itself one single unifying demand. Of the couple; upon the world, upon time; to experience again that perfect equilibrium. A wild, strong, brazen, narrow-eyed resoluteness, cast in desire, treading on the fingers of restraint, knocking aside whatever makes the passage of the will improbable and even impossible. Rosa Burger and Bernard Chabalier would not have many opportunities to live together whole days followed by nights when their bodies kept vigil over one another in sleep like the side-by-side tomb effigies that stand for loving bodies left deserted by death. If days and nights are going to have to be counted on the fingers, the score is important. Rosa found London a brilliant idea because ideas in this urgent context have only to be practicable to be brilliant. She herself had some complementary to his essential basic one, the reason for him to go to London. A hotel was risky; no matter how obscure, someone who knew him or her might be staying there; after all, there are many reasons for seeking obscurity. A flat was available to her—a key to a flat in Holland Park was always available to her, she had never used it. Never been to England, to London—was Holland Park all right? Bernard was charmed by the idea of showing the *jeune anglaise* (French people in the village where he had met her made no fine distinctions of origin between English-speaking foreigners) round London. Holland Park was ideal! A short ride on the Underground to the West End.

How far from the London School of Economics?

Laughter and words capering—Ah that's right off our route, we'll never find that, don't worry—But my colleague, now, *he* lives in Holland Park, he's going to get me a room in the house of some friends, êh, it's cheaper than staying in an hotel . . . and if there's a phone-call (Rosa already understands the pause, the inference, old Madame Chabalier has had an 'infarctus'—heart attack—twice, and there must always be a means of reaching her son) there's nothing remarkable about someone else in the house having answered the phone, no?—

Yes. And yes again. Yes to everything, as what can't be done begins to be achieved with the zest of practical solutions following step-by-step, carefully planned, because carelessness costs wounds, no one must be hurt if Bernard Chabalier and Rosa Burger are to remain intact and unreachable.

On the 7th of September Bernard Chabalier assembled the type-written pages and hand-written notes scattered in coded disorder round the room where he had worked and made love, both well— he paused to grant it; a remarkable witness, that room he would not wish to be confronted with again, under changed circum-stances, ever—and went back to Paris. It was one week before the re-opening of the lycée where he was, like all French schoolmasters, a professor. That was reasonable enough. It was one week before the re-opening of his children's schools; that was the reason. He could return one day and walk into his classrooms the next—he had taught what was to be taught many times, but his own children liked him to go along when pencils and exercise-books and new shoes were to be bought in preparation for the school year. He had talked to Rosa about his awareness that he did not know, beyond a certain elementary level, how one would have to behave to be what he called a 'continuing' father, equal to needs one would have to divine; for the present he simply did what seemed to please the children most obviously? He did not tell her that the date he and she agreed upon for his departure was a specific instance. That was the sort of thing she had, would have to divine in the kind of life he and she were living and going to live; no need to lift the fact clear of supposition that a 'professor' needs a week to assume that identity. Loving the girl, anywhere outside the pure state, the principle that no one must be wounded reversed her position from possible perpetrator to possible victim. If nothing were said, and yet she understood why he was committed to himself to leave on that day, this would be another of the unspoken facts that would graft Rosa Burger and Bernard Chabalier closely upon one another.

He left on a day that denied the date on the airline ticket. Holiday crowds had gone but the ancient stone bones of the village held the marrow of summer. The blue of the sea, triumphant over its pollution, was solid. By contrast the mountains powdered away into delicate haloes of sun-gauze; no memory of snow, it would never come back. From Madame Bagnelli's car, a smell of geraniums through the windows instead of petrol fumes, and the old men playing their ball-game under the olive trees in the parking ground empty of cars, as Rosa saw him doing there when he grew old. She drove, and perhaps her concentration (still not able to trust her reflexes to keep to the right side of the road instead of the left—which was the rule where she came from) held at bay the desperation that attacked him, so that beside her his hands shook and he breathed with open mouth.

But he was coming to meet her in London in a few weeks. In the meantime he would look for the small apartment for her in Paris in the *quartier* of the lycée; she would go to London and install herself, waiting for him, in the flat that was available to her always. He would take a week's leave—he had not had a day's sick- or study-leave in ten years, he did not care a damn if the term had only just begun—and then they would come back to Paris on the same day, if not the same plane, which is to say, together. It was no parting; it was the beginning of commitment to being exactly that: together. They were no longer one of the affairs of the village. He would telephone her every day; once again, they discussed the best times—she, too, was very good at the connivance of privacies. She did not cry but he was in awe of all she had known in order to learn not to weep; and could not unlearn. It took over again, now; but suddenly she turned from her tight little profile as the angle of a mirror is changed to present full-face and the big calm lips and eyes the colour of the lining of black mussel shells (it had taken him weeks, more than somewhat influenced by the surroundings in which he moved with her and even—at last!—he acknowledged himself as an example of the French preoccupation—the things they ate, to decide the colour). —You are the only man I've loved that I've made love with. So I feel you can make everything possible for me.—

—What things?—

She took the tongue of ticket stuck out by the meter at the

barrier to the airport parking ground, and did not react the moment the gate lifted. He watched her mouth with the passionate attention of the pleasures he found there. That jaw was almost ugly; she attempted as little to disguise the unbeautiful as to promote the beauties of her face. Her lips moved to find shapes for the plenitude struck from her rock—pleasure in herself, the innocent boastful confidence of being, the assurance of giving what will be received, accepted, without question. Before she drove on she tried. —I can't say. Things I didn't know about. I find out. Through you.—

—Through me! Oh my darling, I can tell you—sometimes with you I feel I am that child sent out of the room while the adults talk, now grown-up—lived my whole life—out there . . .—

How much his turn of phrase delighted her! They laughed together at him, in Madame Bagnelli's old car that brought them to a stop; to the destination of the day. Laughter became embraces and in a state of bold intoxication with each other, totally assuring, they parted, for a short while—less than two hours later, from Charles de Gaulle airport where he had just landed, Bernard Chabalier, having found some excuse to get away for a few minutes from whoever it was (Christine with or without children, aged mother) who had met him, telephoned Rosa Burger. He said it this time with blunt wonder: You are the dearest thing in the world to me. She cried in some unrecognized emotion, another aspect of joy; a strange experience.

She left for London ten days later by train because this was the cheapest way. She had earned a little money practising her old healing profession on people to whom she had been recommended, at the yacht harbours; but the folder of traveller's cheques she had brought to Europe was almost empty. She felt no particular concern. She had telephoned Flora Donaldson in Johannesburg and explained that after spending the summer in France she now wanted to visit London. A normal sort of itinerary for a holiday abroad; Flora, as Rosa knew she could expect of any one of her father's associates and/or friends, asked no questions that would suggest anything otherwise and expressed no surprise at or reproach for his daughter having gone abroad without telling anyone of the intention, explaining in what possible manner it could have been realized, or saying goodbye to someone who regarded herself, with justification, as the closest of family friends, who had stood outside the prison door with the girl when she was fourteen and suffering her first period cramps. She did not tell Flora with whom she was staying or where, in France. Flora told her from whom to ask the flat key in Holland Park and found a way to indicate that if money were needed, that could be arranged too. Her voice sounded, out of the past, very close, and soprano with excitement as it always became at the prospect of involvement with problems of evasion and intrigue. Rosa found a way to thank her but explain money was not needed. Flora Donaldson suddenly began to ring out as if she could not be heard properly: —But how are you? How are you? Really all right? How are you?—

The little Rôse left behind the summer dresses Gaby Grosbois had made her because English autumns were known, in the South of France, to be like winter elsewhere, and she would be returning to stay with Madame Bagnelli next summer. Oh and long before: —You will come for Christmas, or Pâques—at those times Bernard—it can be a bit difficult for you in Paris. Any time, this is always your home. The mimosa is already out, Christmas week, here— The warm cheek-kisses, the hug smelling of delicious soup vegetables and wood-varnish. And the nightingales? —Of course! In May, you come in May and they'll be here.—

The London street was not tunnelled through dirty rain and fog they had told about. The trees were a heavy quiet green. Rugs of sunlight were laid by the long windows across Flora Donaldson's Spanish matting. A ground-floor flat with a shared strip of garden sloping down towards it from the plane trees. Black birds (magpies? Christmas-card birds of the Northern Hemisphere) called sweet exclamations from a soft domestic wilderness of uncut grass and daisies.

More like a house! She was excited, on the telephone. A kind of wooden clock-face with a movable cow-tail to indicate how many pints the milkman should leave outside the door. A wall of books and a freezer full of food; one could withstand a siege. But the French did not know what England was like—England was the sun, and birds and lovers hidden in the grass. She was indoors hardly at all. She walked in the parks and took the boat to Greenwich. She knew no one and talked to everyone. Bernard Chabalier had to postpone his arrival for another two weeks because one of his fellow professors developed *oreillons* and the lycée was short-staffed. (What on earth . . . ? He did not know the name of the illness in English but described the symptoms—mumps, that's what it was, mumps.) He not only telephoned every day except Sundays at home but also wrote long letters; the delay merely gave her longer to enjoy the anticipation of their being together, alone, among all these gentle pleasures. She was taking an audio-visual French course at a student centre—it cost little and was excellent. She had been to the French Consulate and was awaiting information about the validity of her B.Sc. physiotherapy degree in France. He had spoken confidentially to the Anti-Apartheid Committee chairman in Paris about arranging permanent residence and a work permit for her, probably using some such terms as 'an unnamed member of a white family of prominent victims of apartheid'. Even between Paris and London, on the telephone or in letters, he was not more explicit than simply to let her know he had 'talked to friends', as if—another lover might pick up tics from his mistress in a desire to identify with the way of life that formed her before he knew her—he had taken on the customs of a country he never knew.

Whereas apart from the precaution of registering at the student centre under a surname not her own—but that was for private rather than political reasons—Rosa Burger was relaxedly communicative and did not find herself in any conversations whose subject required discretion: exchanges with young mothers about the ingenuity of children making houses of sticks and leaves; discussions with barge-men about the fish who had come back to the Thames: arguments with fellow students about the meaning of this scene or that in a Japanese film everyone was seeing. Her quick responses did not extend to allowing herself to be picked up in bars—she had the invincible smiling trick of being able to turn aside such attempts that is possible only for a woman already in love. But she did go to a party with a young Indian couple who were learning French along with her. The girl came from India but the man spoke English with the accent Rosa recognized as he did hers. At the party there were other South African Indians; she had told the young couple her real name but asked them to respect her privacy for the time being—the other guests did not know her as anything more than a student from home. She met them again at the young couple's flat. These casual encounters had the curious and unprevised effect of making her think, or day-dream, about looking up the people it had been easy for her to undertake to avoid, because she could not have imagined herself wanting to do otherwise. Now she saw herself talking to them, accompanied by Bernard Chabalier. The next time one of the faithful in exile telephoned the flat on the chance that Flora might be there, Rosa no longer answered as an anonymous tenant; accepted the enthusiastic assumption that she would come round; sat on a Saturday afternoon in Swiss Cottage, a political refugee talking over old times. It was assumed that like them, she would be carrying on the struggle in one way or another; someone said she had mentioned France as her base. She went to another gathering; this time it turned out to be in honour of a Frelimo delegation in London to seek aid from the British government. Some of Samora Machel's men had been to school or university in South Africa. In the common Southern African revolutionary cause between the blacks of Moçambique, Angola, Rhodesia and South Africa, the Frelimo government was part of black South Africans' own self-realization, proof of themselves. Black Moçambiquan migratory labourers still worked alongside South African blacks in the gold mines and as servants in hotels and houses all over South Africa. The exiles from both countries had sat in refugee camps together, trained as guerrillas together in distant parts of the world, taken sides in each other's internal power-struggles, splits and realignments; they spoke one another's languages, and the white man's English that had culturally industrialized the whole tip of their

continent even where the language of the colonial power was
Portuguese. It was not easy to say which among the black men in
the loudly crowded room was from Moçambique and which from
South Africa. Among those in the uniform of leadership, at least:
the well-cut suits or Mao jackets were favoured indiscriminately by
the same kind of authoritative, path-clearing face, whether ANC or
Frelimo, moving from group to group. A speech was made about
Frelimo and the beginning of the end of colonialist-imperialism in
Southern Africa. A speech was made about the African National
Congress and the fight against racism and world fascism, linking
Vorster with Pinochet. 'A few words' were spontaneously said—
and developed into an elegy with the eloquence of one (of the
faithful) who had drunk just enough to gauge his moment—about
the great men who had not lived to see oppression in Southern
Africa breached—Xuma, Luthuli, Mondlane, Fischer, and of
course Lionel Burger, who was particularly in the thoughts of
many people tonight because 'someone closest to him' and his wife
Cathy Jansen, another fine comrade—was present among them.
Lionel Burger's role in the struggle; the callousness and cow-
ardliness of the Vorster government, keeping an ageing, dying
man in jail, in contrast with the courage of that man undefeated to
his last breath who refused to allow any appeals for compassionate
concessions on his own behalf, who asked nothing of Vorster less
than justice for the people. The white racist government had stolen
his body but his spirit was everywhere—in Moçambique; in this
room, tonight. An elderly white Englishwoman came up and
kissed the girl. She was taken off to be introduced to the Frelimo
contingent. A middle-aged ANC man reminisced about campaigns of the 1960s, working with Burger. She smiled and
thanked, like a bride at a reception or an actress backstage.
Bernard Chabalier was privately present to her, keeping her surely
in another order of reality.

A *Guardian* journalist asked whether there was any chance of an
interview? An independent television producer wanted to arrange
to talk to her about including Lionel Burger as a subject in a
television series with the provisional title, 'Standing on The

Shoulders of History'. Was there access to photographs, letters, as well as (so fortunately) the testimony of many exiles right here in England who could talk about him? She mentioned a source in Sweden. The man solicitously drew her over to the table where hot sausages were being fished from a vast pot. There were some young black men eating clannishly, their knot turning backs upon the room. He broke in among them, chatting about his project, introducing the one or two he knew, murmuring the polite English burble that disguised a lack of names for the rest. They made the laconic response of people intruded upon. She was looking at one who, while he stood with tall shoulders hunched towards his plate, chewing, stared at her as if she threatened him in some way. He had given her a thin, hot dry hand for a second, then it was stabbing at tough sausage-skin with a fork. She took her plate of food; the group that now included the television man and herself was again invaded by others, she became part of a new drift-away and nucleus. But she took no part in the conversation contained within this one. She ate slowly, and drank in regular swallows from her glass of wine. Presently she put aside plate and glass as if at a summons; the person talking beside her thought she had been waved to by someone outside all angles of vision but her own. She went back to the clique of young black men. Gritting words along with mouthfuls, he was talking, low, in Xhosa, to his neighbour, but the touch she had had from him earlier interpreted itself and she interrupted: —Baasie.— The answer to a question.

A piece of skin or gristle that wouldn't go down. He swallowed noticeably. The tendons connecting mouth to jaw pulled on the left side as he tried with cheek muscles to dislodge something caught between two teeth. The movement became distorted; into a smile, resuscitated, dug up, an old garment that still fits.

—Yeh, Rosa.—

She came on awkwardly (he put away his plate).

She resorted to that foreigners' greeting, brought from every café, bar and street-corner encounter, strained up to brush him on this cheek and that. He wiped his mouth as if her mouth had been there. —Yeh, Rosa. I saw you when you came in.—

The conversation seemed to follow some formula, like a standard letter copied from a manual that deals with birthday greetings, births and deaths.

—Are you living here, then—have you been away for a long time?—

—A couple of years, on and off.—

—And before that?—

He frowned to dismiss the importance of any chronology; or to establish a constant in its vagueness. —Germany, Sweden. I was around.—

—Studying something? What's Sweden like? I've had an invitation to go there, but I've never done anything about it. They seem to be very helpful people.—

He gave a sad, sour laugh. —They're okay.—

—Were you working, or—

—Supposed to be studying economics. But the language. Man, you've got to spend two years learning that language before you can take a university course. You can't understand what's going on at lectures.—

—I should think not! It must be terribly difficult.—

—Oh you just give in, give up.—

—And Germany?—

—It's all right. I mean, from Afrikaans—it's not so hard to pick up a bit of German.—

—Are you still busy with a course, here, or have you graduated?—

He seemed uncertain whether to answer or not; not to have an answer. —Well, here, once you live in this place (a laugh, for the first time, his whole face trembled) —I haven't really got back to it properly. I have to pass some exams and so on, first.—

—Yes . . . I wonder if I'd be allowed to work, here. If my qualifications would be recognized.—

—But you've been to a university, isn't it?— Like many blacks from their home country—his and hers—for whom English and Afrikaans are *lingue franche*, not mother tongues, he used the Afrikaans phrase translated literally, instead of the English equivalent.

323

—Yes, but not all degrees are international. In fact very few. I took some sort of medical one. Not what I really wanted to do . . . but . . .— The reasons were implicit, for him.

—Oh I'd thought you were a doctor, like your father?— The television man was back, and a young couple attendant, waiting to be introduced to Rosa, listening with polite movements of the eyes from one face to another in order to miss nothing. —Incredible the way he just went on with his job, inside the jail, is that true? The warders used to come to him with their aches and pains, they preferred him to the prison doctors? They weren't afraid he'd poison them or something?— He laughed with Rosa; turned to the couple. —Fantastic man, fantastic. I'm inspired about doing him in the series. This is his daughter, Rosa Burger—Polly Kelly, Vernon Stern. They run the universities' AAA, that's nothing to do with the RAC—Action Anti-Apartheid—

There was no need to introduce anyone else; the couple signalled greetings all round, they had met the company before. Rosa found an urgent way through the talk. —When will we see each other.— Before there was an answer—Come to me. Or I'll come to you. We can meet somewhere—you say. I don't know London. Are you very busy?—

—I'm not busy.—

She borrowed a pen from somebody who fished it out of a breast-pocket without breaking the train of a conversation about mi-gratory labour with Kelly and Stern. She wrote the address of the flat and the telephone number, and put the scrap of paper into his hand. He was glancing at it when someone else spoke to her and her attention was counter-claimed. He was here and there in the room all evening, not far from her, and once or twice she smiled, thought he might have felt her eyes on him, but he and she were not brought together in the crowd. He had always been slight; the type that will grow up tall and thin. A little boy with narrow, almost oriental eyes and the tiny ears of his race—her brother's ears were twice the size when they did the anatomical comparisons children make in secret out of sexual curiosity and scientific wonder. There was an unevenness in his gaze across the room, now; standing close up, she had noticed that the right eye bulged a little, flickered in and out of focus. A scar cut across his frown; an old scar with pinhead lumps where stitches had been—but he hadn't had it, that far back. The university couple followed her from group to group; she found herself the centre of women who wanted to know how women's lib could have an explicit function in the South African situation (she should have referred them to Flora), and passed, by way of various people who claimed her, back to her Indian friends, where her father's association with their leaders, Dadoo, Naicker, Kathrada, was being explained to the *Guardian* journalist. Very late, she was talking alone to one of the Frelimo men whose passion for his country was a revelation, seen from the remove of the Europeans who had accepted her as one of themselves, who understood nationalism only in terms of chauvinism or disgusted apathy. A sensual longing pleasantly overcame her, the wave of relaxation after a yawn; for Bernard; to show off this revelation of a man to Bernard Chabalier. —When your delegation goes to France, I'd like you to meet someone there.—

He was enthusiastic. —Anyone who's interested in Moçambique, I am interested . . . You understand? Anyone who will help us. We need support from the French Leftists. And we get it, yes. But what we need more is money from the French government.— The pretty white girl said she couldn't promise that . . . but the three of them could eat together, drink some wine. Their dates of arrival in Paris, so far as they could predict from present intentions, accommodatingly overlapped. She promised she would confirm this after her usual telephone call from Paris next day.

The telephone ringing buried in the flesh.

Bernard.

Staggered—vertigo of sleep—hitting joyfully against objects in the dark, to the livingroom.

The voice from home said: Rosa.

—Yes.—

—Yeh, Rosa.—

—It's you, Baasie?—

—No.— A long, swaying pause.

—But it is.—

—I'm not 'Baasie', I'm Zwelinzima Vulindlela.—

—I'm sorry—it just came out this evening . . . it was ridiculous.—

—You know what my name means, Rosa?—

—Vulindlela? Your father's name . . . oh, I don't know whether my surname means anything either—'citizen', solid citizen— Starting to humour the other one; at such an hour—too much to drink, perhaps.

—Zwel-in-zima. That's my name. 'Suffering land'. The name my father gave me. You know my father. Yes.—

—Yes.—

—Is it? Is it? You knew him before they killed him.—

—Yes. Since we were kids. You know I did.—

—How did they kill him?—You see, you don't know, you don't know, you don't talk about that.—

—I don't . . . because why should I say what they said.—

—Tell it, say it—

—What they always say—they found him hanged in his cell.—

326

—How, Rosa? Don't you know they take away belts, every-thing—

—I know.—

—Hanged himself with his own prison pants.—

'Baasie'—she doesn't say it but it's there in the references of her voice, their infant intimacy—I asked if you'd come and see me—or I'd come to you, tomorrow, but you—

—No, I'm talking to you now.—

—D'y'know what time it is? I don't even know—I just got to the phone in the dark—

—Put on the light, Rosa. I'm talking to you.—

She uses no name because she has no name for him. —I was fast asleep. We can talk tomorrow. We'd better talk tomorrow, mmh?—

—Put on the light.—

Try laughing. —We'd better both go back to bed.—

—I haven't been in bed.— There were gusts of noise, abruptly cut off, background to his voice; he was still somewhere among people, they kept opening and shutting a door, there.

—The party going strong?—

—I'm not talking about parties, Rosa—

—Come tomorrow—today, I suppose it is, it's still so dark—

—You didn't put the light on, then. I told you to.—

They began to wrangle. —Look, I'm really not much use when I'm woken up like this. And there's so much I want . . . How old were we? I remember your father—or someone—brought you back only once, how old were we then?—

—I told you to put it on.—

She was begging, laughing. —Oh but I'm so tired, man! Please, until tomorrow—

—Listen. I didn't like the things you said at that place tonight.—

—*I* said?—

—I didn't like the way you went around and how you spoke.—

The receiver took on shape and feel in her hand; blood flowing

327

to her brain. She heard his breathing and her own, her breath breathing garlic over herself from the half-digested sausage.

—I don't know what to say. I don't understand why you should say this to me.—

—Look, I didn't like it at all.—

—I said? About what?—

—Lionel Burger, Lionel Burger, Burger—

—I didn't make any speeches.—

—Everyone in the world must be told what a great hero he was and how much he suffered for the blacks. Everyone must cry over him and show his life on television and write in the papers. Listen, there are dozens of our fathers sick and dying like dogs, kicked out of the locations when they can't work any more. Getting old and dying in prison. Killed in prison. It's nothing. I know plenty blacks like Burger. It's nothing, it's us, we must be used to it, it's not going to show on English television.—

—He would have been the first to say—what you're saying. He didn't think there was anything special about a white being a political prisoner.—

—Kissing and coming round you, her father died in prison, how terrible. I know a lot of fathers—black—

—He didn't think what happened to him more important.—

—Kissing and coming round you—

—You knew him! You know that! It's crazy for me to tell *you*.—

—Oh yes I knew him. You'll tell them to ask me for the television show. Tell them how your parents took the little black kid into their home, not the backyard like other whites, right into the house. Eating at the table and sleeping in the bedroom, the same bed, their little black boss. And then the little bastard was pushed off back to his mud huts and tin shanties. His father was too busy to look after him. Always on the run from the police. Too busy with the whites who were going to smash the government and let another lot of whites tell us how to run our country. One of Lionel Burger's best tame blacks sent scuttling like a bloody cockroach everywhere, you can always just put your foot on them.—

Pulling the phone with her—the cord was short, for a few moments she lost the voice—she felt up the smooth cold wall for the switch: under the light of lamps sprung on the voice was no longer inside her but relayed small, as from a faint harsh public address system in the presence of the whole room.

She hunched the thing to her head, clasping with the other hand the wrist of the hand that held it. —Where did they take you when you left us? Why won't you tell me? It was Transkei? Oh God. King William's Town? And I suppose you know—perhaps you didn't—Tony drowned. At home.—

—But he taught us to swim.—

—Diving. Head hit the bottom of the pool.—

—No, I didn't hear. Your little boss-kid that was one of the family couldn't make much use of the lessons, there was no private swimming-pool the places I stayed.—

—Once we'd left that kindergarten there wasn't any school you could have gone to in our area. What could your father or mine do about that. My mother didn't want your father to take you at all.—

—What was so special about me? One black kid? Whatever you whites touch, it's a take-over. He was my father. Even when we get free they'll want us to remember to thank Lionel Burger.—

She had begun to shiver. The toes of her bare feet clung, one foot covering the other, like those of a nervous zoo chimpanzee. —I just give you the facts. He's dead, but I can tell you for him he didn't want anything but that freedom. I don't have to defend him but I haven't any more right to judge him than you have.—

His voice danced round, rose and clashed with hers—Good, good, now you come out—

—Unless you want to think being black is your right?—Your father died in jail too, I haven't forgotten. Leave them alone.—

—Vulindlela! Nobody talks about him. Even I don't remember much about him.—

The shivering rose like a dog's hair along its back. —I want to tell you something. When I see you and we talk. Not now.—

—Why should I see you, Rosa? Because we even used to have a bath together?—the Burger family didn't mind black skin so we're different for ever from anyone? You're different so I must be different too. You aren't white and I'm not black.—

She was shouting. —How could you follow me around that room like a man from BOSS, listening to stupid small-talk? Why are we talking in the middle of the night? Why do you telephone? What for?—

—I'm not your Baasie, just don't go on thinking about that little kid who lived with you, don't think of that black 'brother', that's all.—

Now she would not let him hang up; she wanted to keep the two of them nailed each to the other's voice and the hour of night when nothing fortuitous could release them—*good, good*, he had disposed of her whining to go back to bed and bury them both.

—There's just one thing I'm going to tell you. We won't meet, you're right. Vulindlela. About him and me. So long as you know I've told you. I was the one who was sent to take a fake pass to him so he could get back in from Botswana that last time. I delivered it somewhere. Then they caught him, that was when they caught him.—

—What is that? So what is that for me? Blacks must suffer now. We can't be caught although we are caught, we can't be killed although we die in jail, we are used to it, it's nothing to do with you. Whites are locking up blacks every day. You want to make the big confession?—why do you think you should be different from all the other whites who've been shitting on us ever since they came? He was able to go back home and get caught because you took the pass there. You want me to know in case I blame you for nothing. You think because you're telling me it makes it all right—for you. It wasn't your fault—you want me to tell you, then it's all right. For you. Because I'm the only one who can say so. But he's dead, and what about all the others—who cares whose 'fault'—they die because it's the whites killing them, black blood is the stuff to get rid of white shit.—

—This kind of talk sounds better from people who are in the country than people like us.— Impulses of cruelty came exhilarating along her blood-vessels without warming the cold of feet and hands; while he talked she was jigging, hunched over, rocking her body, wild to shout, pounce him down the moment he hesitated.

—I don't know who you are. You hear me, Rosa? You didn't even know my name. I don't have to tell you what I'm doing.—

—What is it you want?—the insult thrilled her as she delivered herself of it—You want something. If it's money, I'm telling you there isn't any. Go and ask one of your white English liberals who'll pay but won't fight. Nobody phones in the middle of the night to make a fuss about what they were called as a little child. You've had too much to drink, Zwelin-zima.— But she put the stress on the wrong syllable and he laughed.

As if poking with a stick at some creature writhing between them—You were keen to see me, eh, Rosa. What do you want?—

—You could have said it right away, you know. Why didn't you just stare me out when I came up to you? Make it clear I'd picked the wrong person. Make a bloody fool of me.—

—What could I say? I wasn't the one who looked for you.—

—Just shake your head. That would've been enough. When I said the name I used. I would have believed you.—

—Ah, come on.—

—I would have believed you. I haven't seen you since you were nine years old, you might have been dead for all I know. The way you look in my mind is the way my brother does—never gets any older.—

—I'm sorry about your kid brother.—

—Might have been killed in the bush with the Freedom Fighters. Maybe I thought that.—

—Yeh, you think that. I don't have to live in your head.—

—Goodbye, then.—

—Yeh, Rosa, all right, you think that.—

Neither spoke and neither put down the receiver for a few moments. Then she let go the fingers that had stiffened to their own clutch and the thing was back in place. The burning lights witnessed her.

She stood in the middle of the room.

Knocking a fist at the doorway as she passed, she ran to the bathroom and fell to her knees at the lavatory bowl, vomiting. The wine, the bits of sausage—she laid her head, gasping between spasms, on the porcelain rim, slime dripping from her mouth with the tears of effort running from her nose.

L ove doesn't cast out fear but makes it possible to weep, howl, at least. Because Rosa Burger had once cried for joy she came out of the bathroom and stalked about the flat, turning on all the lights as she went, sobbing and clenching her jaw, ugly, soiled, stuffing her fist in her mouth. She slept until the middle of the next day: it was another perfect noon. This spell of weather continued for some short time yet. So for Rosa Burger England will always be like that; tiers of shade all down the sunny street, the shy white feet of people who have taken off shoes and socks to feel the grass, the sun wriggling across the paths of pleasure boats on the ancient river; where people sit on benches drinking outside pubs, the girls preening their flashing hair through their fingers.

THREE

Peace. Land. Bread.

Children and children's children. The catchphrase of every reactionary politician and every revolutionary, and every revolutionary come to power as a politician. Everything is done in the name of future generations.

I'm told even people who have no religious beliefs sometimes have the experience of being strongly aware of the dead person. An absence fills again—that sums up how they describe it. It has never happened to me, with you; perhaps one needs to be in the close surroundings where one expects to find that person anyway—and our house was sold long ago. I didn't ask them for your ashes, contrary to the apocryphal story the faithful put around and I don't deny, that these were refused me. After all, you were also a doctor, and to sweep together a handful of potash . . . futile relic of the human body you regarded as such a superb example of functionalism. Apocrypha, on the other hand, has its uses. It's unlikely they would have given me the ashes if I had asked.

I cannot explain to anyone why that telephone call in the middle of the night made everything that was possible, impossible. Not to anyone. I cannot understand why what *he* had to say and his manner—even before the phone-call, even in the room where we met—incensed me so. I've heard all the black clichés before. I am aware that, like the ones the faithful use, they are an attempt to habituate ordinary communication to overwhelming meanings in human existence. They rap out the mechanical chunter of a telex; the message has to be picked up and read. They become enormous lies incarcerating enormous truths, still extant, somewhere. I've experienced before the same hostility: being treated as if I were not there—the girl and the young man once at Fats' place, for example; and then I didn't feel mean and vile and find weapons

339

ready to hand. Like liberal reaction to understand and forgive all, this vengeful excitation is foreign to me. The habit of sorting into objectively correct and false assumptions the position taken—the sane habit of our kind saves me from the ridiculousness and vanity of personal affront. '*A war in South Africa will doubtless bring about enormous human suffering. It may also, in its initial stages, see a line-up in which the main antagonists fall broadly into racial camps, and this would add a further tragic dimension to the conflict. Indeed if a reasonable prospect existed of a powerful enough group among the Whites joining in the foreseeable future with those who stand for majority rule, the case for revolt would be less compelling.*' Your biographer quoted that to me for confirmation of a faithful reflection of the point of view. Then why be so—disintegrated, yes; I dissolved in what I heard from him, the acid. Why so humiliated because I had—automatically, not thinking—bobbed up to him with the convention of affection, of casual meetings exchanged with the cheeks of the Grosbois, Bobby, Georges and Manolis, Didier—a rubbing of noses brought back from a trip to see Eskimos. What did that matter?

What was said has been rearranged a hundred times: all the other things I could have said, substituted for what I did say, or at least what I remember having said. How could I have come out with the things I did? Where were they hiding? I don't suppose you could tell me. Or perhaps if I had grown up at a different time, and could have had an open political education, these things would have been dealt with. I could have been helped. Katya was surely ineducable, in that sense. Our Katya—she exaggerates for effect; I would gladly be censured, by you or the others, for being able to say what I did. 'Unless you want to think being black is the right.' Repelled by him. Hating him so much! Wanting to be *loved*!— how I disfigured myself. How filthy and ugly, in the bathroom mirror. Debauched. To make defence of you the occasion for trotting out the holier-than-thou accusation—the final craven defence of the kind of people for whom there is going to be no future. If we'd still been children, I might have been throwing stones at him in a tantrum.

I took my statements (I thought of them that way; I had to

answer for them, to myself) one by one, I carried them round with me and saw them by daylight, turned over in my hand while I was sitting at my class, or talking softly on the telephone to Paris. How do I know what it is he is doing in London? Maybe he goes illegally in and out of South Africa as his father did, on missions I should know he can't own to. 'This kind of talk sounds better from people who are in the country than people like us.' To taunt him by reminding him that he is thousands of miles away from the bush where *I thought he might have died fighting*; I! To couple his kind of defection with mine, when back home he's a kaffir carrying a pass and even I could live the life of a white lady. With the help of Brandt, I don't suppose it's too late for that.

Is it money you want?

But those five words that came back most often presented themselves differently from the way they had been coldly thrust at him to wound, to make venal whatever his commitment is. They came back not as the response to the criminal hold-up, but as the wail of someone buying off not a threat but herself.

There's nothing unlikely about meeting a man on holiday whom one comes to love, but such a meeting—with Baasie— is difficult to bring about. There was no avoiding it, then? In one night we succeeded in manoeuvring ourselves into the position their history books back home have had ready for us—him bitter; me guilty. What other meeting-place could there have been for us? There have been so many arrests, trials, interrogations, fleeings: failures. The Future has been a long time coming, and who's going to recognize the messiah by the form he finally takes? Isaac Vulindlela called his son 'suffering land' and probably never translated the name for you, his comrade, either, and you called your daughter after that other Rosa—ah, if you'd heard us at each other . . . What a bastard he is! What a bitch.

But at least you *know*; you still know—there is only one end to the succession of necessary failures. Only one success; the life, unlike his or mine, that makes it all the way to the only rendezvous that matters, the victory where there will be room for all.

A squabble between your children.

My Chabalier—of course I told him about the meeting, the phone-call in the middle of the night. The family history, Baasie and me. *My poor darling. You of all people.* But he was drunk, êh— poor devil. You really should have put down the phone. To hell with the stupid cunt, then. I don't care who he is! . . . Maybe a bit crazy? You know, an exile, black, it's hard. Je hais, donc je suis. What else is there for such a one? An exile, living it up in London, sponging . . . just drinking themselves to death . . . self-pity, even in Paris there are some, hanging about out of favour with this regime or that.

All these things; and once my love said (I wish it had not been over the telephone. If I could have seen his face, the gestures—I might have found, at that point, how to explain what was happening to me, I might have found he was moving to come between it and me)—he said: —There are some things you can tell only in the middle of the night . . . and what you mean is that next day they will have disappeared for good—probably next time . . . if you ever see him again it will be all right.— But there was only the voice of Bernard Chabalier. The chance was gone. *Don't be upset, my darling.* Of course you lost your temper. Your father! It's absurd. Everyone, black and white . . . no matter what political differences. Whatever happens. A noble life. What does it matter if some crazy chap comes along with his own frustrations in the middle of the night—that's all it amounts to . . . We really shouldn't even get excited. But it's natural, you were outraged.

He hit upon the word I sometimes use to describe *your* kind of anger; but of course mine was not like that. A foreigner, he had probably picked up the word from me.

The fact is that after a few days my obsession with what had been said to me that night and what I had said or should have said, should have done (nearly twenty years, and then that borrowed, bar-room embrace!) left me. Deserted me. I solved nothing but was no longer badgered. There's no explanation for how this comes about. Silence. In place of the obsession were the simple, practical facts of a life being planned. A little apartment had been found with a tiny balcony not big enough to put a chair out on but enough for a pigeon to have found a ledge where to lay an egg. That was sufficient to tip the decision in favour of taking the place—the pigeon already in residence on its egg. It was impossible to be lonely in the company of that pigeon, êh. There was no view because unfortunately the rooms faced one of the narrow side streets (quieter, anyway) but the building was actually on a very old forgotten square, almost like a courtyard, where there was a church with a clock that whirred before it chimed. Two chestnut trees. No grass, but a bench. A good baker nearby. A hole-in-the-corner shop run by a nice Arab couple, maman and son, where yoghurt and groceries and even cheap wine could be bought at all hours—apparently they never close. The metro to dive into at the corner—and it was one of the old ones, green copper curlicues, genuine art nouveau—two stops exactly from the lycée.

I wrote down the address and left the piece of paper where I would keep seeing it. I read it over often. I had no sense of having been in the kind of streets that led there, only a few blocks from a High School. Paris. 'Paris is a place far away in England.'

It isn't Baasie—Zwel-in-zima, I must get the stress right— who sent me back here. You won't believe that. Because I'm living like anyone else, and he was the one who said who was I to think we could be different from any other whites. Like anyone else; but the idea started with Brandt Vermeulen. You and my mother and the faithful never limited yourselves to being like anyone else.

I had met a woman in her nightdress wandering in the street. She was like anyone else: Katya, Gaby, Donna; poor thing, a hamster turning her female treadmill. I remember every detail of that street, could walk it with my eyes shut. My sense of sorority was clear. Nothing can be avoided. Ronald Ferguson, 46, ex-miner, died on the park bench while I was busy minding my own business. No one can defect.

I don't know the ideology:

It's about suffering.

How to end suffering.

And it ends in suffering. Yes, it's strange to live in a country where there are still heroes. Like anyone else, I do what I can. I am teaching them to walk again, at Baragwanath Hospital. They put one foot before the other.

R osa Burger's return to her native country within the period for which her passport was valid coincided with two events rivalling each other in prominence in the newspapers. Orde Greer was on trial for treason. He was accused on three counts: of having written one of the (discarded) versions of the text of a leaflet, alleged to be inciting, distributed in Cape Town by means of a pamphlet-bomb exploded in a street; of harbouring certain manuals pertaining to urban guerrilla warfare, including Edward Luttwak's *Coup d'État* and the writings of General Giap; and— the chief indictment—having attempted to recruit a young man of a well-known liberal family, doing his compulsory military service, to supply information and photographic material relating to South Africa's defence installations and equipment. The trial was well under way. The State had almost concluded its evidence when Rosa Burger attended a session. The trial was held in Johannesburg because Greer was not considered a sufficiently prominent personality for there to be any risk of whites crowding the court, and with the growing political separatism between white and black radicals it was thought that the mobs of blacks who rally where political trials of their own kind are in progress would be unlikely to gather. In fact hundreds of blacks congregated outside the courts each day; the trial was transferred to a remote maize-farming town in the Eastern Transvaal before the Defence was heard.

At the stage at which Rosa was present the court was still sitting in Johannesburg. Someone made room for her on the very end of a bench in the last row of the visitors' gallery; she had in her coat-pocket a scarf handy, but found since her father was on trial the talmudic convention by which women were expected to cover their heads in the presence of a judge had lapsed. Orde Greer was being cross-examined on the State evidence of the recording of a long-distance telephone call monitored by a device he was not aware had been installed, in his flat, by the post office on the instructions of the Security Branch, BOSS. The court heard the whirr of the tape then Orde Greer's voice, not sober, at one point maudlin, asking what had he done? What had he failed to do? The call was identified with documentary evidence that the person to whom it was addressed, and who had replaced the receiver at once on (presumably) recognizing the voice and hearing the first few sentences, was a former South African Communist, an expert on explosives as a result of his experiences as a Desert Rat during the war and now believed to be directing urban terrorism in South Africa. The Prosecution put it to Greer that first having been recruited some time in 1974, he had been dropped by the Communist Party because of unreliability. He had a drinking problem, didn't he? His masters' lack of confidence in him was vindicated beyond all doubt by this preposterous telephone call asking for further instructions in the underground work they had entrusted him with . . . Acting on a sense of 'disappointed destiny' he had been 'devilishly inspired'—had he not?—to prove himself to his masters, to reinstate himself in their good books. He had even conquered his drinking, for a time. He consulted a doctor about his drinking problem, visiting Dr A. J. Robertse, a Durban psychiatrist, on 25th February 1975, while on an assignment to that town in the course of his work as a journalist. He had told Dr Robertse that he was under stress due to marital problems. But he had no 'marital' problems; he was not, had never been married, his problems were with his masters, the Communists in London, who no longer trusted him because of his drinking. He had determined to show himself worthy of them, and it was therefore he himself, acting on his own initiative but strictly within the aims and objects of the Communist Party, who had tried to obtain military information by persuading a young National Serviceman that if he were indeed a liberal vociferously opposed to the policy of apartheid, he ought to be willing to steal documents, make sketches, take photographs that could lead to the destruction of the army by whose strength the policy was maintained—in short, that this young man's duty was not to defend his country but to become a traitor to it.

Rosa Burger was not able to attend the trial again. A week after her return she took up an appointment in the physiotherapy department of a black hospital. She followed the proceedings, like everyone else, in the newspapers. The Defence admitted that Orde Greer had written a text which appeared in a somewhat different form as a leaflet distributed by means of a harmless explosive device ('no more revolutionary than a firework set off on New Year's Eve'). The difference in the texts was crucial: Greer's version (Exhibit A of the documentation seized on the occasions when his flat was raided by the police) included no exhortations to violence, whereas the text of the leaflet actually disseminated had several statements, clearly added later and by someone else, that possibly could be interpreted to be of this nature. The well-known phrase used by Greer—was it not heard in every pulpit, employed to put the righteous fear of God into every Christian community?—'day of reckoning' was by no means a threat of violence or an encouragement to violence. It was, on the contrary, a reminder that everyone would have to account to his own conscience for his convictions and actions, in the end.

There was long argument between Defence and Prosecution on the definition of 'manual': was Clausewitz's classic on strategy a 'manual' or an historical work on the waging of warfare, a special kind of military memoir? And if the latter, were not General Giap's writings a modern counterpart? As for the Luttwak book on the do-it-yourself *coup*—could anybody take such a work seriously? Was it not patently the sort of radical chic with which people living in politically stable countries titillated themselves, a subject of cocktail-party expertise?—The judge asked for a definition of the term 'radical chic', and this provided an item for a journalist whose assignment was sidelights, preferably ironical if not bathetic, on the trial.— And taken in the context of the reading matter of a man who was demonstrably an exceptionally wide reader—a man who earned a modest salary and must have spent a good percentage of it on the 3,000-odd books, on all subjects, that were the main furnishings of his tiny flat—was the presence of the Giap and Luttwak books of any significance? The defendant would say he had been sent both books by publishers, for review during the period when he had been acting literary editor of a journal.

Finally, the Defence provided a sensational poster for the evening paper by keeping quiet, until the appropriate moment, about a discovery made: the 'expert on explosives' identified by the State as the man to whom Greer was talking in the incoherent taped telephone conversation had been in Stockholm on the date on which the call was faithfully recorded by the device secretly attached to Greer's telephone. The number was that listed under the man's name in the London telephone directory, yes, but the subscriber himself was not living in England at the time. There was no proof that the person who answered the telephone was a member of the Communist Party, in fact there was no proof of any identity that could be attached to that voice; and whoever it belonged to had replaced the receiver promptly, as one normally does when one gets a nuisance call. The defendant would not deny the evidence that he was not sober when the call was made. In fact he would submit that he had no memory of having made the call.

But it was the main count—the alleged recruitment of a young liberal doing his military service stint—that roused fly-bitten, carious-breathed antagonisms sleeping beneath the table, in the white suburbs. Quiet dinners among intelligent people turned shrill and booming as men and women gave vent to their secret judgments of each other's political and personal morality under the guise of disagreement about the political and moral significance not so much of Orde Greer's action as that of the young man whom he had approached. This young man had at first agreed to do what Greer asked, and was in a position to do so because he was some sort of assistant-cum-driver to a military press attaché, often accompanying his officer with the top brass on official inspection of secret installations around the country, humble enough in status to be ignored as a piece of furniture, but with ears and eyes wide open, and hands with access to files and photographs kept as classified information. After a brief period during which he produced nothing for Greer except a confidential guide to behaviour when among foreign rural blacks—a leaflet issued to South African troops during the invasion of Angola—he apparently grew afraid or decided for some other reason that he was not willing to continue his commitment to Greer. With fist closed at rest beside a wine-glass, if not thumped, someone insisted that the proper course for that young man, if he was so repelled by the idea of serving in 'that army', if it went so strongly against his principles, was to become a conscientious objector. Not a spy. The liberal position was to oppose the present regime openly, not betray the right of the people of the country to defend themselves against foreign powers who wanted to take advantage of this situation.— A younger man laughed fiercely: When would people learn that this playing-fields morality showed a complete misunderstanding of what repression *is*. —You say you want to free the blacks and ourselves of this government, and at the same time you expect people to 'play the game', be 'decent'—Christ! Apartheid is the dirtiest social swindle the world has ever known—and you want to fight it according to the rules of patriotism and honesty and decency evolved for societies where everyone has something worth protecting from betrayal. These virtues, these precious 'standards' of yours—they're just another swindle, here, don't you see? The blacks haven't ever been allowed into your schools, your clubs, your army, for God's sake, so what do the rules mean? Whose rules? You say you're against white supremacy—then you can't confine your conscience to moral finesse only whites can afford. That chap had every right to use his compulsory army service to take any information he could get that would contribute to destroying that army and all it stands for. What's 'done', what 'isn't'; I just want to smash these bastards here every way we can. Do you want to get rid of them or don't you? That's all I ask myself.— William Donaldson interrupted the argument with a choice of Grand Marnier or Williamine while his wife Flora followed with the serving of the coffee.

Orde Greer was found guilty on the main count of the indictment and sentenced to seven years' imprisonment. The one occasion on which Rosa had seen him in court he was smartened up like a scruffy boy made presentable for a summons to the headmaster's office. His beard was shaved off. His hair, still long, had been combed wet until tamed. He wore a tan corduroy suit provided by someone who didn't want to go so far as to put him entirely out of character in navy pin-stripe. She did not think he saw her in the gallery. His gingerish, unattractive face (for a long time the eyes in their deep archways, the thin, twirly intelligent mouth, the high bifurcated forehead with the frizz of hair behind the ears would be the image with which the faces of all men would be matched)—Orde Greer's face was quiet and privately enquiring, as if he and his accusers were going through some process of scrutiny together, as one. She had this transparency of Greer across her mind when she read that in his opportunity to address the court he had said (inevitably) he had acted according to his conscience. Then he had interrupted himself—saying no, no—that was just a phrase, what he meant was according to 'necessity'. People were detained every day merely for expressing too freely their conviction that theirs was an unjust, hypocritical and cruel society. 'I've spent many years being proud of hob-nobbing with the people who were brave enough to risk their lives in action. I spent too many years looking on, writing about it; I would rather go to prison now for acting against evil than have waited to be detained without even having done anything.'

The other front-page story became one only when it was learned that a South African was involved. Before then it was a European affair, concerning the hijackings, kidnappings of industrialists and murders of embassy officials and politicians for which responsibility was claimed by, and sometimes imputed to international terrorist groups. A man known as Garcia, believed to be of Bolivian origin and belonging to the Armed Nucleus For Popular Autonomy (NAPAP), the Japanese Red Army, the Baader-Meinhof gang, or perhaps some new grouping including these and others, was thought to be the brain behind the most recent series of urban terrorist activities. He remained at large and had been sheltered by a number of women, each unaware of the others' existence, with whom he had love affairs in London, Amsterdam and Paris. The one in Paris turned out to be a South African girl employed by the Citrus Board to promote the sale of oranges. The story dominated the Sunday papers; she was Marie Nel, daughter of a prominent Springbok Flats farmer, who with his wife also ran the dorp hotel. There were photographs of its façade, showing the bar and the name above it: C. J. S. Nel, Licensed to sell wine and spirituous liquors. There was a photograph of Marie Nel of the startled flashlight kind taken by itinerant photographers in nightclubs; the occasion appeared to be Christmas or New Year, and the venue must have been a South African city—a smiling Indian waiter in the background.

The story took on another week's lease of life when one of the journalists, no doubt in the course of snooping about the dorp, learned that Mrs Velma Nel was the sister of Lionel Burger. To many readers this seemed some sort of explanation. The differences between the anarchic phenomenon of a Baader-Meinhof gang or something called the Japanese Red Army which had little to do with Japan, and the ideas of a Lionel Burger who wanted to hand over his country to the blacks, were blurred by the equal distance of such ideas from these readers' comprehension. Marie Nel's cousin, daughter of Lionel Burger and only surviving member of his immediate family, was working as a physiotherapist in a Johannesburg hospital. An old photograph reproduced from the newspaper's files showed a young girl coming out of court in the course of her father's trial.

Not even a postcard from the Musée de Cluny.

The unicorn among the beautiful medieval ladies, the tapestry flowers, shy rabbits; the mirror. *O dieses ist das Tier das es nicht gibt.* At the conjunction of the Boulevard Saint-Germain and the Boulevard Saint-Michel. An old abbey on the site of Gallo-Roman thermae, and she would walk into the court-yard described and up into the half-round hall where you can sit on the shallow well of steps and look at the six tapestries. On an azure island of a thousand flowers the Lady is holding a mirror in which the unicorn with his forelegs on the folded-back red velvet of her dress's lining sees a tiny image of himself. But the oval of the mirror cuts off the image just at the level at which the horn rises from his head: a horn white as his coat, plumed tail, mane and curly beard, a tall horn delicately turned. Two tresses of her golden hair are bound with a fillet of pearls up round her oval face (like the gilt frame round the mirror) and twisted together on top of her head imitating the modelling of his horn, which at the same time is itself an artifice, êh, bone fashioned to imitate a spiral . . . A smiling lion holds an armorial pennon. Rabbits are there, a dog, a spotted genet. Foxes, cheetahs, lion cubs, a falcon pursuing a heron, partridges, a pet monkey tethered by a chain to a little roller—that was done to prevent it from climbing trees—these are to be made out round the representation of the other four senses:

The Lion and the Unicorn listening to music played in the garden by the Lady on her portable organ.

The Lady weaving sweet-smelling carnations into a chaplet while her monkey sniffs at a rose inquisitively pilfered from a basket.

The Lady taking sweets from a dish held by her maid; she may be going to feed them to her parakeet—the monkey is secretly tasting something good.

The Lady touches the Unicorn's horn.

A sixth tapestry shows the Lady before a sumptuous pavilion or tent, amusing herself with a box of jewels. In medieval Bestiaries he is called a 'monocheros'; he is there, paired with the Lion this time, holding aside with a hoof one of the flaps of the tent and gracefully rampant (the ridiculous position of a begging dog), supporting her standard. A legend is woven in gold round the canopy of the tent, *A mon seul désir*.

Here they are: to love you by letting you come to discover what I love.

There she sits, gazing, gazing.

An old and lovely world, gardens and gentle beauties among gentle beasts. Such harmony and sensual peace in the age of the thumbscrew and dungeon that there it comes with its ivory spiral horn

       there she sits gazing

              bedecked, coaxed, secured at last by a caress—O the pretty dear! the wonder! Nothing to startle, nothing left to fear, approaching—

There she sits, gazing, gazing. And if it's time for the museum to close, she can come back tomorrow and another day, any day, days.

Sits gazing, this creature that has never been.

The children Rosa was teaching to walk who were born crippled were getting excellent rehabilitative care, better than her doctor half-brother could dream about providing in Tanzania. In the second half of 1976 those who were born deformed were joined by those who had been shot. The school riots filled the hospital; the police who answered stones with machine-guns and patrolled Soweto firing revolvers at any street-corner group of people encountered, who raided High Schools and picked off the targets of youngsters escaping in the stampede, also wounded anyone else who happened to be within the random of their fire. The hospital itself was threatened by a counter-surge of furious sorrow that roused the people of Soweto to burn and pillage everything the whites had 'given' in token for all, through three centuries, they had denied the blacks. The million or more (no one knows the exact figure) residents of Soweto have no municipality of their own; a white official who had done what he could, within the white-run welfare system for blacks, to help them endure their lives, was stoned and kicked to death. Other white officials had narrow escapes; several were rescued and hidden safely by blacks themselves, in their own houses. There was no way of identifying one's white face as one that was different from any other, one that should be spared. The white doctors and other personnel among the hospital staff drove back and forth between the hospital and the white city of Johannesburg every day, privileged to pass through police roadblocks that isolated the Soweto area, and at the risk of being surrounded and dragged from their cars as they moved along the road where the armoured police vehicles the people called Hippos had gone before them, raising fists useless against steel plates and guns.

354

After the funerals of the first wave of children and youths killed by the police, at each successive burial black people were shot while gathered to pay homage to their dead or at the washing of hands at the house of the bereaved that is their custom. The police said it was impossible to distinguish between mourners and the mob; and they spoke more truly than they knew—mourning and anger were fused.

Although the white personnel at the hospital had knowledge of events and consequences in the black townships only touched upon by the reports in the newspapers gathered, among dangers and difficulties, by black journalists, no one of the white hospital staff could go into the places from which the patients came. Extracting bullets from the matrix of flesh, picking out slivers of shattered bone, sewing, succouring, dripping back into arteries the vital fluids that flowed away in the streets with the liquor from bottles smashed by children who despised their fathers' consolations, these white people could not imagine what it was like to be living as their patients did. Rosa was visited one Sunday night in her flat by an acquaintance, Fats Mxenge. He apologized for turning up without warning, but it was not wise to use the telephone although (of course) he was one of the few people in Soweto to have one. He had a message; when it had been delivered he sat in her flat (a one-roomed 'studio' affair she had moved into when she returned from Europe) and accepted the brandy and hot tea she offered. He looked around him; someone brought aboard out of a tempest and seeing drawn curtains, lamplight, the turntable of the player circling where a record had just been lifted. He tossed off the brandy and then stirred the tea, knees close, stirred and stirred. Shook his head in summation—gave up. They exchanged the obvious. —Terrible, it's terrible, man. I just want to get my kids out, that's all.— She began to talk of some of the things she had seen at the hospital, not in her department: a little girl who had lost an eye; she was used to working with horrors (she used the word 'deformities') about which something could be done—nerves slowly brought back to feeling, muscles strengthened to flex again. —The left eye. Seven or eight years old. Gone for good.— She was not able to describe the black hole, the void she was seeing where the eye ought to be. —Last week the man who lives in the next house to us—you know our place? you've been there with Marisa—just there, the next house, he went out to buy something at the shop, candles, something his mother wanted. Never came back. She came over—she says, what must she do? Go to the police, my wife told her, ask them where he is—she thought he's arrested. So the woman goes to the police and asks, where is my son, where can I look for him. D'you know what they told that woman? 'Don't ask us here, go to the mortuary.'—

—I pass by on my way home. There's been a queue outside every day.— A bus queue of black men and women waited, orderly, to lift up sheet after sheet to find the familiar face among the dead. There were babies, of course, asleep, warm and wet against backs under the blanket, there are always babies. There were the usual shopping bags that lug newspaper parcels of sustenance to courts and hospitals and prisons; one woman had a plaid Thermos flask sticking up out of her bag—the queue was long, and some people would have to come back next day.

—The police must've shot him between our place and the shop. Shot dead. She identified him all right. Just there in his own street, man. It was about nine at night when he went out, that's all. You lock yourself in and stay home as soon as it's dark. You don't move, man. I won't go back tonight, a-a-h no! I can tell you—when it's dark I'm afraid to go across my yard to the lavatory. I never know when I'm going to get a bullet in my head from the police or a knife in me from someone else.— He shook back shirt cuffs with square gilt and enamel links. He was dressed for success and happiness, his usual snappy clothes, like a woman who has nothing to hand in an emergency but the outfit she wore to dinner last night and left hanging over the chair when she went to bed. —Every morning I expect to find my car burned out. We've got no garages in our places. What can I do? It stands in the street. The students are going around setting fire to the cars of reps and so on, people who have good jobs with white firms . . . Who doesn't work for whites? If they know the owner of such-and-such a car is a

sports promoter who arranges boxing matches with whites . . .
They can come after me . . .— His laugh was an exclamation,
protest. —What this government has done to us. Can I just— She
pushed the brandy bottle over to him and he helped himself. She
tipped the last drops of tea out of her cup and poured brandy into
it, taking a first sip that burned along her lips voluptuously while
she listened. —I want to get my kids out, that's all. Margaret and
the baby can go down to Natal with the old lady—her people are
there. I want to put the older kids in boarding-school somewhere
. . . But you know what the students are saying? They're going to
go to the trains when the kids leave for schools in the country and
they're going to stop them, they're going to drag them off the
trains. They say no one must break the boycott. And they'll do it,
I'm telling you, they'll do it. I'll take mine away by car. They don't
listen to me or their mother, there's no school, they run in the
streets and how d'you know every day they're going to come back
alive?—

—I don't know what I would do.— She was white, she had
never had a child, only a lover with children by some other woman.
No child but those who passed under her hands, whom it was her
work to put together again if that were possible, at the hospital.

SOWETO STUDENTS REPRESENTATIVE COUNCIL

Black people of Azania remember our beloved dead! Martyers who were massacred from the 16th June 1976 and are still being murdered. We should know Vorster's terrorists wont stop their aggressive approach on innocent Students and people who have dedicated themselves to the liberation of the Black man in South Africa—Azania. They shall try at all costs to suppress the feelings of the young men and women who see liberation a few kilometres if not metres There's no more turning back, we have reached a point of no return as the young generation in this challenging country. We have proved that we are capable of changing the country's laws as youths this we shall persue until we reach the ultimate goat— UHURU FOR AZANIA.

Remember Hector Peterson the 13 year old Black child of Azania, a future leader we might have produced, fell victim to Kruger's uncompromising and uncontrollable gangsters of the riot squad. What does his parents say, what do his friends say, what does the stupid and baldheaded soldier who killed—actually murdered him in cold blood—say, of course he is less concerned. What do you say as an oppressed Black and brother to Hector? Remember our learned scientist 'who decided to commit suicide all of a sudden' Tshazibane? We suspect that somebody somewhere knows something about this 'suicide' For how long will our people persue with these 'suicide attempt' and 'successful suicides'.

Remember Mabelane who 'attempted to escape from John Vorster Square by jumping through the 10th floor window' apparently avoiding some questions? Remember our crippled brothers and sisters who have been disabled deliberately by people who have been trained to disrespect and disregard a black man as a human being? Remember the blood that flowed continuously caused by wounds inflicted by Vorster's gangsters upon the innocent mass demonstrating peacefully? What about the bodies of our dead colleagues which were dragged into those monsterous and horrible looking riot squad vehicles called hippos? We the students shall continue to shoulder the wagon of liberation irrespective of these racists maneouvers to delay the inevitable liberation of the Black masses. June the 16th will never be erased in our minds. It shall stand known and registered in the minds of the people as STUDENTS' DAY as students have proved beyond all reasonable doubt on that DAY that they are capable of playing an important role in the liberation of this country without arms. We are also aware of the system's conspiracy:

1.   To discredit present and past leadership with the hope of distracting the masses from the leaders.

2.   To capture present leadership with the hope of retarding the student's struggle and achievements.

FORWARD FOREVER . . . BACKWARD NEVER!!!

issued by the S.S.R.C.

O ur children and our children's children. The sins of the fathers; at last, the children avenge on the fathers the sins of the fathers. Their children and children's children; that was the Future, father, in hands not foreseen.

You knew it couldn't be: *a change in the objective conditions of the struggle sensed sooner than the leaders did*. Lenin knew; the way it happened after the 1905 revolution: *as is always the case, practice marched ahead of theory*. The old phrases crack and meaning shakes out wet and new. They seem to know what is to be done. They don't go to school any more and they are being 'constantly re-educated by their political activity'. The parents who form committees to mediate between their children and the police are themselves being detained and banned. It could happen to Fats; a black heavyweight can win a title from a white heavyweight now and black and white teams play together on the soccer fields, but that isn't what the children will accept. It has even happened to Mrs Daphne Mkhonza, who used to come to Flora's lunch parties. There are new nightclubs in Johannesburg where fashionable get-ups provide consumers' equality and apparently privilege the self-styled black and white socialites from police raids. But these are not the kind of pleasures on which the children are set. The black men with yearnings to be third-class, non-Europeans-only-city-fathers, who sat on the Advisory Boards and school boards set up by the whites have resigned at the threat of a generation's retribution. The people who were Uncle Toms, steering clear of the Mofutsa-nyanas, Kotanes, Luthulis, Mandelas, Kgosanas, Sobukwes who went to jail for the ANC and PAC have begun to see themselves at last as they are; as their children see them. They have been radicalized—as the faithful would say—by their children; they are acting accordingly; they are being arrested and detained. The real Rosa believed the real revolutionary initiative was to come from the people; you named me for that? This time it's coming from the children of the people, teaching the fathers—the ANC, BPC, PAC, all of them, all the acronyms hastening to claim, to catch up, the theory chasing events.

The kind of education the children've rebelled against is evident enough; they can't spell and they can't formulate their elation and anguish. But they know why they're dying. You were right. They turn away and screw up their eyes, squeal 'Eie-na!' when they're given an injection, but they kept on walking towards the police and the guns. You know how it is they understand what it is they want. You know how to put it. Rights, no concessions. Their country, not ghettos allotted within it, or tribal 'homelands' parcelled out. The wealth created with their fathers' and mothers' labour and transformed into the white man's dividends. Power over their own lives instead of a destiny invented, decreed and enforced by white governments. —Well, who among those who didn't like your vocabulary, your methods, has put it as honestly? Who are they to make you responsible for Stalin and deny you Christ?

Something sublime in you—I couldn't say it to anyone else. Not in your biography. You would have met in your own person with what happened to blacks at Bambata, at Bulhoek, at Bondelswart, at Sharpeville. But this time they are together as they never have been, ever, not in the defeat of the 'Kaffir' wars, not at Bambata's place, at Bulhoek, at the Bondelswarts' place, Sharpeville. It's something peculiarly their own? You used me as prison visitor, courier, whatever I was good for, you went to prison for your life and ended it there, but would you have seen yourself watching Tony and me, hand-in-hand, approaching guns? You will never tell me. You will never know. It's not given to us (don't worry, the reference is to the brain's foresight, not to a niggardly God; I haven't turned religious, I haven't turned anything, I am what I always was) to know what makes us afraid or not afraid. You *must* have been afraid sometimes; or you couldn't have had your sweet lucidity. But you were a bit like the black children—you had the elation.

I ran away. Baasie was repulsive to me; I let repugnance in: the dodge-em course between diverticulitis, breast cancer, constipation, impotence, bones and obesity. I was scared. You would laugh. You knew about such things all along; when people are dead one imputes omnipotence to them. I was scared. Maybe you will believe me. No one else would. If I were to try out telling, which I won't. And the consequent effect is not the traditional one that I don't 'defend' myself against anyone thinking ill of me; quite the contrary, I'm getting credit where it's not due. When I came up behind him in the street, Dick said, I knew it was you, girl. Your daughter was expected. The man in France was the one I could talk to; and when it came to the point, this was the one subject I couldn't open with him. Not that he lacks the ability to imagine—what? This place, all of us here. He reads a lot about us. Our aleatory destiny, he calls it. He could project. He had plenty of imagination—a writer of a kind, as a matter of fact, as well as professor (but he laughs at the academic pretensions of that title). Once while I was drying myself after a shower he suddenly came out with an idea for a science fiction book that would make money. Suppose it were to happen that through chemicals used to kill pests, increase crops etc. we were to lose the coating of natural oils on the skin that makes us waterproof, as the oil on duck's feathers does—we begin to absorb water—we become waterlogged and rot . . . On another level, it could even be seen as an allegory of capitalist exploitation of the people through abuse of natural resources . . .—I would never have thought of that.

J. B. Marks, your first choice as best man, died in Moscow while you were in prison. I managed to tell you. Now again I have the impression of passing on bits of news as I did through the wire grille. I won't see Ivy; she was gone, on orders, before the Greer trial. If she had stayed she would have been on trial, once more; she was named in absentia as a co-conspirator in the indictment. The prosecutor said she was the one who recruited Orde; Theo appeared and pleaded that his client's outraged sense of injustice, coupled with the experience of a political journalist in this country that attempts at constitutional change are constantly defeated, led him to the hands of people who understood this outrage.

And so, at last, you. It's to you . . .

All the while the air is thick with summer, threaded with life, birds, dragonflies, butterflies, swaying lantern-shapes of travelling midges. After heavy rains the concrete buildings have a morning bloom in the sun that makes them look organic to me. The freeway passes John Vorster Square at the level of the fifth storey and in the windows of the rooms with the basic units of furniture from which people have jumped, I see as I drive there are hen-and-chicken plants in pots on the sills. Your lucidity missed nothing, in the cell or round the swimming-pool, eh. A sublime lucidity. I have some inkling of it. Don't think I'm gloomy—down in the dumps. Happiness is not moral or productive, is it. *I* know it's possible to be happy while (I suppose that was so) damaging someone by it. From that it follows naturally it's possible to feel very much alive when terrible things—dread and pain and threatening courage— are also in the air.

I've been to see the Nels. They were glad I came. I had always been welcome any time. There's a Holiday Inn where the commercial travellers mostly go, now. But the off-sales trade is unaffected. The Vroue Federasie has its annual meeting in a private room at the Holiday Inn, Auntie Velma told me (distracted for a moment from her trouble), even though it's licensed premises. And the chief of the nearby Homeland comes to lunch in the restaurant with the white mining consultants who are looking into the possibility that there's tin and chrome in his 'country'.

The Coen Nels are bewildered. I hadn't realized it could be such an overwhelming state of mind. More than anything else— bewildered. They were so proud of her, in a quasi-government position, speaking a foreign language; the brains of your side of the family, but put to the service of her country, boosting our agricultural produce. So proud of Marie, her sophisticated life—all this time imagining Paris as the Champs-Elysées pictured in the cheap prints sold to backveld hotels.

363

At the farm I asked to be put in one of the rondavels instead of the main house. They didn't argue on grounds of offended hospitality; when people are in trouble they somehow become more understanding of unexplained needs or whims, don't they. Walking at night after these dousing rains, the farm house, the sheds sheer away from me into a ground-mist you can lick off your lips. Wine still isn't served at the table but Uncle Coen made us drink brandy. I moved unevenly through drenched grass, I bumped into the water-tank, I thought only my legs were affected but I suppose my head was. I put my ear to the side of the stone barn wall where bees nest in the cavity, and heard them on the boil, in there. Layer upon layer of night concealed them. I walked round, not through, the shadows of walls and sheds, and on the bonnets of the parked cars light from somewhere peeled away sheets of dark and shone. Like fluttering eyelashes all about me: warmth, damp and insects. I broke the stars in puddles. It's so easy to feel close to the soil, isn't it; no wonder all kinds of dubious popular claims are made on that base. The strong searchlights the neighbouring farmers have put up high above their homesteads, now, show through black trees. Headlights move on the new road; the farmlands are merging with the dorp. But it's too far away to hear a yell for help. If they came out now from behind the big old syringa trees with the nooses of wire left from kids' games in the branches, and the hanging length of angle iron that will be struck at six in the morning to signal the start of the day's work, if they loped out silently and put a Russian or Cuban machine-gun at my back, or maybe just took up (it's time?) a scythe or even a hoe— that would be it: a solution. Not bad. But it won't happen to me, don't worry. I went to bed in the rondavel and slept the way I had when I was a child, thick pink Waverley blankets kicked away, lumpy pillow punched under my neck. Anyone may have come in the door and looked down on me; I wouldn't have stirred.

O ne day there may be a street named for the date. A great many people were detained, arrested or banned on 19th October 1977; many organizations and the only national black newspaper were banned. Most of the people were black—Africans, Indians, Coloureds. Most belonged to the Black Consciousness organizations—the Black People's Convention, South African Students' Organization, Soweto Students' Representative Council, South African Student Movement, the Black Parents' Association, and others, more obscure, whites had never heard of before. Some belonged to the underground organizations of the earlier, long banned, liberation movements. And some belonged to both. All—organizations, newspaper, individuals—appeared to have been freshly motivated for more than a year by the revolt of schoolchildren and students on the issue of inferior education for blacks. Hundreds of teachers had accepted the authority of the children's school boycott and resigned in support of it. No persuasion, bribery, or strength of threat by the government had yet succeeded with the young and the elders to whom they were mentor; and the government, for its part, refused to abolish the separate system of education for blacks. However the situation was summed up the explanation remained simplistic. The majority of children in Soweto had never returned to school after June 1976.

A few white people were detained, arrested, house-arrested or banned on 19th October 1977, and in the weeks following. The Burger girl was one. She was taken away by three policemen who were waiting at her flat when she returned from work on an afternoon in November. The senior man was Captain Van Jaarseveld, who to make her feel at home with him under interrogation in one of the rooms with two chairs and a table, reminded her that he had known her father well.

She was detained without charges. Like thousands of other people taken into custody all over the country, she might be kept for weeks, months, several years, before being let out again. But her lawyer, Theo Santorini, had reason to believe—indeed, a public prosecutor himself had indicated in a moment of professionally-detached indiscretion during one of their frequent encounters when the courts adjourned for tea or lunch—that the State was expecting to gather evidence to bring her to Court in an important breakthrough for Security—a big trial—at last—of Kgosana's wife. —That one— he said; and Santorini smiled his plump, sad cherub smile. That was the important one. For many years he had been engaged with the same prosecutor in the running battle for tattered legalities by which he had got Marisa Kgosana acquitted time and again. The government—police probably even more so, because as they complained to her lawyer, she 'gave them a hard time', offering not so much as one of her red fingernails' length of co-operation when they were only doing their duty—the Minister of Justice wanted her out of the way, inside, convicted for a long stretch. The public prosecutor, so far as Kgosana was concerned, made a suggestion for her own good, quite objectively, in the form of a warning to Santorini. It would be better for this client of his not to risk airing, in answer to allegations being made about her at the Commission of Inquiry into the Soweto Riots then in session, any line of defence that might be useful to the prosecution in the event of a future case brought against her. He would do best not to press for her to be 'produced'—for Marisa was in detention, too.

Prisons for women awaiting trial and women detainees are not among the separate amenities the country prides itself on provid-ing. Where Rosa and Clare Terblanche found themselves held there were also Coloured, Indian and African women; different colours and grades of pigmentation did not occupy adjoining cells or those served by the same lavatories and baths, nor were they allowed into the prison yard at the same time, but the prison was so old that actual physical barriers against internal communication were ramshackle and the vigilance of the female warders, mini-skirted novices dedicated to the Chief Matron as to the abbess of an Order, could not prevent messages, the small precious gifts of prison economy (cigarettes, a peach, a tube of hand-cream, a minute electric torch) from being exchanged between the races. Or songs. Early on, Marisa's penetrating, wobbly contralto announced her presence not far off, from her solitary confinement to Rosa's, and Clare's. She sang hymns, piously gliding in and out of the key of 'Abide with me' to ANC freedom songs in Xhosa, and occasionally bursting into Miriam Makeba's click song—this last to placate and seduce the wardresses, for whom it was a recognizable pop number. The voices of other black women took up and harmonized whatever she sang, quickly following the changes in the repertoire. The black common law prisoners eternally polishing Matron's granolithic cloister, round the yard, picked up tiny scrolled messages dropped when Rosa and Clare were allowed to go out to empty their slops or do their washing, and in the same way the cleaning women delivered messages to them. Marisa was at once the most skilled of political old lags and the embodiment, the avatar of some kind of authority even Matron could not protect herself against: Marisa got permission to be escorted to Rosa's cell twice weekly for therapeutic exercises for a spinal ailment she said was aggravated by sedentary life in prison. Laughter escaped through the thick diamond-mesh and bars of Rosa's cell during these sessions. Although detainees were not allowed writing materials for any purpose other than letters which were censored by Chief Warder Magnus Cloete before being mailed, Rosa asked for sketching materials. A 'Drawing Book' of the kind used in kindergartens and a box of pastels were delivered by her lawyer and passed scrutiny. The wardresses found *baie, baie mooi* (they talked with her in their mother tongue, which was also hers) the clumsy still lifes with which she attempted to teach herself what she had claimed was her 'hobby', and the naïve imaginary landscape that could rouse no suspicions that she might be incorporating plans of the lay-out of the prison etc.—it represented, in a number of versions, a village covering a hill with a castle on the apex, a wood in the foreground, the sea behind. The stone of the houses seemed to give a lot of trouble: it was tried out in pinks, greys, even brownish orange. She had been more successful with the gay flags on the battlements of the castle and the bright sails of tiny boats, although through some failure of perspective they were sailing straight for the tower. The light appeared to come from everywhere; all objects were sunny. At Christmas detainees were allowed to send home-made cards to a reasonable number of relatives or friends. Rosa's was a scene banally familiar to Chief Warder Cloete from any rack of greeting cards—a group of carol singers, and only the delighted recipients could recognize, unmistakably, despite the lack of skill with which the figures were drawn, Marisa, Rosa, Clare, and an Indian associate of them all; and understood that these women were in touch with each other, if cut off from the outside world.

Theo Santorini did not repeat, even to those closest to Rosa Burger's family over many years, the strong probability that the State would try to establish collusion of Rosa with Marisa in conspiracy to further the aims of Communism and/or the African National Congress. The charges would allege incitement, and aiding and abetting of the students' and schoolchildren's revolt.

His discretion has not prevented speculation. What Rosa did in her last two weeks in London is unclear. She did have contact with Leftist exiles, after all. She was at a rally (informers are inclined to up-grade their information) for Frelimo leaders, where her presence was honoured by a speech, delivered by one of his former close associates, lauding her father, Lionel Burger. That much was under surveillance, and will certainly appear in any indictment. She apparently abandoned without explanation an intention to go into exile in France, where the French Anti-Apartheid Movement was ready to regard her as a cockade in its cap. She told no one, no one, how she occupied her time, between the meeting with old associates at the rally or party and her return. It's reasonable to suppose she could have been planning with others, putting herself at the service of the latest strategy of the struggle that will go on until the last prisoner comes off Robben Island and the last sane dissident is let out of an Eastern European asylum. Who could believe children could revolt of their own volition? The majority of white people advance the theory of agitators (unspecified), and the banned and underground organizations adopt the revolt as part of their own increased momentum, if not direct inspiration. Sailors gag on stinking meat, children refuse to go to school. No one knows where the end of suffering will begin.

A woman carrying fruit boxes and flowers stood among a group at the prison doors.

She had pressed the bell with more force and a few seconds longer than would seem necessary. The few people outside could hear it ringing thinly in there. Nevertheless there was a wait for any response; she chatted with them—a black prostitute holding bail-money in a gold plastic purse and moving a tumour of chewing-gum from one side of her jaw to the other, two women arguing in whispered Zulu expletives, a youth accompanying an old relative smoking a pipe with a little chain attaching its cover. They were patient. The youth danced, as one hums inaudibly, on heel and toe of blue, red and black track shoes. The woman was white, she knew her rights, she was used to regarding officialdom as petty and ridiculous, not powerful. —Are they asleep?— The high, penetrating voice of a rich madam. —How long've you been here? You shouldn't just stand—they're supposed to answer, you know.— The blacks were used to being ignored and bypassed by whites and were wary of any assumption of common cause, except for the young prostitute, who knew white men too intimately to be impressed by the women they were born of. She pulled a face. —They did come, but they say we must wait.—

—Wait! Well we've waited long enough.— The white woman put her thumb on the bell and made a play of leaning all her weight against it, smiling back at everyone jauntily. Her hair was dyed and like the dark windows of her sunglasses, contrasted with her lined white forehead; she was a woman in her mid-fifties with the energetic openness of a charming girl. The hand that pressed the bell wore jade and ivory. The prostitute giggled encouragement —Ouuu, that's beautiful, I'd like to have a ring like that. For me.—

—Which one?—No, this little one's my favourite—you see how it's made? Isn't that clever—

The speak-easy slot in the doors opened and a mime's face appeared in the frame, two taut thin bows of eyebrows, eyes outlined in black, cheeks chalked pink.

—I've got some things for detainees.— The woman was brisk; the painted-on face said nothing. The slot shut and the woman had just turned her head in exasperated comment to her companions when there were oiled sounds of bolts and keys moving and a door within one of the great doors opened to let her in. It closed at once, behind her alone; the wardress who owned the face said—Wait.—

The woman's cream pleated skirt and yellow silk shirt reflected light in the dark well of brick and concrete, so that some creature with rags tied to protect the knees, washing the floor, gazed up. An after-image appeared before the eyes that returned to mop and floor. The scents of fine soap, creams, leather, clothes kept in cupboards where sachets hung, a lily-based distilled perfume, and even a faint natural fruit-perfume of plums and mangoes was an aura that set the woman apart in the trapped air impregnated with dull smells of bad cooking and the lye of institution hygiene, the odour under broken nails leached to the quick. The visitor had been here before; nothing was changed: except the outfit of the wardresses, black and white—they were got up in what seemed to her to be the remaindered uniforms worn five years ago by air hostesses—she travelled a good deal. Under the stairs on the left were suitcases and cardboard boxes tied with rope and labelled, even a few coats; possessions taken from detainees on their reception, awaiting the day or night of their release. She saw the bright sunlight enclosed in the jail yard. The fat ornamental palms, the purplish shiny skin of the granolithic. She skilfully glided a few steps forward to take a quick look, but there was no one out for exercise—supposing they were to be allowed anywhere near the entrance, anyway.

Tiny skirt winking on a round high bottom, the tilted body on high heels led her to the Chief Matron's office.

Like—like . . . to describe Chief Matron to people afterwards it was necessary to find some comparison with an image in a setting that was part of their experience, because she was a feature of one in which they had never been and an element in a scale of aesthetic values established by it alone. Like the *patron*'s wife in a bar or dance-hall in a nineteenth-century French painting—Toulouse-Lautrec, yes—but more like those of a second-rater, say, Félicien Rops. Her desk was wedged under barathea-covered breasts. She wore service-ribbons, and gold earrings pressed into fleshy lobes. The little wardress's eyebrows were a fair imitation of her red-brown ones, drawn high from close to either side of the nose-bridge. Her little plump hand with nails painted a thick, refined rose-pink tapped a ballpoint and moved among papers she looked at through harlequin glasses with gilt-scrolled sidepieces. There were gladioluses in a vase on the floor. A wilting spray of white carnations with a tinsel bow stood in a glass on the desk—perhaps she had been to a police ball.

The visitor carried two wooden fruit-trays and a big untidy bunch of daisies and roses from her own garden. —Rosa Burger and Marisa Kgosana. Their names are on labels. Plums, mangoes, oranges and some boiled sweets—loose. In open packets. I can't bring a cake, I understand?—

—No, no cake.— The tone of someone exchanging remarks on the oddities of the menu in a cafeteria.

—Not even if I were to cut it right open, in front of you?— The visitor was smiling, head inclined, flirtatious, corner of her mouth drawn in contemptuously.

The Chief Matron shared a little joke, that was all. —Not even then, no, it's not allowed, you know. Just put the boxes on the floor there, thank you so much, we'll see they get it just now. Right away.— No one was going to equal her in ladylike correctness. —Sign in the book, your name please.—

—And the flowers are in two bunches . . . could you perhaps put them in a bucket of water? It was so hot in the car.— A couple of Pomeranians were sniffing at the visitor's shoes. The Chief Matron reproached them in Afrikaans: —Down Dinkie, down boy. You'll tear the lady's stockings—Flowers are not allowed any more. I don't know what . . . it's a new order just came through yesterday, no more flowers to be accepted. I'm very sorry, ay?—

—Why?—

—I really can't say, I don't know, you know . . .—

—My name's on the boxes.—

—But just put it down here please—the wardress jumped to offer a large register almost before the signal—Let me see, yes . . . that's right, and the address—thank you very much— The manner was that of getting amiably over with a mere matter of form: the necessity for well-intentioned sympathetic ladies to commit themselves in their own hand to acquaintance, to association with political suspects. The Chief Matron moved her lips over the syllables of the name as though to test whether it was false or genuine: Flora Donaldson.

People detained under Section 6 of the Terrorism Act are not allowed visitors, even next of kin. But when later Rosa Burger became an awaiting-trial prisoner she was entitled to the privileges of that status, and in the absence of any blood relative, Flora Donaldson sought and was given permission to see her. Other applicants were refused, with the single exception of Brandt Vermeulen who, no doubt through influence in high places, was suddenly there, when Rosa was taken to the visitors' room one day. These were not contact visits; Rosa received her visitors from behind a wire grille. It is not known what Brandt Vermeulen talked about in the category of 'domestic matters' to which the subject of prison conversations is confined, under surveillance of attendant warders. He is a fluent, amusing talker and a broad-minded man of many interests, anyway, not likely to be at a loss. Flora reported that Rosa 'hadn't changed much'. She remarked on this to her husband, William. —She's all right. In good shape. She looked like a little girl, I gather Leela Govind or somebody's cut her hair again for her, just to here, in her neck . . . About fourteen . . . except she's somehow livelier than she used to be. In a way. Less reserved. We joke a lot—that's something the bloody warders find hard to follow. After all, why shouldn't family matters be funny? They're boring enough. You only realize quite how boring

when you have to try to make them metaphors for something else
. . . Theo tells me Defence's going to give the State witnesses hell.
He thinks she's got a good chance of getting away with it this
time—the State may have to drop charges after the preliminary
examination. In which case she'll probably be house-arrested as
soon as she's released . . . well *all right*, anything rather than
jail?—there're a lot of things you can do while house-arrested,
after all, Rosa'll get out to go to work every day—

A letter came to Madame Bagnelli in France. It bore the stamp of
the Prisons Department in Pretoria but this aroused no interest in
the handsome postman who stopped in for a pernod when he
delivered the mail, because he could not read English and did not
know where Pretoria was. In a passage dealing with the comforts of
a cell as if describing the features of a tourist hotel that wasn't quite
what the brochure might have suggested—*I have rigged up out of
fruit boxes a sort of Japanese-style portable desk (remember the one old Ivan
Poliakoff had, the one he used when he wrote in bed) and that's what I'm
writing at now*—there was a reference to a water-mark of light that
came into the cell at sundown every evening, reflected from some
west-facing surface outside; something Lionel Burger once mentioned. But the line had been deleted by the prison censor.
Madame Bagnelli was never able to make it out.

A NOTE ON THE AUTHOR

Nadine Gordimer's many novels include *The Lying Days* (her first novel), *The Conservationist*, joint winner of the Booker Prize, *July's People*, *My Son's Story*, *None to Accompany Me*, and most recently *The House Gun*. Her collections of short stories also include *Something Out There* and *Jump and Other Stories*. In 1991 she was awarded the Nobel Prize for Literature. She lives in South Africa.

A NOTE ON THE TYPE

Linotype Garamond Three – based on seventeenth century copies of Claude Garamond's types, cut by Jean Jannon. This version was designed for American Type Founders in 1917, by Morris Fuller Benton and Thomas Maitland Cleland and adapted for mechanical composition by Linotype in 1936.